THIRD MAN BOOKS

T0395110

THE ROOT AND SKY SERIES
BOOK 01

Sheree Renée Thomas

DEDICATION

To the Deep Creative Wellspring
where Rhythm meets Root
and Mojo becomes Song.
May the Magic linger on and on.

Published by
Third Man Books, LLC
623 7th Ave S
Nashville, Tennessee 37203

Art direction: Jordan Williams, Amin Qutteineh
Cover/book design: Amin Qutteineh
Cover/interior illustrations: Caitlin Mattisson

FIRST PRINTING

ISBN: 979-89-89908-94-3

THIRD MAN BOOKS

thirdmanbooks.com

CONTENTS

THE BEAUTIFULEST (Or, Peace to All Who Enter)

Ninety-five degrees on Friday, Memphis baked, the afternoon heat thick enough to swim through, but here on this street corner where the concrete shimmered, stood a different kind of cool. The building housing The Beautifulest commanded attention, painted a defiant, spirit-soothing haint blue against the Southern sky. Flanking its entrance two statues rose like sentinels: women sculpted larger than life, stone skin gleaming, full breasts proud, their hair rendered in cascades of impossibly complex braids, eternal guardians of the threshold. Giant combs, some intricately carved from fragrant dark wood like ancient Afrikan artifacts, others sleek chrome arcs hinting at futures yet unspun, adorned the haint blue facade, symbols of the power held within.

Approach these sentinels
pass under the silent judgment of the combs
and face the entrance...

The heavy Dogon granary doors, carved with swirling fractals that whispered and breathed, muffled the hot Memphis afternoon outside. But beyond them, the air vibrated. Not just with the rhythmic thrum of a sub-bass beneath a syrupy UGK sample, perhaps drifting from a passing car, but with the quiet hum of power. "Peace to All Who Enter," the sign above declared, the letters themselves an ancient script shimmering with a faint holographic afterglow.

The Beautifulest wasn't just a salon, it was a world-renowned cathedral of hair. The hypnotic scent hit first—a heady mix of fragrant, mango-infused shea butter, sweet almond oil, and something sharper, more mystical: burnt myrrh and a hint of...*ozone*? Golden light, filtered through arched, jewel-toned stained-glass windows depicting Yoruba deities, Haitian divinities with Afros and braided swirls that spiraled and stretched to the heavens, pooled on the ochre-painted walls. And those walls weren't smooth. They pulsed with fractal patterns, repeating triangles of gleaming metal inlay, echoing the braids themselves.

Hi-hats in triplets rang through the air from vintage speakers as Willie Hutch sang out, "*I choose you, babyyyyyyyy...*" and a chorus of angels backed him up. Uzoma bobbed her head, nodding at the old school towers, her skin the color of polished ebony, as she hovered near a workstation. As the salon's primary specialist in the ancient art of braids and natural hairstyles, Uzoma was a revered guardian of healthy hair care. She was an undisputed expert at cultivating nu growth, a renowned Edges Resurrectionist, and a "Kitchen Queen" whispered about in awed tones for her skill in nurturing the often-delicate hair at the nape. Holographic projections danced around her head, a sonic halo, guiding her hands as she planned a complex cornrow design. It wasn't just aesthetics. The lines pulsed with calculated light, each angle a potential energy pathway. She muttered to herself, Igbo syllables snapping like code: "*Isi gbụ, isi gbụ*...make the path, make the path."

Further down, Naiser, taller and leaner, moved with a capoeira grace, even standing still. Her braids, thick as pythons, swayed with her subtle shifts, the cowrie shells woven into their ends clicking, a quiet threat. Little brass bells, ancient and burnished, were woven throughout the dark strands above her temple, and even the smallest movement sent out a gentle chime. While all braid conjurers at The Beautifulest were versatile, Naiser also possessed a distinctive expertise in the art of cutting hair, shaping and liberating strands with precision. She kept an array of lethally sharpened shears of all sizes nestled in a supple leather satchel belt slung low across her hips. Each tool hummed with potential. She practiced a flowing form, her hands tracing arcs in the air, testing the weight and balance of her braided weaponry.

Presiding over all was Nefertari. Enthroned in her styling chair like royalty. Her expertise was legendary, encompassing all textures and styles—from the most elaborate locs and gravity-defying braid sculptures to the softest, cloud-like Afros. Clients traveled from every corner of the nation, and sometimes beyond, seeking her renowned wig conjure. Nefertari's wig transformations and make-overs were considered top-tier sorcery, weaving new identities and restoring confidence with each perfectly placed strand. To the emissaries of the 'Africa Corps,' whose very presence carried the scent of plundered earth and the silent screams of distant conflicts, Nefertari offered no haven for their gold. With a wisdom as old as the Nile's first flood, learned at the feet of Auset herself, she made it known her doors were closed to those who feasted on the continent's pain—just as they had always been to Langley's intrusive whispers and the neo-colonial overtures of France's DGSE.

A woman who looked like she'd stepped straight out of a per-aa's dream, skin like sunset obsidian, her face lined with the wisdom of a thousand years, her locs a crown of coiled power. Those locs, thick as a grown man's fist, defied gravity, a swirling monument laced with tiny mirrors and golden threads that caught and threw the light. *Those bells.* The source of the ambient chiming. A constant, comforting (or warning) chime from her every gesture. Power rolled off her wrists in waves, ancient, regal, the most Burtiful presence in the room.

A framed photo hung on the wall, one of many. Staged, admittedly cheesy. But Nefertari, the matriarch of hair mastery, understood well the necessity of stagecraft. Indeed, in one cherished, slightly faded photograph, Nefertari stood beside the true Auset, the divine songstress whose voice could soothe agitated spirits, years before the current pop starlet currently signed to Saditty Entertainment's LushLife label, began frontin' in more ways than one with a manufactured image and borrowed glory. Another prominent photo featured Nefertari, arm around the popular singer currently known as Isis, both beaming. A bittersweet image. A painful contrast, this one, because one (Auset) truly channeled life through her art, while the other (the pop starlet Isis) merely mimicked it. Word on the street was that this particular faux Isis was another mediocre using stolen mojotech to engineer and fuel her meteoric rise. It made Nefertari' s heart hurt to look at, how the industry consumed great talent, chewed it up, only to spit it all out sooner than later. What made it tragic is that the girl could sing, and would have been perfectly fine if she had remained true to her own heart's rhythms—instead of plugging in to download someone else's.

Then the world tilted.

A shattering crack ripped through Willie Hutch's soulful promise, silencing the angels mid-chorus. It wasn't just sound that ruptured, it was the feeling of peace fracturing like stressed glass. The heavy Dogon doors, ancient wood and living fractal carvings, exploded inward off their hinges, like a barbecue-laced spaghetti Western, spraying splinters and jagged shards across the amber floor. Raw, unfiltered Memphis sunlight stabbed into the sanctuary, momentarily blinding, carrying the loud, raucous noise of Beale Street within.

Standing silhouetted in the ruined doorway, sucking the light into herself, was a *child*—no more than a teen girl. *Aminata*. All sharp, defiant angles and vibrating fury. Her locs, usually a testament to emerging skill, were a disaster. A tangled, tortured crown that spat sparks, half-done or half-destroyed, bound by sheer, ragged, stubborn will and the frantic energy pouring off her. She smelled like chaos, walked like it, too. Chaos made flesh, dropped careless into a legendary house of order.

The air thickened, became hard to breathe, the sweet scents of shea and myrrh overwhelmed by the sudden intrusion of street dust and something sharp, like ozone after a nearby lightning strike.

The red brick dust didn't hold.

And Uzoma's holographic guides winked out, the sonic halo dissolving around her head. Naiser instantly shifted from fluid grace to coiled readiness, her braids swaying with intent, the cowrie shells clicking like shaken bones. Nefertari's bells fell utterly silent, the sudden absence a heavy weight, a broken rhythm.

When it tore through the stunned quiet, Aminata's voice was pure gravel and grief, raw and cracking. A menace for her age. *"You."* Aimed like a poisoned dart, straight across the room at the enthroned Matron. "You did this."

The accusation hung there, thick with more than just teenage rage. Betrayal. Heartbreak. A lifetime of slights packed into that single syllable.

Aminata stepped fully inside, ignoring the ruined doors, her eyes locked on Nefertari. "My crown," she choked out, gesturing vaguely at her own disheveled hair. "My Promise night. You jacked me. On purpose."

Nefertari rose slowly from her great chair, not frail, but ancient, carrying the weight of generations, her own magnificent locs gathering the light protectively around her. That knowing sadness seen in the photo flickered again in her deep eyes. "Child," her voice rumbled, calm but carrying beneath the accusation, a deep river flowing steady against a sudden storm. "You speak of crowns in a house where respect is the only currency. You track chaos onto floors polished with peace."

"Peace?" Aminata laughed, a rueful, jagged sound that held no humor, only hurt. "What peace is there when she gets to shine wit' the glory you stole from me and wove for her? The blessing you bit from me? That wasn't no slip of the hand, old one!" Her voice cracked on the title, respect warring with fury. "That was sabotage. You broke us up! *Shadeur!*"

The name was a raw wound in the air. Shadeur, with his poet's eyes and brilliant mind, the boy who had been the sun in her sky. Aminata had spent nearly a full year meticulously designing the intricate Promise Night hair sculpture meant to weave their futures together, a cascade of fractal braids and shimmering beads that whispered of devotion and a shared beautiful life. Each twist, each pattern, she had painstakingly planned, consulting with Nefertari herself at every step, trusting the Matron's ancient wisdom to guide the delicate threads of her destiny. And on the night of all nights, *Promise Night*, when her crown was meant to bind her to her first and only love, she'd seen Shadeur's gaze, once solely hers, captivated, utterly ensnared by Khyasia, whose own hastily assembled crown pulsed with a vibrant, stolen energy. *Hers.*

The charge hung heavy in the air, the implied theft not just of a style, but of favor, of a future, of a love she believed was her destiny, one meticulously woven with Nefertari's own blessing, all laid at the feet of the Matron's skill. It was a bitter counterpoint to Willie Hutch's smooth promise of devotion still echoing faintly from the speakers—*"I choose you"* twisted into the raw cry of the unchosen.

Nefertari's regal face tightened, a flicker of understanding—but not with guilt, as Aminata perceived. It was a flicker of profound understanding, a recognition of the painful, necessary turnings of fate she herself had set in motion. The Matron knew this child's heart, had guided her apprentice's hands, and yes, had made a conscious, agonizing decision to redirect the potent energies woven for Aminata's Promise Night. It was a destiny swap, a dangerous gambit undertaken because Nefertari had glimpsed a far greater, more perilous future for Aminata, a destiny upon whose fragile strands the very fate of their world might one day hang. Khyasia and Shadeur were but a diversion, a necessary heartbreak to forge the strength Aminata would need for the true crown that awaited her, if only she could survive this crucible of youthful despair. But explaining such cosmic foresight to a spirit consumed by righteous fury was impossible.

Some lessons had to be lived, some paths walked in fire.

Nefertari took a small step back, a slow, deliberate retreat behind the chair, a gesture not of deference, but of a sorrowful, resolute preparation for the storm she knew must break.

Aminata, lost in the storm of her own pain, read it as guilt, as confirmation.

The girl-child trembled, vibrating like a plucked galactic diddly bow string about to snap. Her head jerked back, her ruined locs lashing like storm-tossed branches, gathering the volatile energy crackling around her. "You ain't slick! Wasn't subtle even!" she screamed, voice breaking. "Wasn't no accident! Anybody seen that knowed that was *me*. *My flavor*. You messed me up! And on the night of nights!" Heartbroken, the air around her visibly vibrated, the first hint of the storm about to break.

The atmosphere inside the fabled salon, neutral ground for a hundred years—a sacred peace painstakingly forged back in the nineteen-seventies during the empowering surge of the Black Is Beautiful era—held its breath, thick and unstable around Aminata. The vibrant aura grew brighter, fueled by the raw, untamed power pouring off the girl-child. A dangerous heat radiated from her, the palpable energy of someone whose crossroads were utterly cluttered, whose destiny line felt cut. Dust motes dancing in the golden light now shook erratically, caught in her rising turbulent field.

"Aminata, wait." Uzoma stepped forward from her workstation, deactivating the dormant holographic guides. Her voice was calm, steady, a lifeline of logic thrown into the tempest, but her eyes held a new wariness, watching the girl like one might watch a cornered viper. "The blessing pattern woven was precise. The energy matrix for the Promise ceremony stable, mapped according to tradition. There was no intentional flaw, child, no rerouting of destiny..."

Naiser didn't speak, didn't need to. Her shift was subtle but absolute, from graceful readiness to imminent violence. Her body became a living shield between Aminata and Nefertari. The brass bells woven near her temple gave a single, sharp, discordant clang that cut through the air. *A warning.* The cowrie shells adorning her python-thick braids rattled, a dry, menacing sound like desert snake scales skittering across packed earth. Her eyes, fixed on Aminata, held no warmth, only warrior focus, calculating the trajectory of the potential strike, the cost of intercepting it.

Aminata whirled, dismissing Uzoma's calm reasoning with a sharp flick of her wrist that trailed visible static. "Flaw? Stable?" she spat, her voice thick with tears and fury. "You think this about some calculation? Some pattern in your weave?" She jabbed a trembling finger towards her own heart, then flung it towards the salon space where her rival likely received her blessing. "That look was *me! My* flavor! *My* heat! The blessing Nefertari wove special for *my* Promise! And she gave it to *her!* The work meant for *my crown!* Twisted my destiny! Gave *Khyasia* my future—and Shadeur!"

Uzoma flinched internally. *Everyone can't be all up in your crown,* she thought, the old warning echoing sharp and clear. *Cluttering up your crossroads, damaging your nu growth... and your destiny*. This child was radiating pure spiritual interference, a danger not just to herself but to everyone whose energy mingled here.

"Child." Nefertari's weary voice resonated then, deeper, imbued with an ancient authority that seemed to momentarily quell the seething frenzy. She raised a hand, palm outward, fingers steady despite the storm gathering before her. "Cease this now. This path you tread, fueled by a pain I see but warped by misplaced rage, leads only to ruin. Do you understand what you risk to this House?" her voice deepened, taking on the resonance of the very walls around them, "this neutral ground, this sanctuary, built on generations of peace bought with struggle, since the fires of the nineteen-seventies, during the dawning of the Black Is Beautiful age, nearly consumed us all. It will not suffer the breaking of that sacred truce such discord unleashed within its heart."

The Matron's warning, heavy with the weight of that thousand-year war held barely in check, was instead the final spark to the waiting tinder. "Ruin?" Aminata screamed, the sound tearing from her throat, raw and shredded. Tears finally broke free, carving hot paths through the grime and frantic energy on her young face. "You already ruined *me*!"

She threw her head back, a guttural cry ripping from her lungs. Her tempestuous locs writhed around her like living things, a Mami Wata rising from psychic depths, a Medusa crowned in sparking, angry wire. She gathered the unstable energy, pulling light from the shattered shards of the stained-glass windows, leeching power from the ambient magic humming in the salon, even drawing the swirling fractal patterns off the copper wall into herself. The complicated calculations of Uzoma's unfinished designs nearby flickered and drained. The air crackled audibly. The smell of ozone intensified, sharp and metallic. Power, raw and untamed and steeped in adolescent agony, reached its peak. The air thinned, and Uzoma registered the violent drain on the salon's ambient magic. Across the room, Naiser's stillness was that of a predator poised to strike, every muscle taut.

The very Rootwork woven into the foundation of The Beautifulest shuddered.

Then, with a final, ragged scream that blended fury and heartbreak, Aminata whipped her head forward. The gathered maelstrom erupted from her hair, unleashed not through practiced Kemetic Weaving that employed kinesthetic art, or the steady hand of a Crown Conjurer or a Crown Architect, but through sheer, stubborn will. Not shimmering air, not static discharge. A visible lance of sharp, unstable energy. Pulsing violent purple veined with angry red crackled like a downed power line, tore across the suddenly silent salon, a new violation.

The lance, a raw scream made visible, sucked the warmth from the air, leaving trails of angry red sparks like dying embers. It moved with the impossible speed of pure rage, aimed true at the Matron's still, waiting heart. But Nefertari, ancient as the Mississippi mud, fluid as the humid Memphis air, didn't flinch.

Her eyes, pools of starlit obsidian holding centuries of witnessing such fires, narrowed almost imperceptibly. Time stuttered, the silence stretching, amplifying the echo of Willie Hutch's promise. With a movement that was less action and more intention—a sigh of profound sorrow mixed with the unbending will of a queen defending her realm—she raised her hands, palms facing the incoming assault.

Power, deep and resonant as the earth's core, bloomed from her. Nefertari's own magnificent locs flared, the tiny mirrors embedded within them catching the ambient light and weaving it into a blinding, intricate web. Gold threads pulsed, singing with energy, forming a breathtaking, three-dimensional fractal shield—a luminous golden geometry, impossibly complex yet perfectly ordered, rooted in Kemetic precision and the deep mathematics of creation. The untamed lance slammed into the golden shield with a sound like tearing dimensions, like metal screaming against stars collapsing. Purple energy splashed, arcing wildly, scorching the ochre wall behind Nefertari. It instantly shattered a tall standing mirror into a rain of glittering dust that evaporated before hitting the floor. The shield held its steady light, absorbing the brunt of the raw, undisciplined force, yet.

Nefertari winced, a slight tremor running through her hands.

"The truce ends here, child," Nefertari's voice resonated, quieter now, laced with sorrow but utterly final, carrying the weight of broken history, the promise of consequences older than memory. "You have desecrated this House. You have chosen war."

That was the signal. Uzoma and Naiser exploded into motion. Neutral ground violated, Matron attacked. The ancient protocols, the warrior instincts, the fragile peace shattered beyond repair.

Uzoma's hands flew, light weaving between her fingers like luminous thread. Igbo calculations became tangible energy as glowing nets of turquoise light, humming with contained power, sprang into existence. They cast energy like a celestial fisherman seeking to ensnare a thrashing storm. She aimed not to harm, but to contain, to bind Aminata's flailing limbs and thrashing locs before the girl's volatile Rootwork damaged the very foundations. Her own expertise was in growing clients' edges, tending to the delicate roots with reverence, not brutally snatching them away as this raw, undirected energy threatened to do to the entire salon. "Aminata! Hold!" Uzoma shouted, her voice sharp with command and fear. "Think! Before you unravel us all!" Her movements were precise, driven by logic even amidst the chaos, the Crown Conjuror desperately trying to reinforce collapsing order.

Naiser, however, was pure kinetic fury unleashed. She flowed instantly into the ginga, a constant, hypnotic, deceptive motion that ate the distance between her and Aminata, her bells chiming sharply with each step, a discordant battle rhythm replacing the memory of soul music. Her braids became living weapons.

One moment she'd spin low, braids weighted with shells and charged metal sweeping across the floor like a scythe crackling with grounding energy, aimed at Aminata's ankles. The next, she'd launch herself forward, a specific thick braid whistling through the air like a meteor hammer, ending not in blunt force but in a burst of concussive sonic power from the bells woven within. Aimed to disorient, to disarm. Sharpened cowrie shells glinted with captured light. Her movements echoed the ferocious grace of Dahomey warriors, channeled through the fluid unpredictability of capoeira. This was Kinetic Weaving ignited by righteous anger.

Aminata shrieked, batting away Uzoma's energy net with a wild surge of purple static that caused the remaining intact mirrors to crack and the overhead lights to flicker violently. She dodged Naiser's sweeping attack with raw instinct, her ruined locs whipping around her like thorny vines tipped with unleashed energy, leaving sizzling ozone trails in the air.

"Get off me!" she screamed, tears streaming, voice raw with pain. "Stay outta this! This between *me* and *her*! She owe me!"

Her power flared brighter but more erratically with each outburst, drawing ambient energy recklessly, causing the copper wall panels to warp and groan, the air to taste thick like burnt sugar and blood. Nefertari deflected another, weaker pulse from Aminata, her golden shield rippling again, the fractal patterns shifting, adapting. She moved with deliberate, sorrowful grace, her defense almost a lament, a demonstration of the beauty and strength of controlled Rootwork against raw, untamed hurt. It was a silent plea for the child to see beyond the immediate pain to the greater destiny she was unknowingly being guided towards. The tiny bells on Nefertari's locs chimed specific, rich frequencies, complex harmonic waves attempting to disrupt the disordered static Aminata generated. To soothe the storm. And perhaps, to gently nudge the chaotic threads of the child's power towards a more constructive, if still hidden, path.

The Beautifulest groaned around them. Another mirror exploded. A carved wooden styling chair near Uzoma splintered as Naiser dodged a wild, unfocused blast from Aminata. Stuffing from the cushions tumbled onto the floor in great, white clouds. Uzoma threw another net, this one wider, laced with glowing Igbo symbols of binding and balance.

Seeing an opening as Aminata momentarily faltered, Naiser's hand darted to the leather satchel at her hip. With a flick of her wrist, a set of gleaming shears—long, slender, and wickedly sharp—flew through the air. The hair tools now weapons were aimed not to maim but to sever the flow of Aminata's volatile energy by cutting through a key section of her wildly thrashing locs.

Aminata, however, shrieked, a wave of purple force erupting from her, not only deflecting the shears but sending them spinning back towards their owner with terrifying velocity. Naiser was forced to duck, bob, and weave with breathtaking speed, the redirected shears slicing through the air where she'd been milliseconds before. Close enough to snip a few stray strands from one of her own braids, which sizzled and fell to the floor like singed whispers.

For a moment, it seemed they might overwhelm Aminata's raw power through sheer skill and coordinated effort. The teen staggered back under Naiser's relentless pressure, momentarily blinded by a pulse of pure golden light from Nefertari's shield. That deep wellspring of adolescent agony fueled her as the image of Shadeur smiling at Khyasia flashed behind her eyes. *Khyasia*, radiant in a glory Aminata was certain had been spun for her, Shadeur's attention a bright, painful affirmation of the theft. Seeing her chance closing, Aminata did something unexpected. Something desperate—before Promise Night, she would not have dared. But betrayal had emboldened her, imbuing her in this moment with an odd calm, discipline.

She didn't lash out again. Instead, Aminata inhaled sharply, a ragged gasp sucking energy inward. She pulled it all back into herself: the crackling static, the radiating heat from the scorch marks, the very fear choking the air. Her eyes rolled back briefly, pupils flaring void-purple. She became the terrifying eye of her own storm, a nexus of unstable, concentrated power.

Uzoma cried out, a true scream this time, "No! Child, don't concentrate it! You'll break yourself! You'll break everything!"

Before Nefertari could recalibrate her shield for this terrifying implosion/explosion dynamic, before Naiser could land a truly disabling blow, Aminata unleashed it all. Not a lance this time, not a wild surge. A focused, coherent beam of pure destructive void, purple force erupted from her forehead, her third eye, channeled through the ruined crown of her locs.

Arcing, the beam bypassed the golden shield. Maybe it found a harmonic weakness in the shield, something Nefertari hadn't anticipated from such raw fury. Or maybe Nefertari herself moved. *Yes,* Aminata narrowed her eyes to see, the elder had shifted fractionally, instinctively angling her shield. Perhaps she sought to protect Uzoma from a ricochet that could unravel the Architect's careful matrix.

The force struck Nefertari high on the chest.

But there was no explosion. Only a sickening *thump,* a sound like a heart stopping, a sudden cancellation of light, sound, energy. The golden fractal shield dissolved instantly into fading motes. The vibrant power surrounding Nefertari vanished. The tiny, ever-present bells fell utterly silent. Nefertari crumpled. Not dramatically, but with a terrible, boneless finality. Her regal, lush crown fell limp around her shoulders as the Matron collapsed back into the elegant throne-like chair behind her. Once a titan among the Conjurors, the magnificent queen spirit was abruptly unplugged from the world. Her eyes fluttered closed.

The light, the life, the ancient, grounding, Burtiful power that had radiated from her dimmed, winked out, leaving a void that sucked the very breath from the room.

Silence crashed down, heavier than any sound. The void left by Nefertari's extinguished light pressed in, stealing the air, the warmth, the very hum of ambient magic that had always defined The Beautifulest. Dust motes hung suspended in the fractured golden light bleeding from the violated jewel tones of the shattered stained-glass windows, witnesses to the unthinkable.

First to react, logic battling horror was Uzoma, the Architect. A sharp, indrawn gasp, and she surged forward, not towards Aminata, but towards the fallen Matron. Her movements were clipped, efficient, hands already tracing diagnostic patterns in the air, whispering Igbo terms for spirit locus and life-thread integrity.

"Matron? Nefertari? Nne nne?" she murmured, kneeling beside the still figure, her clinical focus a thin dam holding back a flood of grief and terror. Was the spirit merely pushed into a liminal space? Trapped between worlds? Or severed completely, cast adrift? She reached into a small conjure bag tied securely at her waist, fingers searching frantically for chalk, for Goofer Dust, maybe even a protective railroad spike consecrated under a Memphis moon. *Anything* to draw a hasty circle, to anchor the Matron if some part of her still lingered near the cooling flesh.

"Need to secure the crown," she muttered, her voice tight with strain, eyes scanning Nefertari's now-limp locs for any flicker, any residual spark of the immense Memphite Rootwork the Matron commanded. Leaving the head, the seat of the spirit, exposed like this... unthinkable. A gaping door for any wandering negativity.

Naiser's reaction was pure sound and fury. A low, guttural roar ripped from her throat, echoing the primal violation that had just occurred. Her capoeira grace vanished, replaced by the locked stance of a predator about to spring. Every line of her body radiated killing intent, focused solely, utterly on Aminata. The brass bells woven near her temple didn't chime. They jangled with sharp, discordant rage, an alarm signal screaming across the sudden silence. Her voice, when it came, was a low snarl, vibrating with power barely held in check. "You, child, will *pay*." Her braids writhed, charged metal and shell adornments glinting like fangs in the fractured light.

Frozen for a heartbeat, Aminata stared, the purple energy fading around her forehead like a dying bruise. The frenzied power ebbed, leaving behind a nauseating emptiness, a ringing silence where her rage had been. She saw Nefertari slumped in the chair, magnificent and terrifyingly still. The silence of those ever-present bells screamed louder than her own attack. "Matron?" she whispered, the sound thin, lost in the vast quiet. *Did I...? Is she...? Dead?* The face of Shadeur smiling at Khyasia dissolved, replaced by the weight of Nefertari's last warning, the knowledge of the broken truce, the desecrated sanctuary, the unleashed war. This wasn't about jacked up hair or a boy, not anymore. A cold dread, colder than the Mississippi in winter, seized her. Triumph flickered for a nanosecond, instantly extinguished by the horrifying magnitude of what her pain had wrought.

What have I done?

Fluid and deadly, Naiser took a step forward, the floorboards barely registering her weight. That predatory focus snapped Aminata from her shock. An apprentice barely begun, she knew she wasn't battle-ready for a warrior such as Naiser. It was enough that she had survived. Panic itching surged the broken paths of her scalp, primal and overwhelming. *Get out. Now.* She didn't think, didn't plan. With a final, desperate cry that was half sob, half gasp, she flung her hands out, unleashing not a focused beam, but a blinding flash of residual purple static and pure, terrified energy. It wasn't an attack, just a shield, a desperate get-away burst meant to disorient.

Naiser recoiled instinctively, shielding her eyes with a hiss. Uzoma cursed, pulling her own protective energies tight around herself and the unmoving Matron. In that split second of confusion, Aminata turned and fled. She scrambled through the ruined doorway, tripping over splinters of ancient Dogon wood, out of the sanctuary she had violated, and into the musical revelry and wet heat of the city's most famous street beyond.

Inside The Beautifulest, the silence returned, heavy and accusing. Uzoma frantically worked over Nefertari. Sprinkling a fine circle of powder around the chair, she whispered urgent protective prayers, trying to anchor what remained of the Matron's spirit. Eyes ringed with slow tears, she prayed it hadn't fled entirely into the discord. Near the wall, electrostatic energy ringed Naiser who stood rigid, trembling slightly, her fury momentarily checked by the stark reality of their loss. Gaze fixed on the empty, shattered doorway, she muttered words that did not sound like prayers, flinging her voice to where the scent of Aminata's panic and ozone still hung. The holographic sign above it, "Peace to All Who Enter," flickered violently, then went dark. Outside, beyond the broken threshold, the subtle warding spells woven into the haint blue paint began to fray visibly, the illusion wavering, the deep wound inflicted on this sacred space beginning, inevitably, to bleed out into the world.

Within the violated Beautifulest, the guilty silence stretched, thick with the scent of ozone, burnt sugar, and spilled conjure powders. Uzoma continued her frantic work over Nefertari, her face a mask of concentration etched with desperation. The chalk circle around the Matron's chair glowed faintly, a fragile dam against the encroaching disorder. Nefertari remained horribly still, her spirit stubbornly anchored or perhaps already gone beyond reach. Maybe she slipped sideways in time, as the deepest Memphite Rootwork allowed for the true masters. Those who could walk the woven threads of lineage to commune with their ancestors, or even seek counsel, as legend claimed Nefertari could, from the future daughters whose possibility resided within their own spirit. Or was the thread simply... cut? Uzoma couldn't tell yet. Raw discordant energy from Aminata's attack had dangerously scrambled the readings. Her tears fell unheeded onto the amber floor. Each drop a prayer unanswered. Leaving the crown vulnerable like this was courting disaster.

Near the shattered doorway, Naiser's trembling ceased. The electrostatic crackle around her faded, replaced by a cold, hard stillness that was somehow more frightening than her earlier rage. Her grief hadn't vanished, but had transmuted into diamond-hard resolve. She slowly, deliberately, reached up, testing the tension of a specific braid, running fingers over the sharpened edge of a cowrie shell. Her eyes, fixed on the empty space where Aminata had vanished into the Beale Street revelry, held the flat, implacable focus of a hunter settling in for a long pursuit. The muttered words she'd flung after the fleeing girl had not been prayers, but promises. Oaths sworn in the old way. They had maybe hours, less perhaps, before word fully spread, before *they* arrived – the other factions, drawn by the scent of spilled power and broken peace like sharks to blood. The clock was ticking, loud as a drumbeat in the sudden quiet.

Outside, beyond the fraying wards of the haint blue building, Memphis itself shuddered. Traffic lights flickered blocks away. Down by the river, the water turned sluggish for a moment, the currents confused. Across town, in a high-rise overlooking the city lights, an Elder of a rival Crown Architect house paused, head tilted, sensing a profound disturbance in the Rootwork grid, a power vacuum opening where none should be. Perhaps Khyasia, still basking in the glow of her Promise night blessing, felt a sudden, icy tremor beneath the triumph, a discordant note in the energy Nefertari had woven, making her glance nervously towards downtown where The Beautifulest stood sentinel. The ripples were spreading fast. The consequences were already knocking at the door.

Uzoma finally sat back on her heels, the chalk dust white against her dark knuckles.

"She's... stable," she whispered, the word tasting like ashes. "Her spirit is still tethered. Barely. But anchored." She looked up at Naiser, her usual calm shattered, revealing the fear beneath. "But the truce, Naiser... the truce is broken." The peace bought in nineteen-seventies, that monumental Black Is Beautiful period....gone like smoke, yet leaving behind the scent of burning and the pain.

Naiser nodded once, sharply. Her gaze didn't leave the doorway. The discordant jangle of her bells had ceased. Now, with a flick of her wrist, a single bell chimed, clear and cold as judgment.

"Peace was a dream," Naiser said, her voice low and hard as river stone. "A place to rest, perhaps, but not a place to live when the remembering has not been done. Now, the reckoning begins. We secure the Matron. Then I find the child."

Uzoma looked at the fallen Matron, the magnificent queen unplugged from the world carrying the weight of that unspeakable, unbroken history in her very stillness. Uzoma's eyes rested upon the warrior coiled beside her, then towards the violated threshold. No turning back. History wasn't a story told. It was the ancient ocean beneath the river, and its currents were pulling them all under now. The thousand-year war, held sleeping for a precious generation, stirred once more in the heart of Memphis, awakened by a heartbroken girl wielding power she didn't understand. The foundations shuddered, not just with Rootwork, but with the promise of shed blood and futures rewritten in fire and fury. The story, the real story, was just beginning.

SEE ME! LOOK ME!

Music was rebellion. Not just the bass thump that shook the chain-link fence around Goat Park, heavy enough to vibrate in your bones, nor the quick-fire bars that spilled from tinny speakers daring the world to listen. No, the real rebellion lived in the beat translated through bodies–*their* bodies, young and hungry and electric with refusal right there on the cracked concrete stage they claimed from the city. It lived in the sharp, precise angles Chanel's arms carved through the humid summer air, fractals of defiance that sliced through indifference and judgment.

It flowed in Bijou, all liquid grace and impossible slides, hips tracing stories older than the pavement beneath their feet, water finding its level against the hard edges of an unkind world. And it sparked brightest in Na Na – Sanaa then, choreographer and heart-fire – who pulled their threads together, who wove steps that spoke truth to power, that laughed in the face of doubt. Each synchronized stomp, each defiant gesture, each shared grin mid-motion was their living argument, their claim on joy in a world quick to snatch it away.

An urgent claiming, maybe, fierce and necessary, because Black girl joy felt like borrowed time, a bright spark vulnerable to the slightest wind, shadowed always by the hard truth that the world saw you last, protected you least.

It was their attack on the invisible chains—the ones forged of low expectation, of quiet, violent erasure, of being told your rhythms didn't matter, nor your heart, nor your truth. They danced freedom into existence, breath by breath, beat by beat.

Together.

The memory flared, hot and sudden, behind Chanel's hard eyes now, years removed from the asphalt playgrounds and basketball courts of her youth. The taste in the air wasn't New York heat thick with possibility. It was the stale, recycled chill of an airport terminal somewhere far from home, the scent of jet fuel and anxiety clinging to her clothes. That vibrant rebellion felt like another lifetime, a bright dream that receded with brutal speed. The music hadn't freed Na Na. It had become the intricate, glittering bars of her gilded cage. The chains were no longer invisible. They were digital, proprietary, soul-deep. But the echo of that dance, the muscle memory of that shared, fierce joy—that was the pulse beneath Chanel's own skin now. That remembered rhythm was the map, the fuel, the reason. The real attack, the one that mattered, hadn't even begun yet.

Chanel pushed the phantom beat down, locking it away behind a wall of cold resolve inside her chest. Sentiment wouldn't breach the fortress built around Na Na. Grief wouldn't unlock the doors. She sat stiffly on the edge of a sagging motel bed, the scratchy polyester blanket beneath her rough as sandpaper against her jeans. The room smelled faintly of stale cigarette smoke and the harsh chemical cleaner that fought a losing battle against it. A single fluorescent tube flickered erratically overhead, casting a sickly yellow pallor on the water-stained acoustic ceiling tiles and the peeling wallpaper patterned with faded, indeterminate flowers. Outside the grimy window, the endless drone of highway traffic provided a bleak, impersonal soundtrack. She needed leverage, information, a crack in the wall of silence. Where to pry?

Not family. Useless. She'd learned that from clipped phone calls filled with awkward silences or suspiciously smooth assurances. Na Na's cousins, her aunts—suddenly flush, their social media feeds glossy with trips and trinkets neither earned nor deserved—recited vague lines about Na Na being "so busy," "living her dream." Their eyes, glimpsed over spotty video feeds, held the flat, dead sheen of coached denial, or maybe just the willful ignorance that came easy when the checks kept clearing. Bought and paid for, content to trade silence for comfort while Na Na vanished into the machine. And Nana Sylvie, the fierce matriarch who would have demanded truth, who would have burned down walls with her righteous fury – Nana Sylvie was years gone, ashes and beloved memory, leaving an unfillable void where Na Na's staunchest protector should have been. The thought made the cheap, anonymous room feel even colder, emptier.

Bijou? Chanel traced the outline of a coffee cup ring stained onto the cheap laminate nightstand, absentmindedly pushing back a heavy fall of spiraling locs from her face. Later. Maybe. When she had something solid, something more than desperate hope and a gut full of dread. Bijou had her own battles, her own chains forged in hardship. Chanel couldn't pull her into this vortex without a clearer path, without something tangible to offer besides more danger.

So, the source. The deal itself. The moment the gilded cage door swung shut. Who held the pen? Who brokered the sale? *Morris Finley.* Slick, percentage-hungry Morris, whose smarmy face flashed in her memory. The flickering neon sign from the gas station across the highway pulsed rhythmically outside the thin motel curtains, casting shifting, unreliable shadows across the floor – red, then green, then dark. Chanel wasn't just looking for information; she was hunting, fueled by a cold, simmering rage directed squarely at him. Word on the virtual street, pieced together from fragmented online whispers, was the label ditched him shortly after the ink dried, his purpose served. Good riddance, maybe, but the damage was already done. But he was *there* at the beginning. He saw the clauses, met the executives, knew the initial promises. And Chanel suspected, deep in her gut, that he *knew*. Knew how foul that deal smelled beneath the gloss, how predatory the gleam was in those corporate eyes. Knew, and didn't care enough about Na Na – about a brilliant young Black girl from the neighborhood – to throw up a flag, to whisper a warning, not when that kind of money was shimmering right there. More money than any of them had ever been within sniffing distance of. Chanel could almost forgive the hunger, that desperate grab for the brass ring after years of hustling pennies. Almost. But not the abandonment. Not signing the deal and then walking away – even if he *was* pushed out later by Ice and her whole crew of yes-men, those sycophantic handlers and PR hacks with their fake smiles and empty hype. Not leaving Na Na defenseless, a lamb tossed to the lions just as they were sharpening their claws. Guilt, resentment, maybe just plain carelessness fueled by whatever cheap high he chased these days – Finley was the only loose thread visible in this whole damn tapestry. He was the place to pull.

The decision settled, hard and unwelcome as the lukewarm coffee she'd choked down hours ago. Find Finley. Pry the truth out of him. *Make him answer for it.* Whatever it took.

It took days, chasing digital ghosts and faded contacts from rooms much like this one, fueled by stale gas station snacks and sheer, grinding will. Days navigating dead-end forums that smelled metaphorically of desperation, calling numbers that rang into oblivion, following whispers that evaporated like smoke in the indifferent city air. It felt like wading through drying concrete, thick and suffocating. But Chanel pushed, the memory of Na Na's stolen light a burning coal in her chest, until finally, a grimy lead solidified. It pointed her here, to a crumbling apartment building in a neighborhood slumped under the weight of forgotten promises, staring up at a bank of dirty buzzers beneath a sky the dull grey color of dishwater. She found his name, faded but legible, and jabbed the button beside it.

The buzzer shrieked back at her thumb, a high-pitched, grating sound that felt like frayed nerves made audible. Pushing open the door that grudgingly gave way, Chanel was hit by the atmosphere inside – air thick as old soup, carrying a cloying sweetness battling something sour underneath. Mildew, maybe, or just the accumulated funk of neglect. Dust motes, fat and lazy, swam in the single blade of weak afternoon light cutting through a grimy window blind coated in what looked like years of city soot. The light illuminated a landscape of defeat: towers of yellowing trade papers listing precariously on scarred surfaces, takeout containers fossilizing on a low table, a couple of stained coffee mugs hosting ancient dregs, even an overflowing glass ashtray though the air didn't smell of recent smoke. Peeling paint curled away from the wall in one corner like a cynical lip.

And there he was, Morris Finley, architect of Na Na's gilded cage, slumped in a threadbare armchair whose pattern had surrendered to stains and time. His breath hitched wetly in the silence. Beside him, on a stack of folders threatening to avalanche, sat the half-empty vial of iridescent blue – liquid Kush, the neon signpost of his surrender.

Chanel's eyes swept the room, taking in the squalor, and snagged on a dusty shelf angled crookedly above a silent, dark-screened vintage monitor. Framed photos crowded it, mostly glossy 8x10s showcasing Finley's rictus grin alongside various artists – some Chanel vaguely recognized, others lost to obscurity. Standard industry poses, forced smiles under harsh lighting. But one, smaller, slightly cleaner, stood out. It was him and Na Na. Sanaa, really – captured maybe just weeks after signing. Her hair was intricately braided then, beads catching the light, her smile wide, incandescent, eyes blazing with the fierce, joyful hope that had been her signature. Seeing that untamed exuberance, that belief radiating from her friend before the world clipped her wings, made Chanel's breath catch sharp in her chest. A wave of hot grief threatened to spill over, but she blinked it back fiercely. Tears would have no impact on this soulless wonder before her; they were a currency he couldn't spend.

Finley's eyes, filmed over like cracked marbles, finally registered her presence. A flicker, not of recognition, but maybe of startled prey sensing a predator.

"Whoa now," he rasped, voice like dragging gravel. "Security-" He stopped, squinting. "Didn't buzz."

"Security?" Chanel's voice was low, tight, vibrating with contained energy. She took a step forward, the grit of the floor unseen but felt beneath the sole of her boot. "You think *security* matters now, Morris? I'm here about Sanaa."

The name hit him like a physical blow. He flinched, shrinking deeper into the chair's stained embrace. "Na Na," he mumbled, the sound thick with something – guilt, perhaps, or just the kush slurry in his throat. "Big star. Shining bright. Ice, well, Ice polishes her diamonds."

"Stop talking like a damn press release!" Chanel snapped, the sound cracking sharp in the dead air. "I know better. *We* know better. Where is she?"

Finley recoiled, eyes darting nervously. "Safe! She's safe. Top of the world. Contract makes sure—"

"Contract?" Chanel laughed, a harsh, brittle sound. "You call that a contract? Or a digital slave trade? We know she's wired, Morris. We know she ain't free. We know Ice is sucking the marrow from her bones, byte by byte!" She leaned in, invading his space, her energy suddenly sharp, focused like a blade, radiating contained power, forcing him to meet her glare. "They called it her big break. Nah, it was *breakage*. You broke her, Morris. Or helped them do it."

He whimpered, trying to turn away, fumbling for the vial. Chanel moved faster, her hand clamping down on his wrist. It felt frail, bird-like. "Don't," she warned. "Not yet. Talk to me. Where. Is. She?"

Tears, oily and unnatural, began to leak from Finley's eyes. "Can't," he gasped. "NDA. Proprietary tech. They watch."

"Who watches the watchers when they're counting blood money?" Chanel shot back, paraphrasing something her Pops used to say. "Tell me something real, Morris. For her. For Na Na." She glanced involuntarily back at the photo on the shelf, the image searing itself behind her eyes. "For the girl who carried constellations in her damn shoulders before you sold her off as satellite data."

The mention of constellations snagged something in his ruined memory. "Data stream," he whispered, shuddering. "Pure kinetic gold. They map it. Map it onto the new girl now too."

Chanel's blood ran cold. "New girl? They're replacing her?"

Finley nodded, misery etched onto his face. "Tymphany. Fannie. Sounds like money, right?" He gave a weak, wheezing laugh. "Na Na's just legacy tech now. Still valuable, but phasing out."

He looked directly at Chanel then, a moment of horrifying lucidity in the chemical storm. "Tour. Africa. Last one for the setup. Ouaga...Ouagadougou." He stumbled over the syllables. "Mobile unit keeps her close. Med-bay container. Gotta be near the stage. Needs the, the source code." He gestured vaguely at his own chest, then collapsed back, spent.

Chanel released his wrist, stepping back, the sour air catching in her throat. Ouagadougou. Mobile unit. Replacement. The pieces clicked into a grim mosaic. Legacy tech. Source code. *Another Black body mined for its rhythm,* she thought, the bitterness rising like bile. *Soul digitized, packaged, sold off. And when it runs thin? Find another vein.*

Finley was already reaching for the blue vial again, his escape hatch. Chanel watched him for a second, a storm of pity and disgust warring within her. He was a casualty too, in his own way, poisoned by the system he'd fed. But Na Na was the one chained.

She turned, her locs swirling briefly with the abrupt movement, pulling her resolve around her like armor. She had names, places,

pieces. Enough to start. Enough to find Bijou. Enough to fight. She
walked out without looking back, the agent's ragged breathing fading
behind her, replaced by the determined, fractured rhythm pounding
in her own chest. *Step, find, fight*, it seemed to beat. *Step, find, fight.*
Bring her home.

* * *

The automated floor buffer hummed a low, monotonous
rhythm across the polished expanse of the corporate lobby. Its oper-
ator moved with it, not guiding it so much as orbiting it, her motions
fluid, economical, almost unnervingly graceful even in the unflat-
tering grey coveralls of the night cleaning crew. Years had passed,
hardships etched fine lines around her eyes, but Chanel would know
that flow anywhere. Bijou. Bijoutiful Wata Wata. Still moving like
water, even here, surrounded by steel, glass, and the sterile quiet of
late-night commerce in a city that never truly slept. A small cleaning
drone zipped past Bijou's ankles, efficiently scrubbing edges, its quiet
whir a counterpoint to the buffer's drone.

Chanel watched from the shadowed alcove near the bio-scan
entry turnstiles she'd slipped through moments before Bijou's
shift likely locked them down. Seeing Bijou like this – competent,
focused, yet carrying an undeniable weariness in the slump of her
shoulders when she paused – sent a complex pang through Chanel.
Respect warred with a fierce, protective anger, not *at* Bijou, but *for*
her. For the dreams deferred, the fire banked low by necessity. She
remembered Bijou's ex, that dusty fool whose name she refused
to even think, remembered the fear in Bijou's eyes back then, the

pregnancies used like anchors. Seeing her here, free of him at least, raising her kids, working these brutal hours – it was survival, fierce and hard-won.

Chanel stepped out of the shadows, a cascade of thick locs framing a face set with determination. "Bijou?"

The buffer drone hummed on, but Bijou froze mid-sway. She turned slowly, her eyes narrowing in the ambient glow from the lobby's recessed lighting. Recognition dawned, followed immediately by a complex mask of surprise, wariness, and something that might have been old hurt.

"Chanel?" Bijou's voice was lower now, huskier than Chanel remembered. "What in God's name are you doing here?" She glanced instinctively towards the security console, her hand hovering near the comm panel on her wrist-comp worn over the coverall sleeve.

"Just... passing through," Chanel lied lamely, moving closer. "Saw the light, saw you. Been a long time, B." She kept her voice soft, non-threatening. "Heard about Mercie – she doing good on her own?"

Bijou nodded curtly, her gaze still guarded. "She's good. Smart like her mama." A flicker of pride, quickly shuttered. "Look, Chanel, it's late. I got three more floors, and these bots need supervising or they start buffing the executives' synth-leather chairs. Whatever this is..."

"It's about Na Na," Chanel cut in, the urgency overriding her attempt at a gentle approach.

Bijou flinched, physically recoiling as if struck. Her face hardened. "Na Na?" she repeated, the name tasting like ash. "What about her? Enjoying her millions? Forgot all about the broke-ass fracters and wata dancers she left behind in the dust, right?"

"It ain't like that, B," Chanel said quickly, holding up a hand. "She didn't sell out. She's trapped. Like, seriously trapped." And then the words tumbled out, the story gleaned from Finley – the tech, the crystal cave turned mobile med-bay, the nanites, the isolation, the replacement waiting in the wings, Ouagadougou.

Bijou shook her head. "You warned her if she wasn't careful, they would take everything. Give'm an inch, they take your world, the moon and the stars." She listened, head tilted, her face impassive at first, the mask back firmly in place. But as Chanel spoke, describing the electrodes, the ashen skin, the hollow voice, cracks appeared. Disbelief warred with dawning horror. "Wired?" she whispered. "Like... like some kinda ghost in the machine?"

"Worse," Chanel confirmed, her voice grim. "She *is* the machine. Or the battery for it. And they're about to toss her when she's drained."

Bijou turned away sharply, walking towards the towering glass windows overlooking the glittering, indifferent city sprawl below. She rested her forehead against the cool surface. "So she didn't just leave us," she said, her voice muffled. "They *stole* her." Then anger flared again, hot and quick. "Stole her creative mojo, her style, *errything*. But where were *you*, Chanel? You were always the one saying she gave too much away! You didn't stop her?"

"Stop her how?" Chanel shot back, stung. "She was blinded by the lights, the money! We all were, almost. You think Morris "The Mouth" Finley gave a damn? He saw dollar signs! And then she was gone, vanished behind layers of corpo bullshit!"

"And you just let her go?" Bijou whirled around, eyes blazing now. "Just like you let the dream go? We were supposed to be *it*,

Chanel! The three of us! But Na Na chased the money, and you..."
Her voice faltered. "...And I had babies."

The raw pain in that last admission silenced Chanel for a beat.
She saw the years of struggle etched on Bijou's face. *Dance teaches
you how to fall,* Bijou used to say back when they were practicing
drops and freezes till their bodies screamed. *Life teaches you how
to get back up when falling ain't part of the choreography.* Bijou
had done more than get back up, she'd clawed her way upright while
carrying the weight of the world.

Chanel softened her tone, stepping closer again. "Nobody *let*
anything go, B. Life happened. Tricks got played. Yeah, maybe Na
Na made a bad choice trusting those snakes, maybe I shoulda fought
harder then, I don't know. But you know Na Na. Once she gets her
mind set on something, that's it. And you?"

She met Bijou's fierce gaze. "You survived. You protected your
kids from that trifling piece of crap. That ain't giving up, that's fighting a different kind of war."

Bijou looked away for a moment, her gaze sweeping over the
silent, gleaming lobby floor as if seeing reflections of a past she'd
fought hard to scrub clean. The hum of the buffer drone receded,
replaced by sharper, more discordant echoes in her mind. When her
eyes returned to Chanel's, they held a raw, ancient weariness, yet
beneath it, a glint of unbreakable steel.

"A different kind of war is right," Bijou said, her voice low
and textured, like gravel smoothed by a relentless tide. "You think
I wanted to trade the rhythm of the Wata-flow for the drone of this
damned machine? Trade cosmic slides and hydro-pulses for chasing

dust bunnies in these empty halls?" She made a sharp, dismissive gesture that still held a dancer's contained power.

"He knew," she continued, her voice dropping further, the name of her ex hanging unspoken in the sterile air. "He knew every beat of my heart was a step away from him. So he changed the tempo. One kid, then another. Said it was love, said it was family. Called it building a future. Felt more like building walls, brick by tiny, demanding brick, right around my feet until I couldn't 'fract or flow or even breathe right."

"There's a dance to survival too, Chanel," Bijou murmured, a flicker of something – not quite bitterness, more like stark under-standing – in her eyes. "It ain't got the lights or the crowds. No roar-ing approval when you land a move just right. It's the quiet shuffle in the dark, the rhythm of just keepin' on when every muscle, every bone, every piece of your soul is screaming to just. Stop. You learn to make your spine out of what's left when everything else is taken. You learn that your body is still a sacred space, even when it's been a battlefield. And these kids..." A fierce, protective light, the one Chanel had seen earlier, blazed up. "They're my best choreography. My most important performance. Worth every damn sacrifice."

She took a deep, steadying breath, the practiced calm of her current life settling back over her like a well-worn shield. The ghosts of her past receded, leaving only the present, and Chanel, standing before her with an impossible plea.

She paused, letting the words sink in. "But this thing with Na Na... this is the same system that grinds us all down, choose your poison. Exploitation ain't just bad contracts. It's dusty partners trapping you with babies they don't love or help take care of, it's cleaning corporations working you to the bone for pennies while you watch bot cleaners do half the job. It's all chains, B. Na Na's are just... higher tech." She gestured helplessness, frustration. "I gotta get her out. And I can't do it alone."

Bijou stared at her, conflict churning in her eyes. The fight seemed to drain out of her, replaced by a profound weariness, then a flicker of the old steel. She sighed, a long, slow release of breath that carried years of held tension. "Ouagadougou, you said?"

Chanel nodded, hope flaring cautiously.

Bijou tapped a command sequence into her wrist-comp, pausing the buffer drone. She ran a hand over her face. "Big tours like that, they always hire local temp crews for load-in, setup, tear-down, hospitality, sanitation. Agency I work with sometimes handles international placements. I got seniority. I could bust a move."

A ghost of a smile touched her lips, sharp and knowing.

"You still got it?" Chanel asked.

Bijou traced the programmed path of the main buffer, her own movements mirroring its steady, monotonous glide across the vast lobby. That practiced glide stuttered and stopped as she instinctively sank into a forgotten flow, then fractured the air with a signature twist so sharp and liquid it momentarily stole the light.

"Got it? People like us? Cleaners, caterers? We're invisible but we see everything." She looked directly at Chanel, the old spark, the Bijoutiful Wata Dancer's fierce intelligence, bright in her eyes. "I got it all right her, Chanel." She pointed at her heart and mind. "Alright. Tell me everything Finley said. Everything."

* * *

The airplane door opened onto a wall of heat. Not the humid, sticky embrace of a New York summer, thick with exhaust and possibility. This heat was different. Ancient. Dry as bone, baked deep into the red earth Chanel could see shimmering beyond the tarmac, carrying the scent of dust, charcoal smoke, and something else – something floral, sharp, and unfamiliar. Sunlight hammered down, unfiltered, bouncing off the metal stairs, making her squint hard. Beside her, Bijou drew a sharp breath, her hand instinctively going to shield her eyes.

> *Step onto the stairs.*
> *Feel the metal radiate stored sun,*
> *almost too hot to touch.*
> *Descend.*

Each step closer to the ground felt like a step into a different rhythm, a world operating on a syncopation Chanel hadn't learned yet. The air buzzed. Not just with heat anymore, but with sound – the whine of unseen engines, shouts in languages that slipped past her ears like water (French? Mooré? Others?), the distant, insistent beat of music she couldn't quite place. A different kind of energy pulsed here, looser, maybe, but no less intense than the concrete jungle they'd left behind. *It breathes different here,* Chanel thought, a pithy observation cutting through the sensory flood. *Like the earth itself ain't forgotten how to exhale fire.*

They walked across the tarmac towards the low-slung terminal building, the heat pressing down like a physical weight. Bijou moved beside her, silent for once, her usual fluid grace subtly altered, perhaps, by weariness or the sheer weight of this new reality. Chanel glanced at her friend's profile – jaw set, eyes scanning, taking it all in with a practiced economy of attention honed by years of navigating tough spots. *What's she thinking?* Chanel wondered briefly. *Mercie? The job? The sheer insanity of us being here?* The distance between them felt both vast and infinitesimal in that moment, bridged only by the desperate mission that had dragged them across the globe.

Inside the small terminal, the air conditioning fought a losing battle. Fans stirred the thick warmth, circulating the scent of jet fuel, disinfectant, and faintly, miraculously, roasting peanuts. Chaos, but with its own internal logic. People moved with purpose – flowing robes, crisp uniforms, worn Western clothes. Lines formed, dissolved, reformed.

A staccato rhythm of stamps on documents, murmured questions, quick scans under indifferent official gazes.

They navigated immigration, their pre-arranged visas linked to Bijou's agency contract smoothing the way, Chanel's freelance "cultural consultant" cover story barely warranting a second glance. Their carefully prepared narratives felt thin, fragile, like kite paper in a hurricane under the weight of their real purpose.

Finally, outside the terminal doors. The full force of Ouagadougou hit them. A kaleidoscope of color and motion. Mobylettes and small motorbikes buzzed everywhere like metallic insects, weaving improbable paths through pedestrians and battered taxis. People surged around them, a living river clad in breathtaking color. Vibrant wax prints bloomed with intricate patterns – spirals, sunbursts, geometrics that throbbed with life. Richly dyed bazin fabrics shimmered with a subtle sheen, tailored into flowing grand boubous or sharp, modern designs. Women walked with regal postures, heads held high, some balancing burdens with an impossible grace, their faces – a thousand variations of beautiful, deep-brown skin – some serene, some animated, like masks carved from luminous ebony. Men conversed in clusters, their movements sharp or languid, wrapped in crisp white or vivid patterns. Bright fabrics flashed everywhere. The air was thick with dust kicked up from the unpaved edges of the road, mixed with the rich smell of grilling meat – *dibi*, maybe, smoky and spiced – and the sweeter, nutty scent of shea butter.

Chanel felt momentarily breathless, submerged in a sea of unapologetic Black beauty, so dense and vibrant it made the still-real pockets of Harlem, the deep belly of Brooklyn, feel like a muted echo. This was that energy, that style, that inherent grace, times three, times ten, rooted deep in the earth beneath her feet. Chanel felt something shift inside her, deeper than the jet lag or the mission's tension. This air, this light, this red earth beneath her feet – it felt impossibly, profoundly *real*. Africa. Not a picture, not a story book myth, but the actual soil her ancestors were stolen from, a land they could only dream of returning to. A fierce, unexpected wave of emotion – awe, belonging, a sorrow too deep for tears – washed over her, rooting her to the spot for just a second beneath the vast, ancient sky. This place held history in every dust mote.

Bijou finally spoke, her voice low, dry. She wiped a bead of sweat tracing a path through the fine red dust already settling on her temple. "Right," she sighed, the sound carrying the weight of the journey, the kids left behind, the impossible task ahead. "Feels like we landed on the sun." She scanned the clamoring taxi drivers and hopeful porters. "First things first. Gotta find the agency contact,

check in for this 'job.' Get our bearings before we even think about..."
She didn't need to finish the sentence.

Chanel nodded, pulling herself back to the present, the mission
snapping back into sharp relief, overriding the momentary awe but
somehow deepened by it. The vibrant, pulsing life of the city faded
into background noise again, fuel now added to the fire.

"Yeah," she agreed, her voice tight with purpose. "Check in.
Blend in." *Then,* she thought, the old rhythm kicking back in, sharp
and determined, *we find the cage. And we break it open.* The real
attack was finally about to start, here, under this vast, unforgiving sky.

Step one. Find the contact.

* * *

Finding the contact was less cloak-and-dagger and more a
masterclass in Bijou's quiet efficiency. While Chanel scanned the
throng of hopeful taxi drivers and vendors outside the Ouagadougou
airport, her senses still buzzing from the sheer sensory overload of
their arrival, Bijou had already palmed her wrist-comp, its surface
momentarily shimmering with a complex, untraceable encrypted
handshake with a local network node.

"He's expecting us," Bijou said, her voice a low counterpoint
to the surrounding cacophony. "Designated pick-up. Zone C, blue
kiosk. Name's Moussa. Agency uses him for all their Sahel gigs.
Reliable. Discreet."

Reliable and discreet looked like a man barely out of his
teens, leaning against a faded blue refreshment kiosk shaped like an
oversized mango. He wore a crisp, locally tailored shirt in a vibrant

geometric print that could have been a signal in itself, and his eyes, quick and intelligent, flicked over them with an assessing gaze that missed nothing. He didn't approach until Bijou gave a small, almost imperceptible nod, a gesture Chanel herself almost missed.

"Akwaaba," Moussa said, his French accented with the melodic lilt of Mooré. Welcome. His smile was fleeting, professional. He gestured with his chin towards a battered but clean electric van, its solar panels glinting on the roof. "Punctuality is a virtue, yes? Especially when the curtain rises soon."

The ride to the sprawling "Harmattan Arena," a new, modular mega-structure on the outskirts of Ouaga 2000, was a blur of sunbaked streets, acacia trees draped in fine red dust, and the ubiquitous dance of mobylettes. Moussa, true to Bijou's assessment, was a man of few words. He handed them ID badges—"Hospitality Services – Level 2 Access"—attached to utilitarian grey lanyards.

A barely perceptible, holographic watermark of an intertwined "LL" pulsed faintly beneath their names. LushLife Records. The sight of it, even so subtle, sent a prickle of unease across Chanel's skin; SaDitty's empire was built on shadows and ruthlessly enforced contracts, and Na Na was caught deep within its silken, suffocating web. Beneath the "LL," almost an afterthought, was a smaller, starker insignia: a geometric ice-crystal design. The official tour mark.

The chips embedded within, he explained, were geo-fenced and time-restricted. Any deviation from their assigned zones or schedules would trigger an instant alert to "Ice Central Security," a notoriously humorless private firm whose operatives patrolled the venue with the predatory grace of desert foxes.

"Your supervisor is Madame Assetou," Moussa continued, his eyes meeting Bijou's in the rearview mirror. "She oversees all local temp staff for Zones 3 and 4. Catering, sanitation, general support. Strict, but fair. She values invisibility above all. Blend in, do the work, ask no questions. Your assignments will be on your work-slates when you clock in." He paused. "And your 'cultural consultancy,' Madame Chanel?" He gave Chanel a pointed look. "Best pursued during designated break periods. The Client is very particular about focus."

Chanel merely nodded, absorbing the implicit warning. The "Client"—Isis—was clearly a micro-manager of her gilded empire.

The backstage entrance of the Harmattan Arena was a jarring contrast to the vibrant chaos of Ouagadougou. It was a sterile warren of temporary corridors, humming with the thrum of massive generators and the chilled breath of industrial air conditioning. Cables thick as pythons snaked across rubber-matted floors, and stern-faced crew members in identical dark grey utility wear hurried past, their expressions uniformly stressed. Automated cleaning drones, smaller and more utilitarian than the one Bijou operated back in the States, zipped along the edges, their sensors blinking. Holographic signage in French, English, and surprisingly, Mandarin, flickered overhead, directing traffic and issuing stark warnings about restricted areas.

Occasionally, the main directive signs would cycle through a series of sponsor displays. The same intertwined "LL" that was on their badges flashed larger here, unavoidable, confirming LushLife Records' omnipresent ownership. The name, Chanel thought, was a cruel joke given the stories that circulated about SaDitty's iron grip and the artists trapped within. Then, more dominant, the geometric ice-crystal symbol blazed under the legend: "ISIS: The Crystalline Dominion Tour—

An Ice Central Production, under exclusive license from Lush-Life Records." The branding was as cold and unforgiving as the artist herself was reputed to be, a clear visual declaration of the power structure they were walking into, and how deeply Na Na was embedded in this high-tech, high-stakes spectacle.

Bijou took it all in with a practiced calm, her eyes already mapping layouts, noting camera placements, the flow of personnel. "Just another gig," she murmured to Chanel, a wry twist to her lips, but Chanel saw the old spark, the Water Dancer's intelligence, already calculating, adapting.

"Yeah," Chanel replied, her own gaze sweeping their surroundings, cataloging the layers of security, the almost fanatical order. "Just another cage. Bigger, maybe. More high-tech. But a cage all the same."

Moussa led them to a crowded check-in area, a cacophony of languages and nervous energy as other local hires were processed. He pointed them towards a bank of chrono-scanners. "Work-slates will activate once you're clocked. Madame Assetou will find you. Bonne chance." And with another fleeting smile, he was gone, disappearing back into the flow as easily as he'd appeared.

Holding their breath, they stepped up to the scanners.

*　*　*

The chrono-scanners blinked green, their work-slates activating with a soft chime and a flood of holographic data: complex

43

SHEREE RENÉE THOMAS

schematics of their assigned sanitation zones, a dizzying schedule
of timed tasks, and sternly worded compliance protocols in three
languages. Madame Assetou, a tall, imposing woman with eyes
that missed nothing and a gele headwrap that defied gravity, found
them within minutes. Her briefing was brutally efficient, her French
a rapid-fire staccato that emphasized speed, precision, and above
all, discretion.

"Zone 3 for you, Bijou – VIP suites, pre-show. Zone 4, Chanel
– tech corridors, loading bays. Stick to the maps on your slates. No
deviations. No chatter. Eyes down, work fast. The Client expects
perfection." Her gaze lingered on Chanel. "Your 'cultural consultancy'
begins after your assigned duties are complete, and only in designated common areas. Am I clear?"

"Crystal, Madame," Chanel said, meeting her gaze with a
practiced deference that cost her some effort.

Their new uniforms were the same anonymous grey as the rest
of the support staff, designed to fade into the high-tech background.
Bijou, equipped with an array of sophisticated sonic cleaners and
nano-polishing tools, disappeared into the hushed luxury of the VIP
wing. Chanel, armed with an industrial-grade refuse handler and a
cart of sterilized containment units, plunged into the labyrinthine
tech corridors. The air here was colder, thrumming with the constant
hum of cooling systems for racks of servers and power conduits
that pulsed with barely contained energy behind transparent
plasteel panels.

Every movement was a calculated risk, every glance a piece
of reconnaissance. The work was relentless, demanding, clearly
designed to keep temp staff too busy and too tired to be curious. But

44

they were more than temp staff. Chanel, while efficiently managing waste streams and biohazard disposal from tech stations, let her gaze linger on junctions, access panels, unusual power signatures. Her slate, officially displaying sanitation routes, covertly ran a passive scan for anomalous energy readings or shielded enclosures – anything that might indicate a hidden med-bay.

It was Bijou who struck gold first. During a mandated fifteen-minute hydration break, her wrist-comp pulsed twice against Chanel's – a coded signal. They met in a crowded, noisy catering hub, the air thick with the smell of synth-protein being flash-fried and the clatter of automated food prep units.

"West wing, sublevel two," Bijou murmured, her back to Chanel as she ostensibly refilled her water flask. "Near the main hydro-plant access. Saw a dedicated fiber-optic line, heavy shielding, separate climate control feed – all overkill for standard tech storage. And two Ice Central guards who don't rotate with the regular patrols. They look... permanent."

Chanel nodded, her heart hammering. "Finley's med-bay."

Just then, a ripple of activity moved through the hub. Voices hushed. Crew members straightened, their movements suddenly more alert, almost reverent. Through a parted service curtain, Chanel caught a glimpse: Isis. In the flesh. Not the larger-than-life stage persona, but a smaller, almost icily precise figure in a stark white, minimalist jumpsuit. Her face was a pale oval, expressionless, eyes hidden behind dark, reflective lenses. She was flanked by two imposing figures in black, their movements radiating lethal efficiency. Trailing slightly behind her, looking like a brightly colored, nervous bird, was a young woman Chanel didn't recognize – Tymphany, probably – her face a mask of anxious awe as Isis gestured sharply at something on a data-slate one of the black-clad figures held.

The glimpse was fleeting, but the message was clear: the absolute control, the casual display of power, the almost interchangeable nature of the talent. Na Na was indeed "legacy tech."

"Showtime soon," Bijou said, her voice carefully neutral as the entourage passed. "They'll be locking down sublevels for talent prep."

Chanel's jaw tightened. "Then we better know exactly where we're going before they do." As she turned to head back to her zone, a supervisor – one of Ice Central's ubiquitous mid-level enforcers – stepped directly into her path, his eyes narrowed.

"Problem, consultant?" he asked, his voice smooth but edged with steel. "Your break concluded ninety seconds ago. And your sanitation cart is blocking a primary access route."

Chanel forced a quick, apologetic smile. "No problem at all. Just disoriented. Big place." She maneuvered the cart out of the way, her mind racing. That was close. Too close. They were being watched, every second accounted for.

The cage was located. Now they just had to figure out how to pick the damn lock while the wolves were circling.

* * *

The air outside, even filtered through the venue's industrial ventilation, hummed with Ouaga, the scent of roasting peanuts, diesel fumes from a thousand sputtering mobylettes, something dusty and floral Chanel couldn't name. Inside this sterile, white room tucked away behind the glittering stage machinery, the only smell was antiseptic and the faint, unnerving odor of ozone, like a storm was brewing right here in this box. And there, perched on the edge of a narrow cot like a bird with clipped wings, was Na Na.

Not Na Na. Not the Sanaa whose body sang electric even standing still, whose skin soaked up the Brooklyn sun and glowed richer than the cocoa butter Mama slathered on them. This woman was... diminished. Her skin, usually the color of deep earth after rain, looked ashen, dry, stretched taut over bones that seemed too sharp. And the patches... Gods, the patches. Not just a few like Chanel had imagined from the agent's rambling description. Dozens. Small, silver-dollar sized bio-interface electrodes, adhered starkly against her dull skin, networked by near-invisible filaments. They dotted her arms, her neck, the smooth plane of her forehead partially visible beneath a thin cotton wrap. Like some ghastly, clinical ivy consuming her.

Chanel's gasped, air vanished from her lungs. All the fury that had propelled her across continents, the righteous anger at Ice, the frustration with the useless agent, the fear—it all collapsed inward, leaving only a hollow ache that swiftly filled with tears. They welled hot and fast, blurring the horrifying image of her friend.

"Oh, Na Na..." The name was a choked whisper, rough with unshed grief and the dust of her journey.

Sanaa looked up. Her eyes, usually bright and alive with rhythm, seemed clouded, distant. Recognition flickered, slow, like a faulty connection. A small frown creased her brow, the expression achingly familiar. Then, her own eyes widened slightly, mirroring Chanel's tears.

Chanel didn't wait. She crossed the small room in two strides and knelt, pulling Sanaa into a fierce hug, mindful of the damn patches. As Chanel held her, a small, hard object pressed almost imperceptibly against her side, tucked deep within the folds of Sanaa's thin cotton wrap. For a fleeting second, an image flashed in Chanel's mind – a glint of dark metal, the elegant, ancient loop of an ankh, a gift from another lifetime, another Isis, heavy with promises that had long since turned to dust. The recognition was a ghost of a pang, instantly swallowed by the overwhelming flood of the present crisis, the fragile weight of her friend in her arms. Sanaa felt terrifyingly light, fragile. Her returning embrace was weak, hesitant, like a marionette learning its strings.

"Chanel?" Sanaa's voice was thin, reedy, lacking the resonant timber Chanel remembered. "You... you shouldn't be here. It's not safe."

"Safe?" Chanel pulled back slightly, her hands framing Sanaa's face, thumbs brushing away tears, careful to avoid the electrodes. "Look at you! What has she *done* to you, Na Na? We dreamed of stages, yeah, but not like... not like *this*." Her voice broke on the last word.

Sanaa's gaze drifted, focusing somewhere over Chanel's shoulder. "She gives me the world," she murmured, the phrase sounding rehearsed, hollow. "Everything I wanted."

"Bullshit!" Chanel said, her voice low but intense, shaking Sanaa gently. "This ain't you. This ain't dancing. This is," she paused, the pain in her voice, "draining. She's draining the life out of you! We gotta get you out."

A single tear traced a path down Sanaa's cheek, navigating around a patch near her temple. "Out?" she whispered, the concept sounding foreign. A flicker of the old fire sparked deep in her eyes, almost immediately extinguished by weariness. "How did you even get in? And where will I go? There's nowhere else."

"There's *us*, Na Na," Chanel insisted, gripping her friend's thin shoulders. "There's always us. Me. Bijou. We find a way. We *always* find a way."

* * *

Chanel's words hung in the sterile air, a lifeline tossed across a chasm of despair. Na Na clung to it, to Chanel's hands, her eyes still clouded but with a pinprick of light now struggling to break through the fog. But the room, this white box, felt like it was closing in, the hum of its unseen machinery a countdown timer.

"Okay," Chanel whispered, her voice urgent, already shifting into tactical mode. "Okay, Na Na, listen. Stay as still as you can. Conserve your energy. Don't react to anything unless it's me or Bijou. Can you do that?"

A faint nod from Na Na. Her breathing was shallow, a butterfly's flutter.

Chanel squeezed her hand one last time, then rose. Every instinct screamed to get Na Na out now, but a raw snatch-and-grab was suicide. They needed a plan, and for that, she needed Bijou. She touched her temple, activating her internal comm, a sub-vocal link so discreet it was almost thought-based.

"Bijou? Status. I'm with her. Condition critical, but she's aware."

Bijou's voice, when it came, was a calm anchor in Chanel's ear, laced with the faint background noise of a service corridor. "Copy, C. Just finished my sweep of the sublevel access points near target.

Assetou's got us on a tight leash, but there's a sanitation disposal chute near the west loading dock that services this wing. It's a long shot, shielded, but the schematics show it bypasses two major security checkpoints if we can override the biometric lock on the terminal hatch. Old system, probably overlooked in the latest upgrades. Primitive, but effective if we're small enough."

Chanel's mind raced. A disposal chute? The indignity was galling, but the practicality was undeniable. "Small enough for cargo, or small enough for...?"

"Small enough for two, maybe three if one is... compact," Bijou replied, her meaning clear. "There's a standard 'biohazard' containment unit – the large rolling kind – scheduled for sterilization cycle just before Isis's overture. If we can time it right, swap the unit, get Na Na inside... It's our best window. Peak chaos backstage. Everyone's focused on Isis hitting her first mark."

"Uniforms?" Chanel breathed, already seeing it. The ultimate invisibility.

"Already sourced two extra sets of the Level 1 'Enviro-Crew' coveralls and particle masks from a 'misplaced' supplies locker. Untraceable. They look just like the poor schlubs who have to clean the... chutes." Bijou didn't need to elaborate on the filth.

"And Isis?" Chanel asked, the image of the cold, crystalline performer flashing in her mind. "Her movements?"

"Locks down her Green Room Suite an hour pre-show. Total radio silence. No one in or out except her personal tech and that... replacement," Bijou said, a subtle distaste in her tone. "Tymphany. They run a full systems diagnostic on her right before Isis takes the stage. That means for about twenty minutes, all eyes in Ice Central

Security are on that feed. It's the narrowest of openings, C, but it's there."

Chanel looked at Na Na, so fragile on the cot. Getting her into a containment unit, through a disposal chute... it was a desperate gamble. But it was a gamble. "The Monument of Heroes," Chanel suddenly whispered into the comm, a flash of inspiration from their arrival, the image of that lonely, defiant structure. "If we make it out, that's our rally point. North side. You remember the landmark from the ride in?"

"Red earth and resilience. Got it," Bijou confirmed. "Now, getting you out of that room to help me prep... that's the next trick."

Before Chanel could reply, her wrist-comp, synced with Bijou's, gave a soft, urgent pulse. A new holographic icon appeared on her internal heads-up display: a flickering janitorial cart icon now showing a green pathway leading away from the med-bay towards a nearby service lift. Bijou was already moving, already making it happen.

"Diversion in three," Bijou's voice came again, calm but clipped. "Automated sanitation alert, Zone 4 corridor D. Minor spill, bio-foam containment protocol. It'll pull the guard from your door for at least five minutes. Be ready to move, Chanel. And be invisible."

* * *

Chanel didn't waste a nanosecond. The soft chime of a distant alarm—Bijou's diversion—was her cue. She gave Na Na's hand a final, reassuring squeeze. "Stay with me, sister. We're walking out of this hell."

Moving with the silent grace of a predator, Chanel cracked the med-bay door. The corridor outside was momentarily empty, the usual Ice Central guard drawn away by the manufactured bio-foam alert blaring further down the hall. The air thrummed with the distant, bass-heavy pulse of Isis's overture beginning to build – a percussive, militaristic beat that sounded like the arena itself was developing a monstrous heart.

She slipped out, her internal HUD already highlighting the green pathway Bijou had mapped. It led her through a series of humming service tunnels, the scent of ozone and hot circuitry thick in the air. She found Bijou near a junction, already wrestling a large, wheeled biohazard containment unit out of an alcove. Two bundled Enviro-Crew coveralls and particle masks were tucked beside it.

"Perfect timing," Bijou breathed, already shrugging into one of the grey, shapeless suits. "Guard bought the diversion. Assetou's having a fit on the comms, but she's directing resources away from us. Now, the hard part."

Returning to Na Na, getting her into the cramped, cold interior of the containment unit without alerting any passing tech or remote surveillance, was a masterclass in their old synchronized artistry, reborn in desperation. Bijou, with her fluid strength, created a moving screen with her body and a discarded equipment tarp while Chanel, whispering encouragement, gently lifted Na Na. Na Na was terrifyingly light, her body trembling, but a flicker of her old fight showed in her eyes as she tried to help, to fold herself into the confined space. The particle masks would help obscure their faces if anyone got too close.

Once Na Na was inside, curled on a thin, sterilized pad Bijou had scrouged, they sealed the unit. It looked like any other piece of refuse equipment. Humiliating, yes, but freedom had never cared much for dignity.

Pushing the heavy unit, they moved. Chanel took point, Bijou covering their rear, her eyes constantly scanning, her hand never far from the sonic stunner she'd "borrowed" from a security locker. The route to the disposal chute was a tense gauntlet of near-misses: a crew of roadies arguing loudly in Lingala as they muscled a massive set piece, forcing Chanel and Bijou to flatten themselves into a darkened doorway; a pair of Ice Central guards striding past, their heavy boots echoing, so close Chanel could smell their synthetic-leather body armor.

The air grew warmer, heavier, as they neared the loading dock and the disposal chute terminal. It stank of stale food waste, industrial solvents, and something else... an almost primal fear, as if the chute itself had devoured countless secrets.

Bijou quickly keyed in the override sequence on the chute's ancient control panel. The heavy terminal hatch hissed open with a gust of fetid air, revealing a dark, sloping maw.

As they began to maneuver the containment unit towards the opening, a side door slid open. Isis. Standing there, flanked by her two black-clad shadows, her dark lenses fixed directly on them. Time froze. The thumping bass of her show vibrated through the floor, a counterpoint to the sudden, suffocating silence.

Chanel tensed, ready to fight, to scream, to do anything. Bijou's hand subtly moved to her stunner.

Isis didn't move. Her head tilted, a slow, deliberate motion.
Her gaze flicked from the containment unit to Chanel's eyes, then
to Bijou's. There was no readable expression on her face, but for
a heartbeat, Chanel thought she saw something flicker behind the
lenses – not malice, not mercy, but something akin to... appraisal?
Or perhaps, the cold calculation of an empress discarding a piece that
no longer served a purpose on her grand, galactic chessboard.

Then, one of her shadows leaned in, whispering something.
Isis gave the smallest of nods, turned, and swept back through the
door without a word, her entourage following, the door hissing shut
behind them. Leaving Chanel and Bijou, hearts pounding, in the
sudden, echoing silence.

They didn't question it. Didn't dare to breathe. With a
shared, desperate look, they heaved the containment unit into the
disposal chute. It rumbled, then slid away into the darkness with a
sickening finality.

"Now us," Bijou said, already kicking off her Enviro-Crew boots
to reveal the lighter, more agile stealth-runners beneath. "Go! Go! Go!"

* * *

The slide down the disposal chute was a stomach-lurching,
bruising symphony of darkness and speed, the rank breath of refuse
and recycled air a suffocating cloak. They spilled out, Chanel and
Bijou, onto a jagged mountain range of compressed trash bales
behind the Harmattan Arena's remote perimeter fence. The bass
thump of Isis's concert was a distant, angry god, its rhythm a fading
tyranny against their skin. For a breathless eternity, they just lay

there, stardust and grime their new twin attires, adrenaline singing a high, sharp lament in their veins.

Then, a frantic scramble, a shared instinct. They were at the containment unit, its plasteel shell scarred from the descent. Bijou, her fingers nimble despite the tremor of reaction, fought with the latches in the thin, unforgiving security light spilling from the distant arena. Finally, with a gasp, she wrenched the hatch open.

Na Na was a crumpled bird inside, bones fragile as spun glass, eyes wide with a universe of terror and the dazed bewilderment of a soul returned from some far, cold star. Chanel reached in, her touch a prayer. "We got you, Na Na. We got you, starlight. You're out. You're breathing free air now."

Together, their movements a practiced, desperate choreography, they eased her from the cold, metallic womb. The moment Na Na's bare feet kissed the rough, unforgiving earth of Ouagadougou, a tremor, profound and elemental, ran through her. She inhaled – a ragged, shuddering bloom of a breath – as if tasting the night for the first time in a lifetime. The air itself was a wild tapestry: the ancient, resinous incense of unseen fires, the sharp, sweet tang of overripe mangoes from a hidden market stall, the metallic zing of distant mobylettes, the velvet thrum of a million unseen wings, all under the vast, diamond-dusted canvas of the African sky – a boundless, living ceiling so unlike the sterile, measured confines of her cage.

It was a deluge, a glorious assault on senses long starved. Her legs, unaccustomed to the simple act of bearing weight, buckled. Chanel and Bijou were there, a vise of love, one on each side, their arms a fierce, protective cradle. Na Na buried her face, a broken bird seeking shelter, first in Chanel's shoulder, then Bijou's, her thin body wracked with sobs that were almost soundless, tremors from a deep well of unshed grief, shaking her from the roots of her hair to the soles of her feet. Tears, hot and liberating, streamed down Chanel's face, carving paths through the grime and sweat. Bijou's own eyes glistened, jewels in the dim light, her warrior's expression softened by an almost unbearable wave of tenderness.

Lifting her head, her face tear-streaked and fragile against Chanel's shoulder, Sanaa's voice was a mere whisper, raspy from disuse and emotion. "So many times, so many nights alone in that... that box." She gestured vaguely, a shiver running through her. "The silence, or just the machines, and her voice in my head." Her eyes found Chanel's, then flicked to Bijou's. "That ankh she gave me, the pretty lie of it, with its hidden dagger...It had a sting in its tail, you know? A way out." Her breath hitched. "I thought about it. Gods, I thought about it. When the applause felt like thunder for a ghost, for pieces of me she'd stolen and replayed. When I couldn't feel my own rhythm anymore." She paused, drawing a shaky breath of the free night air. "But then, I'd remember Goat Park. The concrete. Your strength, Chanel, like pure fractal fire. Your flow, Bijou, always like wata finding its way home. I kept thinking, *they wouldn't stop. My sisters... they'd find a way.* You... you were the beat I held onto when everything else went silent." Her voice broke completely then, a raw sound of pain and profound gratitude.

They stood, a trinity forged anew in shadow and light, three fractured rhythms finding a shared, defiant beat under the immensity of the night. The raw, untamed joy of her liberty was a fragile, incandescent flame, casting long, dancing shadows of the profound exhaustion, the lingering terror of their audacious act.

Chanel, raising her head, seeking an anchor in the swirling tide of emotion, saw it. Looming in the near distance, a stark silhouette against the city's softer, more diffuse glow beyond the arena's harsh glare, rose the proud, unyielding shape of the Monument of Heroes. It pierced the darkness like a spear, a silent testament to battles fought with fire and spirit, to sacrifice that still whispered on the wind, to the relentless, unkillable dream of sovereignty. It felt, in that heartbeat, like an ancestor made stone, watching over them, its presence a solemn kora strumming a chord of acknowledgment for their own small, desperate act of rebellion, their own claim on freedom.

"Look," Chanel whispered, her voice a raw thread of sound, nudging Na Na with infinite gentleness. "Look, Na Na. You see it? That's for the fighters."

Through the prism of her tears, Na Na lifted her head. Her gaze, still a clouded mirror, slowly found the monument. A flicker, a nascent spark, danced deep within her eyes – recognition, perhaps, of a strength she'd forgotten she possessed, or just the dawning, overwhelming truth of a world that existed beyond her cage, a world that still held such defiant beauty.

"We gotta move," Bijou murmured, her voice a grounding earth-tone, practical but infused with a gentle urgency, her arm a steadfast bulwark around Na Na's waist. "They'll know. That Ice Queen, SaDitty's dogs… they'll be hunting soon. Real soon."

Chanel nodded, wiping her eyes with the back of a dirt-streaked hand, the grit a reminder of their passage. Out, yes. Free, for this breath. But they were fugitives, embers scattered from a forge, with a sister soul still bearing the fresh, deep wounds of her captivity, no tangible resources beyond the fire in their spirits, and

the crushing weight of SaDitty's LushLife empire, Isis's far-reach-
ing machine, poised to descend. The path ahead was a vast, unlit
savanna, fraught with unseen dangers.

But Na Na, drawing a breath that gathered strength from
the very air, took a small, unsteady step, leaning into their shared
support. And then another. Away from the fading, profane pulse
of the arena, towards the beckoning, mysterious shadows and the
distant, hopeful lights of Ouagadougou. The Monument of Heroes
stood at their backs, a silent blessing, a promise of resilience etched
against the night. They were three sparks, three heartbeats, three
dancers moving into the fragile hope of a new, uncertain dawn, the
first notes of their own unwritten song just beginning to stir in the
warm, African night.

DON'T STOP, CAN'T STOP

The air in the penthouse suite hung thick with the scent of expensive cigars and fear. Crimson silk, draped over every surface, pooled at the feet of Samuel "Saditty" Pope, his skin the color of polished ebony against the opulent backdrop. He paced, a caged panther, the hum of the city below a distant lullaby. His empire, built on the broken dreams and shattered spirits of countless young Black artists, was crumbling. Hip Hop, R&B, neo-Soul, he'd ruled them all. A remarkable collection of gleaming Grammy's and BET Awards covered a wall unit built like a bank vault. Cracks, however, marred the once-pristine surface, like fissures in his carefully constructed image. But the lawsuits—especially the multi-billion dollar case his LushLife spirits company had pending against Reine North America, the French conglomerate bleeding him dry—the public outcry, the whispers that followed him like a shroud— they were suffocating him. Saditty, the Midas of the music industry, whose touch turned talent to gold, now found himself a pariah, his gilded cage shrinking with every passing day.

The massive screen on the far wall flickered to life, the sound initially low. It was a segment from "Moguls & Monsters," a new docu-series promising to dissect the rise and fall of music industry titans. Saditty paused, a muscle ticking in his jaw. He knew this episode. Knew it and hated it.

The screen sharpened on a younger Saditty—Samuel—an impeccably dressed teenager, his wrist dwarfed by a watch. The camera panned to a group of boys sliding down an icy hill in Yonkers.

A voice, warm with nostalgia, filled the room. *"We lived seventeen steps from each other,"* Pretty Tony's voice. *"First time me and Krusha saw him come outside, he looked like a little old man. Had this watch on bigger than him. We laughed, man. Had to make him feel ridiculous."*

The scene shifted to a dimly lit basement apartment, where a younger Saditty sat at a table, sketching furiously. His mother, tall and elegant, dressed in a simple but stylish dress, watched him with a mixture of pride and worry.

"My mom, she was the queen," a slightly older Saditty narrated. *"Triple threat: singer, dancer, dresser. She had that street hustler energy, cuz she had to—a widow, single mother, making it work."*

The documentary cut back to Pretty Tony. *"I ain't gon' lie. Truth is, we bullied him,"* he said, his face etched with shame, a hint of regret. *"You could tell he was used to his mama's love. But ain't no love on the streets. Guess he figured right then he had to buck up."*

The image dissolved into chaos.

"He busted Chris Krushner in the head with a bottle," Pretty Tony said, his voice quiet. *"Split him wide open like a jackfruit.*

Beat him 'til the white meat show. But when Chris, now known as Krusha, healed...they was friends ever since. We all was."

The documentary shifted again, this time to an interview with Trudy Archer, former editor in chief of *BoomBap!* magazine, her expression tight with controlled fury. *"He left me a horrible message,"* she said, her voice shaking slightly. *"Said he would see me good and dead in a trunk if I didn't show him the final edits from our shoot."*

Saditty snarled, stabbing the remote, but the images continued to flicker on the screen, a relentless assault of the past. His carefully constructed image, the one he'd cultivated for decades, was being dissected, exposed, ripped apart. Tonight, though, a sliver of doubt wormed its way into his thoughts, fueled by desperation. He needed a talisman, a symbol of his enduring power, something to silence the ghosts, and haters haunted his gilded prison. Rumors had reached his ears – whispers of a mythical figure in the tattoo world. *Artis La.* A name spoken in hushed tones, a legend whispered in smoky back-rooms. Their work, it was said, was the best in the industry, a blend of artistry and...something more. Those who bore Artis La's super-natural ink were said to be unstoppable – their fortunes soaring, their power absolute, their influence undeniable.

Some spoke of ancient rituals, of a connection to unseen forces, of magic woven into the very ink. Others whispered that the tattoos were a front, and that the stars had inked irrevocable deals with the devil. Saditty scoffed at such superstition. He believed in power, dominance, absolute control. Flesh. If Artis La could provide power made flesh, then Saditty would find them, no matter the cost. All he needed was the appearance of the thing—in his long career, he'd learned that fools and fans would believe anything. Just the rumors that he'd become a client of Artis La would raise his failing stock in some quarters. He would risk everything to maintain his music empire, to silence the whispers, to rise above the ashes of his tainted reputation. He would rise again.

More powerful. More ruthless. Unstoppable.

Though he kept a cool facade in public, he was losing control. The lawsuits were piling up, and so were the bodies—all the skeletons in his deep, dark closet threatening to bone dance back on out. Seeing Pretty Tony's pained look on the screen, and even some lying folks he didn't even know, made him even more desperate. But friend or foe, they all threatened his carefully built tower of power, and *that* was unacceptable.

Because if nothing else, Saditty craved that power. He craved the invincibility that would silence his detractors, crush his enemies, and solidify his reign over the music world. It wasn't just about the money anymore—though God knows he needed it with the Reine wine and spirits lawyers breathing down his neck. It was about the silencing. Climbing the mountain didn't erase the hate, it just changed the angle of the daggers. First, it was his color and culture. Then, it was his crown. He'd thought the fortune would be armor, the kind his mother, sharp and proud even in poverty, never had. Armor against the world's contempt for a Black boy from the 'hood. The viral docu-series was just the latest in a recent string of accusations, the damning headlines, the whispers of his predatory behavior—they were chipping away at his carefully constructed facade. He needed a counter-force, a weapon to wield against the tide of misfortune.

Artis La. He had to find them. But no one knew the true identity of Artis La, a phantom artist who flitted from location to location, their whereabouts a closely guarded secret.

❊ ❊ ❊

The air hung heavy with the scent of jasmine and something older, something primal. Saditty, despite his tailored suit and the simmering rage within him, felt a prickle of unease. He stood before a door that looked like it had been carved from a single block of obsidian, the surface shimmering with an inner light. His personal security guard, a hulking brute named "Krusha," shifted impatiently behind him. Krusha subtly touched the small, worn gris-gris bag tucked inside his jacket, his gaze darting uneasily towards the foreboding portraits lining the hallway they'd passed.

"You sure about this, Saditty?" Krusha rumbled, his voice a low growl. "This place...it ain't right."

Saditty's lips curled in a sneer, but his eyes flickered nervously toward the door. "Superstition," he sneered, though the obsidian door pulsed with an unseen energy, vibrating slightly. "Find a discreet spot and wait. I'll be out soon enough," Saditty commanded, dismissing Krusha with a flick of his wrist.

Krusha nodded, his face a grim canvas, but his feet remained planted. He didn't move towards the alley. Instead, his gaze locked on the obsidian door, a slab of polished night that swallowed the streetlight and exhaled a darkness all its own. The air itself felt wrong, thick with cloying scents—jasmine tangled with something metallic, something that clawed at the back of his throat. He'd followed Saditty into countless hells, handled business that stained the soul, but *this felt different*. A cold dread, smelling of turned earth and old secrets, settled in his gut.

He'd stumbled into something ancient and knowing, something with teeth.

When Saditty, shielding his own flicker of unease with brittle ego, shouldered through the obsidian entrance, Krusha hesitated only a heartbeat. Duty, loyalty—or maybe just the primal fear of letting Saditty walk into that maw alone—won out. He pulled the collar of his black wool peacoat tighter, a useless gesture against the chill that had nothing to do with the night air, and slipped through the door just after his boss. He positioned himself quietly near the entrance, a reluctant shadow swallowed by a place thrumming with unseen life.

The interior was a sensory overload. The air throbbed with a low, rhythmic chant, barely audible yet deeply unsettling. Plants, some familiar, others alien, clawed at the air, their leaves shimmering with an unnatural luminescence. Cobalt blue glass bottle trees, adorned with strange symbols and dried herbs, stood sentinel in every corner. Portraits of figures both human and otherworldly hung from the walls, their eyes following Saditty's every move. Framed images of skin, bearing intricate tattoos that writhed and shifted, hung alongside the portraits. There were also framed photographs— staged shots of Artis La with various clients, their faces beaming with a disturbing mix of awe and something akin to religious fervor. Saditty recognized a few faces—up-and-coming rappers, soul singers, pop stars, all eager to bask in his reflected glory. Then, his breath hitched. One photo, featuring a radiant young woman named Sanaa, her eyes full of youthful exuberance and hope, made a sharp pang of something akin to guilt jolt through Saditty, a feeling he quickly suppressed. These were the works of Artis La, each a testament to their power.

And then, he saw her.

Seated upon a throne that resembled a Betye Saar sculpture—a vibrant collage of found objects, antique dolls, and symbolic arti-facts—sat a woman whose beauty was both mesmerizing and terri-fying. Her skin, the color of polished mahogany, glistened with an inner light. Her hair, a cascade of thick braids adorned with seashells and gold, framed a face that shifted and changed, a mask of shifting expressions. Her eyes, the color of deep dark walnut, held an ancient wisdom that chilled him to the bone.

Most startling of all were her nails. They were impossibly long, curved and sharp like the talons of a hawk, making him wonder how she could possibly wield a tattoo machine. A small, intricate symbol, etched into the back of her left hand, caught his eye. He recognized it as the Vèvè of Ogun, the Lwa of war and iron, its lines shimmering with an inner light. The air crackled with a faint energy, raising the hairs on Saditty's arms.

A knot tightened in Saditty's stomach. He had heard whis-pers of Artis La's connection to the Lwa, of their power being more than just artistic. Fear, cold and insidious, coiled around his heart. He wanted to turn, to flee, to pretend this entire encounter had been a fever dream. But his ego, bruised and battered, refused to allow it. He would not be intimidated. He would have his power, his invincibility.

A low chuckle, like dry leaves skittering across pavement, escaped the woman's lips. "So, the mighty Saditty Pope seeks the blessing of the Warrior," she purred, her voice a mesmerizing blend of honey and venom. "Tell me, Mr. Pope, what does the Warrior demand?"

As her words hung in the charged air, Saditty shot a quick, sharp look at Krusha, catching the nervous glint in his bodyguard's wide eyes and the tightness in his clenched jaw.

"You mean one of the warriors up in Brooklyn?" Saditty's bravado faltered slightly. Saditty flexed his gold and platinum-ringed fingers, chuckling under his breath. He wasn't buying any of Artis La's mumbo jumbo, hocus pocus. *You can't bullshit a bullshitter.* "Let's keep it a stack. I want a tattoo, and not no regular shmegular shiz. I can afford whatever you chargin'. Save the bubble-bubble-toil-and-trouble theatrics for one of your basic tricks. I'm not the one, understand?"

When Krusha audibly sucked in his breath, Saditty turned and stared, pulling his sunglasses down to the bridge of his nose. He registered Krusha fully then—not just the fear radiating off him, but the fact that the fool was still inside when he'd been told to wait. Disobedience piled on top of weakness. *Is this nigga shaking?*

"What's gotten into you, Krush? You're supposed to be the head of my security, and you're in here acting like a scared little bitch." He turned back to Artis La. "Excuse my language, ma'am."

"No need." Artis La's voice was soft, low yet oddly menacing. Her knowing smile stretched across her plum-stained lips. "But your friend has more wisdom than perhaps you realize. When you enter the realms of the gods, it is wise to mind yourself and pay attention."

"Ha!" Saditty's laugh was louder than before, but held a tremor. "Gods, huh? I am a God." He stroked the dark waves on his close-cut hair. Freshly lined, cut to perfection, he was a hulking vision in white. "Can't nobody tell me nothing about gods when I live and walk among them, right here in the real world where don't nothing but power matters. If I need a physical situation handled, somebody's teeth knocked out, legs broken, something like that. I'll call this nigga. That's what I pay him for. Other than that, I think I can manage the *gods*."

He popped his collar, a heavy gold chain and the expensive watch gleamed on his wrist. "I'm tired of all this playing around." He waved dismissively. "You want my business or what?"

"*What*, Mr. Saditty," the mysterious woman said. "Right this way."

Artis La turned her back on Saditty and Krusha and disappeared behind a black, velvet curtain that covered an unseen door. Saditty watched her appreciatively, staring at the thin gold chain of charms and seashells that wrapped around her waist and hips. "If she wasn't so weird, I'd tap that," he said, licking his lip. "Crazy coochie is the best coochie."

Krusha did not look so sure.

"You coming?" Saditty asked, looking incredulous. "A'ight, scary ass, stay here. You know the drill. Don't let nobody out. Don't let nobody in."

✳ ✳ ✳

Saditty adjusted the drape of his immaculate white jacket, squared his shoulders, and pushed through the heavy, black velvet curtain. He expected... something. More eyes, perhaps. More unsettling symbols.

Instead, the space beyond the curtain felt like stepping into the heart of a held breath. Quieter. Denser. The air, still scented with jasmine and metal, now carried an undercurrent of something else—ozone, like the air before a lightning strike, and a faint, coppery tang he couldn't quite place. *Blood? Old magic?* The low chant that had throbbed in the outer room was absent here, replaced by a silence so profound it felt like a physical presence pressing against his eardrums.

This room was smaller, more intimate, yet somehow vaster. Walls the color of dried blood absorbed the minimal light emanating from pulsing, vein-like lines embedded within the plaster itself—lines that subtly shifted between deep reds and greens. No windows. Instead of the chaotic profusion of the entry, this space held a focused intensity. Stunning pieces of Haitian metal art hung on the walls—intricate, darkly gleaming figures hammered from old steel drums in the style of Croix-des-Bouquets, depicting intertwined serpents, fierce warriors wielding manchèts, and complex Vèvè symbols that vibrated with latent power. One striking abstract sculpture, all sharp angles and repurposed iron, reminded Saditty of something he'd once glimpsed in a high-end gallery catalogue featuring artists from Pétion-Ville—an unsettling echo of sophisticated artistry in this raw, primal space.

A single, intricately carved chair, looking disturbingly like it was fashioned from bone and shadow, faced a low table inlaid with mother-of-pearl patterns that shifted like oil on water. Positioned strategically around the chair were several tall, freestanding mirrors, their frames fashioned from dark, heavy wood and more hammered metal, angled to offer fragmented, multiplying reflections. On the far wall, several framed examples of Artis La's work hung, but these were different from the client photos outside—abstract, powerful swirls of ink on preserved skin, radiating palpable energy. Safe choices, perhaps. Tattoos for the tourists of power, not its true seekers.

Artis La stood beside the table, waiting. Away from her bone-shadow throne, she seemed both smaller and more concentrated, her presence undiminished. Dark waters, her eyes locked onto his, offering no welcome, only assessment.

"Alright," Saditty began, forcing his voice into its usual commanding register, shoving down the unease that prickled his skin. "Enough with the mood lighting. I need something strong. Something permanent. Something that screams power so loud it deafens these haters and whispers sweet nothings to the bank." He gestured vaguely at the framed pieces on the wall. "Something better than that basic shit."

Artis La didn't react immediately. She tilted her head, her heavy braids clicking softly, adorned with shells and gold. "Power has a price, Mr. Pope," she said, her voice still that low, mesmerizing hum. "And permanence..." She pursed her lips, as if choosing her words carefully. "Permanence is a cage of its own making. Perhaps one of these speaks to your—ambition?" She indicated the swirling designs on the wall with a subtle lift of her chin. They were beautiful, undeniably skillful, radiating a contained, quiet strength.

But Saditty's eyes weren't on them. His gaze was snagged by something else, positioned almost like an altar against the back wall: an ancient, leather-bound book, thick as a tombstone, resting inside a heavy glass case that shimmered faintly, as if protecting the world from the book, or the book from the world. Its cover was dark, worn smooth by countless hands or perhaps something else entirely, marked with symbols that were vaguely familiar yet disturbingly alien. He couldn't look away. That was where the real power pulsed. Not in the tasteful swirls on the wall—*that was Mickey Mouse bullshit*—but in that book.

"Forget these," Saditty snapped, his voice tight with impatience and a sudden, consuming avarice. He pointed a diamond-ringed finger towards the glass case. "I don't want off the rack. I want that. Whatever's in that *book*. The real deal. The kind of ink that makes kings and breaks enemies."

Artis La followed his gaze. A flicker, gone almost before it registered, passed through her deep eyes. Was it amusement? Pity? Or something else, something ancient and calculating? "That book," she said slowly, turning back to him, "is not for casual perusal. It contains patterns of power, yes. But they demand... reciprocity. They have appetites."

"Everything got an appetite," Saditty scoffed, though the coppery tang in the air stronger now. "Mine's bigger. Open the case."

She studied him, truly studied him then—his arrogance, the fear tightening the corners of his eyes despite his posture, the soul-deep paranoia that saw threats and challenges everywhere. She saw the rot beneath the riches. A faint, knowing smile touched her lips again, not cruel, perhaps, but inevitable. Like a river deciding its course. She hadn't chosen this for him, not directly. He was choosing it himself, demanding it, blinded by the very flaws that made him vulnerable to the justice held within those pages.

"Very well," Artis La said softly, the sound like stones settling at the bottom of a well. "If that is your choice. So be it. But know this: the ink demands its due. Always." Moving towards the glass case, her talon-like nails clicked faintly against the smooth, shimmering surface as she prepared to unlock it.

With a touch that was both infinitely delicate and unnervingly strong, she murmured a low word, and whatever unseen force held the case fast relented. The glass front slid open with a whisper of displaced air, revealing the ancient, leather-bound book within.

"The registry of Kay Fè holds many paths, Mr. Pope," Artis La murmured, her voice echoing slightly in the suddenly resonant space. "The House of Iron requires balance. What is forged in flesh must be tempered in spirit." She lifted the book with a reverence that was at odds with Saditty's crude demands. It looked impossibly heavy, bound in hide darker than midnight, scarred and worn, yet radiating a heat that warmed the air around it.

She placed it carefully on the low, mother-of-pearl inlaid table. The vein-like lights in the walls pulsed a little brighter, casting shifting patterns across the room. "You seek power," Artis La stated, less a question than an observation, her brown eyes pinning him. "Dominance. A shield forged against the consequences you yourself have hammered into being."

She opened the massive cover. The pages weren't paper, not exactly. They looked like thinly stretched parchment, or perhaps something older, tougher—skin?—each filled with designs that pulsed with a life of their own. They were intricate, terrifying, beautiful. Vèvè intertwined with symbols he didn't recognize, faces of spirits both benevolent and terrifyingly alien, patterns that writhed like serpents before his eyes.

"Many come here," Artis La continued, her voice a low chant as she slowly turned a page, revealing a swirling pattern of protective energy, "seeking Ogou Fèray's strength, his manchèt to clear their path." She turned another page, showing a complex design of interwoven lines. "Or perhaps Simbi's magic, wisdom from beneath the waters." Her fingers longer now, impossibly long and sharp, hovered over these designs, offering them without emphasis.

Saditty barely glanced at them. His eyes were drawn deeper into the book, searching for the raw, untamed power he craved. He felt Artis La watching him, gauging his hunger, his blindness. He waved impatiently at the pages she'd shown. "Nah, nah. Stronger. More... direct."

Artis La paused. Then, with deliberate slowness, she turned another page.

And there it was.

The design leaped out at him, stark and fierce against the ancient canvas of the page. It depicted a woman, stern-faced, eyes burning with an intensity that felt like judgment, like fire. Scars, like ritual markings or the slashes of a manchèt, adorned her image. In one hand, she held a blade; in the other, something that looked like a heart, gripped tight. It wasn't just a drawing, it felt like a presence looking back at him, challenging him. *This* was raw power. Unflinching. Absolute.

"Ezili Dantò," Artis La identified, her voice devoid of inflection, yet the name itself vibrated in the air. "Petwo Lwa. Fierce protector of women, of children. Her rage is the fire of the forge itself, Mr. Pope. She answers injustice with a blade sharpened on suffering." She paused, her gaze heavy. "This is a deep *mak*, demanding much of the flesh it inhabits. Ogun's fire is in this one, yes, but it is Dantò's justice that wields it."

Saditty heard the words—protector of women, justice—but they registered only as abstract concepts, secondary to the raw, undeniable power radiating from the image. He saw the fierceness, the blade, the unyielding stare, and interpreted it through the lens of his own needs: dominance, intimidation, a weapon. Maybe even—a flicker of something buried deep, unwelcome—the kind of fierce protection his mother always offered him, the kind only a mother could extend even to cover the sins blooming dark inside him. He missed the warning, the specific nature of the Lwa's protection, the implication of whose side she inevitably took. Saditty saw only a reflection of the ruthlessness he aspired to embody.

"That one," he said, his voice hoarse with desire, tapping the page with a demanding finger. "That's the one. Ezili Dantò. Put her on me."

Artis La held his gaze for a long moment, her expression unreadable. Then, she gave a single, slow nod. The choice was made. The path, forged in his own arrogance, was set. "As you wish," she said softly. "The ink awaits the flesh."

Artis La closed the ancient book—the heavy midnight cover falling shut with a soft thud that felt unnaturally loud in the charged silence of Kay Fè. The whirling patterns on the table ceased their shimmering. She didn't lead Saditty to another room, the transformation happened around them. With a gesture—a fluid ripple of her long, talon-fingered hand—the intricately carved chair reshaped itself, lowering, extending, becoming less a seat of consultation and more an altar for the flesh. The very air hummed with a higher frequency now, the coppery tang intensifying.

Saditty watched, a knot tightening low in his belly, but he forced a smirk. *Showmanship. That's all it was. High-priced theatrics for high-paying clients.* He settled himself into the chair as commanded by her silent gesture, arranging his large frame with deliberate nonchalance, already imagining the power—the raw, undeniable *presence*—the Ezili Dantò tattoo would grant him. He'd wear it like armor. Reluctantly, maintaining a shred of dignity, he shrugged out of his expensive white jacket and then his shirt, tossing them aside, already imagining the power—the raw, undeniable presence—the Ezili Dantò tattoo would grant him. He reveled in the idea, exposing the expanse of his back to Artis La's assessing gaze.

Artis La prepared her instruments. Her movements were hypnotic, the subtle glint of gold in her heavy braids catching the room's pulsing light as she drew tools from carved wooden boxes that looked as ancient as the book. The machine itself gleamed—a dark, polished metal that drank the light—but it felt different from any Saditty had seen before. The needles, when she fitted them, were impossibly fine, yet menacingly sharp. The ink wasn't in plastic bottles, she poured it from dark ceramic vials into small, shell-like cups—a black so deep it was starless, and reds like arterial blood, crushed hibiscus. There was a ritualistic quality to her movements—precise, economical, imbued with intention. Her brown eyes holding that profoundly disturbing ancient wisdom, focused entirely on the task, as she murmured something low in a language Saditty didn't recognize—Kreyol? older still?—while wiping his skin with a cool, astringent-smelling liquid that made him flinch involuntarily. He caught his own reflection in one of the angled mirrors—tense, pale beneath his dark skin ashen, looking disturbingly vulnerable on the bone-and-shadow chair.

"Relax, Mr. Pope." Artis La's voice was a silken thread in the quiet. Her face, that mask of shifting expressions, was uncannily still now, concentrating. "Tension makes the forge hotter—makes the flesh resist the mark."

"I ain't worried," Saditty lied, clenching his jaw. "Get on with it. I ain't got all night."

She offered him a thin smile, all lip, no eye shine. "For a work of this size, it's customary to do it in sessions, Mr. Pope. But since you have chosen to journey on..." Her liquid voice trailed off.

Then came the buzz—not the high-pitched whine he expected, but a lower, resonant hum, something ancient stirring deep within the metal machine. It vibrated through the chair, up his bones. The first touch of the needle wasn't just pain—it was a sharp, stinging shock, a single, venomous insect burying itself deep. He caught the briefest glimpse of her hand near his skin in the mirror's reflection—the dark, polished mahogany contrasting with the gleaming needle, the intricate Vèvè of Ogun seeming to pulse faintly on the back of her hand—before he snapped his gaze away. He grit his teeth, refusing to give her the satisfaction of a groan or a reaction. *Power has a price*, she'd said. Fine. He'd pay it.

She began the outline—long, deliberate strokes. The stinging intensified, multiplying—a thousand tiny bee stings tracing fire across his skin.

He could see fragmented glimpses of the work beginning on his back in the strategically placed mirrors—lines of fire against his dark skin, the start of something potent and permanent. He focused on the ceiling, on the pulsing, vein-like lights, refusing to watch the needle's dance. He thought of his enemies, of their shock and fear when they saw this *mak*—this brand of dominance. He thought of reclaiming his throne.

But then the sensation shifted. As Artis La worked closer to bone—his shoulder blade, the curve of his bicep—the vibration became pronounced, a deep shudder that resonated not just in his skeleton but somewhere deeper, unsettling his core. And the pain wasn't just sharp anymore. It carried a strange heat, a burning quality, as if the ink itself was molten. He could feel her focus—that unnerving, almost predatory concentration emanating from her still form—and watching the blood-red ink bloom on his skin in the mirror, a terrifying thought slipped through his mind: *She knows.* She knew what this symbol meant, what it would cost, what justice it carried—and she was etching it into him anyway. His carefully constructed arrogance began to feel thin, brittle, like a layer of ice over dark, churning water.

He tried to anchor himself—focus on the sheer physical sensation, compartmentalize it, the way men do. *Just pain*, he told himself. Just needles and ink. Like the dozens he already wore, hidden beneath bespoke suits. But this *felt* different. The burning deepened as Artis La started laying in color—that impossible, vibrant red—feeling less like a surface scratch and more like she was embedding embers beneath his skin. The machine—Kay Fè's spirit-infused tech, he thought wildly—didn't just hum, it *keened*, a low thrumming harmony that resonated somewhere behind his ribs, shaking loose things he'd buried deep.

Scratch, burn, vibrate.

The needle felt like it was dragging claws across raw nerves. And with a particularly sharp sting near a cluster of old scar tissue—a faded reminder of some long-forgotten street brawl—came the first flash. Not a thought, but an imprint burned onto the inside of his eyelids—*Sanaa's eyes*. Not hopeful and vibrant like in the photograph hanging outside, but wide, terrified, reflecting the harsh studio lights from that last session...

He flinched—a barely perceptible tightening—but Artis La didn't miss it. Her own eyes lifted fractionally, meeting his in the reflection of a nearby dark-framed mirror he hadn't noticed before. Her expression remained placid, knowing.

"The flesh remembers, Mr. Pope," she murmured, her voice barely louder than the machine's keen. "The ink—*Ogun's Mark*—simply gives memory a voice. Especially *this* ink."

Her ink. He remembered the whispers now, dismissed before as jealous rivals or fanboy hype. How Artis La's pigments were legendary—colors too vibrant, too deep, holding light in ways physics couldn't explain. Some swore she mixed her inks with sacred offerings—*loko* leaves, water from hidden, sacred springs in Haiti where the spirits danced, soil from holy ground near an ancient mapou tree—to bless the wearer, to connect them directly to the Lwa. Others, the ones who spoke low in darkened corners after too much rum, whispered darker origins—graveyard dirt, powdered bone, *lanmò*— claiming she bound ancestral spirits directly into the *mak*, linking the wearer to the specific traits, the unfinished business, the *power* —and perhaps the hunger—of the dead themselves.

Looking at the blood-bright red blooming on his skin in the mirror, feeling the *thrum* of the machine vibrating through him, the darker rumors didn't seem so far-fetched. Whose strength—whose rage—was he inviting into his skin?

As she switched to a cluster of needles for shading, the pain morphed into a furious scratching—a thousand claws digging trenches across his back. Another sharp puncture, deeper this time, seeking bone. *Flash*—a different face. Younger—*Lavinia?*—her mouth a distorted rictus, lipstick smeared, her mouth forming a silent O, *no!,* the cheap, moldy motel air thick with something broken as he walked out, demo tape in hand. Terrified tears streaking knock-off Jordans pounding rain-slicked pavement—the runner he'd sent Krusha to handle years ago, the one who tried to leak Sanaa's contract details. *Gone.* Saditty squeezed his eyes shut, trying to force the image away, but the memories lingered like retinal burn.

"Breathe," Artis La instructed calmly, though her dark eyes seemed to track the ghosts flickering behind his own. Her hand moved with relentless precision, the needle dancing. "You invited the spirit, do not fight its arrival now."

He wasn't just fighting the pain, he was fighting his own history erupting from the archive of skin. Each sting, each vibration of the needle unlocked another cell, releasing specters he thought long buried. The burning wasn't just ink, it was the friction of his past grinding against his present. The House of Iron indeed—a forge burning away his defenses, tempering him into something new, something terrifying, whether he wanted it or not. His heart hammered against his ribs, a frantic drumbeat against the machine's steady, soul-deep hum. The unease wasn't just growing—it was blooming, dark and insidious, fed by the very ink she was laying down, watered by the blood blooming on his skin. He wanted to scream—to tell her to stop—but the sound lodged in his throat, a knot of fear and pride. He could only endure as the needle continued its relentless excavation.

* * *

Krusha remained frozen just inside the obsidian door, a mountain of muscle barely contained by his black wool peacoat, feeling utterly useless and increasingly unclean. Saditty had told him to stay put, but every instinct screamed at Krusha to drag his boss out of this place—this house of disturbing power. The silence from beyond the black velvet curtain was somehow worse than if he could hear screams. All he *could* hear was the faint, sinister *thrum*—the vibration of that strange machine—seeping through the thick velvet, a sound that felt like it was burrowing into his teeth. That, and the cloying scent of jasmine tangled with something metallic, maybe ozone, maybe old blood—or maybe just guilt.

He shifted his weight, the expensive leather of his shoes creaking softly on the polished floor. His eyes scanned the foyer again, trying to find something normal, something solid to anchor him. But everything felt charged and wrong here. The pulsing, unnatural light from the alien plants, the cobalt blue bottle trees glinting with captured spirits, the intricate, hammered metalwork figures from Croix-des-Bouquets hanging on the walls—warriors, serpents, symbols that writhed if he looked too long. His hand instinctively went to the worn gris-gris bag inside his coat—a prayer Madear taught him whispered under his breath.

His gaze drifted to the framed photographs he'd noticed earlier—Artis La's previous clients. He saw Sanaa's hopeful face again and quickly looked away, a familiar sour twist in his gut—he remembered driving her home that one time, such a gifted dancer and choreographer, how quiet she was, how Saditty had laughed later. Her talent was an instant money maker, a bank Saditty'd sold off to another less talented artist. The look on her eyes when she'd realized she signed away her own future... Krusha focused instead on the older photos interspersed among them—sepia-toned, black-and-white, some with the faded pastels of the 70s. Different eras, different fashions, and in each one, standing beside the client—was her, *Artis La*. Or someone identical—always those same knowing, ancient brown eyes and that faint, spectral smile.

Krusha felt a chill independent of the room's temperature trace a path down his spine. He leaned closer to one, a black-and-white shot. It had to be Artis La, impossibly young. He scanned the other walls. There she was again, beside a musician Krusha knew had died in the 90s. And again, a tintype photo—*her* face unmistakable. It looked impossibly old, like centuries had passed since it was taken. Impossible.

He backed away, bumping slightly against one of the iron sculptures. It felt cold, unforgiving. Who the hell was this woman? Immortal? Ageless? Or a lineage—a family passing down the secrets of Kay Fè, the mastery of ink and flesh? Either answer felt terrifying. He glanced towards the black velvet curtain, hearing the low thrum from the machine behind it, steady, relentless. He thought of the runner with the terrified eyes, the wet *thud* when he'd cornered him in that alley—another job done, another soul stained. Krusha edged closer to the obsidian door, the urge to flee warring with the ingrained duty to stay—and the paycheck that kept his own family fed—to wait for the man who paid him. The man who was currently submitting himself to whatever ancient power resided in this house, marked by a woman who maybe wasn't a woman at all. He shuddered, pulling his peacoat tighter, wishing he'd stayed outside like he'd been told—wishing he'd quit years ago.

* * *

Each searing pass of the tattoo machine was met with a stoic resolve, Saditty's jaw clenched, the pain swallowed before it could find voice. Time dissolved—measured only in the jarring rhythm of the machine, the searing paths of pain, and the ghost-flicker behind his eyes. Each flash carved itself deeper not just into his mind but into the ink itself—Sanaa's terror, Lavinia's brokenness, the runner's panicked flight—their faces swimming in the blood-bright reds and starless blacks blooming across his back, visible in the mocking fragments of the mirrors. He felt marked, not just on his skin, but through it—claimed by something ancient, something tied to the graveyard dirt and ancestral rage he now felt terrifyingly certain was mixed into Artis La's pigments.

He was sweating freely now, the initial cigar scent long over-whelmed by the metallic tang of blood and the cloying sweetness of jasmine that emanated from Artis La herself. He risked another look at her reflected face—her brown eyes were dark pools utterly focused, her expression unchanged. Was that satisfaction he saw there? Or just the dispassionate focus of a master artisan—or a priestess preparing a sacrifice? But then, with a pained groan, he remembered, he was no sacrifice, and the woman had done nothing but what he himself requested—no, *demanded*.

Then—silence. The deep, soul-shaking hum of the machine finally ceased. The sudden absence of its vibration left his bones buzzing, his skin screaming with a million phantom needles. A profound, burning ache settled deep beneath the surface, a testament to the sheer trauma inflicted.

"The first pass is complete," Artis La announced, her voice startlingly clear in the renewed quiet. She began wiping his back with something cool and damp, the relief almost agonizing against the raw, burning skin. "It has taken root."

Taken root? The phrase sent another shiver down Saditty's spine—not of cold, but of violation. He felt heavy, altered. He wanted desperately to see the finished work—no—he wanted desperately not to see it, to pretend it wasn't there, branding him.

He pushed himself up from the chair, muscles protesting. He tried to recapture his swagger, but his legs felt unsteady. His gaze, against his will, riveted on his reflection in one of the angled mirrors. There, across the expanse of his back, was not just ink, but a sweep-ing, breathing mural of deep blacks and furious reds, pulsing with its own malevolent light. It was vast, intricate, terrifyingly complete. It felt...alive. Heavy, like a shroud woven of judgment. A strangled gasp caught in his throat, but he quickly swallowed it, forcing his face into a mask of disinterest.

"Good," he forced out, the word scraping his dry throat. He wouldn't let her see how shaken he was. He reached for his jacket, pulling it carefully over his raw skin. "Looks powerful. That's what I paid for."

Artis La simply inclined her head, offering that same faint, knowing smile that never reached her eyes. "The power is there, Mr. Pope. Kay Fè provides the conduit—the *mak*. How you wield it—*or how it wields you*—that remains to be seen. Remember balance."

Saditty just grunted, eager to escape the cloying intimacy of the room, the weight of her gaze, the phantom touch of the needle. He needed air. He needed noise. He needed to reassert control. He turned, pushing back through the black velvet curtain without a backward glance, stepping out of the forge and back into the slightly less oppressive—but no less strange—atmosphere of the outer parlor, bracing himself to face Krusha. The burning on his back felt like a living thing, clinging to him, whispering promises—or maybe threats—he couldn't yet decipher.

* * *

Saditty hadn't slept—not really. He'd paced the penthouse, the vast space feeling tight, suffocating. He'd downed half a bottle of expensive cognac, his own label, of course, trying to numb the incessant, burning throb radiating from his back, but the liquor only sharpened the edges of his unease. He'd refused to look at the *mak* again after leaving Kay Fè, avoiding the bank of mirrors in his entry-way. He vaguely recalled Artis La pressing a small, dark container into his hand just before he stumbled out, murmuring something about aftercare with Haitian vetiver to "settle the spirit of the ink." He'd shoved it into his pocket without a thought, desperate for fresh air. Finally, sometime before dawn, he'd collapsed onto his ridicu-lously large bed, the crimson silk sheets feeling alien against his skin.

He woke with a gasp, not from a nightmare, but from a sensation—a spreading dampness beneath him, sticky and warm. Panic seized him. He scrambled upright, heart hammering, and stared down at the sheets. A dark, viscous pool stained the luxu-rious silk—a horrific tableau of black and deep red, like ink and blood mingled with pus. It emanated from where his back had rested, concentrated streaks weeping from where he imagined the Lwa's heart and burning eyes were etched into his flesh. It looked like a river of gore staining his expensive bed, as if the *mak* itself were bleeding him out, draining him where he lay.

"What the hell—" The words choked off. This wasn't normal tattoo leakage—he knew that much from his previous ink. He'd felt the initial ooze before, but never this. Never this volume, this dark mingling of ink and lifeblood.

He stumbled out of bed, legs shaky, ignoring the ruined sheets. He lurched towards the massive master bathroom—a space walled in floor-to-ceiling Italian marble and strategically angled mirrors designed more for vanity than practicality, but perfect for viewing every angle. He needed to see the damage. He braced himself, expecting raw, inflamed flesh, maybe torn skin from the intensity of the session. Angling himself awkwardly, using the reflections-within-reflections, he finally got a clear view of his entire back.

The sight stole his breath. Beneath the smear of dark fluid still marking the surface, the skin wasn't raw. It looked... healed. Utterly, impossibly, completely healed. No redness, no swelling, no peeling—none of the tell-tale signs of fresh ink that usually lasted weeks. The lines of the Ezili Dantò tattoo were sharp, settled, the colors terrifyingly vibrant, as if they'd been part of him for years, not hours. He could see the detail now—the fierce, burning eyes seemed to hold actual depth. It looked like an eyeball might blink, rendered in fiery reds and ghostly blacks, and the manchèt-like scars looked almost three-dimensional, raised as if carved into him, embedded not merely inked. It looked ancient, powerful, and chillingly permanent. A cold sweat broke out on his skin, unrelated to the night's humidity.

Tattoos didn't heal like this. Not overnight.

He found the small, dark container Artis La had given him on the marble countertop where he'd blindly emptied his pockets. He opened it. Inside was the thick, greenish-gold butter, smelling faintly of smoke, damp earth, and the sharp, distinctive rootiness of Haitian vetiver. Not the usual clean, antiseptic scent. It smelled like it was going to hurt.

Hesitantly, using a plush towel to wipe away the disturbing ooze first along the edges of his back—the fluid thick and staining— he scooped a small amount of the butter. It felt unnaturally cool against his fingertips. Reaching awkwardly, using the angled mirrors to guide him, he began to smooth it over the vast, seemingly healed tattoo. The deep ache lessened slightly under its touch, the coolness soothing the phantom burn, but the skin felt too smooth, the energy radiating from it palpable, alien.

That's when he heard it. A faint whisper, thin as cobwebs, seeming to curl around the edge of the running water sound from a faucet he hadn't turned off.

Samuel...

He froze, hand flat against the Lwa's face on his back. His birth name—not Saditty. Samuel. The name his mother used. He scanned the empty, opulent bathroom, eyes darting between reflections. Nothing. Just steam, marble, and his own wide eyes staring back.

Imagination. Stress. Lack of sleep.

He dipped his fingers back into the vetiver butter, forcing his hand to move, to complete the task. As the cool balm slid over the Lwa's fierce, burning eyes inked into his flesh—

Sammy, why? Why'd you let him?

Clearer this time. Right beside his ear. A girl's voice—reedy, spectral, choked with tears he suddenly remembered all too well. *Lavinia*. The first one, really. The one back in Yonkers, before the deals, before the Grammys, before Saditty Pope consumed Samuel whole.

"Who's there?" he choked out, spinning around, finding only empty space and mocking reflections.

Only the hiss of steam and the drip of water answered. But the air felt thick, charged. The paranoia, which had been a familiar companion he usually managed, clamped down hard—cold, sharp, undeniable. He wasn't alone. The House of Iron had followed him home. The *mak* wasn't just on his skin, it was in his head. It was a conduit. And the spirits—or his guilt, what was the difference anymore?—were starting to whisper through.

Saditty stumbled back from the bathroom mirrors, the ghost-breath of Lavinia's whisper cold against his neck. He wouldn't be undone in his own house, wouldn't be haunted by regrets he refused to claim. *Guilt.* The word itself felt foreign to him, ill-fitting—a garment meant for weaker men. He was Saditty Pope, predator, not prey. He stalked into the living area, the crimson silk robe pooling around his feet like shed skin, the city lights outside a distant, indifferent galaxy.

He tried to anchor himself in the tangible—the weight of his phone in his hand, the familiar cadence of legal threats. "Updates on Reine," he snarled at his lawyer, pacing. "I want them crawling." But the words felt hollow, brass shields against incoming cannon fire. Even as he spoke of depositions and breaking contracts, his eyes betrayed him, darting to the shadows that seemed deeper today, pooled beneath furniture like spilled ink. Was that the glint of judgment from a Grammy's wink, or just the unforgiving shine of his own ambition staring back?

He cut the call short, the silence rushing back in, thick and expectant. Then came the whispers again—not just the sighing drift of air conditioning, but something more intentional, focused like old women worrying beads, sharing dark secrets in the corners of the room. Whispers like dry cane leaves rustling with forgotten names. He couldn't make out words, only the sibilant accusation, the sound of judgment sharpening itself just beyond his hearing.

Sammmmmmmmy.

He spun, finding only emptiness and the city skyline glittering beyond the windows—a cold constellation of other people's lives. He caught his reflection in the dark glass of the entertainment center—and for a terrifying instant, a face superimposed itself over his own—not the runner this time, but Sanaa, her eyes wide with a grief that shattered her youthful hope, the talent he'd shackled indefinitely for another artist's use and name. That sham of a pop star, Isis. Sanaa was a face in the glass, brief as mercy, sharp as consequence. *Gone.* A forgotten promise, betrayal.

And he hadn't cared before because he was making money either way, off each one of them.

"Krusha!" he roared into the intercom, the sound raw, tearing through the expensive silence. "Sweep the floor! Check the goddamn perimeter! Somebody up in here!" He needed the mundane, the physical assertion of security, even as he felt the true siege was internal.

Krusha's voice, tight, weary, crackled back. "Still clear, Saditty. Locked down."

He tried to build a fortress of gold. He forgot that true hauntings were born in the blood, nested in the bone.

Locked down.

Saditty laughed, a harsh, grating sound. As if stone and steel could hold back ghosts born of his own making. He poured the cognac. The amber liquid smelled faintly of the vetiver butter on his hands—smoke and earth and something sharp that promised pain. *Stress*, he insisted again. *Lack of sleep. I been goin' hard. Need to rest.* Maybe they were messing with him—some industry rival playing psychological games. A head trip. Or maybe it was the

Illuminati conspiracy heads kept crying about. It felt more plausible than acknowledging the alternative—that the house he built to keep the world out couldn't protect him—from the rot within its walls, or within himself.

He hurled the tumbler. Crystal shattered against marble, a small violence in the face of the larger, creeping one. The whispers rushed into the vacuum left by the sound, clearer now, fragmented—*liar... abuser... thief... blood-money...* He clamped his hands over his ears, the thrumming from the *mak* on his back pulsed in time with the accusations. His empire felt vast but hollow, a gilded drum echoing only his own frantic heartbeat.

This penthouse—his monument to music mastery—was a tomb closing in. He couldn't fight shadows with money or muscle. He couldn't cuss a ghost out. He needed something else. He needed the source, the smithy where this spiritual shrapnel had been forged. *Kay Fè. Artis La.* The thought tasted like bitter bile, like surrender, but the whispers were getting louder, promising worse to come. He had to go back. He had to face the woman who wielded Ogun's fire, even if it meant walking deeper into the furnace and the flame.

The decision, once made, felt like leaping off a cliff—terrifying, but decisive. The whispers hadn't stopped—they merely retreated to the edge of hearing, waiting. The burning ache from the *mak* on his back was a constant companion. Sleep was impossible. He couldn't stay in the penthouse—his tomb-in-waiting—any longer.

"Get the car," he snarled into the intercom, his voice cracking with a freshly ignited, violent fury. "Now! And hurry! Take me back to that damn alley! I want to talk to that wench face to face! She's got another thing comin' if she thinks she can pull this kind of stunt on me!"

* * *

The ride was taut with Saditty's seething rage. Krusha drove, his massive shoulders tight, knuckles white on the steering wheel. He hadn't asked questions when Saditty emerged from the elevator, face ashen and drawn, demanding to be taken back to *that place*. Krusha's own face was a mask, but Saditty caught his eyes flicking nervously to the rearview mirror, not checking traffic, but checking *him*—checking the back seat as if something might manifest there. The silence in the luxury SUV felt louder, more accusing, than the whispers had been. It was the loaded quiet of men sharing a dangerous secret—a secret Saditty was only beginning to understand the true cost of.

As they neared the non-descript street, the address burned into Saditty's memory, his heart began to pound again—a frantic rhythm against the cage of his ribs. He half-expected the air to change, to thicken with jasmine and old magic as they approached. He peered through the tinted windows, searching for the shimmering obsidian door, the strange glyphs he hadn't noticed until Krusha pointed them out, the malevolent energy that should have clung to this block like humid air.

Krusha slowed the vehicle, pulling towards the curb exactly where they had stopped before—how long ago was it? Last night? A lifetime? Saditty's breath hitched.

Nothing.

Where the obsidian door had pulsed with inner light, there was now just...brick. Old, grimy, unremarkable red brick, tagged with faded graffiti Saditty was sure hadn't been there before. No shimmering surface, no heavy velvet curtain glimpsed just beyond. The narrow space between the dingy laundromat and the boarded-up check-cashing place held only overflowing black dumpsters and the lingering scent of despair—spoiled milk, stale refuse, and city grime.

"Hell naw," Saditty whispered, shoving the car door open before Krusha had fully stopped. He stumbled onto the sidewalk, ignoring the late-night drizzle that had begun to fall. He scanned the storefronts. But his mind raced, refusing to accept what his eyes were showing him. "It was here! Right here, damn it."

He walked towards the brick wall, running his hands over the rough, cold surface. Solid. Mundane. Only red brick dust in his hand. No hidden seams, no shimmering energy, no hint of the otherworldly space he had entered—the space where Artis La had marked him, where the spirits whispered through ancient ink.

The House of Iron was gone. And all that was missing was the reason—a portal of logic and possibility his mind could not cross.

"Krusha!" he yelled, spinning around, frantic. "You saw it! You were here! The door—the carvings—tell me you saw it!"

Krusha had gotten out of the SUV, standing heavily by the open passenger door, breathing hard, his face ashy, his eyes wide with a fear that mirrored Saditty's own growing terror. He looked at the brick wall, then back at Saditty, then quickly away, unable to meet his boss's desperate gaze. "Saditty, I..." Krusha swallowed hard. "Mane, I don't know what we saw last night. But there sho'll ain't nothin' here now. Ain't never been nothin' here but brick, far as I can tell."

The denial—or perhaps the terrifying truth—in Krusha's words hit Saditty like a physical blow. Vanished. Kay Fè—the House of Iron—had simply ceased to exist, taking Artis La and her ancient book with it. The forge was cold, the smithy gone—but the shrapnel remained, embedded deep in his flesh.

A wave of vertigo washed over him. He thought he would pass out. If the source was gone, what did that mean? Was the *mak* still active? Was Ezili Dantò still bound to him? Or was he simply left marked, ruined, haunted by an echo with no source, no recourse? The uncertainty was a new kind of terror. He wasn't just haunted. He was cut adrift, branded by a power that had shown its face and then dissolved back into the mundane world, leaving him alone with the consequences.

The way he had left so many others.

The city lights pulsed and jeered, cold constellations mocking his plight. He pressed a hand to his back, the burning ache suddenly feeling less like power and more like a phantom limb haunting him— an undeniable presence attached to a body that was no longer there.

✳ ✳ ✳

The ride back to the penthouse was a blur of rain-streaked city lights and suffocating silence. Krusha drove with grim focus, his eyes fixed straight ahead, refusing to meet Saditty's frantic gaze in the rearview mirror. Saditty himself slumped in the back, the vast space suddenly coffin-tight. Kay Fè was gone. Vanished like smoke, a fever dream—except for the brand seared into his flesh, a burning anchor tethering him to a nightmare he couldn't wake from. The ache intensified, a constant, agonizing reminder of the power he'd grasped and the abyss he'd fallen into. He wasn't just haunted now, he was marked, owned by an echo.

Back in the penthouse, the opulent emptiness mocked him. The whispers hadn't returned—not yet—but the silence was worse, pregnant with waiting malice. He paced, agitated, the crimson silk underfoot feeling like slick blood. He tried to work, to lose himself in the mechanics of his empire, but the numbers swam, the contracts blurred. He even tried to return to his first love, his art. The memory of the watercolor brushes broken by Pretty Tony, Chris before he was renamed as Krusha, and the other faceless bullies tumbled back, unbidden to him. And all he could paint were the traces of the lives he'd ruined, their faces rising up from the wet paint like pigmented phantoms. Every shadow writhed with potential menace. Every reflective surface threatened to show him another face—the dancer's grief, the young, much too young "first love's" silent scream, the runner's terror, so many others—and worse, the unyielding judgment in Ezili Dantò's eyes, now permanently etched onto his back, onto his soul via his skin. And what burned more was that it was a curse he'd foolishly put on himself. But his rare self-awareness did not last long.

His paranoia found focus—shifting from the supernatural he couldn't fight to the people he could control. His staff became targets. He fired his chef via intercom for the "repugnant" smell of garlic—a scent that had never bothered him before but now grew thick with graveyard earth. He screamed at his financial advisor over a minor dip in futures, his voice cracking with a hysteria barely masked by rage. He was a king raging against the tide by commanding the sand.

Then came the call he'd been both dreading and craving—his lead counsel on the Reine North America lawsuit.

"They blinked," the lawyer said, voice tight with suppressed excitement. "They want to discuss a settlement. Substantial figures, Mr. Pope. Very substantial."

For a moment—a single, treacherous heartbeat—a wave of incredulity and relief washed over Saditty. *It worked.* The thought flared, bright and desperate. The *mak*. Artis La. Kay Fè. Maybe the gamble, the terror, the price paid in flesh and sanity—maybe it had secured his hard-earned, hard-hustled bag after all. Maybe this power, however terrifying, could still be wielded.

But the relief curdled almost instantly, replaced by a chilling insight. The universe didn't trade like that. Power invoked demanded its own terrible exchange rate. This settlement felt less like a victory and more like bait, like the spirits—or the Lwa herself—were merely fattening the calf before the slaughter. What good was securing the bag if his soul was already lost?

"Handle it," Saditty snapped, cutting the attorney's connection, the good news feeling like another turn of the screw. The brief flicker of hope only made the surrounding darkness feel deeper, more absolute. The old feeling returned, which was, the absence of feeling. He needed to hit something, to break something, to assert dominance over something tangible. Anyone would do.

He found Krusha in the security monitoring room, hunched over the screens, the reflection of static flickering in his weary eyes.

"Anything?" Saditty demanded, his voice dangerously soft.

Krusha jumped slightly, startled. "N-no, mane. Still quiet. Locked down."

Saditty stared at him, at the fear Krusha tried so hard to mask, the complicity etched around his eyes. He saw the man who'd followed him into Kay Fè, the man who'd seen something but now claimed only brick, the man who'd handled the runner. The man who used to bully him. Krusha knew. He knew the rot. And that knowledge, that shared witnessing, suddenly felt like betrayal.

"Quiet?" Saditty echoed, stepping closer, invading Krusha's space. The air crackled. "You call this quiet? Somebody runnin' my house, talkin' crazy and you call that quiet?" He gestured wildly around the penthouse, though the room itself was still. "You don't hear them? You don't see them?" His voice rose, cracking. "Or are you with them now, Krush? Keeping secrets? Enjoying the show? You ain't never liked me! Even when was kids."

"Saditty, no—" Krusha began, holding up his hands, his face paling further. "He ain't like that. I don't know what you're talkin' 'bout—"

The denial, the fear, it ignited something vicious in Saditty. He lashed out, not with words, but with fists. A brutal, unexpected explosion of violence born of terror and impotence. He struck Krusha hard, again and again, the sickening thud of knuckles against flesh a counterpoint to the phantom whispers in his own head. He kept hitting, knowing Krusha would never hit him back. It was the desperate violence of a cornered animal, mistaking its own cage bars for the enemy. Krusha crumpled, stunned, offering no resistance—just shock and a dawning horror that went beyond fear of his boss.

Saditty stood over him, chest heaving, fists bruised, the adrenaline momentarily silencing the dread. But as he looked down at Krusha's stunned face, at the blood trickling from his lip, there was no triumph, only a hollow, echoing emptiness. He hadn't defeated the ghosts. He'd just created another victim, right here in his sanctuary. The violence hadn't purged the fear. It had only fed it, proving the rot was real, was him.

And then—a new sensation. A searing heat blooming across his back, sharp and sudden, like coals pressed against his skin. He gasped, stumbling back, clutching at his shoulders. It wasn't the dull ache from before. This was active, aggressive pain—an agonizing burn centered directly on the *mak*. It felt like the ink itself was boiling, like Ezili Dantò was stirring beneath his skin, her rage igniting. The forge wasn't cold anymore. It was inside him now, and he was the fuel.

Saditty ripped off his shirt, frantic, stumbling towards the bathroom mirrors again. In the reflection, the tattoo glowed—the reds incandescent, the blacks deeper than voids, the entire image pulsing with a malevolent heat that radiated outwards, making the air shimmer around it. The burning eyes of the Lwa blazed, fixed on his own reflected terror. Eyes darker than the womb. The manchèt scars looked raw, weeping not ink this time, but something that sizzled like acid on his skin. Sin. His sins.

"Get it off!" he screamed, clawing at his own back, nails scraping uselessly against the impossibly healed skin. "Get it off!"

The pain intensified, blinding him. It wasn't just burning—it felt like judgment made manifest, like every sin, every betrayal, every act of cruelty was being cauterized onto his soul through the

Lwa's fiery gaze. He collapsed against the marble counter, sobbing, incoherent, the fortress of his ego finally, irrevocably breached—not by whispers or shadows, but by the unbearable fire blooming from within.

Saditty lay broken against the cold marble, breath hitching, the fire on his back a living entity consuming him. The world was pain, shame, and the sudden, terrifying silence that followed his screams. His ego, that fortress built of swagger and cruelty, lay in ruins around him, breached not by rivals or lawsuits, but by the unbearable weight of his own history ignited by the *mak.*

Through the blur of tears and the shimmering heat haze rising from his own skin, the steam in the bathroom parted like a veil. A figure stood just beyond the threshold—still, quiet, radiating an unbearable sorrow.

Lavinia.

Achingly real. Not a fleeting flash this time, but the solid presence of the Yonkers teenager he had deliberately forgotten. Clutching phantom books, eyes fixed on him—not with ghostly malice, but with the bottomless grief of the first betrayal. *She* was the cracked foundation upon which his entire empire tilted.

He tried to speak, to curse, to command her away—but only a pathetic whimper escaped. Samuel—the scared boy who traded cruelty for safety—was all that remained. Her presence stripped him bare, forcing him to witness the genesis of his monstrosity. Her silence was the preface to the entire despicable book of his life, each subsequent sin merely a footnote to this original desecration. He had violated her and her trust. The rationalizations—the game, the power, what everyone did—crumbled to dust before the unwavering sorrow in those eyes. He saw the lineage of his victims stretching out behind her—an accusation more profound than any scream. The Lwa on his back pulsed, a searing echo of Lavinia's judgment, illuminating the full, unbearable architecture of the rot that was him. His denial finally, irrevocably, surrendered.

A sound tore from Saditty's throat—a laugh choked with a sob, a howl of utter psychic annihilation as Lavinia's sorrowful presence finally dissolved, leaving only the echo of his complete undoing. The judgment wasn't just on his back, it was branded on his soul. The rot was the throne.

As this final realization crashed down, a new horror bloomed, immediate and invasive. He looked down at his arms, slick with sweat and the weeping fluid from his back, reflected sickeningly in the blood-smeared marble floor. New lines were appearing—angry red welts rising on his skin, forming new tattoos across his chest, his arms, his stomach. Faces surfaced through his flesh like horrifying stigmata—Sanaa's grieving eyes, the runner's terrified grimace, others he couldn't name—their spectral forms etching themselves onto him now, weeping faint trails of that same dark, ink-blood mixture. Their whispers emanated directly from these erupting marks, a cacophony of accusation...*liar... thief... abuser... predator*...a chorus of the damned sung in his own skin.

"No! Shut up! Get off me!" Saditty clawed frantically at the images appearing on his chest. His nails left bloody gouges but failed to erase the spectral ink that bloomed beneath. He lurched towards the remaining angled mirrors, smashing his fist into them, shattering the glass, trying to break the reflections, the accusations—but the faces remained on him, weeping, whispering, crying out, indelible.

Saditty stumbled back, panicked, crashing blindly out of the bathroom and into his adjacent private study—a shadowy room curated with expensive African art. His private collection was impressive. It included powerful spiritual masks and sculpted figures, alongside shelves containing tools for mounting his collection. He tripped over an overturned box, scattering heavy brass framing nails, picture wire, and a small tack hammer across the thick rug. He saw the glint of the nails—long, sharp, brutally functional.

Down the hall, Krusha, drawn by the crash and the renewed, terrifying screams, forced himself upright. He crept towards the master suite, peered cautiously around the doorframe into the study—

Saditty wasn't just screaming. He was on his knees amidst the scattered art supplies, grabbing the spilled nails with frantic, trembling hands. His eyes were wild, fixed not on Krusha, but on the spectral faces weeping dark ink from his own arms and chest. With a roar of pure fury aimed at silencing the unbearable chorus erupting from him, he took one of the long framing nails and drove it violently into the weeping eye of a face emerging on his forearm. Not as ritual, not as effigy—but as a desperate, mad attack against the haunting itself. He sucked in pain, his breath ragged, arm bleeding as he tried to nail the accusing spirits down, to physically stop the whispers tearing out of his skin, his own flesh.

Krusha saw the spurt of blood, the horrifying logic within the madness—Saditty wasn't just destroying himself, he was trying to kill the haints haunting him, the ghosts manifesting on flesh. He saw Saditty fumble for another nail, eyes blazing with insane purpose, preparing to strike another emerging face. A strangled gasp of recognition tore from Krusha's throat. He turned and fled—bolting down the hall, lumbering past the silent luxury, the ghosts now seemingly confirmed as terrifyingly real and inescapable. He slammed the elevator button, hoping to escape the House of Iron's final claim before the contagion reached him too.

Alone now, surrounded by scattered nails, shattered glass, and the accusing faces blooming across his skin, Saditty Pope—Samuel—continued his gruesome work. He grabbed another nail, then another. He was a portrait of pain. Like a human Nkisi, he took shape accidentally, horrifically. His form was born from a desperate attempt to silence the past by attacking its manifestation on his own flesh. The burning on his back raged, the Lwa's judgment fueling the frantic, bloody rhythm of the hammer he now dimly registered finding in his hand.

The hammer rose and fell, a frantic, unsteady rhythm against the backdrop of Saditty's ragged breathing and the phantom whispers only he could hear now. Blood spattered the pristine marble, the scattered African masks. Some grinned now in the dim light, the thick rug darkening like cursed earth. He drove nail after nail into his own flesh—into the weeping eyes of Sanaa, the silent "O" of Lavinia, the terrified grimace of the nameless runner—pinning down the accusations, trying to silence the chorus erupting from his skin. Each impact was a grotesque prayer hammered against the gates of madness, an attempt to impose order on the spiritual chaos consuming him.

The pain was immense, a universe collapsing inward, eclipsing even the constant fire on his back, but it was secondary now to the manic focus of his task—to stop the voices, to erase the memory of their names, to nail down the ghosts that refused to let him forget.

He became a thing of iron and agony, studded with metal, leaking blood and the dark, viscous fluid of the *mak*. A walking testament to every sin, every soul he'd hammered down in his ascent, now made brutally manifest on his own shuddering flesh canvas. He was no longer Saditty Pope, the mogul, nor even Samuel, the broken boy. He was simply the vessel, the *Nkisi,* like the one watching from a top shelf, bristling with the captured torment of his own making. The Ezili Dantò tattoo on his back blazed, no longer just burning *him*, but seeming to *fuel* the horrific transformation, its power now fully, devastatingly, rooted. Her fierce womb-dark eyes, now unseen by him but felt as a constant pressure, bore witness.

Did he finally scream when the last nail went in, pinning down the final whisper, sealing the last spectral eye shut? Or did he simply slump forward, a grotesque sculpture of judgment and self-destruction, bleeding out onto the expensive rug in his ruined study? Perhaps he remained there, impaled and immobile, eternally conscious within the prison of his flesh, the whispers finally silent only because they were now trapped inside him forever. The man who claimed godhood—now just a king left alone on a throne of his own agony.

The specifics mattered less than the silence that eventually fell in the penthouse—heavy, final, stained.

News reports in the following weeks were confusing, contradictory. Samuel "Saditty" Pope found dead in his penthouse—an apparent psychotic break leading to extreme self-harm. Gruesome, but explainable to a public already primed by the "Moguls & Monsters" exposé. But then came the other whispers—stranger tales. Krusha, his long-time bodyguard and childhood friend, hospitalized after a sudden, inexplicable illness that left strange, scar-like marks across his skin before his own untimely death. Other former associates—executives, lawyers, rivals who'd been complicit in Saditty's rise or benefited from his fall—reported disturbing phenomena: uncontrollable tremors, phantom whispers, vivid nightmares featuring faces they didn't know but somehow recognized. And in some cases, faint, angry red lines appearing on their own skin, sharp as a machete blade—like nascent tattoos, like judgment spreading.

* * *

The mak demanded its terrible balance
and the House of Iron always
collected its due.

* * *

Months later, whispers surfaced from a hidden courtyard within New Orleans' Vieux Carré—tales of an obsidian door appearing where none was before and of an artist named Artis La, a woman with ancient brown eyes and a knowing smile, and long, talon nails wielding impossible ink shimmering across a sea of hungry flesh.

SPECIAL 66

T he ferry groaned against the dock, a sound of old bones settling into discomfort. Stepping off felt like being swallowed whole. The air itself, thick enough to chew, carried a metallic sharpness, the undeniable odor of rust. But there was something else beneath it, heavy and sweet, teetering just on the edge of rot. Like overripe peaches, left too long under a sun that knew too much. It was the scent of memory made foul, the taste of promises made, and bodies broken by another time that still lingered in the air. Mama always said that smell meant trouble brewing, not the kind you could see coming down the road with a name and a face, but the kind that snaked up from the roots of things, deep and unseen, twisting around your ankles before you even knew you were caught.

The island presented itself as a shrug of decay, a place where things came to be undone, a testament to promises broken and dreams left to fester. Flat tires lay scattered, forgotten offerings to some indifferent god. The dead carcasses of abandoned cars littered the landscape. Their hollowed-out shells gaped like the mouths of old ghosts, monuments to wrecked dreams given solid, rusting form. Beyond the sun-dried cow bones and scattered ribs, the charred ruins of a church lay half-buried at Mourner's Beach, its pews exposed to the indifferent, relentless gaze of the Atlantic tide. The iron bell, never salvaged, stood sentinel over the wreck, a dark tongue silenced but not forgotten. Folk said a spirit haunted that bell, a girl who died there in a fire on the eve of her wedding, her joy consumed by flames. They said she'd married the devil himself under those waters, a quick, hot ceremony, and he'd claimed her, body and soul. So the church and its bell and the spirit trapped within remained, half buried in the sand, half free in the salt spray. Like the town itself, I thought, and the people who called this place home. Parts of them still visible, walking around in the daylight, others lost to the shifting sands of time and sorrow, buried in places the map forgot.

My feet, accustomed to the predictable hardness of city pavement, sank into the red dirt road leading away from the dock. Each step felt less like forward motion and more like walking backward, peeling back the layers of years I'd tried to outrun, layers of distance I'd put between myself and this place, this blood-soaked ground. I carried the Bonecarver blade wrapped in my mama's old headscarf, tucked deep in my bag. It was a weight that felt both foreign and deeply familiar, a promise and a burden I hadn't fully understood until now, a piece of my own history I'd stolen away.

The road, red dust clinging to my shoes, eventually led towards Mourner's Beach, and there, nestled near the sand and the half-buried church, stood the place the islanders spoke of in hushed, reverent tones: From Scratch. It was a low-slung building, weathered by salt and time, but stepping inside was like entering a different world entirely. The air was thick with the comforting smell of fried fish, simmering greens, and warm cornbread, a stark, almost jarring contrast to the decay outside. The walls were a museum to labor, adorned with antique cooking implements, rusted graters, heavy iron skillets, wooden spoons worn smooth by generations of use. From the rafters hung intricately woven sea island baskets, their sweet-grass scent a subtle counterpoint to the savory aromas, each one a testament to generations of hands and stories. Amongst the tools and faded photographs of island families long gone, I noticed something else tacked to the wall—a scattering of missing persons flyers. Their edges were curled and yellowed with age, the faces on them blurred by time and salt spray. A surveyor who'd cheated the family out of land, a mainland politician who'd cut the ferry hours and enacted other petty slights, trying to force the last remaining families from the land that was their home and haven. Their disappearances weren't mysteries here. They were quiet, grim warnings. Warnings that echoed the historical hunger, the insatiable appetites of those who thought Black lives were endlessly consumable, meant to be flayed and boiled, exploited and monetized. forgotten. And domi-nating one wall, reaching almost to the ceiling, hung a giant wooden knife and fork, carved with intricate, almost unsettling detail, like tools fit for gods or giants. It was a place that celebrated the history of cooking, the skill passed down, but there was an undercurrent, a tension that hummed beneath the surface of the easy chatter, a sense that the labor here was more than just sustenance.

I found a quiet corner, trying to blend in, watching the island-ers come and go. Their faces were a mix of weariness and resilience, eyes that held secrets the mainland couldn't fathom. A woman with kind eyes served steaming plates, her movements practiced and efficient, a quiet grace in her work. A group of men sat at a worn table, their voices low as they discussed the tides and the weather, their hands, gnarled and strong, speaking of lives lived close to the bone of the island. It felt, for a moment, like a normal place, a brief, fragile illusion.

Then, a man I didn't recognize, clearly from off-island with the crispness of his clothes and the way he held himself, approached the counter. His face was unfamiliar, as were most on this island I hadn't seen since a childhood funeral, a distant memory of hushed whispers and Mama's fear. He was just another tourist, I thought, another outsider seeking a taste of the island's "authenticity." He didn't have the round forehead, the high cheekbones, or the deep-set eyes that ran in my family, the subtle markers of our bloodline that I'd come to recognize even in distant cousins. He carried himself with the entitled swagger of someone who believed every place was put there for his convenience, every local a prop in his personal narrative. He had a demanding air about him, the kind of man used to getting what he wanted. As he placed the order, his gaze met mine across the bustling diner, and a slow, unsettling leer spread across his lips, followed by a subtle, almost imperceptible wink. It was a gesture that made my skin prickle, a moment of unsettling familiarity that I couldn't quite place.

"Yeah, I heard about this spot," he said, his voice cutting through the diner's hum like a rusty blade. "Heard you got something special. Gimme Special 66."

A hush fell over the diner, sudden and absolute. The woman behind the counter froze, her smile faltering, her eyes widening just a fraction. The easy chatter died, replaced by a palpable silence that pressed in on all sides. Heads turned, slow and deliberate. I saw the knowing looks exchanged between the customers, a flicker of alarm in their eyes, a shared understanding of a boundary being crossed. The laminated menu on the counter, thick with offerings of seafood platters and Gullah rice, did not list "Special 66." It was not a dish you ordered like fried chicken or shrimp and gravy biscuits. It was something else entirely.

The air grew heavy, thick with unspoken understanding, with the weight of history and consequence. The man, oblivious or perhaps deliberately ignoring the shift, tapped his fingers on the counter, waiting with an arrogant patience. From a table near the back, a voice, low and urgent, a thread of fear and deference woven together, broke the silence.

"Call Nana. Now."

The whisper carried across the room, sharp and clear. It was clear this wasn't just a meal; it was a request that resonated with the island's deepest secrets, a request that went directly to the source of its power. The atmosphere in the diner, moments before comforting, now felt charged, expectant, humming with a dark energy. I felt the weight of the name, Nana, the same name that had drawn me back to this island, the same name that belonged to the house waiting for me up the road. The dread I felt earlier returned, sharp and cold, mingling with the sudden, chilling realization that the legend of "Special 66" is not just folklore; it is something real, something that commanded silence and summoned ancient power. No one else moved, but the air was too thick to breathe, too heavy with the

island's secrets. I had to escape the suffocating weight of their knowing, of the dark promise that had just been uttered.

Leaving the charged air of the From Scratch Diner behind, I
made my way towards Nana Fey's house. It jutted out from the trees
like a giant piece of driftwood thrown ashore by a storm of ages,
thick-walled and leaning, covered in vines that seemed to hold it
together and consume it all at once, a green, creeping hunger that
reached for the sky. There was no fence, just an airless yard that
felt heavy with unspoken history, with the weight of generations
of secrets pressed into the soil. Seeing it again, after all these years
away, the old dread, slick and cold, welled up inside me, that chilling feeling that no one here truly lived or died without Nana Fey's
permission, without her ancient, squinting eyes seeing their beginning and their end. The last time I was here, I was small, barely big
enough to see over the top of a coffin, and it was for a funeral I barely
remembered, only the hushed whispers that followed me like flies
from the dock and the way Mama clung to me, her eyes wide with a
fear I hadn't understood until much later, a fear that tasted like ash
and something bitter.

She had vowed never to return, not as long as she drew breath,
and she kept that vow until her dying day. She said every night she
slept in that house, the dreams came for her, twisting and dark. Now,
standing before it, I felt the sharp edge of those nightmares pressing
in, the air thick with the weight of them, humid and suffocating.
I was back, but I wasn't sure if the I who returned was the same
person who had left, or if the island had already started to claim the
soft parts of me I thought were safe on the mainland, the parts that

hadn't been steeped in this particular kind of darkness. The parts Mama tried to protect.

The vines on the house reached for me, hungry, wanting to turn everything back, back to the beginning, before even the Old Ones discovered this island, before the Persimmons and their hateful plantation, forced prison and sadistic torture ground covered in a word that pantomimed gentility. Back to a time when things were raw and untamed, wanting to reclaim me and all the years I'd spent waiting, afraid, for this inevitable return.

Nana Fey's house held its breath, or maybe it just didn't need to breathe the same air as the rest of the world. Stepping inside was like entering a different kind of heat, one that pressed in from the walls themselves, thick with the smell of old wood, dried herbs and spices, and something else I couldn't name, something that prickled the back of my neck like unseen eyes. No photographs hung on the walls. No smiling faces trapped behind glass, no mirrors to catch your reflection and remind you who you were supposed to be. Every surface, the rough-hewn table, the worn floorboards, the very doorframes, carried scars, nicks and gouges that spoke of time and use, hinting at a different kind of work, a craft that left its mark on everything it touched. Wherever my eyes landed, I saw the quiet evidence of Nana Fey's life's work. It felt like a Bonecarver's touch, yet no delicate carvings or keepsake talismans met the eye—none of the intricate work the name might usually invoke. Here, that touch was in the stark raw materials, the heavy tools of severance hinted at behind closed doors, and the pervasive sense that bone itself—stripped bare, perhaps, for some relentless, primal purpose—was central to this place, to her.

Butcherboy, his presence a constant, unsettling hum in the background, gestured with his head towards a narrow hallway leading away from the main kitchen area. "Your room's this way," he said, his voice low and rough, like gravel shifting under a heavy boot. He didn't offer to help with my bag, just turned and started walking, his steel-toe boots thudding softly on the worn floorboards. I followed, the air growing heavier with each step away from the front of the house, the silence amplifying the sound of my own breathing.

As we walked towards the back, I caught glimpses of other structures in the yard through dusty windows – a low, squat building that looked like a smokehouse, its wood dark and aged, and further out, a larger, more mysterious blood red barn, its doors heavy and barred, like the gate to a place best left undisturbed. I knew, with a chilling certainty that settled deep in my gut, that this barn was where the undone were kept, the family whispers about zombies, the living dead they said Nana Fey had bound to her will through some ancient, terrible pact. According to the island's lore, these were not mere spirits, but bodies drained of their own life force made to serve the insatiable appetites of another. A chilling echo of the forced journeys across the big waters in the holds of ships. Dark, bottomless maws that swallowed Black bodies whole. The thought, though ridiculous, sent a shiver down my spine, despite the oppressive heat.

He stopped outside a door at the end of the hall and pushed it open. "Here."

The room was small, the air close and still, carrying the faint scent of dust and something else, something vaguely sweet and decaying. An old iron-frame bed stood against one wall, covered with a thin, faded quilt that looked as old as the house itself. In one corner stood a dark, heavy chiffarobe, its wood old and scarred, like it had stories carved into its surface. Its mercury-distorted mirror warped, a vintage warning. Against another wall, a tall, leaning bookcase sagged under the weight of its contents. It wasn't filled with fiction or trinkets, but with books – antique cookbooks, their spines worn smooth, their pages likely brittle with age, a library of culinary history rooted in this very soil. Titles I recognized from whispers and old stories were crammed together, names that spoke of generations of Southern Black women's kitchens: The Carolina Rice Cook Book, What Mrs. Fisher Knows About Old Southern Cooking, and nestled amongst them, a title that caught my breath, a direct link to a cherished memory – Vibration Cooking. Mama had a copy of that one, worn and loved, filled with her own handwritten notes in the margins, a testament to her own kind of kitchen magic. Seeing it here, amongst these ancient tomes, felt like a piece of Mama reaching out to me, a fragile connection to a life that felt impossibly far away, a life that had tried to outrun this island and failed.

Butcherboy didn't linger. He just stood in the doorway for a moment, his eyes scanning the room, then mine, a silent assessment. "Dinner when Nana calls," he said, his voice flat, and then he was gone, leaving me alone in the quiet, syrupy air of the room, the weight of the old cookbooks and the mysterious barn pressing in.

That night, the house settled around me, its old bones creaking and groaning like a ship in a storm. Sleep came fitfully, thin and easily broken, the humid air feeling thick with unseen things. And when it came, it brought nightmares, not the simple, linear fears of the mainland, but dreams woven with island logic, surreal and disturbing, a kind of dream logic that bypassed the conscious mind and went straight to the bone. I was walking through a field of cow bones, the ground shifting like sand, and the bones began to hum, a low, vibrating sound that grew louder, turning into whispers. The whispers were in a language I didn't understand, ancient and guttural, but they spoke of deals made in darkness, of prices paid in flesh, of promises whispered to Old Scratch under a blood-red moon. I saw shadows dancing around a giant black pot, figures with milky eyes and jerky movements, their hands reaching, always reaching, dragging themselves across the ground as if they wore invisible chains. The air in the dream was thick with the smell of sulfur and something burning, something like hair and rot, a Lovecraftian miasma that clung to everything. I saw my mother's face, her eyes wide with that familiar fear, her mouth opening to scream a warning that never came out, her image dissolving like smoke.

I woke with a gasp, the dream clinging to me like the humid air. The smell of sulfur and burnt hair was still in the room, faint but unmistakable, a chilling echo of the nightmare. My heart hammered against my ribs, a frantic drumbeat in the darkness. Old Scratch. The whispers about Nana Fey's deal, trading something ancient and terrible for the power to keep her enemies close. Turning them into zombies, into indefinite labor, the way generations of our family line had been forced to work mercilessly. The only freedom death. The cloying ache in the air, a suffocating darkness made me scream on the inside. It wasn't just folklore. It felt real, a horrifying possibility rooted in the very ground beneath me, in the groaning bones of the house, in its very scent.

I lay there in the dark, the smell slowly dissipating, and my mind drifted back to another night, years ago, when I was small.

Mama and Daddy were arguing in the next room, their voices low but sharp, a familiar rhythm of disagreement. It was about returning to the island for a funeral, full of distant cousins whose names I barely knew. Mama said it was important, that we had to show their respects together as a family, that it was the right thing to do, a tie that couldn't be broken. But Daddy's voice was tight with resistance, a weariness that went deeper than just the thought of travel or expense.

"I don't see why we got to waste the time or the money flying down there to that weird island," he'd argued, his voice laced with a deep-seated aversion. "Don't play crazy now, Dahlia. Last time you said it was just going to be another fake funeral, made public just for show, because everybody know Nana and her sister ain't dead, ain't neither of them great-great—how many greats they supposed to be?— ain't none of them great grandmamas ever really dead." He spoke of two sisters, sharing one bloodline, forever feuding over darkness and the light, their ancient rivalry a living thing on the island, a battle fought with roots and bone and whispers. He wanted no part of it, he said, no part of the island's magic or its curses, whether it was fable or true, his voice firm with a fear he wouldn't name.

Lying there, the smell of sulfur still faintly in the air, the weight of the Bonecarver blade heavy in my bag, I understood his fear in a way I never had before. This island, this family, the power they wielded, it was real, and it was terrifying. Two sisters, two paths, and I was caught somewhere in the middle.

Nana Fey cooked, her movements slow and deliberate. No one really knew how old she was—every generation on the island remembered her being alive, hunched over that stove in this kitchen next to the giant fireplace we'd had since slavery. Hundreds forced to clear forests, drain swamps, and build canals for the island's prized rice. Skills they brought with them from home, and skills the Persimmons certainly could never teach them.

Nana's stove looked as if it had been engulfed in flames, scorched by otherworldly fires. Her kitchen was rumored to be built around the very place they said Old Scratch emerged, baring his offer. Perhaps not a bargain for a soul, but for an appetite, a right to the bitter feast of vengeance, a taste of what had been made "delectable" for centuries. Her skin, the color of dark chocolate with a dash of caramel, was creased with deep wrinkles that covered her face like palm lines. A thick, silvery-white braid coiled atop her head like a dollop of fresh, whipped cream, and her eyelids drooped so low, she seemed to squint even when looking directly at you. I wondered how she could see me, let alone her "receipts," what she called her recipes. Her apron, a simple thing with faded flowers embroidered years ago, was stained, but the powder blue house dress beneath it was spotless. Attached to a thin black leather string was a red pouch pinned with seven safety pins. She placed a plate of rice and shrimp, biscuits and thick gravy before me. The food smelled heavenly, spicy, rich, and buttery, a cruel contrast to the tension in the air.

Welcome did not come with words from her, couldn't or wouldn't. The only sounds were the quiet scrape of forks against plates, the soft clink of cobalt blue cups as I stacked them on the speckled enamel drainboard, the color of red earth. I washed the dishes in near silence, the water running over my hands a small, temporary comfort. This was our unspoken agreement, laid out without a single direct word: she cooked, I cleaned.

Now and then, one of us might offer a brief observation.

"Smell like rain."

"Glad to be rid of this heat."

Anything but the words that needed to be spoken, the reason I had been summoned here, the truth that strained just beneath the surface of every breath.

I had been spared all these years, kept away by Mama's fierce protection and the hushed whispers of brave cousins who somehow diverted the call. This time, however, it was my turn. I was Nana Fey's new apprentice, here to take the place of the last one, whose grave was still fresh on the island. This house, this air, this silence – it was all part of the apprenticeship, a steeping in the island's particular reality.

I felt the pull of history, the absence of family members, an ache in the old house. One daughter lay under a stone in Guinee Field, her story a sorrowful note in the island's song. Another's ashes were scattered on ocean tides, carried away but never truly gone. Other seed, other cousins, were scattered too, in the wind, in the sandy dunes by the ocean, hiding on the mainland just as I had hidden for so long. All that was left here was me, and even I felt incomplete, unfinished, like all the other things on this island. The life I remembered, the person I thought I was, felt distant, unreal. I was emptiness covered with skin, concentrated grief as flesh scraped from bone, waiting to be filled or perhaps carved into something new.

Adding significantly to the unsettling atmosphere was a constant sound from another part of the house—the rhythmic, high-pitched whine of knives being sharpened. My tight-lipped cousin, the butcher, Butcherboy as they called him, was always at it, a relentless, almost manic sound that spoke of a chilling fascination with blades, a percussive backdrop to the house's heavy silence. I imagined him hunched over, his eyes fixed on the steel, the sound scraping at the edges of my nerves. Sometimes, I felt his gaze, even when I couldn't see him, a foreboding, assessing look, that made my skin crawl. One afternoon, seeking a moment of quiet away from the oppressive heat, I leaned over the sink, letting my hands run through the cool water and caught his reflection in the grimy windowpane. There he was, bullfrog eyes frowning at me, the veins pulsing in his neck, fresh perspiration rings under his arms. It was a fleeting, disturbing glimpse of a man with eyes too intent, a jaw set hard, the sound of his work echoing in the humid air. Startled, I backed away, my heart hammering against my ribs. I heard him sharpening again, then grinding of his whetstone as if he were a demented John Henry, hammering at the wheel of the earth instead of mountains. Other times I heard him cursing, his gruff voice directed at faces I could not see. Muttering about offenses only he knew.

Out in the backyard, beneath the reaching live oaks shrouded in Spanish moss, amidst the small talk and the long silences, sat the giant black pot. Pot was too genteel a word. It was a grim-black cast iron cauldron, the size of sorrow, almost big enough to take it all in. It was covered now beneath a stack of faded quilts, a hulking, silent presence that had been in the family since the days the elders didn't speak of anymore, the time of chains.

Some people on the island whispered that Willie J had tried to persuade her once dear sister Nana Fey not to call up dark powers, but instead, to lend her gifts to the amplification of light. But it was clear the two paths did not meet. That Nana Fey, a legendary beauty in that day, was said to stand at the intersection of three roads, where she demanded to parlay with none other than Old Scratch himself. None living but perhaps her own sister knows what she bartered, but surely something precious, perhaps her own mortal peace. Her soul's peace for power? The power to snatch others' eternal rest? These were the zombies, the undone, forced to serve the family who had once served their kind.

To my horror, it appeared that one of them shuffled near the edge of the yard. A figure in ragged, archaic clothes, a tattered embroidered waistcoat like something drawn in an old waterlogged history book. Atop his head looked like the remnants of a moldy powdered wig. It was a chilling echo of the original Persimmons Family who owned the vast number of enslaved Africans om the island. All forced to work on their plantation, to make the island's considerable acres profitable.

He moved with a slow, jerky gait, his eyes milky and vacant, forever bound to this place. He shuffled closer, his hand, pock-marked, gnarled and grey, reaching out, dragging a piece of charcoal across the dusty ground. He grunted, a low, guttural sound, trying to form words that wouldn't come. Just a hoarse rasping. On the fresh earth in an ancient calligrapher's script, a message began to form: Have mercy. Forgive me. Free me. Butcherboy watched from the porch, a grim set to his jaw. "He stopped trying to escape a long time ago," he muttered, the sound of his voice low and rough.

Seeking escape from this dreadful sight, a living undead affirmation, and respite from the oppressive heat and the heavier air of Nana Fey's house, I stumbled away, my mind reeling under the palmettos and giant oaks. I walked with no firm destination in mind, only the desire to remove myself from the shattered man's presence and sour stench, and Butcherboy's merciless eyes. I soon found myself following a faint, less-traveled path by the wild woods that wound towards a different part of the island.

The air shifted here, losing some of its thick, humid weight, carrying instead the clean scent of sea air, turned earth, sweetgrass marshes, and growing things. It felt like stepping out from under a shroud. The path led me towards a small, unassuming yard, less imposing than Nana Fey's leaning structure, but alive with a quiet, vibrant energy.

There, amidst rows of herbs I didn't recognize and plants that pulsed with a life of their own, was Nana Fey's sister, Willie J the Bonecarver. She sat on a sky blue painted tree stump, her knotted hands moving with a swift, graceful motion across a piece of bone she was whittling. It was hard to imagine such nimble skill in a woman folk said was centuries old, but the grooves in her skin, the deep lines marking her neck and jaw, tribal marks from a home she never forgot, and those high cheekbones, told a story a hundred years couldn't begin to hold. Her eyes, rheumy and water-filled like murky marbles in the light, met mine. They held a different kind of sight than Nana Fey's or Butcherboy's assessing squint, a sight that seemed to look through you, not to judge, but to see.

I stopped at the edge of the yard, hesitant, the dust of Nana Fey's path still clinging to my shoes. Willie J didn't stop her work, but her voice, when she spoke, was like two trees falling or the wind sulking beneath a sagging roof—low and resonant.

"Seed scattered," she murmured, not looking up. "Hard to take root, far from the birthing ground."

My heart hammered a different rhythm than the one the butcher cousin's sharpening knives had set. She knew who I was, knew why I was here, perhaps even knew the weight of the stolen Bonecarver blade I carried hidden in my bag.

"Long time we ain't seen you, child. Since you was knee-high to a duck. Heard you got something for me. The blade told me."

I don't know why, but panic rose and settled right between my eyes. The blade. Bonecarver. She knew. This wasn't going to be as easy as I imagined. I had already broken one promise to Mama. Keeping the other was going to be harder than I thought. "No," I lied.

She finally set the bone down, smoothing the shiny bit with the back of a rusted knife. Her hands, though ancient, moved with a surprising strength. She looked directly at me then, and her gaze felt like cool water on sunbaked skin.

"Island got two hearts, Cuffie," she said, her voice a low rumble. "One beats for what's broken. Other beats for what can still grow."

She didn't elaborate, didn't ask why I was at Nana Fey's, didn't offer solace or judgment. She simply held my gaze for a long time, a silent question hanging in the humid air between us. The scent of the herbs in her garden, sharp and clean, filled my lungs. It was a different kind of power here, quiet but deeply rooted. Not shiny but bright.

"Some things," she said, picking up her bone piece again, her fingers tracing its contours, "can be easily mended. Some things... they just break different. But they don't have to stay broke."

She returned to her carving, the soft scrape of bone the only sound now. The moment felt complete, a brief, potent encounter. I didn't need more words. The glimpse she offered, the quiet strength of her presence, the hint of a different way the island's power could manifest – it planted a seed of doubt in my mind, a fragile, unsettling thing that contrasted sharply with the heavy certainty of Nana Fey's house and the path she was leading me down. I turned back the way I came, but the air no longer felt quite so thick; a different kind of possibility had entered it.

The oppressive calm in the house shattered like dropped glass. It began with the sharp ring of an old red rotary telephone, a jarring sound that cut through the wet silence. Nana Fey, who moved with the slow deliberate pace of moss growing on stone, blood lichen on the branches of the live oak-pine was suddenly alert, her ancient ey¬es snapping open. The air in the kitchen, thick with the smell of simmering greens and something else I still couldn't place, seemed to vibrate with a sudden, electric energy. Butcherboy, whose constant knife sharpening had become a chilling backdrop to the house's quiet, fell silent mid-stroke, the sudden absence of the sound more unnerving than its presence.

Nana Fey spoke into the receiver, her voice low and guttural, a language of clicks and murmurs I didn't understand. But the words that came next, spoken with a chilling clarity, needed no translation.

"Gimme Special 66."

The house transformed. The slow, waiting energy of the past days evaporated, replaced by a coiled tension, a predatory readiness. Movements became sharper, gazes more intense. Nana Fey's squinting eyes held a fierce, focused light I hadn't seen before. Preparations began in the backyard. Nana Fey moved towards the giant black pot, throwing back the faded quilts that covered it, revealing the dark, patient maw. She began to build a fire beneath it, her hands, gnarled with age and work, arranging kindling and wood with practiced efficiency. The smoke rose, thick and acrid, mingling with the sweet, heavy air of the island.

Then, her voice, sharp and commanding, cut through the rising smoke. "Come. Help me hold this fire."

My stomach twisted. Help? I hadn't been taught to cook, not like this. My mother's frantic warning echoed in my ears: Don't let them feed you Special 66. Now I was being asked to help make it. The brief, quiet encounter with Willie J, her words about mending and growing and brokenness, flashed in my mind, a stark, unsettling contrast to the heat and smoke and the grim purpose settling over Nana Fey's yard. Fear, cold and sharp, pierced through the creeping dread. I felt utterly ill-equipped, a child handed a weapon she didn't know how to hold. Dusk was beginning to paint the sky in bruised purples and oranges, the light fading fast, and with it, any hope that this was just another quiet evening on the island. The air grew thick with anticipation, the buzz of mosquitoes and the violent heat of the island amplifying the tension.

The time for waiting was over.

Dusk deepened, dark brushstrokes a skyborn warning. The fire beneath the giant black pot began to lick at the iron, casting dancing shadows that twisted the familiar shapes of the yard into something menacing. The air grew thick with the smell of woodsmoke and the heavy, sweet scent of the island, a combination that now felt less like nature and more like a prelude. My heart hammered against my ribs, a frantic bird trapped in a cage, the quiet moment with Willie J feeling impossibly distant, a fragile dream against the encroaching reality of Nana Fey's purpose.

Then, the sound came. Not the familiar groan of the ferry or the hum of an engine on the main road, or the bellow of the wild cows, but the low rumble of a vehicle turning off the path, its tires crunching on the red dirt as it approached the house. It felt like a heartbeat in the stillness, growing louder, closer. Headlights cut through the twilight, two yellow eyes staring from the darkness beyond the trees. They stopped just outside the yard, the engine falling silent, leaving only the buzz of mosquitoes and the crackle of the fire.

Two figures emerged from the vehicle, moving with a grim efficiency that chilled me to the bone. And between them, something else. A shape, bound and struggling, making low, whimpering sounds that were barely human. They dragged it from the back of the vehicle, a heavy, resistant weight, rolling it onto the ground like a package meant for the pot. It was a man, tied at the wrists and ankles, his face obscured in the dim light and the shadow of his own terror.

My blood ran cold. This was the "meat."

Nana Fey watched from the edge of the firelight, her face unreadable, a silhouette against the rising smoke. Butcherboy stepped forward, a dark shape detaching itself from the shadows near the house. He moved towards a small, squat shed I hadn't paid much attention to before, a structure that seemed to sag into the earth, its door secured with multiple heavy locks. The sound of the locks being undone, a series of metallic clicks and scrapes, echoed unnervingly in the quiet yard.

The door creaked open, releasing a smell that hit me like a physical blow. The sickening, unmistakable odor of death, thick and cloying, mingling with something foul and stagnant. My gorge rose. I stumbled back, clapping a hand over my mouth and nose, the humid air suddenly suffocating.

They dragged the bound man towards the shed, his whimpers turning into desperate pleas. "Please... I'm sorry... I said I'm sorry."

His words were muffled, frantic, swallowed by the night and the island's indifference. They shoved him inside, into the darkness and the stench. I caught a glimpse of the interior before the door slammed shut. Rough-hewn walls, dark and stained, and scratched into the wood, faint but horrifyingly clear in the fleeting light, were marks. Fingernail marks, clawed into the wood in desperate, vertical lines. And lower down, scrawled in something dark and viscous, words. Help me. Written in excrement.

Terror, pure and paralyzing, seized me. I wanted to run, to scream, to disappear into the thick, vine-covered walls of Nana Fey's house, to run back to Grandmama Willie J and beg her forgiveness. Why had I answered Nana Fey's dark call Could anything she offered me bring my brother back? What was happening now? What was this place?

Then, Nana Fey's voice, sharp and unwavering, cut through my panic. "Look."

Someone, I don't know who, perhaps Butcherboy, grabbed my arm, a grip like iron, and forced me forward, towards the shed door. Forced me to look through the narrow gap between the warped wood and the frame. Forced me to see the trembling man huddled inside, his face now visible in the faint light filtering from the yard.

And I saw him.

My breath hitched, a ragged gasp torn from my burning lungs. The world tilted. It was him. The man. The vigilante who saw my brother as an easy target. The one who got away with murder. Literally. The one who profited from our pain, auctioning off the very gun he used, racking up a million in donations of appreciation from the other ghouls who saw our grief as sport and comedy. He was here. Delivered. Whimpering in a shed filled with the evidence of past horrors. Begging for his life, the way, my brother begged for his. He, too, was now the "delectable Negro," his life a prize to be carved and consumed, a literal manifestation of a parasitic hunger that had fed on our people for centuries.

The horror wasn't just what was happening; it was who it was happening to. Grief, rage, and a sickening understanding washed over me, a tidal wave of emotion that threatened to drown me in the humid air. This was the meat. This was Special 66.

A shadow crept from the periphery of the yard, stepping into the firelight. It was the man from the diner. His crisp clothes seemed out of place against the flickering inferno, yet he stood there with an unnerving calm, his eyes fixed on the spectacle. He caught my gaze, and this time, the leer was unmistakable, broad and triumphant, accompanied by a slow, deliberate wink that sent a fresh wave of icy understanding through me. He wasn't just a tourist. He was part of this macabre ceremony, an orchestrator, a collector, another one of my distant cousins.

The rage, a hot ember, ignited. Grief, a constant ache, sharpened into a desperate, consuming need for reckoning. The injustice of it all, the sheer, sickening wrongness of his freedom, of my father's failing mental health, of my mother's brokenness and heartbreak that finally killed her, of my brother's tragic absence, it crashed over me, a tidal wave that swept away everything else. Fear? Conscience? Pity?

The thought of what can still grow, what could be mended? They were whispers against the roar in my ears. All that mattered was the fire in my veins, the sudden heat, an overwhelming desire for this specific, singular man to pay.

Butcherboy, a dark shape against the firelight, moved with a chilling purpose. The sound of his relentless knife sharpening, the sound that had scraped at my nerves for days, now felt like a prelude, a sharpening not just of steel, but of intent. He approached me, his eyes unreadable in the shifting light, and placed something cold and heavy in my hand. A knife. It felt solid, real, a stark contrast to the spectral dread of the island.

His voice, low and flat, cut through the night. A different kind of blade. "This is meat for anyone who comes seeking Special 66."

The man in the shed heard him. His whimpers escalated into desperate shouts, curses hurled into the darkness, directed at me. "No! You can't! I'm sorry! I said I'm sorry."

Sorry. The word was a spark that ignited the tinderbox of my fury. Sorry didn't bring my brother back. Sorry didn't mend my mother or my father. Sorry didn't erase the years of pain, the spectacle. The image of Willie J, her quiet strength, her words about mending, flickered for a second, a fragile counterpoint to the raw power surging through me. But it was swallowed by the heat, the smell of smoke and rot and too sweet peaches, and the burning, absolute certainty that this was a necessary thing. This was the only language this man would understand. This was the only justice this island offered when the courts and the public failed.

My hand tightened around the knife handle. It felt... right, even more than the Bonecarver axe I was supposed to return to Willie J.

Mother had willed it, praying that I would make her misdeed right. But something else called me tonight, something that had been rooting inside me ever since I received Nana Fey's handwritten letter. Vague promises were made. Promises she intended to keep.

My hands shook. I was filled with a horrifying, sickening rightness that silenced the last vestiges of doubt. The rage, the grief, the years of unspoken pain – they channeled into this single point, this blade in my hand. The man's screams from the shed faded, replaced by the pounding of blood in my own ears, the frantic beat of my own heart. The sound of my mother's wail, the keening that rose when we first received the news. The wail that ripped through the ceiling and flung up into the sky when the jury set the man free. In that moment, standing in the humid air of Nana Fey's backyard, under the bruised twilight sky, the desire for vengeance, for a brutal, visceral justice, was greater than the sum of all my fears and every whisper of conscience I had ever known. The island held its breath, waiting.

The air, moments before thick with the man's desperate cries and my own surging fury, settled into a heavy, unnatural quiet. The sound of the knife, the visceral finality of the act – it hung in the waiting air, a silent testament to the justice served from scratch. My hands trembled, not just with the receding tide of adrenaline, but with the unsettling weight of what they had just done, what they had just become capable of. The rage still burned, a low ember, but beneath it, a cold, hollow space began to open. The image of Willie J's face, her ancient eyes holding a different kind of knowing, flickered again, a brief, unwelcome light in the darkness that now seemed to cling to me. Replaced by the satisfying sight of the craven man—who had stolen my brother's life and used our family's pain for celebrity, simply because he could—finally recognizing me. No tears this time, just clear-eyed focus reflecting the great pit's riding flames.

Without a word, Butcherboy reached for a gleaming hook on a nearby post. He began the work of preparing the meat, his movements efficient and chillingly practiced. As he plunged his hand into the bucket of brine, the fire beneath the giant black pot roared now, eager, casting grotesque shadows that danced across the yard and the walls of the silent shed. The smell of woodsmoke intensified, mingling with the iron scent that rose from the very earth, and soon, another aroma began to emerge – rich, savory, and unnaturally divine. It was the smell of something cooking, yes, but it carried a depth, a complexity that spoke of more than just flesh and spice. It smelled like history, like infinite sorrow, like a very old debt finally being paid.

Nana Fey watched the pot, her face impassive, a study in ancient patience. The steam rising from the cauldron curled into the bruised-lit sky, carrying its strange, compelling scent. When the time was right, a time only she seemed to know, she moved with that slow, deliberate grace towards the pot. She took out special bowls, not the everyday kind, but heavy, dark, perhaps ceramic bowls that seemed to absorb the firelight rather than reflect it. With a large, iron ladle, she dipped into the bubbling depths of the pot. The sound of the stew, thick and viscous, being ladled into the bowls was a low, wet slurping that turned my stomach even as the strange divine aroma drew me closer. It smelled savory but wrong at the same time.

She presented a bowl to me, the steam rising into my face, carrying that intoxicating, disturbing smell. "Eat," she commanded, her voice flat, leaving no room for argument. "This is from scratch. You made it with your own hand."

My hand, the one that had held the blade moments ago, trembled as I reached for the bowl. It felt heavy, warm against my cold fingers. The stew within was dark, thick with pieces of meat and root vegetables I couldn't identify in the dim light. The smell was overwhelming now, a mix of the divine and the deeply unsettling. Every instinct screamed for me to recoil, to run, to purge myself of the horror. Not to taint or pollute myself. But grief and incandescent rage had already done that. The need for justice, any kind of justice in this world, not just the next, the strange, dark satisfaction that had surged through me during the act—it held me captive. And beneath it all, a morbid curiosity, a need to understand the taste of this terrible reckoning.

I lifted the bowl to my lips, the rough edge cool against my skin. I remembered every slight and humiliation he had put my family through the moment he took my brother's life. The first sip was thick, coating my tongue with a flavor that was both intensely savory and something else entirely, something that bypassed the usual pathways of taste and went straight to the bone. It tasted like the long-denied feast, the return of what was taken, a reversal of the delectable flesh that once fed appetites across oceans and generations. It was the island's soil, the salt of the Atlantic, the bitter root of injustice, the sharp tang of spent fury, the heavy sweetness of sorrow. It was all of it, distilled into this single, potent mouthful.

Nana Fey watched me, her ancient eyes fixed on my face. "What does it taste like?" she asked, her voice barely a whisper, yet it filled the entire yard.

I swallowed, the strange, powerful flavor lingering on my tongue, settling deep in my gut. The horror was still there, the chilling knowledge of what I had done, but it was intertwined now with something else, something that felt like a release, a heavy burden finally lifted. The question Willie J had planted, about mending and breaking, felt distant now, muted by the overwhelming reality of this moment.

I looked at Nana Fey, at her ancient, unreadable face, and the word came to me, not from my mind, but from the very marrow of my bones, from the blood that now felt irrevocably tied to this island and its dark legacy.

"Justice," I said, the word a low, chilling affirmation in the humid night air. "It tastes like justice."

My voice was steady. The deed was done. The meal was complete. And I knew, with a certainty that settled deep and cold in my soul, that I was no longer the person who had stepped off the ferry. I was now a part of the island's receipts, its recipe, an ingredient in its long, slow, simmering history of vengeance served from scratch.

The last mouthful of stew settled heavy and warm in my belly. The taste of "justice," sharp and deep, lingered on my tongue, a brand seared into my senses. The horrors of the shed, the raw violence of the act, the sickening sweetness of the cooking meat – they were still there, yes, but now they were woven into the fabric of something else, something ancient and powerful that had claimed me. The rage that had driven me was a low hum now, a steady current beneath the surface. Grief remained, a constant ache, but it felt different, somehow contained, given a brutal form of release.

Nana Fey watched me, her ancient eyes, half-hidden by drooping lids, seemed to hold the weight of centuries. As if she was remembering whatever it was that had driven her to barter away her own soul's peace. There was no judgment in her gaze, only a quiet, knowing acceptance. She had set the table, prepared the meal, and guided my hand towards this inevitable end. The path had been laid out long before I stepped off that ferry, long before her letter was written, long before my brother was taken, long before Mama vowed never to return. It was written in the scars on her walls, in the rust and embedded dust on the black pot, in the very soil of this island.

The thought of Willie J, her gentle strength, her words about mending and growing, felt like a distant memory from another life-time, a faint echo across a widening chasm. Her path was one kind of power, a quiet cultivation. Nana Fey's is another, a fierce, consuming reckoning. And in that moment, with the taste of justice still fresh in my mouth, I knew which path I had been pulled onto, which legacy had claimed me.

I looked out into the sweltering night, the fire beneath the pot now embers, the air thick with the aftermath. The island felt different now, not just a place of decay and dread, but a place of terrible, ancient power, a power I was now a part of. I had come seeking answers, perhaps, or just a place to hide from the mainland's wide pain. Instead, I had become an ingredient in the island's oldest recipe. The person who stepped off the ferry was gone, consumed by the heat, the history, and the taste of Special 66. I was here. Rooted. A new, dark bloom in Nana Fey's spice garden. The grieving, I knew, would go on, but now it had a flavor and a purpose, served from scratch.

On this night, every illusion has dropped away, my world taken apart, seam by seam, rewoven the way spider webs on the island change every nightmorning, wet with dew. Time here is deceptive. There is nothing to measure it by any longer. A breath can take a lifetime, a lifetime a second, and the grieving, the grieving can go on years and years.

FAST

THE INVITATIONAL

A carpet of green dotted the ground filled with mottled, moss-covered trees. Taller and taller, they leaned and twisted alongside the crooked road until they split the earth and lifted the ground beneath them. The clumps of soil and twisted roots looked like wide, gaping mouths. Judaea Autrey shuddered as the yellow school bus careened down Interstate 72, bumping and stumbling along. A layer of fog wrapped itself around the twisting trees that sped past her window in a gray blur. The curtain of chaotic growth was strangely familiar, as if from a forgotten dream.

"I don't believe what they said about you," Qori whispered, her hair braided in a neat bun atop her head. The signature gold and green B.T.W. Warriors jacket was zipped up to her neck. Like everyone on the Booker T. Washington track team, Qori competed in multiple events. She was a nimble runner, gliding over hurdles like a gazelle. She also raced with Judaea in the 100-meter dash, the 200.

More importantly, she was the first leg in the 4x400 relays. And right now, she was Judaea's only kinda-sorta friend.

The increasing fog and murk outside the window evoked a roiling ocean, storm-driven, boundless. Judaea nodded at Q, then rested her forehead against the cool glass as the school bus lurched and tumbled. Slow tears of frustration mingled with nerves. Even without the nausea and the weird food cravings, Judaea was always a little on edge before a race, her thoughts focused on the win, the preparation.

In her mind she floated. Leaned forward in victory as her heart burst open, the plastic tape breaking across her chest. But there was no applause. In their last meet, she had fumbled, adding fuel to Raven's simmering hate. Judaea used to think she liked her, that they had a bond, beyond the track and field, connected by care given and time spent as friends.

But the baton inexplicably had fallen from her hand. She could hear the crowd gasp, feel the judgment of the others pressing against her back. She'd crumpled in her lane, deflated.

Now, she picked at a hole in the worn leather seat, the faint, cloying scent of stale Gatorade and old sweat a lingering ghost in the bus's recycled air. She wished she could fall in, just disappear. The faded leather felt clammy against her legs. She sat up, fingers splayed against her abdomen. The muscles were hard, taut, but something quickened beneath her touch. Scanning the bus, she saw her other teammates huddled in the back, whispering—laughing a little too loudly, laughing at her. Though she was a few rows away, she could hear the hushed, concerned tones of her coaches, probably discussing her downfall, planning the day's logistics. The whole while she wondered if she could even make it through another Invitational.

The two-and-a-half-hour drive from Memphis to Florence, Alabama was usually the highlight of their year. The girls would face fierce competition across the region from the fastest teens in the region, some with Olympic dreams. Only the best made it to the annual Track & Field Invitational. Before the summer, Judaea had counted herself among them. Now she wasn't so sure. The Warriors racked up medals in most of their heats, but the 4x400 relay was their signature event—and that was the one she had jacked up.

Just one more month to go. Long enough to finish the season, to hang up her shoes and quit. No point in fooling herself. After the scandal surrounding He-Who-Shan't-Be-Named—a forced encounter that Raven twisted into a stolen crush—Judaea found herself adrift and friendless on the team. She didn't have any real ones left, except for Q, a gentle soul too scary to even be seen talking to her.

While Assistant Coach Fuller steered, Coach Harris walked from the front of the bus to the middle and stood in the aisle right next to Judaea's seat. Without saying a word, she leaned to the side and peered out of Judaea's window. Her lanyard dangled from her neck, a "Run Fast, Turn Left" shirt visible beneath her green tracksuit.

"Welcome to North Alabama," Coach said, sucking her teeth. Judaea raised her head to see a tattered familiar orange and blue flag propped up against a rickety wood table in a field by the road.

"Bootleg," Judaea muttered. Coach Harris laughed and sat in the empty seat beside her.

"Hey Warrior, why do you weep?" Coach asked. "Fresh off your birthday, I'd think you'd still be celebrating, sharpening your oyster knife."

Judaea wiped her eyes, smiled warily. Coach Harris was always cracking jokes or saying something strange. But now she was trying to diffuse the tension that had been on the bus since the girls arrived at the BTW parking lot on Lauderdale early that morning.

"Zora Neale, Shakespeare?" Coach continued. "How does it feel to be colored me?"

"Wonderful," Judaea said with a wry smile. She turned to face her. "If you like spending your birthday at home with your mama."

"Look," Coach whispered. "I know you're having a rough patch with the girls, but don't let anyone take your crown, Judy, or get you out of character. Words are their own violence. They hurt, but don't let them define you." Judaea met her eyes, breath quickening.

Don't cry, don't cry, she repeated silently. *That'll only make things worse.*

"They'll come around," Coach said. "You're sisters...*of the yam!*" She poked Judaea playfully. "Sisters by choice, not by blood..." Coach waited, her eyes sincere under the matching cap.

"United on the field," Judaea finally managed, unconvinced.

"Good." Coach Harris rose and stood in the aisle, her arms resting on the worn seats.

"Warriors!"

"United!" the girls shouted. "United on the—"

"Gross!" Raven cried. They all turned to look. A deer lay stiff on the side of the interstate, its torso ripped into bloody shreds. Tongue lolling, eyes glazed, it looked as if it had been devoured instead of hit by a car.

"Damn!" Raven continued, her wine-tipped locs spilling down her back. "I thought Memphis couldn't drive!"

"Language!" Coach Harris said. She waited for them to settle down. "Listen, we may not be the biggest school out there today, the most experienced, or the fastest—"

"Heh!" Raven snorted. "We the fastest!"

"But what you are is very well prepared. Every week you put in the work, no matter what, and that determination makes you more than warriors. It makes you winners." The girls rolled their eyes, smirking.

"That's right!" Coach Fuller said, smiling in the mirror. He smoothly guided the old bus into the slow lane, allowing a truck to pass. Assistant Coach Fuller was new to the team, making this his first Invitational. He'd worked well with the girls, but ever since the dance, Judaea felt uneasy being around people she didn't know well. Hard enough to trust the ones she did know. She wasn't sure if she liked him yet or if she trusted him. She'd have to wait and see. But then she remembered. *Doesn't matter anyway.* After today, she wouldn't be running anymore.

"Ali said champions aren't made in the ring, in the gym, or on the field," Coach Harris continued, her eyes warm. "They're made from something deep inside you. A desire, a dream, a vision. Like Fatouma, who came here and had to learn a whole new language…"

The long jumper looked up, surprised, her bantu knots a dark crown spiraling around her head. At five-eleven she towered over her teammates and sat mildly pleased, clutching the equipment bag she loved so well. Her javelins were stored in a tube stretched across the row of seats in front of her. Raven's pole vault lay on the floor in its long, protective case in the aisle. For this Invitational, Fatouma would use a regulation rubber-tipped javelin, but she carried metal-tipped steel and aluminum since she practiced with all.

"Jërëjëf, Coach," Fatouma said, smiling, "bari laa jéeg naka ci wax ñaar languages. English was easy."

Raven blew Fatouma a kiss and they burst out laughing.

"I see, trilingual. Well, it wasn't easy, coming far from home, from what you know and love, but you practiced and never gave up. Now your home is here with us. Your team, your fellow track sisters."

"Raven, Fatouma, Qori, Judaea, each of you have something special to give, and not just competing. Individually you've all improved and excelled, but together you're even greater. So whatever beef you have, I'ma need you to work it out, squash it." She walked over to her hurdler, jumper, and pole vaulter, making sure to establish eye contact. "Because talent can win races, but teamwork and intelligence wins championships. United."

Raven and Fatouma watched Coach Harris walk back toward the front of the bus to join Coach Fuller. As soon as her head turned, they laughed loud as hell and Judaea heard snickers. "...No Booty Judy..." She sank in her seat, the morning light making her head and eyes hurt. She'd become so sensitive to light lately. As the girls whispered behind her back, she knew it was going to be a very long, bad day.

Judaea shook her head but could not shake the feeling. Instinctively, she touched her stomach again. Something stirred that wasn't supposed to be there. She was no expert and was relatively attentive in health class, groaning at the gross parts and giggling at all the rest. But what Judaea suspected was impossible. It had to be, and none of it was fair.

It wasn't. *He'd kissed her.* It happened so fast that she was shocked and she froze in the hall. If anyone bothered to ask her how it felt that night, she couldn't tell them. She couldn't even remember much beyond the alcohol on his breath, the fact that he barely pronounced her name, just the shock and the confusion of it all, the embarrassment and the urge to get away.

She had gone to her locker to change her shoes; her feet were killing her in the silver heels she wasn't used to wearing. She thought she looked cute that night for the dance. She had no idea he was following her. Judaea thought he'd been looking for Raven, but then he was on her, grabbing and pulling. She tried to push him away, but he kept trying to kiss her. Of course, that's when Raven walked in, convinced that her friend had stolen her crush. And Judaea's life crashed all around her. Within fifteen minutes, her reputation was over. The whole school was calling her everything but a child of God. *And all over a kiss, thrust upon her, that she didn't want in the first place.* Thinking about it still made her nauseous.

As Coach passed, she paused and stared down at Judaea for a moment. But Judaea didn't look up. She didn't want to risk seeing the same accusing eyes that had followed her out of the spring dance that night. The same questioning eyes that made her stop volunteering in the school office and start taking her lunch in the library with Ms. Glendale. She already knew what those eyes said: *fast tailed girl, man thief, crusher of crushes.* Judaea worried that those questioning eyes could belong to her mother, so she never told her what happened, no matter how many times she asked.

Fast was the name they'd laugh and call toddlers, whose milestones were ahead of the pack. *Fast* was the name for little girls who chose their own barrettes or took them out without permission. *Fast* for girls who wore red, or who wanted to choose their own clothes, for girls whose bodies grew too fast without society's permission, whose growing curves attracted the wrong kind of attention. *Fast* was for girls who got their cycles early, whose breasts and hips developed beyond the boundaries of their age and the ill-fitting clothes, *fast* for girls who everyone thinks they know but never see.

* * *

CHANGEOVER

Judaea heard the crowd before she saw it. Coach Harris was worried about the weather. A bank of clouds covered the sky and loomed overhead, a bad omen, just like the dead deer. She went to get the team checked in while Fatouma and Coach Fuller carried the equipment. Qori were up ahead toting the extra towels, medical kit, and garbage bags. Judaea knew Raven had a stash of gummy worms, but she wouldn't be offering her any. So, Judaea walked alone, her lucky running shoes slung over her shoulder. Qori slowed down so she could catch up.

"Don't let Raven bother you," she said, a digital watch wrapped around her wrist. "Fatouma doesn't even care. She just goes along to get along. Raven will be over this before you know it."

"I don't even like that boy, and I didn't do nothing wrong," Judaea said, frustration making her voice crack.

Before Q could respond, Raven spun around, rage transforming her face. She mouthed a word that made Judaea turn and run. She rushed past the other teams filing in, hot tears burning her cheeks. Before she knew it, she was at the concession stand. Normally she didn't eat before a race—too nervous—but her stomach roiled. She needed something salty to settle it.

Judaea felt the woman's gaze before she looked up.

"Can I help you?"

She stood behind the counter, dressed in white, a strange smile on her face. The skin on Judaea's arms rippled with an electric shock she had not felt before. She gasped, unsure what to say, the air unfurling from her lungs, words tumbling out as she tried to recover.

"Breathe," the woman said. "It will pass."

The stranger spoke without moving, so still, as if frozen in time, but she was staring at Judaea as if she knew her, an expression of disbelief and deep curiosity etched on her face. She was memorable, an interesting face you would not forget, with flawless skin and strong features carved like an ancient sculpture.

Nascent recognition, an ancestral hum stirred at the edges of Judaea's consciousness, though she was certain she had never seen this woman before. *At some point, we're all from the same tribe,* her mother once said.

"How about some water?" The woman handed her a bottle when Judaea did not reply. There was a familiarity about her. Judaea's brain itched with the effort to recall the memory.

Do you know who you are?

"Excuse me, what?" Did she hear that? The question unnerved Judaea because she did not. So much of her identity was connected to running, to the team and the friendships she thought she had. Who was she if none of that was part of her life anymore?

Your roots are here with us. It wasn't a question. Suddenly Judaea wanted to get away. The woman said so much without words, but Judaea did not understand. "Where you from? Where yo people from?" the woman asked.

"Tennessee?" Judaea said, suddenly unsure. Nothing made sense anymore. She gulped the water, trying to relax. She had heard about anxiety attacks but never felt one before that awful night.

"The change can be hard at first, but you'll get the hang of it. We all do eventually," she stated with quiet, knowing certainty. She held out her hand. "I'm Maryse. From the Colony."

Judaea paused, stared at the smooth, open palm then shook her hand gingerly. The woman studied her, as if weighing her reaction. *Rivers, reeds, earth, trees.* The image surprised her. "Colony? Where is that?" Judaea asked.

"Not far from here," the woman said. "You will come when you need to." She leaned over, wide eyes full of what looked like concern, care, comfort. The very things Judaea felt missing from her life right now when it had all gone wrong.

"Have they had the talk with you yet?"

The talk? Judaea shook her head. Confusion flickered across her face. She gripped the bottle. What did this stranger know about her that she didn't? Wasn't that the question that bothered her the most? People knowing secrets that she hadn't even revealed to herself.

"I don't understand."

"But you will. You're not alone," the woman said and refused her money.

* * *

They were warming up when Judaea made it to their section. She walked by Raven who pretended not to see her. Pods in her ears, Fatouma gave her a curt head nod as she stretched her hamstrings.

"What happened to you?" Qori asked, signaling her to sit.

"I don't know." She'd already gone through the first three stages before the meet began. The nerves and odd sense of fatigue, the dread and now that old excitement and anticipation flowed through her. Stretching with Q, she was just beginning to feel like herself. A smile emerged beneath the mask of wariness until Raven's dusty self stood up at Coach Harris's raised hand. Her eyes were cold fire.

The next two hours went in a blur of adrenaline and cheers. She could feel the strange sorcery of her body's music, getting her hyped with each win. Coach Harris was pleased. Their times had all improved. Fatouma performed as if she could leap over mountains. Qori had mastered the tricky, gravity-defying rhythms of the hurdles, sprinting and leaping without fail. No nicks, no knocked over barriers, while Raven catapulted herself to greater heights than she had known. Personal Best improved, they all looked satisfied, but then the moment came that they had been waiting on. *The relays.*

Coach Fuller led a prayer and Coach Harris dapped them up before the girls entered the track for the relay. This was the last event of the track meet, and the first and second legs would run in the inside lanes. Coach Harris liked to run the second-fastest runner first, the third fastest runner, second, the slowest runner next, and then the fastest, last as the anchor. That meant that Qori would get them started. Fatouma would set it off, leaving Raven and Judaea to finish—and win.

Raven was bouncing in place, kicking her feet. Judaea stared at her. *Truce?* But Raven rolled her eyes dramatically, wrapping her Kool-Aid colored locs in a hair tie. Judaea frowned. *How are you going to be the slowest and loud,* she thought, then she chastised herself. She didn't need any more negative energy at this moment. She had to concentrate. She started to walk to her spot when she heard her name.

"Judy!" Raven said. She turned, hopeful. "You better not fuck this up."

* * *

BLIND PASS

There are a hundred ways a race can go wrong.

Even at the highest levels of competition. Shoes fall off. People crash into each other. Some fall into forward rolls, while others toss the baton in desperation, stumbling, unable to reach their teammates in time. But no one was prepared for the Warriors of Booker T. Washington to win then lose their race—

disqualified.

The ride home was so silent, all Judaea could hear was the labored hum of the engine. Coach Harris looked stricken, as if the life force had drained out of her. The only thing she said was, "Running is not a contact sport, ladies." After that, both Coaches had shuttered up like Sphinxes. No eye contact, no admonishing words, nothing about the public humiliation at an honored event, just staring straight ahead, staring into the increasing fog.

Exhausted, mildly malnourished, and demoralized, the girls sat separated by several rows, silently grieving, seething. This time, even Qori was upset. Neither she nor Fatouma had spoken a word to Judaea and Raven. Judaea's temples throbbed, and she was officially over all of them. She wrapped her head in her jacket and closed her eyes. They rode in silence for some time until Coach Fuller slowed down. "We're gonna have to make a stop," he said. "I can't hardly see anything, and we need to gas up."

They drove on but never made it to the exit.

"Did we miss it?" Coach Harris asked. Her Warriors cap rested on the dashboard; auburn hair hung loose around her shoulders. "I didn't see anything but this damn fog. It should have let up by now."

Coach Fuller shook his head. "GPS acting up. Said nine minutes away, but now it keeps rerouting us." He sounded worried. "I hope it's not taking us too far off road."

"Not with folks out here with Confederate flags on the damn highway like broke-down lemonade stands."

He glanced in his mirror. The two gladiators looked as if they had fallen asleep. "We told them to *think* like Ali, not be out there *thumpin' like Ali*," Fuller whispered, shaking his head. Qori was reading and Fatouma was busy wiping down the equipment with a soft cloth. "The sooner we get them home, the better," Coach Harris said.

"Agreed."

After rerouting a few more times, Coach Fuller finally found an exit, but the closer he got to the destination, the further it was away. He finally gave up on following the app and drove following instinct.

"This can't be right," Coach Harris said, staring at her own phone. "This fog is still playing with the signal, reception is so poor." Just when they were going to back up and turn around, they passed an old Victorian house back off the road and then arrived at what appeared to be at one time, a gas station.

"I thought we were stopping right off the expressway," Raven said, yawning. "When we getting off this cheese bus? It looks like *Deliverance* out here."

"Those pumps look half a century old," Coach Harris said to Fuller.

He shrugged, pulling into the lot only to be met by protests.

Qori closed her book and peered out the window. "Coach! Where are we?" Her laughter was forced, anxiety crept through her voice despite her best efforts.

* * *

The gas station sat on top of a hill surrounded by neglected grass, gray asphalt, and a quartet of rusty gas pumps. The storefront window smeared with grit advertised cold beer, cigarettes, and lottery tickets. A faded sign hanging overhead read, Jonah's Ark. The air around it felt still, watchful, carrying a scent that wasn't just old gas and dust, but something else—something ancient and aware.

"Ain't nobody in there," Raven said.

"This place looks ancient. Can't we go somewhere else," Qori added.

The girls marched toward the gas station, bunched together behind Coach Harris despite the tension between them. The debacle at the track meet was still in the air, but resentment and worry kept them silent. Behind them the yellow bus idled beside a dirty gas pump. Coach Fuller leaned against the vehicle's side, scanning the foggy sky, while the black hose and metal nozzle filled the empty tank with diesel fuel.

Behind the cash register sat a middle-aged man with midnight skin and dark aviator sunglasses that hid his eyes.

"There *is* somebody in there," Judaea said.

Qori glanced at her, disappointment still on her face. Judaea knew she had let everyone down when she let Raven's smart mouth get the best of her. If she still had a crown, as Coach Harris had suggested earlier, then she had dropped it on the track in the inside lane.

"Is he sleeping?" Qori asked.

"Let's see," Coach Harris said. "The quicker we go, the quicker we can get back on the road and head home."

A curious heat and pressure fought for space, coiled just beneath Judaea's navel. She had to use the restroom and prayed that it didn't look like a murder scene.

Inside the gas station the competing scents of Good Vibes Clean's Frankincense and Myrrh and mildew leapt from the floor tiles and the dusty shelves. Behind the counter, a man stood, his stillness unnerving, his dark eyes hidden behind aviator sunglasses that seemed to absorb the dim light. When the door opened, a bell jangled and the man behind the counter jumped to his feet.

Tall and wiry with long, sinewy arms, he reminded Judaea a little of Coach Harris, though she might not appreciate the comparison. A fitted maroon baseball cap was pulled down over his forehead,

and a gnatty gray beard covered his face. He wore a multicol-
ored-striped tank top.

Across his chest, the man wore more silver necklaces than
Judaea had ever seen in her whole life. *Was silver in?* Heavy silver
cuffs were stacked along his wrists and forearms. Silver rings
adorned his fingers. He reminded Judaea of the overdressed elderly
men from her neighborhood who hung out, greeting everyone and
watching out for troublemakers.

"Lawd have mercy," he said, smiling at Coach Harris. "I done
fell out and woke up in heaven." A huge smile stretched his scraggly,
gray beard and revealed a black space where three missing teeth had
once resided.

Coach Harris chuckled and shook her head before directing her
girls through the store.

"Get what you're gonna get so we can go. Don't take all day.
You're not shopping for groceries. We're trying to get home."

Inventory-wise the store was ordinary. It had more beer than
juice, more sugar and salt than actual food. The girls made their way
down the aisles grabbing snacks. Raven selected a bag of skins, and
Qori fixed some hotdogs. Fatouma filled a huge, plastic cup with
cherry flavored slush.

Judaea was ravenous, more than usual after a race. She
grabbed cookies, water, and chips until they could stop to get real
food. She didn't get the hot dogs because the water smelled funny.
Still, something in the store was curious to her. The wall near the
restrooms was covered from top to bottom with religious icons. Not
just crosses and crucifixes—more silver, of course—but brightly

colored corazóns, little straw dolls, those evil eye medallions, Fatima's hands. And lots more silver.

When she got to the counter, the strange man was still flirting with Coach Harris, but he stopped suddenly and frowned when he saw Judaea. Several rifles and shotguns were leaning against the wall behind him. "You got people 'round here?" he asked.

"Mane!" she exclaimed. "You're the second person to ask me that today."

"Really?" His frown disappeared. *Now* he looked interested. "Who asked you that?" he said, bagging her snacks.

"Some woman in Florence."

He nodded. Coach Fuller walked in, headed for the restroom, but the stranger waved him over. "Hey, I'm Jonah, you can call me Joe. *Everybody* know not to mess with me 'round here," he said loudly. Everyone froze. "I'ma do you a solid. Y'all make sure to get out of Dumas County before sundown. I don't know how y'all got here, but I'ma tell you exactly where to go."

Coach Harris looked uncomfortable, confusion on her face.

"This a sundown town?" Qori asked, strangely excited. "Like in the *Green Book*?"

"I see somebody paid attention in history class," Coach Harris said.

"I told you this place looked crazy," Raven whispered, joining them.

Fatouma looked as if she'd had quite enough. "Coach, can we just go? This has been the worst trip ever!" Three medals hung around her neck, but she didn't feel like a champion now.

"What's going on here?" Coach Fuller asked, bristling up. He wasn't a fighter, but he would do so if he had to. The last thing he needed was for something else to happen on their first trip with him.

"Y'all ain't got time," Joe said. "What *ain't* happening here?" he added.

"GPS didn't say anything about no Dumas County," Fuller said, suspicious.

"Exactly," Joe said. "Ah, you off the grid now, brother. We ain't on no maps."

Fatouma placed her items on the counter and stepped back as if whatever Joe had was contagious. The others dropped their items and waited.

"Well, you ain't got to worry about us," Fuller said, heading to the restroom. "We'll be out of your hair." Coach Harris waved him off, letting him know she was okay.

"Make sure you take this one with you," Joe said, squinting at Judaea.

Fatouma and Qori looked at each other. Raven rolled her eyes.

Joe rang them up, repeating the directions again. "Folks peculiar 'round here. Especially after dark. Trust me, you don't want to know." His voice was low, the tone flat, carrying the weight of truths he knew but didn't fully share, a warning woven into the simple directions.

✷ ✷ ✷

BREAK-LINE

"I thought he said to go this way," Coach Harris said, trying to see through the thick layer of fog that had descended from the sky. They had driven so long, the sun had fallen and disappeared, replaced by night. She stared at the screen as it cast a frosty blue light over her face.

"You mean Jonah '*Everybody* Know' Ark?" Coach Fuller said, laughing. The road stretched out ahead. "I thought I might have to fire on that man." He raised a fist up playfully.

"He was definitely tripping." Coach Harris scrolled down her screen. "But the app said we'd reach the highway in twenty minutes. We've been driving way longer than that." She peered out the window, then shrugged, unable to penetrate the hazy darkness. "These fog lights ain't it. Might as well drive by candlelight out here."

Judaea turned to the dismal night outside her window. The darkness and the fog were unsettling, the way it formed shapes and moved as if it were a living, conscious thing. She also couldn't shake the feeling that they were being watched, even as the bus shuttled along the road that was now bumpier and more disjointed than she remembered on the way to that weird man's store. Why had he looked at her as if he should be afraid? Why was she afraid now?

Because they were lost. Had to be. *A wrong turn on the crossroads*. Sounded like a lyric from one of those old blues songs. She could hear Coach Harris and Fuller bickering about the map. Coach Fuller had slowed the bus down a bit, trying to navigate in the dense fog through the sharp twists and curves of a road on a route he was no longer sure existed. They didn't want to *say it*, but they most definitely were lost, because there had been no leaning mailboxes on their way in, nor was there the hint of crooked houses set off the road, hidden in the trees.

Something else was hiding in the trees.

Judaea could see it, or more accurately, a silvery silhouette lurking in the dense forest that sprung up all around them. Its movements weren't the easy flow of a predator, but something frantic, a desperate energy cutting through the trees. It loped through the woods, weaving in and out of sight like a shadowy thread. She shivered, sinking in her seat, her back to the window. *So, I'm seeing things now?* She stared at the seat in front of her trying her best to forget.

The bus trundled along, forced to a crawl by the thick fog. The streets had gone from the smooth black top to an uneven gravel, and now a winding dirt road leading to where they did not know.

"Hey, can I see your phone? I don't have a signal," Qori said, leaning in the aisle.

Judaea pulled out hers. "Me either. Fatouma?"

She shouted again, finally rousing her. Fatouma pulled out her pods, shook her head. Judaea started to ask but Raven turned away, muttering under her breath.

"Coach Harris, I need to let my mom know we're going to be late."

"I know, Q. I've been trying to reach everyone as well, but it looks like we're in a dead zone for the moment. Just hold tight."

"Hold tight?" Raven said, worry and irritation rippling across her face. "We've been holding for a minute, Coach. When are we getting off this cheese bus?"

Coach Harris stiffened; her eyes squinted as if straining to see. For a moment it felt as if all the air had been sucked out of the bus. Judaea braced herself for the dressing down she knew was coming. It had only been a question of when.

"*When are we getting off?* You're lucky you don't have to walk home, the way you humiliated yourself today. Raven, *Judaea*," she said, shooting a pointed glance to her left, "you allowed your personal differences to impact your whole team," Coach Harris said. Her eyes were steady, voice even but severe. "I don't have to tell you that I'm disappointed, because I know you're both disappointed in yourselves."

Judaea lowered her eyes. She couldn't have been more embarrassed, but for once, Raven kept her thoughts to herself.

"You owe your team an apology. You owe Coach Fuller and me an apology, and you owe each other the grace to do better," Coach continued. "And am I to understand that you risked friendship and glory over a boy? A dusty, ashy boy?" The expression on Coach's face made it sound like the most ludicrous thing in the world. Judaea could have died on the spot.

Fatouma removed both pods, listening intently. So, the beef was finally out in the open. Qori kept her eyes straight ahead, resisting the urge to see how Judaea was handling this. But Raven was restless.

Even from her spot, Judaea could hear Raven in the back, the anger building in her as she repeatedly kicked the seat in front of her.

"I'm sorry Coach Harris, but how are we supposed to be a team if we can't trust each other?"

Her breathing was quicker and shallower with each word, and it echoed loudly in Judaea's ear. Since the night she'd fought off Raven's so-called crush—an act of self-defense that somehow ruined *her* reputation and not his—Judaea's senses had been off the charts.

"She violated! She violated girl code!" Raven yelled, hurt distorting her voice.

Fresh anger bubbled up inside Judaea. She chomped down on her candy bar, while her stomach began its habitual roil.

"She knew how I felt about him, and she threw herself at him anyway!"

"I did not!" Judaea said. Her head throbbed, throat dry and scratchy. "He attacked *me*!"

"Attacked? You're such a liar."

Angry tears spilled, despite her best effort. No one believed her. They never do. It was her word, a whisper really, against the loud chorus of shame. *She's a fast girl, too fast for her own good.* She stared out the window only to see glowing eyes and a silver shape streaking alongside the bus.

Fear gripped her as she struggled to speak. "Something's out there," she gasped, her voice barely a whisper. "Coach! There's something out there, following us. For real."

"What?" Raven cried. "So now you want to play the victim? Why can't you just admit it? You were jealous!"

Judaea scooted to the edge of her seat. "Look, I don't know why he was acting like that, and I don't care. It's not my fault he don't want you!" she shouted.

"Raven, sit down, *now*!" Coach Harris ordered. "I better not hear another mumbling word from you!"

Suddenly, the silvery shape shot out from the woods, a blur of desperate intent, loping into the road. Judaea screamed. "It's coming!"

Screams filled the bus as Coach Fuller braked hard, rolling over something large. Then Judaea was falling to the floor, her head banging against the side of the seat. The crash's impact sent the school bus careening across the road until it skidded to a halt. Blood splashed across the windshield as the fog circled around them. The girls wailed while Coach Harris struggled to rise.

"Calm down," she said, her voice shaky. She rubbed the back of her head, relief on her face. No bloody gashes. "Are you alright?" she asked, walking to check on each one of them. Judaea stared at the windshield, horrified.

"What was that?" Coach Harris asked Fuller. "A deer?"

He shook his head, eyes wide. "Not a deer. I don't know. It looked like some kind of…"

"What?" Coach Harris asked.

He reached into a bag under his seat and removed a flashlight and a gun. Coach Harris protested. "Brandon, you brought a gun up in here?" Her mouth hung open in shock.

"Hell yeah," he said, "I'm licensed to carry," and ran outside. Coach Harris rushed out the door to follow him. "We could get in trouble!"

"We *are* in trouble," he said, then stopped when he got to the figure in the road. He stumbled backward.

"It's not possible!"

He was muttering when the girls ran to the windows to see. Coach Harris burst into tears.

"How did you run over somebody?"

"I didn't! He wasn't there. It was something else."

"What do you mean, *something else*? There is a full-grown man out here."

With those words, Qori, Raven, and Fatouma climbed out of the bus. Judaea hung back, nauseous.

The girls stood outside, shivering in the night air. They stared at the shuddering man in disbelief. Intricate tattoos, ancient rune-like patterns, covered his body. Blood was caked in his brown hair. He shuddered, moaning.

"Why doesn't he have on any clothes?" Fatouma asked.

"Wait inside," both coaches said at once.

Qori ran back onto the bus. Raven and Fatouma whispered together. "Is he dead, Coach?" Raven asked, panic in her voice. She was wringing her hands.

"What are you doing out here?" Coach Harris said, waving them away. "Please get back on the bus."

"I don't know how he got here," Coach Fuller was saying. "It wasn't a man that I saw," Coach Fuller said, fear in his voice. "It was an animal, a big one."

"Does he look like an animal to you? He needs help!" Coach Harris said, stabbing at her phone. She held it up, as the fog slowly swirled all around her. The taillights from the bus flickered.

"I'm not touching him." Coach Fuller shook his head, emphatically. "That ain't a man or a beast. That's something else."

"Bruh, are you serious?" Coach Harris's voice cracked. She waved her phone in frustration. "We hit him with a friggin' school bus, and he needs our help."

"Yeah, that's my point. How is he still alive?" Fuller squatted down, still looking wary. "Can you hear me, man, do you live near here?"

The man's eyes were hugely dilated. Clear fluid drained from his nose, and his limbs were twisted. Shuddering, he gasped for air, his mouth struggling to form words.

"Thank you," he rasped. Harris and Fuller looked at each other, puzzled. "Go..." the man said, his eyes desperate.

"Go where?" Fuller asked him. "Is there a hospital near?"

"We've got to get him some help," Coach Harris said. She tried to activate emergency SOS on her phone but had no success. The whole area was a giant dead zone. "Dumas County, wherever this is, is with the shit," she said. "I know why Crazy Joe wanted us out of here. We're going to have to move him onto the bus and take him with us."

"Sheeeeeiitttttt," Coach Fuller said, standing up again, gun at his side. "He doesn't need to be anywhere near us or those children. Something's not right here, Yolanda. I know what I saw."

"You don't know what you saw, Brandon. All this fog on the road, you can barely see your own hand."

"Well, this hand ain't touching him, believe that."

✳ ✳ ✳

Qori came and scooched over next to Judaea. "We ran over somebody," she whispered. "Some*body*?" Judaea asked, puzzled. That wasn't a person she saw come out of the woods.

"Some man tatted up. I didn't want to say anything, but it looked like either some occult stuff or some prison tats. You know, like on TV."

"And he buck naked," Fatouma said, standing over them.

"Don't tell her that..." Raven sat down and smirked.

"I need the towels," Coach Harris said. Dark circles and tears weighed down her normally cheerful eyes.

This is the worst trip ever, Judaea thought. It kept getting stranger, and now she knew she was losing her mind, because what ran out of the woods was not what Coach Harris and Coach Fuller brought inside. Whoever he was, he tried to fight them, even in his mangled condition. The girls moved to the back of the bus as their coaches lay him on the floor, cushioning his head with one of their B.T.W. Warriors hoodies.

Coach Fuller cussed the whole time. They'd never heard him so upset. A tiny part of Judaea felt relieved. Maybe he saw what she saw. Maybe she wasn't crazy after all. Maybe the accident would make them all forget how much of a mess she and Raven had made that day, but they hadn't driven for more than five minutes when she heard the first howl. The sound was sharp, mournful, and it made her soul feel lonelier than she thought it ever could. Grief overwhelmed her, a language she understood.

Then a loud bang, and the bus swerved. Later, no one could say where they were hit first. The sound of howling swirled all around them, mixing with the shrieks of the girls.

Coach Fuller and Harris were yelling, their words incomprehensible in the den. Fuller tried to keep the bus on the road, but they were on the shoulder, crashing into a stand of trees. Then the door ripped open, shots fired, and a pained growl that chilled Judaea to her bones.

It held Coach Harris like a ragdoll by her throat and flung her through the air. She landed in a crumple near Qori and Judaea. The girls scrambled, screaming, running to Raven and Fatouma, who clutched and scratched at the emergency exit door. The creature stood on two feet atop long silvery legs, its underbelly and chest covered in wispy fur, its face filled with hideous glowing eyes and a snout bearing canines longer than Judaea's wrist.

"Run!" Coach Fuller yelled. They didn't need to be told. Raven was out the door first. Qori followed, but Fatouma grabbed the equipment bag and jumped out. Judaea stood frozen, disbelieving the sound of the scream that came from her own mouth. She sounded worse than the girls who fall down in horror movies.

The creature growled and snarled, its large ears turned inward, eyes narrowed. He ran toward her but bent down to pick up the dying man. It howled, the sound of unmistakable grief and pain.

Judaea shot out, down the aisle, through the exit door. She could hear the other girls screaming ahead, running breathless through the fog, cutting across the road. A chorus of howls and yelps echoed through the air, sending a chill down her spine. Judaea followed the cries of her teammates as they ran, zigzagging through the trunks, feet pounding fallen limbs and rotten leaves. They blazed a trail through the trees until they reached a low stone wall.

Breathless, Qori was the first over it, climbing as if she had been born leaping over craggy hurdles. The stone wall scraped her knees and scratched up her legs, but she bounded over, pushing through the pain. Further down the wall, Raven and Fatouma climbed over, helping each other up. Judaea caught up, guilt mixing with her fear and terror. Even if she had spoken up sooner, no one would have believed her. Odd feelings and strange sightings didn't make sense in any version of the world they knew.

They met up in a patch of clearing where the fog was less dense and the trees arched above. Fatouma stood, breathless, bag slung over her shoulder.

Q kept looking back, her phone throwing barbs of light in all directions as she spun around, hyperventilating. In the distance they could hear the mournful howling. Their screams assaulted the air, the howling revealing the full moon against the cloud-filled night.

"Q," Judaea said, out of breath. "Don't leave me!"

"Where would we go," Raven replied, silently weeping. She was terrified but still had time, still had that smart mouth even now. Judaea was surprised that her former friend acknowledged her. *Guess we have to be close to death,* she thought and turned on her flashlight app with shaking hands.

There were few options that made sense, given the circumstances. "I don't know what to do," Raven said. "There's no way we're heading back to that road now. No telling what's out there."

"We know what's out there," Qori said, crying all over again. "Coach Harris…" she said, her voice trailing off, "and that thing! What was that?" she asked. "Do you think it killed them?" Fresh tears erupted at the thought of their two coaches being left behind. Coach Harris didn't move after the creature threw her.

Fatouma opened her bag and pulled the javelins out, one by one. She handed one to Raven. Qori shook her head. "What are these going to do? They're rubber-tipped."

"How long have you known me?" Fatouma asked, shaking her head. "Anything can be a weapon if you know what you're doing. Besides," she pulled out some metal tips. "Competition is one thing, but how do you think I really practice?" she asked.

"You mean you jiggy-rigged some weapons for us?" Raven asked.

"What do you think a javelin is for in real life? It *is* a weapon. If you're going to compete, you might as well learn how to properly use it."

"Well, we ain't Greek and this ain't the Olympics," Raven said.

"You really been hunting with a javelin spear?"

"Nope, but I think I can if I had to, and this is probably going to be the most important time to try in my whole life." Fatouma looked dead serious.

The gravity of what they were facing fell on their shoulders like a cold wind. Judaea shuddered. "What else is in that bag that Coach don't know about?" she asked.

Fatouma pulled out the discus, a shot ball, some extra gloves, and some other hardware.

"That is definitely non-regulation," Qori said, cutting her eyes at her. Fatouma shrugged.

"Dad made them for me," was all she said.

"So where do we go now?" Raven asked.

"Here." Judaea's light shone on the makings of a path. Smooth, raised white stones gleamed in the moonlight, leading them through the trees that arched together in a dark embrace.

* * *

They ran down the cobblestone road, gnats filtered through the cone of Judaea's flashlight app.

"Ouch," Raven said, stumbling behind her. She rubbed her ankle, peering in the darkness.

"What is it?"

Judaea turned the light to see a shiny white skull embedded in the dirt. She screamed before she could stop herself. The others huddled around her, gripping her forearm. The light wavered.

"You've got to be kidding me," she said. The whole path was lined with what looked like human skulls. Some were turned up sideways, the eye sockets filled with soil. Qori wept quietly at Judaea's shoulder, pulling her arm away.

"We're not supposed to be here."

"Ain't nobody who did this going to help us," Raven said. "What if they are part of whatever those things were?"

"You might as well say it..." Judaea's head throbbed, her whole body ached from running, but her eyes were beginning to adjust well to the darkness. She could see the fear on Raven's face. It gave her a strange pleasure to see her bully shaking, even in this moment. Now it was her turn to feel afraid.

"Don't!"

"You think not saying it aloud is going to keep it from being true?" Judaea felt the heat of that old anger lighting the edges of her mind. *Your silence won't protect you.* "I think that thing that I saw out the window, that got Coach Harris and Fuller are werewolves. Can't be any other explanation."

"That's fucked up," Raven said.

"It is."

"Well, there's nothing we can do but run," Qori said, "because standing out here, we are dead meat."

"Run? Where in the hell are we?" Raven asked.

"Run anywhere but here," Fatouma said, "and fight if we have to. You can stay here if you want, but I'm not going down easy if I can help it."

They looked at each other skeptically. No one was returning to the bus. No one was left to help or guide them. No motivational speeches. They were on their own. Finally, they trudged down the bone path until they reached a strange tree. The closer they got to it, the stranger it looked.

Something about the tree disturbed Judaea's spirit. It didn't look natural. Its giant roots were exposed, with layers of dirt, a wall that came up to her shoulders. But lights flickered inside the two dark caverns of the tree, like the eye sockets of a skull. *Candles.* Which meant someone had placed them there. Judaea felt the flicker of hope. Maybe someone lived nearby, someone who could help. But she couldn't forget the skulls embedded in the road.

She glanced at the candles warily. They were the big, wide kind, scented, expensive. Such an odd thing to have in the middle of the woods. They looked as if they hadn't been burning long. Probably were lit at sunset. She peered inside.

"What do you see?" Qori asked, curious.

"Some bread, a bowl of water or something, and some flowers. Fresh flowers. Purple."

"Definitely Black people," Q said.

"What Black people you know got bones in their yard?" Raven asked.

Fatouma stepped over to see. "Because those are traditional offerings for an ancestor altar."

"Dia de Muertos," Qori said, "various ATRs—African Traditional Religions—and other faiths around the world where the dead are respected and remembered."

"I don't know nothing about that voodoo stuff," Raven said, shivering.

"Um, you're a Christian, and you celebrate the dead and resurrection every Sunday and Easter," Qori said.

"It's not the same."

"Trust me, it *is*. Holy days, sacrifice—even symbolic— music, rituals, sacred text—same thing."

Qori was cut off by the distant sound of howling. Terror filled every cell in their bodies. This time the chorus included more voices, getting closer. The girls scrambled down the path in silence.

As they ran, the cobblestones turned to dirt and the dirt changed to a neat path leading to a town square. Old structures leaned in every direction. A historical marker on a post was anchored in the ground. Qori raised her phone.

"I told you," she said. The girls gathered around. The sign read, "Old Colony."

Judaea took a sharp breath, the hair on her arms bristling.

"I know this place," she said. "I mean, I met this strange woman at the concession stand, and she told me that she was *from here*."

"Here? There's no one here." Fatouma took a breath, frowned, tasting the dust in the darkness. "Doesn't look like anyone has lived here a long time." She rested her bag on the ground.

It was a ghost town, like one of those historical reenactment places with the people in costumes. Except the creatures that terrorized them were real, all too real and not historic.

"Was she nice strange or creepy strange?" Qori asked.

Judaea had to think about it. "Nice strange," she said after a moment. "Like in that aunty-trying-to-help-you-out kind of way. Except I didn't know what she was talking about. I think she knew about stuff like this. She said her name was Maryse and *this* was her home."

"I sh'oll hate it," Raven said, looking around. The Colony looked like it came from another century. She hugged herself, the Warriors jacket soiled with dirt and debris.

"Point your lights here," Qori said, reading.

* * *

The Colony was formed by a group of 45 Africans, who in 1860 were part of 110 souls bought and transported on the Clotilda ship against their will in one of the last known illegal shipments of enslaved Africans to the United States. 1 died during the Middle Passage. 32 of them formed Africatown near Plateau, Mobile, Alabama. The Colony and First Church was founded as a safe haven to those who would be free,

Beholden to None but the Ancestors.

* * *

An iron sign pointed to the church. Judaea looked at Qori, Fatouma, and Raven.

"If we can get in, maybe we can hide there until morning," she said.

"They're werewolves, not vampires," Raven said. "Wolves ain't scared of churches, are they?"

Judaea shook her head, but she could not shake the feeling. Something about the night was speaking to her in a way that she had never experienced. The strange woman's words returned to her. *The change can be hard at first, but you'll get the hang of it. We all do eventually.*

✳ ✳ ✳

The church was not hard to see from the path. It jutted out amongst a strand of trees, atop a slight hill, like a giant piece of driftwood. Surrounded by a creek, a natural bridge led to its front door. The wooden door was flanked by two stained-glass windows. Thick-walled and sturdy, made of heavy stones, the church's outer walls were covered in vines surrounded by a fragrant garden with a wrought iron fence. When Judaea saw it, she felt as if she had entered a different world, a tree-shaded place where anything could happen, had happened, where even the buzzards knew better than to fly low and the frogs did not emerge without the night's permission.

But Qori was freaking her out. First, she began with the flowers.

"Whatever you do, don't touch those," Qori told them, pointing at the beautiful purple hooded blossoms gathered all around the church. Bent over like little bells, they swayed in the night breeze.

"Maybe it's wolfsbane, monkshood. They're highly poisonous to humans, just by touch they kill you, and werewolves don't like them."

"Don't tell me you learned that in global civ," Judaea said.

"No, *The Little Book of Poisons*."

"I'm not going to ask why you were reading that, but don't you think it's weird they're growing here in this old town, right around the church?"

"They know something for real. We need to get inside and hide," Raven said.

"So, we're breaking into churches now? Adding breaking and entering to the hit-and-run charge?" Fatouma said.

"Does it count if it was a monster?" Judaea was exhausted. Jaw tight, she kicked at the dirt. The air was damp and the fog was not as heavy here. Sweaty and tired, it felt like wet hands crawling over her.

Fatouma pulled out the shot, but no one wanted to take it. Eight pounds, it was heavy on a good day. This was not a good day. Reluctant, Judaea stood before one of the beautiful stained-glass windows, contemplating how much force to use when she heard, *Come inside.* A whisper in her head.

"What is it?" Fatouma asked.

"You didn't hear that?" Judaea lowered the shot, handing it back to her teammate. "Maybe we can open the door?" she asked.

"If only we were that lucky," Fatouma said and raised the iron forged latch, pushing her shoulder against the door. It did not move.

Enter, Judaea heard, more clearly than before. Her palms traced the intricate iron forged-patterns that covered both doors. They seemed to warm under her touch. She did not flinch or pull away. She held the forged iron latch and pushed.

"It was open the whole time?" Raven said. They walked into the sanctuary. An herbal, woodsy scent like a damp forest greeted them. Fatouma went looking for a barrier to help block the door, but there was nothing.

The church was dark inside and simple. Rows of heavy pews arranged before a raised platform. A single lectern before the pulpit with a big book was flanked by ceramic vases full of the blue-purple blossoms. Floor-to-ceiling stained glass windows towered on the north and south walls. Moonlight shone through the top and bottom plain, clear glass panels, but the light accentuated the colors of the more elaborate center pieces.

They seemed to tell a story, starting somewhere in Africa, then across the waters, on to a reedy dock, in chains. The story continued around the church, ending with an image Judaea could not quite understand. The effect was a moving, visual representation of The Colony's history, before and after their settlement in Dumas County. But even with all its light, it was the sculpture hanging from the east wall behind the altar that had Judaea transfixed.

"This is *not* a church," Raven said, staring up at it, her voice low, anxious. She studied several of the stained-glass panels then walked toward the altar area, looking for somewhere to hide.

"It's a figurehead, from a ship," Qori said, gazing at the outstretched hands of the three figures carved in one block of wood. The torsos of an unclothed man, woman, and child, gazing up and out, as if reaching for their lost home. "I've never seen one like this before. It looks old."

"It would have to be, if the founders came on the Clotilda. Where do you think it's from? I mean, before they got here?" Judaea asked, shivering. Qori shrugged, scanning her light across the sculpture. She took a photo. The sound startled Judaea.

"Don't do that."

Fatouma walked briskly to the front, dropping the equipment onto a pew. "We need to see if there is anything we can use as weapons or to help block the door. This place is vulnerable with all of these windows. I didn't realize there would be more."

"There's a whole medieval mote outside..." Raven said.

"I hate to tell you, but regular wolves can swim. I saw it on *National Geographic,*" Fatouma said, glancing at Qori. "Those things out there can probably *float.*"

"They can swim, too? Damn," Raven said from a pew. She had tried to get as far away from a window as she could. She got up from the hard wooden bench and climbed in the baptistery.

"Girl, what are you doing up there?" Fatouma asked.

"Hiding!"

"I know this is an old church because they don't even have a back room. One way in, one way out," Judaea said, looking around. Moonlight shone from the upper panes, illuminating dust motes in the air.

Qori opened the book on the lectern. The inside inscription read:

* * *

Founded in the early 1870s, Old Colony First Church was organized and joined the association at Unity Grove in 1884. During the early

1900s, the church disbanded due to a population shift in Dumas County but was revived in 1952.

* * *

She turned to the page where a thick, leather bookmark rested. The Book of Daniel. Qori read silently, scanning the pages, flipping through the book. Then she called the others.

"This isn't a Bible," she said. "It's more like a collection of sacred texts, some biblical, but others from sources I don't really know. They all have a kind of theme. Like the scriptures around King Nebuchadnezzar. He was powerful but arrogant and God sent him a dream about what might happen if he wasn't humbler and a better king to his people and the land. He asked Daniel to interpret the vision for him, and it wasn't good news. He said he would lose his kingdom and his sanity."

"Girl, we ain't got time for no Sunday School lesson," Raven said, folded up in the empty baptismal pool.

"It might be a clue about what's going on here," Qori said, reading, "He was driven away from people and ate grass like the ox. His body was drenched with the dew of heaven until his hair grew like the feathers of an eagle and his nails like the claws of a bird."

"The 'dew of heaven'?" Raven asked. They all stared at Qori, quiet.

"He was transformed into some kind of beast," Q continued reading, "for seven long years. After that, he changed his spirit and his perspective, and returned to human form again, a better king and a servant to God."

"You mean there is a werewolf story in the Bible?" Raven asked.

"Maybe, depending on how you interpret it. But it sounds like 'the dew of heaven' rained down on him and turned him into something no longer human. And that's not all," Qori said. "Judaea, there's a list of names and dates in the front of this. Dimbo, Plus and Minus Minute, Leeth. Families that go back over a century. Your name is here."

Where you from? Where yo people from? Maryse. Judaea walked up the steps, legs heavy, mouth dry. Her stomach twisted in knots. *You will come when you need to,* the woman had said.

Qori pointed to the page, staring at her oddly.

"Judaea Hosea Autrey, date of birth, November 17, 1870," she read, incredulous.

"One of your great-greats was born here?" Raven asked. "We can't trace our family back that far. You lucky."

"In The Colony," a voice said. Fatouma swung her javelin spear, waving it in a wide arc around her.

The figure appeared out of nowhere, forming out of the darkness, shafts of moonlight on her bare arms. She emerged with her own light, held it high in her hand.

"Maryse," Judaea said. "The woman from the concession stand, the woman in white."

"You don't have much time," Maryse said, directing her kerosene lamp at Judaea, who stood, anxious by Qori, who gripped the book like a shield.

"We walk between worlds," Maryse said. "Protect the living, honor the dead. Judaea, these are not the circumstances in which I would usher you into your knowing, but you don't have much time, child. You will shift tonight," she said.

Instinctively, Raven ducked in the pool, trying to be invisible, but the woman watched as if she could hear Raven breathing. "Come out of there, child." Raven froze, afraid to move, then she climbed out of the pool, wordless.

"Where did you come from?" Fatouma asked. "I checked this whole place."

"There is more to this place than you know," the woman said.

"You're Maryse. We met in Florence." Judaea's voice was blank, as if her tongue and vocal cords could hold no more fear. "You knew they would come for me, didn't you?"

"No," Maryse said, resting the kerosene lamp on an offering table. She lit the candles that lined the sanctuary. A calming scent of vanilla and sandalwood drifted through the air. "I sensed your awakened blood, child, the moment your steps brought you to me, a thread in the ancient tapestry. As for the others, the tragic death on the road, we know it was an accident. Yet, they will seize upon it as an excuse to violate our borders, to shatter the long-held truce."

"An accident?" Judaea said. "That man, that whatever he is, ran out in front of us on purpose."

Maryse frowned, a slight movement across her features, before she was neutral again.

"That thing is what you call werewolves. We are something else."

Judaea felt her heart quickening, her skin rippling, blood-coursing heat again. "I know you can feel it," Maryse said. "If you had been raised amongst us, you would be prepared, but your line left these rocks and woods long ago. It's no surprise the genes were dormant, but you are home again. At least home on these shores," she added.

"Are you saying you're one of those monsters, that *I'm one of them*?" Judaea asked.

"I knew your ass was weird," Raven said, eyes wide. She moved all the way to the pew nearest the front door.

"I'm saying that this kind of thing can skip generations, especially if your bloodline is isolated. You are not one of them. The people in Arkadela are from a different origin, your 'werewolf,' and they conspired with those who brought us here, who tried to enslave us. You are lycan, born of another line, of those who would be free."

"Werewolves, lycans, slavery?" Qori said. "I thought werewolves were lycans? They're not the same?"

Maryse shook her head, no.

"We saw it, that creature," Qori continued, her voice quiet but with the frantic notes of rising panic. "We heard them out there... It killed..." Her voice shook, on the verge of tears at the memory of them running through the fog and the woods, at the memory of them leaving their coaches behind. Coach Harris said teammates have each other's back, Qori thought. *If we did, we wouldn't be here in the first place.*

"Yes, they are mourning a loss. None of our numbers are so great that a life would not be missed, even in an accident, even that accident was intentional," she said, looking at Judaea. "But they are what you call 'werewolves,' and we are something else. The moon does not bind us as it binds them. We can shift at will. We take shape as we choose. This is why they envy us. This is why they fear us. And they are simple-minded in their envies and their cruelty. Always have been, since the first ships arrived on these shores. They think the book you hold contains secrets that would make them as free as us," she said.

Qori watched her, still clutching the volume. "Your name is in here, too. Maryse Monife McCrear."

"Yes, my ancestor was the last *known* living survivor of that wretched ship. So far from home, she resolved to make a life here. When she and the others were freed from their bondage, they were never given their forty acres. Instead, they were told to eke out a life from the rockiest land where no life grew. It was a cruel joke meant to sentence them to failure and starvation, a ruse to send them back into endless servitude. But life was found, and around this stony land, The Old Colony grew." She waved her hand. "The newer one is just over those hills, and we make do. But not all is known, and there are no incantations or spells in that book. There is only us, the blood."

"Lycans?" Judaea asked. She walked over to meet Maryse's gaze. "You mean no one in my family or yours was turned. We..." she hesitated to say it, the ownership of a power or a curse she never asked for and wasn't sure she could handle. "We are..."

"Born," Maryse said.

"You are not human," Fatouma said. "Not if you can change into what we saw."

"You have been seeing us all your lives, in one form or another. Yes, we are human," Maryse said, "but we are also something more." She walked to Fatouma, who lowered her javelin. "See." Maryse pointed at the girl's earrings, golden ankhs. "You wear a symbol long associated with our kind."

"Anubis, the jackal-headed deity of old Kemet. Anpu. There are other names in other cultures and some that are less kind. But we exist here because we seek simple lives, peace. Our neighbors on the other side of the county road have long wished us ill. Tonight, they will use their misfortune and yours, the accident, as an opportunity to strike. There is no time to make you ready, but if you want your friends to live, Judaea, you will—" She stopped mid-sentence, her movement less human and more animalistic.

A dark howl filled the space of silence, leaving them with chills. It was too close to wait out now. The call was answered by a cacophony of howls, growing nearer.

The girls gathered together, huddled almost instinctively, their backs facing the east wall, their eyes turned to Maryse and the wooden door. Moonlight shone through the clear panels at the top and bottom of the stained-glass windows.

This church is fortified, Maryse said to Judaea alone. *In ways our unfortunate neighbors will soon discover. But you must be brave if you wish to save your friends.*

"Save them?" Judaea cried. "I've messed up everything for them today. If it wasn't for me...fighting...we would've been home already."

Raven looked up, guilt on her face.

"The change comes in adolescence, on the cusp of adulthood. It has always been that way," Maryse said. "You would have been home, and still you would shift because it is your time. Except you would have been alone, confused and dangerous with no guidance."

"So, I'm not..." Judaea didn't want to say it aloud, not in front of them, not even here. But Maryse already knew. It was as if the woman could hear the surface of her thoughts.

"The symptoms are very similar when you first start shifting, but no, child, not an immaculate conception."

Judaea could feel the anger and confusion coming off of Raven. Now Judaea understood why she had been so ill, had been having such strange dreams and appetites, hearing what wasn't meant to be heard, seeing what should have remained invisible.

"Raven, I don't know what's going to happen to me or to any of us tonight," Judaea said, "but if we're gonna die, you're gonna hear this. I swear I was never checking for him, I—"

"I know." Raven's voice turned husky, barely a whisper, full of shame. "I know, Judaea. I'm sorry, I misjudged you."

Qori screamed, backing up from the front door. "Look!" she yelled, pointing.

In the lower pane, she could see long, boney feet, barely human, skitter past on curled claws. A red eye glowered, peering through another pane, the snout wrinkled up, revealing canines dripping drool.

"I thought you said this church was fortified, protected."

"It is." Maryse threw back her head and released a sound that made the stained-glass shake. It was answered by an echo of calls that forced Raven to cover her ears, tears streaming down her face. There was nowhere to hide that made any sense.

Hearing the call, Judaea felt suddenly nauseous. She bent over, emptying her stomach, wiping her mouth with the back of her hand. Maryse gathered around Judaea as if she were a midwife, preparing to catch a newborn baby.

"Child?"

"Qori, ma'am."

"Qori, please put the *Histories* down and fetch some water from
the baptistery." She pointed at the faucet and some basins stacked up
in a corner.

She gave Raven the kerosene lamp and directed Fatouma to
empty the fresh flowers into the waters. "Your gloves came in handy,"
Maryse said. "They'll protect your skin from the wolfsbane. By the
way, you did a good job today. I watched your events. You move like
a warrior from the old days." Fatouma only nodded, but one less
furrow in her brow showed that she was somewhat pleased with
the compliment.

"There is another way out of Old Colony, a shorter path that will
take you back to the north wall," Maryse said, candlelight flickering
across her face. "When you get across that boundary, it won't be long
before you make it to the main road."

"72?" Qori asked.

Maryse nodded. "But first, you'll need some protection. Our
neighbors have their strengths, they move alone or as packs, but
we are like a fast wind that moves without wings. They won't see
us coming."

She gathered more wolfsbane and handed it to Fatouma.

"Be sure to soak it all in there. Use everything, the blossoms,
the stems, and the leaves. If this makes contact with any part of them,
it will cause them great pain and they will be out of the game. Aim for
the head, their eyes, or their torso."

"I don't plan to get that close," Fatouma said, crushing the
herbs and sprinkling them in the water. When she finished, Maryse
motioned to the others.

"Children, come." They hesitated, walking only a few steps, just within earshot. "Those medals you wear," Maryse said pointing, "are just a symbol of who you are, a hint of what you can do and be. I watched you compete today. You are special. You run, not for the sport of it, but because running is an extension of your full self. Tonight, you must do more. There is another path over a natural bridge that will lead you back to the low stone wall that marks our borders. You must reach it..."

"Nooooo," the girls wailed. "We can't go back out there," Qori and Raven cried. Fatouma grit her teeth.

"You must. Once you get over the wall, you must run until you reach the road, and don't stop running until you see the sun rising."

"We're not going to make it," Raven said, lowering the lamp, despair in her voice. "Why can't we stay here?"

"Judaea can stay here if she wished, because she is of the bloodline, and she would be safe but not you. This land will change you if you stay. In ways we cannot predict or control. Is that what you want?"

"Hell naw," Raven said. Fatouma grimaced. "Ooh, I'm sorry," she said, staring up at the rafters, crossing herself.

"You've run this race before, many times," Maryse said, assuring her.

"Not with no werewolves on our tails!"

"You run fast enough and there won't be," Maryse said. "We'll take care of them."

Qori looked over at Judaea, who was coughing and gasping for air. A panic attack well earned. "Look at her, she's too sick," Qori said. "We can't leave her behind."

Maryse smiled. "Tonight, Judaea must run a race of her own."

She picked up the basins of water, waved her palm over them and hum-whispered a song whose words held no meaning to them, a song felt more than heard. A vibration filled the air, as if a great fire had been lit.

"When I open this door, take this water and dash it in the face of anything that tries to stop you. They will not," she said, "and you will pass. Judaea, me, and my people will be all around you. Girls, we will have your back, but you are going to have to run." Eyes narrow slits, cheeks stark, Maryse did not waste her words. "Think of it as your most important relay."

The girls stood there, shaking their heads.

"You finna give us some rootwork against some werewolves? Maneeeeee—" Raven said.

Maryse dipped her hands in the waters and rubbed down Fatouma's javelin spears with her fingertips. She doused Fatouma's non-regulation equipment, whispering as she worked. Finally, she rubbed the wolfsbane on Judaea's palms, bare shoulders, and neck. "I thought that was poisonous," Judaea said, heaving.

Maryse studied her, with that same expression in her eyes that she had when they first met at the track meet, *concern, care, comfort.*

"For them, not you."

Then fire, electric shock ripped through Judaea, up her spine and at the base of her neck. Her eyes rolled back, and she could not speak. *Help me!* She screamed but no words came out. Her hands flew to her throat. Qori tried to help but Maryse waved her back. "It is time," was all she said.

Unspoken words lifted in the air. She was aware of a larger presence, other thoughts inside her head, not her own. Suddenly she was plunged into darkness. Judaea screamed. Finally, the sounds erupted and her voice echoed in the wooden rafters above, bouncing off the ancient stones that formed the church.

Bones broken and reformed. Skin sliding into dark shadows, strange, muscled flesh. Nails giving way to claws. Teeth turned to daggers. Eyes, golden discs illuminating the night. She didn't want any part of it and yet, somehow, it was part of her.

It had always been.

She could hear her teammates' concerned cries, could feel her body giving way to another force. The air around her changed. The lens of her eyes shifted until she saw no more, having closed them in fear. Then, the electric shock again, the sensation when Maryse first touched her hand earlier that day. A humming through her new skin and bones, her mind and flesh expanded, and then new eyes opened, vision deeper, wider, sharper than she had ever seen. The sight was beautiful. Finally, she could *see*.

Judaea, now you must run. I will guide you and your friends to safety.

You're not coming with us?

I must guard the Histories, but you won't be alone.

I can't do this without you!

I'll help fight the wolves here, keep them off your trail, and my brothers and sisters—your family, too—will fend them off along the way. We can always sense each other, just like we did earlier today.

It took just a moment for Judaea to realize that they had not spoken any words. She stood, taller than she had ever been, could see

180

and sense more than what should be possible. She turned. The girls' screams were immediate, but distant in her ears. She could see the shock in their eyes, but she was listening to the drumbeat of others, the ones who meant them all harm.

Run!

Maryse opened the door. Transformed, the woman was now a dark, jackal-necked shadow, with a fierce throat that opened up the sky. Shadows streaked and screamed around them as the werewolves howled. Judaea burst through the air, propelled through the door by her thoughts and a force she didn't know was hidden within. She could see!

Pockets of moonlight in the open mouth of night. She was the black shadow against the tree trunks, a hot breeze stirring the branches and the leaves. Paws, claws sank into earth, running swiftly over stones. Inside her head, new voices rose and fell. *Rooted here.* She felt an almost alien sensation, *joy*. Pain was somewhere deep in the distance, a memory waiting somewhere inside for her to feel it. But she did not. Powerful jaws snapping, she would speak in a violent language of her own. She felt nothing but awe for such strength and clarity, so she ran, ran, ran, her heart beating fast.

✳ ✳ ✳

STEEPLECHASE

"Run!" Maryse screamed, her voice suddenly deep, guttural. She offered them the spelled water. They refused to move at first, until Maryse's face began to contort. Her ears elongated into sharp points. The skin on her face morphed into dark, shiny, slick fur, dense like that of a seal or a Dobermann.

They fled, the air outside hot and humid. Howls greeted them, then loud yelps, beastly cries of pain. Some stood on their inhuman feet. Others bounded on malformed limbs, but they all leapt through the air as a dark, tall upright humanoid figure with sleek, black fur and the jackal-like wolf head raked through them, claws sharper than any knives the girls had ever seen beyond the movies.

White fabric clung to the creature's limbs. Maryse.

Qori shrank in horror at the carnage, her eyes darting to find a way out.

Incomprehensible, hacked limbs littered the ground. Black blood and viscera pooled in the moonlight. The girls ducked and darted through the chaos, leaping over the transforming limbs as the creatures turned from beasts to mutilated human arms and hands right before their eyes.

A reddish-brown werewolf spotted Qori who took off, the first leg in a terrifying race, heading down the bridge across the creek. She cried out and tossed the whole basin Maryse had given her, water and all, into his shaggy wolf's head. Its bone-crushing mouth opened wide, hot breath spewed out, its red-black tongue lolling. For a split second, Qori could see all of its back teeth, and then the creature's head burst into flames. It screeched, a bloodcurdling bark of pain as the flames engulfed it.

Qori ran on, but another werewolf leapt at her, landing in the creek with a high-pitched yelp. She screamed, but the werewolf howled louder as the water bubbled around it, as if boiling until it ignited, its body impaled on a pike hidden beneath the dark water's depths. Two other werewolves backed away from the water's edge, turning instead to trap her at the bottom of the bridge. As she ran, another rose from the treacherous water, its head engulfed in flames, its features running like a melted candle. Qori leapt over its massive arm as it swiped at her. She tried to slow herself when the other werewolves stood at their full height at the bottom of the bridge. Facing her, they were seven feet high on their bent hind legs.

Fatouma and Raven ran behind her and tossed their basins of the spelled wolfsbane water, setting the wolves afire. The creatures spun and slashed at the air. One fell down, clawing at the earth. The girls cowered, afraid to jump in the creek but unable to pass. Suddenly, a dark shadowy figure emerged, its golden eyes narrow slits. The lycan sang as it disemboweled the dying werewolves, finishing them off.

Raven shrieked at the sight of the reverse transformations and at the blood-drenched lycan before her. "People!" she wailed. "They're all people!" Looking mournful, Qori shuddered, chewed her nails.

"Fatouma, your weapons!" the creature growled.

Qori and Raven stumbled. "Maryse?" Qori asked.

Fatouma removed the homemade quiver from her back. Her dad showed her how to cut it to length and make her own carrying tube from PVC pipes. She hoped she would make it back home to him and her mother, her little siblings. Until then, all she could do was try. She smacked Raven's back, handing her and Qori each an aluminum javelin. It was lighter, better for the inexperienced. She kept the carbon tailwind one, her favorite, for herself.

She gripped the javelin's shaft, her voice steely, trying to cover up her fear. "Maryse spelled the points, so if something jumps out at you, use it."

A howl rang out, a snarling roar that chilled the air. A ragged wolf running toward them.

"Go!"

Running, the three girls started across the bridge. All around them they could hear the creatures growling, howling, the sound thundering through the hills and trees. They ran in the darkness, not sure which way to go, the sounds of battle distant, a demonic din that followed them into the night.

* * *

SPIKES

A bank of fog thickened around the trunks of trees as they raced through the darkness. Hoarse from crying, out of breath, Raven shrieked as the night rose up around them. A howl rang out though the hills, the sound as if a thousand wolves had descended upon them. A cloud of wraith-like shadowy figures emerged from the fog. Raven raised the javelin spear Fatouma had given her.

Qori and Fatouma watched in horror as a gray werewolf arced through the air. Powerful incisors ripped into the muscled torso of a jackal-headed creature that emerged from the shadows. Shrouded in night, the lycan seized the werewolf by its snout and wrenched open its powerful maw, snapping its jaw. Razor-sharp nails slashed the creature's throat with a sickening sound. The beast's head bounced on the ground, blood spilling on stones. It rolled into the creek before them, mist rising from the waters. Headless, the great body shuddered. The girls could see it transforming back to human even as it fell to the ground. Raven watched as the lycan's wounds, a chunk of flesh shredded by the werewolf's canines, healed right before her eyes. She shook her head in disbelief, paralyzed with fear.

"Raven," an almost familiar voice growled, the sound pitched at a register between human and beast.

"Judaea?" Raven shrank back, horror in her voice. She gripped the spear, not sure where to go. They were trapped on one side by the werewolves, the poisonous water on the other.

"It's me, girl," Judaea said, her voice sounding strange even to herself, as if it was traveling across time. "I would never hurt you!"

"You just ripped a monster apart, and you look a hot mess," Raven said, staring at the creature who had once been her friend and frenemy. Inside her new flesh, Judaea chuckled, her shoulders heaving.

"I can't believe you're one of them," Fatouma said. She gazed at Judaea, her face a mixture of wonder and a twinge of envy. "Or that you still have on that too-tight tracksuit. You're practically busting at the seams. They're going to see you coming a mile away!"

"*You* didn't see me," Judaea rasped. They stared at the dark fur that covered her body. Qori reached out a hand. "No," Judaea said, "you can't touch my hair."

Raven laughed weakly, almost delirious. The only thing that still looked like Judaea was her beautiful eyes, but they were shining, as if lit from a fire within. Her brown skin was no longer visible, nor was her hair, all replaced by dark, shimmery fur. Her features were dog-like, sharp, reminding Raven of the Egyptian statues and figurines she'd seen over the years, the ones with the pitch-black pointy ears.

"I want to go home," Raven said, her voice like a small child. She kept seeing flashbacks of the creatures, hearing the sound of teeth and claws, a frightening din of anger and pain.

Take them through the cemetery, Maryse said to Judaea. *My family will meet you there. It's neutral ground since many lines of Dumas County ancestors are buried there, including the neighbors. But be careful, after the breach tonight, all bets are off.*

"Follow me," Judaea said aloud.

* * *

They leapt over every stone and bush, crashing through the underbrush until Judaea stopped outside a tall iron gate, her pointy ears turned toward a distant sound they could not hear. Her snout reared up, revealing vicious fangs.

"It's too many of them. Get behind me," she barked. But the girls didn't see anything at first, then they felt a vibration in the ground beneath their feet.

Fog eclipsed the moonlight. Thundering through the air, a hulking, copper-colored werewolf landed on giant paws, skidding in the wet grass. The stench of rage emanated off its bloody, matted fur. It snarled and snapped at them, yellowed teeth biting at the wind. Raven yelped and thrust her spear into its chest. A song of pain and rage rose in its mouth as the spelled tip set it ablaze. It spun around, claws flailing, smoke rising with the scent of burning fur and flesh.

Judaea nodded approval, but found herself surrounded by three more, outnumbered and overpowered. "Run!" she roared. Her lycan body flickered in and out of the shadows, weaving around the werewolves in a deadly dance. One clamped its jaws on her arm. She cried out, a sound Raven had never heard before. Other shadows emerged from the trees, slipping through the iron gate. A keening filled the air, the sound of the lycans and werewolves battling all around the cemetery.

When Raven saw Judaea struggling to fight off the beasts, her heartbeat so fast she was sure it would climb out of her throat. She dug in the equipment bag and pulled out the discus Maryse had spelled. With trembling hands, she held it with her fingertips, spun and flung it out wildly like a frisbee. *Worst form in the world,* she thought. But without fail, it lodged in the beast's throat, a ball of flames.

"Thank you, Maryse," she said but nearly choked on her words when blazing eyes burned through the fog. "No!" Qori cried.

Gray with a mangy, striped coat, the beast glowered at them. Malevolent eyes growled, then it lunged at Fatouma. She held the spear up with two hands, to protect her neck. Its great mouth snapped the javelin spear in half like a toothpick. Fatouma scuttled back, digging her heels in the wet earth.

In desperation, Raven swung the shot, bag and all, but it bounced off the creature's back, landing with a thud. She backed up, hand over her mouth, eyes wide.

Without thinking, Qori gripped the javelin, holding the shaft in the crease of her hand. She had watched Fatouma do this a hundred times, and each time, Qori marveled at her skill. But Qori was a runner, a hurdler, not a thrower. She was neither tall, nor muscular, but she was agile, flexible—and brave.

Breathing fast and hard, she held the spear up above her shoulder, lining it up with her head, the tip pointing slightly down. "Please don't miss," she mumbled as she took nine running steps, her legs crossing over as she kept the javelin lined with her eyes. Then she leaned back, her left leg thrust forward, hurling the spear through the air.

Raven screamed in surprise when the javelin hit its target, impaling the wolf. The beast howled, bursting into blue flames. It roared, stumbling blindly, as Fatouma scrambled backwards. The beast snarled, then lunged at her. Jaws wide open, she could see nothing but teeth.

Fatouma grabbed the shot from the bag, and screaming, hurled it with all her might. The beast exploded, spewing blood and bones all over Fatouma's face and hair.

"Ugh!" she wailed, wiping her eyes with her hoodie. The yellow and green Warriors logo stained a deep red. Rain poured from the sky.

"The dew of heaven," Raven said, wearily. She helped Fatouma up, as Qori hobbled over, her high bun dangling to the side. "Where is Judaea?" she asked, looking around frantically. One by one, slow mournful cries echoed. The sound of rage had given way to the sound of grief.

* * *

DEAD HEAT

Judaea heard the call. Stomach roiling, she felt that other self slipping behind her skin, pressing its mask against the inside of her flesh. She dragged herself back outside, barely bone, muscle by muscle she transformed until she was fully human again.

The ground was cold and wet beneath her cheek. The grass smelled sour. She was lying on her arm, the one the wolf had chomped down on like an iron trap. The wound didn't hurt anymore, but she remembered how much it did. The pain she forgot she could still feel, when she had soared in her new flesh. When the werewolf's canines sank in, the pain had radiated in circles, like hair-line fractures through her bones. Bruises distorted, they healed miraculously, disappearing inside her too taut skin.

Soreness wrapped itself around her wrist; the knuckles of her fist ached. She didn't know where she was or how she got there. One minute she was fighting with wolves, the next, she blacked out. *You can't keep running from who you are.* That voice, her mother's, is her oldest memory. It returned to her now.

So small, no more than three. Her father's eyes, frightened, speaking about safety. Her mother tears, pleading. Asking where in the world he could ever go and truly be safe. Where could he call home if it wasn't with them. Her father picking her up, the sensation of being lifted into the air. His tears on her forehead and cheek. Her mother's eyes.

Running from who you are.

That was the last thing her mother had said to her father before they didn't see him again. No news for years. After that, her mother's eyes became the sky. Wide with worry, forever keeping Judaea in her view. Ever watchful, waiting.

Judaea rose on her elbows. She had questions. But first, she needed to find her friends. She prayed they were still alive.

* * *

The fog lifted, the full moon silver in the sky. The girls raced through the ruins, leaping over fallen tombstones, trampling across graves where teacups and watches, and other favored items of the dead rested. They came out onto an open field, to see a battle unfolding before them. Lycan versus werewolf, the dark shadows and the hulking wolves tearing at each other. Some burst into flames, others so eager for blood, they tore at each other. Wild berserkers. The low stone wall was just beyond them.

"Well, now we know why they didn't come," Raven said. "Look like they're getting messed up." Her voice was dry. No more emotion to wring out of her heart after the night of terror.

"We're not going to make it across," Qori said. Her jacket was torn, dirt and cuts lined her face, across her legs. "We don't have anything left. And Judaea..." her voice trailed off. No one wanted to say it, but after they couldn't find her, they all assumed she was dead.

"Damn near," a voice behind them whispered.

Fatouma shook her head as the others ran to her side, staring at Judaea's arm.

"Where did you go?" Qori asked. The disappointment had returned to her eyes. "What happened? We could have..."

"I know," Judaea said, guilt and fear coursing through her. "Maryse led me to you. Her brother and sisters, the whole Colony are out there now, fighting. I don't know how, but we're caught in the middle of a war, and I don't know how to get us out of here."

"You just faded out," Raven said. "I thought you went to get help."

"I blacked out from the pain. It was like I couldn't focus enough to stay in one place. I woke up in the woods behind the cemetery. Maryse was calling me. She said—"

Qoree's scream was cut short. The creature had her by the shoulder, dragging her away. Judaea would never forget the look in her eyes.

Raven and Fatouma screamed her name over and over again.

"Do something!" Raven cried, but Judaea froze. *Not Qori, not Qori, not—*

"Judaea!"

She snapped into focus, her body shifting faster than even the first time. She fell to the ground, bones bending, the old skin replaced with the new. Judaea's senses coursed with a different electricity, rage.

"Run!" she cried, "Get to the wall!" and her shadow swirled through the air, tracking the beast's stench, Qari's screams growing weaker.

* * *

When she descended and reappeared directly in front of the wolf, she was relieved to see that Qori was still alive. She had lost blood, but her spirit held on.

She was a Warrior.

Judaea stared at the werewolf, the eye contact— a direct challenge. She willed her shadow self away, shifting back to human so quickly, she didn't even register the pain this time. The beast released Qori, tossing her limp body aside and lunged at Judaea. She shifted back, spun around, as the werewolf growled and snapped its neck.

She picked up Qori, whose eyes were glazed. "Come on, Qori," she said, "You can make it. We're so close. We're going home."

＊　＊　＊

Judaea tried to carry Qori with her in the shadow form, but she couldn't get far, so they walked, hobbled along, heading north, back to the field. "Can I rest now?" Qori asked, her voice low, her breathing shallow. "My shoulder feels like it's on fire. I feel dizzy."

As they traveled the edge of the field, inching towards the low wall, something needled at Judaea's mind, pinpricks of questions. Why didn't the werewolf kill Qori? Where was it taking Qori? The way it held her, it seemed as if it wanted to injure not kill. It carried her the way a wolf might carry its pup. Maryse had said there were far more werewolves attacking them than anticipated. More than the known number in Arkadela.

The scent of blood and fear reached her before they saw the carnage. The lycans were slicing and cracking bones in a horrific tornado of terror. So many shadows that they rivaled the clouds around the moon, but the number of wolves kept increasing, and

Judaea's heart nearly stopped when she saw Raven and Fatouma being stalked by two different werewolves.

The creatures could have pounced at any time, but they seemed to be waiting, careful. *They want them alive,* she thought. They're actively recruiting, building their numbers. But how? Like lycans, werewolves were born not made.

Until now, she thought. That werewolf they hit on the road had intentionally followed them, through the woods on the shoulder. He jumped in front of the bus... *He wanted to die,* she thought. *They're hunting and turning people against their will.*

She had to get to Raven and Fatouma, but Qori wouldn't make it long alone. Judaea fought back tears. She didn't know what to do. She had started the trip off with no friends and now her teammates were all she had—and she could not choose.

Fate chose for her.

Coach Fuller came flying over the hill in the yellow school bus. Judaea couldn't believe her eyes.

"He's alive!" Qori said, sounding better than she had since they'd been walking. And there was "*Everybody* Know" Crazy Joe hanging out the window, silver chains swinging, rifle blazing.

He picked off the werewolves, one by one, peering through his scope. "Now we know why he was rocking all that silver," Judaea said.

Qori laughed and winced, her shoulder throbbing. "Ouch."

Raven and Fatouma raced through the old field, zigzagging and leaping over the fallen stones, names long erased with time. They ran faster than they ever ran their whole lives, eyes on their escape over the wall. The wolves snapped at them, trying to tackle and corner them as the girls bobbed-and-weaved, high-stepping through the grass.

Fatouma got to the wall first, her shoes slipping on the stones. She found purchase and clambered up. "Come on, Raven!" she cried, reaching back to help her friend.

Raven made a giant leap, trying to scramble up and fail. Fatouma shrieked. "You better get your ass up! You're always talking that shit, you better come on!" she said, tears streaming down her eyes. "Ravennnnnnn!"

Hyperventilating, Raven shot up and tried again, climbing atop the wall and diving to the other side. She got up running, and the girls never looked back.

One wolf ran in a circle, crouched, readying to make it over, but then the yellow bus plowed through it, slamming the creature against the wall.

The other wolf took off, wailing. Judaea and Qori limped down the hill, cheering. The lycans materialized from shadow-wraiths back to their human forms, surveying the aftermath.

"I have never been so happy to see that raggedy cheese bus," Judaea said. Qori rested her head on her shoulder, silent tears rolling down her face.

* * *

FINISH

It took Coach Fuller a while to make it back to the country road. "I don't know how the hell we're going to explain any of this," he said.

"*Everybody* Know" Joe patted his shoulder. "Your Coach was a lovely woman. I'm so sorry for your loss."

"Thank you for coming. I don't know what me and the girls would do."

"I've been out here in Dumas County a long time. It's mostly peaceful. Ain't gonna lie, there's a lot of strange folks out here, all kinds if you get my drift, and we mostly mind our business. My store and that old cemetery is neutral ground—or at least, they used to be."

"I can't tell," Fuller said. Joe snorted.

"S'posed to be that anybody in Dumas County can come and go, get supplies or conversation as they need. But something bad has been brewing for a while. It was only a matter of time before the bad mojo was gon' spill out. I'm just sorry you and your girls got caught in it. But I suspect, Maryse and n'em will sort it." He glanced at Judaea in the mirror. "You keep an eye on those two. They can go either way. It's really up to them."

They drove in silence, exhaustion the only sound on the bus until they saw Raven and Fatouma trudging down the shoulder of the road. They stopped and picked them up. The ride was a bit more cheerful the rest of the way, and they had a new respect for Jonah's Ark after they dropped him off at his gas station.

"How long you been living here?" Fuller asked before he pulled off. "And why the hell do you stay?"

Joe peered at him carefully, as if testing if he could trust him, and then shrugged. "I was given an important mission some time ago, and instead of doing it, I thought I'd take myself a trip. You know, I was young and brash. I disobeyed. Let's just say, I took a drink in a long glass of water and ended up here. Been in Dumas County ever since." They watched him walk under the Jonah's Ark sign and disappear into the store.

When they pulled into the parking lot of The Waffle Club, the girls looked at Coach Fuller like he was crazy.

"We already been fighting enough," Raven said. "If something jumps off up in here, I don't know if I can make it."

"You can, 'cuz you're a Warrior!" Coach Fuller said. "You've been running all night. You mean to say you're not hungry?"

When they walked in, the sign above the counter said, "Serving Delicious Breakfast and These Hands. Choose Your Meal Wisely."

Qori hurt too much to even laugh. Her stomach growled.

"Damn!" the cashier said as they came in the door. "What happened to you?"

"Y'all must've went through Dumas County," somebody said, hunched over a plate of flapjacks. "But don't nobody usually come out of there."

The cashier, the cook, the servers, and all the patrons in the restaurant paused, incredulous.

"If you survived Dumas County, breakfast is on the house," the cashier said, laughing, shaking his head in disbelief. "How did y'all make it?" he asked.

The girls looked at each other and shrugged.

"We were lucky," Raven said. She stroked a scar on her cheek.

"We were smart." Fatouma held up Qori's good hand.

"And we are fast," Judaea said and sat down to study the menu.

MOTHERLODE

1

They don't bury the noise.

The air tasted like old pennies, resignation, and the thick, damp heat that pressed down like judgment in West Tennessee. Akiba stepped out of the transport vehicle, the heavy metal door slamming shut behind her with the hollow boom of a grave being sealed. Sunlight, bleached and hostile, a flat white glare like polished bone, in the open yard hit her eyes, stinging after the dim confines of the transfer cage. She blinked rapidly, trying to clear the spots from her vision, acutely aware of the guard standing too close behind her. Her skin crawled with a prickling heat that wasn't just the Memphis humidity, it was pure, distilled dread. Every muscle was coiled tight, ready to flinch. *Don't show weakness*, she told herself, a mantra she'd been reciting since the gavel fell. *Just get through this*. Getting through this meant keeping her head down, doing what they said, and waiting for the time to be over. That was what she wanted, what she clung to: the end of the sentence, the chance to walk away, maybe find some quiet corner of the world where she could just... *breathe*. But this place wasn't built for 'getting through.' It was built for staying. Built to consume the very idea of a life outside its walls.

Just days ago, they'd sheared off her hair, her low-cropped curls falling to the floor like discarded promises. Now, her scalp felt strangely naked, exposed to the harsh light and the cold, assessing eyes of her captors. A constant, low thrum vibrated through the concrete path beneath her worn shoes, a sound that seemed to bypass her ears and settle directly in her bones. It reminded her of a moment, not long ago, maybe upon waking in a holding cell, when she had simply woke to lifelines. Startled, she'd slowly raised her palms to her eyes in the dim light, and the dark grooves there appeared bizarre, like strange carvings in wood. Now in the dim light, the lifelines seemed deep and obscene, shadows against the pink brown of her palm flesh. They were moving and writhing, a life force of their own. Moving and regrouping, ancient symbols danced across the uncalloused palm. *Or was it her flesh?* Before she opened her eyes, she wasn't so sure. The memory was fleeting, unsettling, a crack in the certainty of her own body, a question of ownership that this place intended to answer with brutal finality.

The uniform they issued felt like being dressed in a historical reenactment of misery: stiff, rough fabric dyed a deep, uneven indigo, like the bruise the sky turns just before a storm. "Indigo flight suit," the intake officer had said, a flat, humorless joke that twisted something sour in Akiba's gut. It had no pockets, of course. Nothing to hold. Nothing of your own to keep close. They even took her small, chipped stone, the one she'd carried for luck since she was a girl. Proof of contraband, they'd logged it. Proof of wanting something they wouldn't give.

Following the guard down the narrow path, she caught the smell first – sweet, earthy, cloying. Indigo plants, their dark, fibrous leaves catching the light, stretched in nauseatingly neat rows. Then okra, its distinctive scent thick and sweet and slightly green-rot, a smell rising from the fields that felt like breathing through a hot, damp rag. It hung thick and still, the kind of heavy wet you only found deep in the Delta, tasting of dust and the promise of rain that never seemed to quite break." Cultivation. Forced labor. The ghosts of history didn't just haunt this place, they worked the fields. The distant hum of unseen machinery was constant, a counterpoint to the insistent, tireless drone of crickets, singing their ancient songs that somehow pierced the oppressive atmosphere, a tiny, wild sound in a place determined to tame everything.

She saw them then, the women in the yard. All in the same indigo suits, their movements slow, practiced. Some stood. Others sat on the sparse benches. And one figure stood apart, near a patch of hardy, thorny bushes beside a low wall.

Madear.

She was taller than most, solid and unyielding as old timber. Her hair, unlike Akiba's raw stubble, was meticulously styled in neat, dark flat twists that framed her face, a testament to a discipline that seemed to defy the environment. There was a stillness about her that was more potent than movement, a settled power that made the air around her crackle. The fear she inspired wasn't just rumor. It was a force you could feel, heavy and ancient. Akiba's gaze flickered over the deep, permanent indigo stains on Madear's hands, hands that looked like they could break stone or coax life from barren ground. *She ain't one to cross*, a whisper from the transport vehicle echoed in Akiba's mind. *Killed her last family*, they say. Akiba averted her eyes, focusing on the cracked concrete beneath her feet. She just wanted to get inside, follow the rules, disappear until her time was up. Survival meant staying invisible.

Near the fence, a softer, sadder sight. A woman with long, dark hair styled in two thick French braids swayed gently. In her arms, cradled like something infinitely precious, was a large watermelon, wrapped in a faded, crocheted doily. *Wanetha.* She hummed softly, her voice a low, broken melody. As Akiba watched, Wanetha bent stiffly and carefully plucked a few tiny wildflowers from the edge of the path – a flash of purple and yellow defiance against the grey concrete. She began weaving them into one of her braids as she murmured to the watermelon, her lips moving silently as if talking to unseen others. *The twins*, the whispers said. *Gone,* but still here to her. "Teched in the head," Madear had said, her voice rough, but something in her eyes when she looked at Wanetha... *pity? Recognition?*

The air grew thin here, carrying a manufactured chill that bit sharper than any winter wind outside. Akiba slowed her steps, though every instinct screamed to run, to sprint past the polished, anonymous doors lining the corridor. This was the wing spoken of in whispers, a place whose very air felt heavier with unspoken dread than anywhere else in the facility. No cheerful murals here, no gentle hum of activity. Only a profound, unnatural quiet punctuated by the rhythmic, mechanical exhale of unseen machines. This violation was sanctioned by the state, brain-dead women used as fetal incubators, implemented against the desperate pleas and rightful claims of families who had already suffered unimaginable loss. Relatives had filed suit, their anguish weaponized against them in sterile courtrooms, attempts to gain custody of children born of this cruelty denied.

Inside, a woman lay utterly still on a narrow bed, her skin the color of faded parchment under the cool, blue-tinged lights. Tubes snaked from her body, disappearing beneath sterile sheets. It wasn't the sight of her stillness that seized Akiba's breath, but the almost imperceptible swell beneath the blankets, a gentle rise and fall that spoke of a life being forcibly nurtured within a body that had already given its last breath. State-sanctioned incubators, kept breathing not for themselves, but for the market, for the waiting hands that would claim the product at a predetermined "birthday." The thought was a bitter, metallic taste in Akiba's mouth. She tore her gaze away, the hushed whispers about profit margins and investor portfolios echoing louder than any sound in this tomb of forced blooming.

Akiba stumbled away from the glass, the sterile air suddenly too thin to breathe. The images seared into her mind made the cheerful screens and mandated lullabies she'd heard about feel like a grotesque, paper-thin mask over a rotting core. Getting through this place felt less possible than ever. The corridor stretched ahead, an endless, gleaming testament to ownership and control, and Akiba walked through it feeling the weight of every stolen breath and every denied plea behind them.

"Inside. Now." The guard's voice was sharp, breaking the moment.

Inside the residential block, the air was different again – cool, sterile, tasting faintly of disinfectant and that cloying sweetness designed to smooth the edges off everything. It made Akiba's thoughts feel distant, muffled, like she was thinking underwater. The hum of the facility was louder here, a pervasive electronic presence. Sometimes, through the thick walls, Akiba thought she could just barely catch the sound of an airplane, high and free, a ghost limb of the outside world passing overhead.

The communal room was stark: concrete, thin mattresses, a screen showing endless loops of placid images. Near a reinforced door, a group of older women sat together, their backs straight, a quiet authority in their stillness. The Big Mamas. Their hair was pulled back in neat, tight buns. They watched Akiba enter, their expressions unreadable, a mix of passive observation and something deeper, harder to decipher.

One of them, her face lined but her eyes sharp, nodded slowly. "New fish," she said, her voice low, a sound of gravel shifting.

Akiba hugged her arms to her chest, the thin fabric of the flight suit itching her skin, the smell of fake sweetness and disinfectant filling her lungs, the image of the woman and her watermelon burned into her mind. This was The Crib. At the Center for Incorrigible Birthers. The name echoed in her mind, cold and clinical, stripping away everything but the state's brutal definition of her existence. She just had to get through it. That's all.

*　*　*

2

The clock on the wall had no hands. Time in The Crib wasn't measured in hours or minutes you could track, but in forced rhythms: the jolt of lights snapping on before false dawn, the bland sameness of the nutrient paste, the migration to the fields as the sun began its climb.

The indigo fields were where the history felt most present. Under the relentless Southern sun, a weight pressing down like a hand on the land as they bent and pulled, the thick indigo leaves scratching against their arms, the fine dust settling on their skin. The dye was everywhere, seeped into the soil, staining their hands a permanent, deep blue, the color of old bruises and forgotten seas. It reminded Akiba of pictures she'd seen in a smuggled book once, pictures of hands just like theirs, centuries ago. *Same dirt,* a voice whispered inside her, *different chains.* It was backbreaking, soul-sapping work, designed to exhaust the body and leave little energy for the mind.

It was the bone-tiring labor in the unforgiving sun and the constant surveillance that wore at her. A guard's voice droned instructions from the edge of the field, a flat, monotonous sound. Akiba felt the familiar despair welling up. Beside her, a woman she didn't know well, dark eyes framed by tightly coiled hair, caught her gaze. The woman's lips curved in a tiny, almost imperceptible smile, a silent acknowledgment of the shared misery, a flicker of defiance that passed between them like a current in the heavy air.

Then came the okra. Fields of it, the plants reaching toward the sky. And the eating of it. Okra boiled, stewed, served cold. Slimy, cloying, ever-present. "Good for the belly," the Big Mamas would announce, their voices flat, their eyes scanning the bowls. "Makes you strong. Fertile." They watched to make sure it was eaten, every last bit. It was food—and a mandate, a biological imperative forced down their throats. Madear, sitting across the sparse table, would sometimes stare at her bowl with a look of pure, contained fury before pushing it away, her movements minimal but clear. Akiba started leaving small amounts too, a tiny act of solidarity, a way to feel less like livestock being fattened for the slaughter.

The air in the residential block felt softened. Like cotton wool stuffed in your head, muffling thought, dulling emotion with that all chemical sweetness. Anger, sorrow – they felt distant, theoretical, like things that happened to other people in another life. It was designed, Akiba knew, to keep them "calm," "stable," suitable vessels. The ever-present hum of machinery was part of it, a low frequency meant to soothe or suppress. The screens on the walls constantly projected images of placidity: rolling hills, calm oceans, idealized depictions of happy families, all interspersed with close-ups of gurgling, pink-skinned babies. It was a relentless, passive assault on their reality.

Evenings meant the mandated "lullaby hour." Sitting in uncomfortable chairs, women were expected to sing soft, soothing songs to the life growing or the potential life within them.

One evening, during the mandatory viewing of a sitcom featuring an overly cheerful family dinner, a ripple of quiet commentary spread through the room. "Look at that fool husband," one woman murmured, barely loud enough to hear. "Don't even know he ain't the one running that house." A low chuckle, quickly stifled, passed between a few women. Another muttered, "All that food. Bet it ain't got no okra." Tiny, shared blasphemies whispered into the air, small acts of reclaiming their thoughts, their voices.

It was grotesque, a marionette performance of maternal affection on demand. They called it "prison blues" amongst themselves, a bitter joke about the required emotional state. Their real blues were the hummed melodies in the fields, low and deep as the Mississippi river's mournful song, the whispered verses shared in the dim light after lockdown – raw, ragged, full of longing and loss, like the old songs Akiba's grandmother used to sing. Sometimes, after the mandated songs ended and the guards had done their final rounds, a low, rhythmic humming would start in one corner of the room, picked up by another woman, then another. Not a lullaby, but something older, something with a steady beat that felt like bare feet on packed earth. A sound that wove them together in the darkness, a secret rhythm against the facility's sterile hum.

Small acts were monumental. Akiba, using a sharpened wire and threads pulled from a frayed hem, began sewing a small pocket onto the inside of her flight suit, a secret pouch against her skin. It was a difficult, painstaking process, her indigo-stained fingers clumsy. She thought again of her palms, the intricate lines she'd seen, moving and regrouping. Were these lines on her hands still her own, or had the Crib begun to redraw them too? Other women did the same, creating hidden spaces for a smooth stone, a shard of interesting glass found in the yard, a carefully preserved wildflower. A place for something that belonged to you. If a guard found it during a surprise shakedown – rare, but terrifyingly possible – the punishment was "The Cradle." The whispers about that unit, the sounds that came from it, were enough to stop breath in your throat. It was a lot to risk for a hidden scrap of autonomy.

Akiba noticed how some women fiercely maintained their traditional hairstyles. Madear's neat flat twists seemed impervious to the general slump Akiba felt. Wanetha, with her long French braids, would sometimes pick wildflowers from the thin, wild strip near the fence and carefully weave them into her hair, talking softly to the watermelon cradled in her arms. "These for my boys," Akiba heard her murmur one evening, her voice thin and reedy. "And this yellow one for you, sweet baby." She stroked the watermelon, her eyes seeing past the fence, past the guards, past The Crib itself. Madear's phrase came back: *She ain't really here with us. She still seeing from the inside.* Akiba didn't understand it, not really, but the image of Wanetha weaving wildflowers for invisible children and a watermelon baby lodged itself deep in her mind. These hairstyles felt like anchors, physical connections to identity the Crib was trying to erase. Later that week, during a quiet hour in the communal area, Akiba saw two women sitting together, one carefully parting and braiding the other's hair into a complex, beautiful pattern. Their fingers moved with practiced, gentle care, a quiet communion in the harsh fluorescent light. No words were needed, just the shared focus, the trust, the simple act of tending to each other's crowns in a place that wanted them all bare and uniform. It was a small, fierce act of preserving something of themselves, something that belonged only to them.

Some women even pulled scarves or bonnets over their heads at night, not just for warmth, but as a small barrier against whatever chemical manipulatives permeated the air. Protecting more than just their hair. Maybe survival wasn't about disappearing. Maybe it was about refusing to disappear completely.

One afternoon in the yard, Akiba saw two women sitting with their backs to the wall, one carefully rebraiding the other's hair into intricate cornrows. Their heads bent together, fingers moving with practiced care, a quiet communion in the harsh light. It was a small thing, easily overlooked, but the focus, the shared touch, felt like building something – a fortress of tradition and care against the relentless uniformity of the Crib.

Sleep offered no true escape. The dreams of fish were constant, shared. Dark water, flashes of silver scales, the silent pull of the deep, muddy bottoms of Delta waterways, the suffocating feeling of being pulled down. "Every night," the woman had said. "That's how it is in the Crib." It was a communal haunting, a shared descent into a watery subconscious where something unknown stirred.

Sometimes, late at night, when the facility's hum seemed to lower just slightly, Akiba could hear the faint chirping of crickets from somewhere outside the walls, a resilient, wild sound. And even fainter, the high, lonesome whistle of an airplane passing overhead – a thin silver thread stitching the outside world to their silence – a reminder of a world she was desperate to get back to, a freedom that felt impossibly distant. She just had to get through. Survive. That was her only want, her only need.

* * *

3

Weeks folded into months, marked by the changing angle
of the sun through the high windows and the increasing tightness
around Akiba's middle. The initial shock of arrival gave way to a dull,
persistent ache of existence, broken only by flashes of visceral terror
or the unsettling strangeness of the Crib's inhabitants. This wasn't
just prison. It was a biological factory, and they were the involuntary
machines. Akiba watched them, trying to understand the unspoken
rules, the subtle hierarchies among the women, the invisible lines
drawn between those who still fought and those who seemed... somewhere else, their minds having found an escape their bodies were
denied. The creeping dread of realizing just how deeply this place
intended to violate them settled over her, cold and heavy.

Wanetha was definitely elsewhere. Akiba saw her often in the
small, fenced-in yard during their limited recreation time. Wanetha
moved with a peculiar, drifting grace, her two long French braids
swaying as she wandered the perimeter. She still carried the watermelon baby, its rind beginning to show faint signs of softening, a
quiet decay mirroring the world around them. She would stop by
the thin strip of earth near the fence where hardy wildflowers, tough
little miracles pushing through cracked clay like tiny fists, somehow
managed to bloom. Defiant bursts of color in the muted landscape.
Carefully, she'd pick a few, examining each petal with intense
concentration before weaving them into her braids, murmuring
the entire time. "A crown for my kings," Akiba heard her whisper
one afternoon, braiding a vibrant purple blossom near her temple.
"And blue for the water where you sleep, little one," adding a single

indigo-stained weed she'd pulled from the edge of the okra patch to the watermelon's doily wrap.

Her chants about Warden Mack were unsettlingly specific, a rhythmic incantation that raised the fine hairs on Akiba's arms. "*Black-black-black* with silver *buttons-buttons-buttons* all down her *back-back-back*," she'd sing, her voice a low, repetitive drone, tracing imaginary buttons down her own spine. It was a child's game twisted into something deeply fearful, linking the Warden's imposing, all-seeing figure to the historical specter of the "pattyrollers," the slave patrols who hunted Black bodies for profit and control. Akiba had read just enough history before the schools crumbled to know those bloodroots ran deep, right into the heart of places like this, right into the uniforms of the guards who watched them now. The chant was a recognition that the authority here wasn't just penal, it was primal, a genetic memory of being pursued, captured, and controlled.

Madear watched Wanetha with that same unreadable expression – a flicker of something that might have been pain, quickly masked by a hardening around her eyes. Madear didn't drift. She sat with her back straight, her indigo-stained hands resting in her lap, watching everything with eyes that missed nothing. Her defiance was a quiet, implacable force, a refusal to be broken by the constant pressure of the place. She moved with an economy of motion, every gesture deliberate, conserving energy. She rarely spoke to the guards unless necessary, her responses clipped and direct, a low growl beneath the words.

Akiba started to see small things, signs she hadn't recognized before, quiet acts that pushed back against the suffocating control. A woman rubbing a specific pattern on her belly when she thought no one was looking, a circular motion ending with a sharp tap. Another tying a knot in a piece of thread while humming a song that wasn't on the approved lullaby list, her lips moving around words Akiba couldn't decipher. Whispers shared in the dim light after lockdown, about dreams, not just the disquieting fish, but dreams of flying, of earth that opened up to swallow guards whole, of ancestors standing just beyond the veil, their hands outstretched. Hoodoo. Rootwork. Not the caricatures from the old fear-mongering news reports, but quiet, private acts of seeking connection, protection, and perhaps a sliver of control in a world utterly devoid of it. These were the hidden currents beneath the Crib's placid surface.

One evening, a small group of women gathered quietly in a corner, sharing something wrapped in cloth. Akiba edged closer, curiosity outweighing her wariness. It was a small, crudely carved wooden comb, smelling faintly of sap, carrying the scent of the wild woods just beyond the wire. One woman ran it through her short, coarse hair, her eyes closed, a look of profound comfort on her face. "From the old oak by the fence," another whispered. "He carves them. Leaves them where he can."

"He?" Akiba mouthed, and the women just exchanged glances, a silent agreement to share only what was necessary. A small act of resistance, a link to something outside, something wild and untamed by the Crib's manicured control. A breadcrumb of connection, maybe even hope, left by someone they couldn't name.

Whispers about "He" and the comb circulated quietly. Later, Akiba overheard two women talking near the fence line, their voices low. "Heard she rub ash from the burning barrel into her wrists," one murmured. "For protection. Old ways." The other woman nodded slowly. "They try to bleach the old out of you here. But the roots run deep."

Akiba hadn't been to the cemetery yet. It was spoken of in hushed tones, a place of sorrow and superstition, a place the Crib pretended didn't really exist, unmarked on any official map. Wanetha's fear of it was palpable, a raw, exposed nerve. Akiba watched Mama Jo, a quiet older woman Akiba knew tended the cemetery, moving among the markers with a serene purpose, pulling weeds that dared to encroach, placing small, smooth stones and wildflowers on the tiny mounds. Wanetha was near the fence, clutching her watermelon, watching Mama Jo in the distance with wide, fearful eyes.

"That's where they keep the ones who didn't fly," a woman near Akiba murmured, her voice low, a grim explanation.

Wanetha suddenly turned from the fence, her eyes fixed on Mama Jo, then darted to Akiba. Her gaze was intense, seeing past Akiba to something else entirely. "She ain't really here with us," Wanetha says, her voice thin but clear, gesturing towards Mama Jo. "She still seeing from the inside." Wanetha taps her own swollen belly, then the watermelon cradled in her arms. "Babies half-born are dangerous. They have power." Her gaze intensifies, seeming to look through Akiba to something ancient and unsettling. "They foots in both worlds, this one and the one beyond—the one where they came from, the one if we lucky at all, we come back to." The intensity fades as quickly as it came, and Wanetha returns to murmuring to her watermelon infant, but the words hang in the air between them, heavy with a meaning Akiba can only begin to grasp. It wasn't just madness. It was a different kind of truth Akiba hadn't encountered before. One that spoke to a violation so profound it reached beyond the physical, into the soul Akiba felt was being stolen, into the world of the ancestors she had only ever heard about in hushed tones.

She remembered her grandmother's hands, the warmth of them, the stories whispered late at night about the ones who came before, the ones who endured, whose strength was a river flowing through generations. That strength felt impossibly distant now, a faint echo against the loud, clinical hum of the Crib. But sometimes, meeting the eyes of another woman across the room, she saw it flicker there – the same deep current running beneath the surface, a shared inheritance they carried in their bones.

The air feels thicker with the unspoken then, heavy with the weight of history and the unsettling possibility of other worlds brushing against this one. Akiba looks at Mama Jo tending the graves of lost children, at Wanetha cradling her fruit and seeing ghosts, and a cold shiver goes down her spine. The cemetery feels like a thin place, where the veil is porous. Where the grief rises from the earth, wet like graveyard mist on a humid morning, thick enough to choke you. It's a repository of the Crib's most profound losses, a place that holds the brutal truth of what happens here, and Akiba feels a morbid pull towards it, a need to understand the depth of the horror.

* * *

4

The initial strangeness of the Crib solidified into a terrifying routine, each day a reiteration of control and violation. Akiba learned the nuances of the system: the different kinds of medical tests ("Wellness Checks," they called the invasive scans and blood draws designed to track their cycles and the viability of their "product"), the mandatory genetic counseling sessions (where they were shown idealized images of the host families and given pamphlets detailing the 'benefits' of contributing to societal repopulation). The chilling efficiency with which pregnancies were monitored and managed felt like a cold, calculated map laid over the secret, wild country of a woman's body, denying the rhythms of blood and moon. This wasn't healthcare as she knew it—it was biological engineering for a specific, horrifying purpose. The laws were clear: following the virus that decimated global fertility, particularly impacting certain demographics among "the right ones"—affluent, primarily white populations—governments desperate to increase birth rates had enacted sweeping legislation. Crimes, even minor ones, committed by healthy, fertile women, especially Black women whose historical resilience and reproductive capacity were now deemed a valuable state resource, were met with extreme sentences. Instead of traditional incarceration, many were remanded to facilities like the Crib, their bodies conscripted into involuntary servitude as state surrogates. It was a horrifying evolution of the historical exploitation of Black women's bodies, now cloaked in medical jargon and societal necessity.

The shared struggle in the Crib, the constant pressure of the system, the micro-aggressions and overt cruelties – it forged a strange, fierce bond between the women. It wasn't always easy. Fear and desperation could breed suspicion and rivalry. But there were moments, quiet and profound, that stitched them together. Sharing a scarce comfort, a whispered joke during forced labor in the fields, a hand offered during a moment of weakness. They saw each other, truly saw each other, in a place designed to render them invisible except for their biological function.

Akiba found herself gravitating towards small groups, listening more than she spoke, learning the unspoken language of survival here. She learned who was reliable, who was lost, who carried the weight of too many ghosts. She saw how women sought comfort in each other, quiet touches, shared glances that spoke volumes in a world where words were policed. She saw two women sitting side-by-side during the lullaby hour, their shoulders touching, their hands clasped beneath the thin blanket covering their laps. A silent strength passing between them, a defiance in their quiet intimacy. There were risks, of course.

The Big Mamas watched it all. Their faces were usually carefully blank, their buns tight atop their heads. But sometimes, just for a flicker, when a baby was being taken, or when a woman cried out in the night, Akiba thought she saw something in their eyes. A deep, banked sorrow. A weariness that went bone-deep, like wood that had been gnawed by termites for a hundred years. They caught the babies, yes. But maybe they were also catching ghosts.

Either way, these were souls the system refused to let them, the surrogate mothers, keep, lives claimed before they could truly begin or snatched away the moment they did. And the deep, human need to grieve, to comfort, to simply touch another soul who understood that loss, was itself a crime.

Rules against "inappropriate contact," violations that could land you in "The Cradle." The very idea of human connection, of choosing who to be close to, was a crime against the system that claimed total ownership of their bodies and relationships. A misbehavior report for intimacy, followed by a hearing, and then days or weeks in "The Cradle" – a chilling punishment where, rumors said, the sounds of crying newborns were played on repeat, a form of psychological torture designed to break the maternal bond the system simultaneously relied upon and feared. But the need for human connection, for intimacy in a place that systematically stripped it away, seemed stronger than the fear of punishment for some. Akiba watched, a knot of longing and fear tightening in her chest. She wanted connection, wanted to feel like a woman again, but the risk... the risk felt immense.

It happened during the mandatory evening viewing of approved programming – old sitcoms showing idyllic, unrealistic family lives. Most women stared blankly or muttered commentary under their breath. Sometimes, though, a wave of shared, dark amusement would pass through the room during the overly cheerful family sitcoms. A roll of eyes caught across the room. A barely stifled snort of laughter that quickly became contagious among a small group. A whispered, cutting remark about the perfect television mothers that only those who lived this reality could truly appreciate. Tiny, shared rebellions that felt like breathing when the air was thin.

But one woman, a newcomer named Cora with defiant eyes, let out a sharp, bitter laugh at a particularly saccharine moment. It wasn't loud, barely more than a scoff. But a guard, patrolling the room with silent, watchful steps, stopped. His head snapped towards her.

"Something funny, 819?" he asked, his voice deceptively soft. Before she could even reply, he crossed the distance between them in two strides and hit her across the face. Hard. The crack echoed in the sudden, shocked silence of the room. Cora stumbled back, clutching her cheek, her eyes wide with pain and disbelief. The guard stood over her for a moment, his face impassive, before nodding to a Big Mama nearby.

"Get her processed for Cradle," he ordered. The Big Mama's face remained neutral, but her eyes held a flicker of grim understanding as she moved towards Cora. No explanation, no warning, just a laugh met with immediate, brutal punishment. Akiba's stomach twisted. A single, bitter laugh. And for that, The Cradle. Survival felt fragile as a spiderweb here. Invisibility felt like a lie she could no longer afford to tell herself. The air in the room felt thicker, colder. The screens continued their cheerful loop of smiling faces, a grotesque counterpoint to the raw violence they had just witnessed. The message was clear: even a sound, a simple expression of dissent, was a punishable offense.

Later that night, the lights dimmed and the hum of the facility seemed to press closer. Akiba lay on her thin mattress, the image of Cora's face burned into her mind. She felt a gentle touch on her arm. It was the woman from the lullaby hour, the one who sat close with her friend. She didn't speak, just squeezed Akiba's arm briefly, a silent acknowledgment of the shared fear, a tiny transfer of strength in the suffocating darkness.

Her own hope for release was a rapidly deflating balloon, pricked by the sharp edges of bureaucratic cruelty. The initial expectation of serving a set term and walking away was being eroded by shifting requirements, trumped-up infractions, and the casual indifference of the administrators who seemed to delight in their power. Papers were lost. New regulations were introduced specifically designed to extend sentences for minor, subjective violations. Her crime, once presented as clear-cut, seemed to morph into something more nebulous, a permanent stain on her record that made her suitability for release perpetually questionable. It was a slow, insidious process of wearing down, designed to make them accept their fate as permanent. The realization settled over Akiba like a shroud, cold and heavy – they didn't want her to leave. Not until she had fulfilled her purpose, birthed however many children the state deemed necessary, and perhaps not even then. The system wasn't about rehabilitation or justice. It was about reproduction, control, and immense profit for the private corporations running these facilities.

She started spending more time near Madear. Drawn by her raw, unyielding strength, perhaps, or by the authentic fire in her eyes in a place that demanded placidity. One evening, Madear was sitting outside on a bench after the meal, staring out at the indigo fields in the twilight, the blue stain on her hands almost invisible in the fading light. Akiba sat a few feet away, hesitant, the air thick with unspoken things.

"They took my first," Madear said, her voice low and rough, startling Akiba. She wasn't looking at Akiba, her gaze fixed on the darkening fields, on the rows of plants grown from forced labor. "Didn't even let me hold him proper. Just cleaned him, weighed him, whisked him away. Like... like he wasn't even mine." Her hands clenched on her knees, the indigo stain deepening under the pressure. "Said I wasn't fit. My crime was trying to make a choice about my own body. Imagine that. In a world where their bodies failed them." Her voice was laced with a bitterness that went bone-deep.

She spoke in fragments, like shards of glass, pieces of a story she rarely shared, a narrative of trauma and injustice.

"Five times. Five babies. To different families. Seen some of 'em again, later. As a nanny. My own blood. Calling some white woman Mama. Taught one of 'em to walk. Had to pretend I was just the help." Her voice was flat, but the pain in it was a physical presence in the humid air between them. "The last one... he was sickly. Cried all the time. Host mother, she... impatient. Didn't know what to do. Didn't have that... that knowing in her bones." Madear paused, a long, heavy silence, the chirping of crickets suddenly loud in the stillness. Akiba held her breath, a sense of creeping dread unfolding in her stomach. "Found him. Quiet. Too quiet." Madear turned then, and the look in her eyes was a raw wound, a horrifying revelation. "She said it was me. Said I neglected him. Said I was unfit. Again. Just like the judge said." Her voice dropped to a whisper that was more terrifying than a shout. "She killed him, Akiba. Her own impatience, her own cruelty. And she blamed me. Blamed the Black *surrogate*."

The truth of it hung in the air, heavy and suffocating, a horror far greater than anything Akiba had imagined. It wasn't about abortion anymore. It wasn't about being "unfit" in the state's eyes. It was murder covered up by policy, by the systematic erasure of a Black mother's truth. The horror wasn't just *in* the Crib. The Crib was built *on* the horror. And in that moment, Akiba felt a cold, hard rage begin to mix with her fear, a dangerous alloy forming in her gut. Rage at the ultimate expendability of Black life, even infant life, in a system built on exploitation. It was about silencing the Black mother who knew the truth, whose testimony meant nothing against the word of a wealthy white woman and the needs of the state. Akiba finally understood the depth of Madear's fury, the root of her violence against the host family. It was born of a grief so profound it had fractured her world, combined with an injustice so monstrous it demanded a reckoning only she could deliver.

Madear looked out at the fields again, at the dark, stained earth. "They called me incorrigible," she scoffed, a bitter sound that held no humor. "Maybe I am." A faint smile touched her lips, brief and sharp, like a broken piece of glass. "Had to protect myself. Protect his truth. Make them pay." The air felt thicker, charged with unspoken history and the terrifying promise of vengeance. Akiba looked at Madear, at her stained hands, the blue like shadows cast by history itself. Her resolute profile stark against the fading twilight, she saw not just a prisoner, but a warrior forged in unimaginable loss, a rootworker whose deep knowledge of life and death had been twisted by the horrors she'd endured. Her own fear began to mingle with something else – a dawning understanding of the system's true depravity, a spark of shared rage, a terrifying sense that simply surviving might not be enough anymore. That sometimes, you had to become incorrigible to fight a system that was inherently corrupt. The Crib didn't just want their bodies. It wanted their spirits, too. It wanted them to break, to give up the fight. But watching Madear, hearing her truth, Akiba felt something in her own spirit begin to harden, to refuse.

* * *

5

The thin thread of hope Akiba had clung to upon entering the Crib began to fray, then snap, piece by agonizing piece. It wasn't a sudden, dramatic pronouncement. It was the cumulative weight of cancelled appointments, misplaced paperwork, the casual dismissal of her questions about her sentence review. Each time she dared to ask, to hope, she was met with blank stares or vague promises that evaporated like mist in the Memphis heat. "The system is backed up, 7677," a clerk droned, not even looking up from a glowing console embedded in the wall. "Review pending. You'll be notified via internal channel." The number they called her by, stripping away her name, felt heavier than the indigo uniform. She saw women who had been here longer, their eyes dull, having long ago given up asking. "They don't never let you go when they 'specting," one woman whispered, her voice flat. "Not 'til you give 'em what they want. And sometimes not even then." The horrifying implication settled in Akiba's gut – her body wasn't her own, and her sentence wasn't measured in years, but in pregnancies. This wasn't a sentence; it was a biological conscription, managed with chilling, high-tech precision.

The system's cruelty wasn't always loud. The sci-fi horror of the Crib was in its clinical control over the most fundamental biological processes. Tiny subdermal implants, inserted upon arrival, tracked everything: heart rate, stress levels, nutritional intake, and most invasively, their entire reproductive cycle. Data streamed constantly to the medical wing, charting ovulation, monitoring uterine health, predicting optimal implantation windows. A sterile, digital cage built around the wild, untamed rhythms of a body that still remembered the pull of the moon and the tides of rivers.

Their diets, controlled down to the calorie and nutrient, weren't for their well-being but for maximizing fertility. Extra folate, calcium, proteins – all calibrated for "optimal gestator performance." The constant okra was part of this, a mandated superfood for the breeding program. Madear, however, maintained her subtle defiance. During meal times, when the Big Mamas' backs were turned or their attention diverted, she would subtly scrape her okra into a folded piece of scavenged paper or pass it to another woman who might be able to dispose of it later. Sometimes, Akiba noted, Madear's defiance was less subtle; she'd seen her crush the despised okra between her stained fingers under the table, the green slime a dark, almost violent contrast to the permanent blue of her skin. It was a small, risky act of rebellion against the mandated diet, a refusal to be fully optimized by the system. Akiba, watching this, felt a growing sense of admiration and a spark of her own dormant defiance.

Conversations about the "new mothers" and their families were overheard fragments, chilling in their casualness. "Unit B's gestator 4 delivered a 9-pound male yesterday. Host family is ecstatic. High genetic compatibility score." They were discussed like livestock, graded on the quality of the "product." Akiba once overheard a conversation between a Big Mama and a medical technician about a "low-value gestator" who wasn't gaining weight properly. Dehumanization, she realized, was baked into the very language of the Crib.

The host families, seen occasionally through reinforced glass or in brief, supervised transfers—affluent, pale, anxious—were the beneficiaries of this system, their infertility crisis solved on the backs and wombs of incarcerated Black women. They were the "right ones," whose desire for children justified this atrocity. "See 'em looking at your belly like it's already theirs," a woman with sorrowful eyes told Akiba one day. "Like you just the oven. Don't even see you." The invisibility was a different kind of violence.

When Cora finally returned, the laughter was sucked right out of her soul. Her eyes were wide and vacant, the sound of the Crib's hum seeming to buzz inside her skull. She flinched at sudden noises. Slowly, quietly, a few women – Madear among them – gravitated towards her bunk. No questions were asked. No demands were made. Just a silent ring of presence, a shared weight of knowing what that unit did to a person. A hand reached out and covered hers, warm and steady.

Akiba was beginning to parse the precarious lines walked by those women who held even a sliver of authority here. She thought of the Big Mamas: their roles were deeply conflicted – one moment offering a gentle, knowing hand through a private sorrow, the next compelled to report any perceived defiance to maintain the Crib's brutal order, or perhaps their own fragile standing within it.

Madear's fury was a low, constant rumble beneath the surface of the Crib's forced calm, ready to erupt like a volcano. Akiba saw it in the rigid set of her shoulders during mandatory "wellness checks," in the way her jaw muscles clenched when a guard spoke down to a Big Mama, in the silent, burning look she gave the screens displaying smiling white babies. It wasn't just anger; it was a profound, elemental rage, the kind that eats away at you from the inside but also hardens you into something unbreakable. Crushing okra wasn't enough anymore; sometimes, during the forced labor in the fields, Akiba would see Madear dig her indigo-stained fingers into the rich, dark Delta dirt with a violence that went beyond weeding, tearing at the earth as if trying to rip the very foundations of the Crib from the ground.

Wanetha's chant became more frequent, more insistent, a haunting soundtrack to their days, especially when Warden Mack was rumored to be in the building. "*Black-black-black* with silver *buttons-buttons-buttons* all down her *back-back-back*," she'd sing, her voice rising and falling, sometimes joined by a few other women in a low, unsettling chorus. The chant, linking the Warden to the "pattyrollers," underscored the chilling reality that the head of this modern breeding facility was a direct descendant, ideologically and functionally, of those who hunted and brutalized enslaved people. Akiba would watch the Warden walk by, her face a mask of detached efficiency, and hear Wanetha's words echoing in her mind, seeing not just a warden, but the latest iteration of a centuries-old mechanism of control over Black bodies. The creepiness of Wanetha's fragmented mind tapping into this deep historical truth was profound.

Akiba's empathy for Wanetha deepened into a fierce, protective instinct. She saw not madness, but a mind shattered by a trauma so profound it had sought refuge in another reality. Wanetha was prized because she bore sons – consistently. Four, whispered some; five, said others. All gone. All taken immediately, because sons were particularly valued by the host families. To be reduced to a producer of male offspring, denied the right to even know them… it was a horror that went beyond physical pain. Akiba started leaving small bits of her own meager food for Wanetha, sitting near her in the yard, offering a quiet presence even when Wanetha was lost in conversation with her watermelon and invisible sons. She started picking wildflowers too, leaving them near Wanetha's sleeping mat or tucking them into her braids when Wanetha wasn't looking. Small acts of acknowledging her, of seeing the woman beneath the brokenness.

One afternoon, Akiba sat near Wanetha in the yard, watching her weave wildflowers into her braids. "Why fish?" Akiba murmured, the question surprising herself. Wanetha looked at her, her eyes momentarily clearing, a flicker of ancient knowing there. "Water remembers," Wanetha whispered back, her voice low and raspy. "Remembers the coming and the going. Remembers the ones they took. Remembers the ones who still swim below the surface, waiting."

Her gaze seemed to pierce through the visible, focusing on something unseen beyond the fences. "They watching. Always watching," she murmured then, a new intensity in her hushed tone. "But they blind to the ones who swim below. The ones who remember the sun on the water. The fire in the sky."

A small, almost soundless giggle escaped Wanetha then, her eyes still distant, staring off at something only she could see. Then, as if the thought was complete, she returned to her braiding. But the words, simple and profound, now layered with defiance and a hidden promise, settled in Akiba's spirit, a new layer added to the unsettling dreams.

Akiba's dreams were still filled with fish, but they were darker now, the water murky, the feeling of being pulled down stronger. She woke up with a gasp sometimes, the heavy air pressing in on her, the hum of the facility a constant reminder of where she was. The small pocket she'd sewn onto her uniform became a focus, a tiny anchor in the swirling despair. Inside, she kept her smooth stone, a dried okra leaf Madear had once pressed into her hand, a single purple wildflower pilfered from the yard – small talismans against the overwhelming unreality of her life.

She spent more time near Madear, drawn to the elder's quiet strength and the magnetic pull of her history and simmering violence. Madear spoke in riddles sometimes, or shared fragments of knowledge – about plants, about the way things were before, about the foolishness of trusting their words. "This ain't just dirt," she'd mutter sometimes in the fields. "This is memory given solid form." She said she knew the old ways the earth remembered, "ways this concrete can't never forget."

She hinted at connections outside, at people who saw the Crib for what it was, people who weren't afraid to fight. "There are others," Madear murmured one evening, her voice barely audible above the defiant crickets just beyond the wall. "Who remember what freedom tastes like. Who ain't forgot how to fight. Ain't forgot how to burn." Her gaze was fixed on the high fence surrounding the facility, a fence topped with glinting wire, then flickered towards the dark bulk of the main building. A reckless, terrifying spark ignited in Akiba's chest, a flicker of something other than despair. Madear wasn't just waiting to get out; she was planning to bring the whole damn thing down. The suggestion of an outside force, of a plan that involved fire, was a dangerous, exhilarating allure. It was incorrigible. Everything in The Crib screamed *don't fight*. But Madear's whisper, barely audible above the crickets, felt like a different instruction. A terrifying one.

A necessary one. Everything in Akiba's being screamed, *Run!* But Madear's eyes, blazing with a fire Akiba now understood, pulled her forward. This wasn't about getting through anymore. This was about making them pay. This was choosing the fire over the cage.

* * *

6

The air was thick and still, heavy with the coming heat of dawn. A tension coiled through the residential block, a silence that felt louder than noise. Whispers had circulated for days, quick, furtive exchanges behind cupped hands. Someone was going to try. Someone was going to fly. The myth of "The People Could Fly," usually a story of spiritual escape, of ancestors shedding the chains of gravity, was taking on a terrifyingly literal meaning tonight. It was a desperate, almost suicidal hope, born of the unbearable weight of reality in the Crib, of laws passed by pens in faraway offices that reached across states and through steel bars to claim dominion over their very cells. They talked about Executive Order 10.1, the "National Biological Security Directive," the one that reclassified certain reproductive capabilities as "critical state infrastructure." That was where it started, the legal language that paved the way for places like this, that normalized the idea that some people's bodies were less their own than the state's. It was designed for them, Akiba knew, for women like her, for Black women whose lives had always been considered more disposable, more open to state control. But the creeping horror was the realization that the logic didn't stop here, that once the precedent was set, the definition of "critical" could always expand.

Akiba felt a nervous energy humming through the women, a mix of paralyzing fear and desperate, vicarious possibility. She didn't know who it was, not for sure, though she had her suspicions about a quiet woman named Lena who kept looking at the sky with a strange intensity. The air in the block felt thin, hard to breathe. She thought of the high fence, topped with glinting, electrified wire, the watchful towers manned by figures who saw them not as people, but as assets to be contained. It seemed impossible. But a part of her, the part that clutched the tiny talismans in her hidden pocket – the smooth stone, the dried okra leaf, the purple wildflower – felt a surge of wild, reckless hope. If one of them could break free, truly break free, maybe...

The sound came just as the pre-dawn light began to creep beyond the horizon. Not a shout, but a scramble near the fence, a thud, then the sharp, piercing shriek of an alarm cutting through the humid air and the hesitant calls of the waking birds. Red emergency lights immediately flooded the yard, harsh and blinding, stripping away all shadows. Shouting erupted, harsh male voices barking orders.

Akiba, along with the others, rushed to the high windows, pressing their faces against the reinforced glass, straining to see through the glare. Below, figures were scrambling near the far fence, two, maybe three women, small and vulnerable against the towering wire and the blinding lights. Guards were swarming from the watchtowers, from doorways, their movements quick, brutal, and terrifyingly coordinated. Their flashlights sliced through the darkness like swords, pinning the escapees in their beams. Their motion marked with a chilling efficiency, a predatory focus that went beyond simply apprehending inmates. They moved like... pattyrollers. Hunting. The historical echo was undeniable, terrifying in its accuracy. This wasn't law enforcement; it was the recapture of chattel, mandated by executive order, enforced with the same brutal logic of ownership.

One of the women, Lena, reached the top of the fence, her body a desperate silhouette against the dawning sky for a split second. A collective gasp went up from the watching women, a single, sharp intake of air. For a fleeting, impossible instant, framed by the harsh lights and the pre-dawn glow, it looked like she might keep going, might gather herself and launch herself into the air, shedding the constraints of earth and wire. Then, a sickening crackle, a flash of blue-white electrical discharge from the wire, and she fell. Not gracefully, but like a broken doll, hitting the ground with a sickening thud, and the acrid scent of burnt hair that Akiba felt in her own teeth.

"No!" someone screamed from the crowd of watching women, a cry of horror and dashed hope. A grim keening filled the air as if it rose from the very bones of the land itself.

The guards were on the others instantly, tackling them with brutal force. Shouts, grunts, the sickening sound of fists connecting with flesh. No attempt at careful capture, just raw, punishing violence designed to injure, to terrorize, to make an example. The guards hauled the struggling women away, dragging their limp or fighting bodies across the manicured lawn Akiba had walked across on her first day, its unnatural green now stained with shadow and the lingering stench of ozone. Lena, the one who fell, didn't move.

Silence fell over the watchtowers, the alarm cutting off as suddenly as it began, leaving a ringing echo in the air. But down in the yard, the guards' voices were harsh, triumphant. "Got the bird," one yelled, a cruel laugh following, flat and chilling. "Wings clipped."

Back inside the residential block, the mandated morning routine began, a desperate attempt by the system to reassert control, to pretend that nothing extraordinary had happened. But the air was thick with the aftermath. Fear was a palpable entity, pressing in on them, heavier than the humidity. But alongside the fear, in the hushed whispers shared throughout the day, in the fields, during the brutal lullaby hour, something else was born.

"Did you see her?" a woman murmured in the fields, indigo staining her cheek where she'd wiped sweat. "At the top of the fence? Looked like she just... hung there. Like she could have flown."

"They caught her," another replied, pragmatic but with a tremor in her voice, her eyes wide with the remembered horror. "Or she fell."

"Yeah, but for a second... she hung there," the first insisted, her eyes distant, seeing past the brutal reality. "Like she almost did it. Like she could have flown."

The story began to spread, fueled by desperation and the need for a different truth. She didn't just fall; she was almost free. She defied gravity for a moment, reaching for the sky. The Crib couldn't hold her completely, not for that one, brief, impossible second. But the wires, the guards, the concrete – they held her body. They broke her wings. And in that moment, Akiba understood with a cold, hard certainty that survival here wasn't about getting out. It was about not letting them break your spirit. The harsh reality was that she was broken on the ground, her body punished for its attempt at freedom, or caught and dragged away to face unimaginable punishment in "The Cradle." But the myth, the desperate, beautiful lie, offered a different truth: even here, trapped and brutalized, the spirit could yearn for the sky. And sometimes, just for a heartbeat, it looked like it might take flight. The creeping dread of their captivity was now mixed with the terrifying knowledge that attempting escape meant almost certain, brutal failure and horrifying punishment. But the myth provided a flicker of something else – a dangerous, resilient spark. It was a story Akiba clung to, a counter-narrative to the one the Crib imposed. She clutched the wildflowers in her pocket, their fragile petals a stark contrast to the violence she had witnessed.

* * *

7

The tension in the Crib had been building for days, a low hum beneath the surface of the enforced calm. Madear was different – sharper, more focused, her eyes holding a dangerous light. She moved with a coiled energy, exchanging subtle glances with a few key women. Akiba watched her, a knot of fear and anticipation tightening in her stomach. She knew Madear was planning something, something big, something that felt terrifyingly close to the fire Madear carried within her. Madear had shared fragments, hints of connections outside, people who understood that the Crib wasn't just a prison, but a wound on the world that needed cauterizing. People who believed that the policies that created places like this, starting with those cold, calculated executive orders and laws, were a sickness that had to be burned out. The kind of dehumanization that started with one group, one kind of body, but would eventually spread, consuming everything in its path. This wasn't just their fight; it was a fight for anyone who didn't want to be defined and controlled by the state, for anyone who feared becoming "critical infrastructure" against their will.

The air grew heavier as the planned time approached, thick with the scent of over-watered earth and something else, something metallic and sharp that Akiba couldn't place. The sky outside the high windows had turned a deep, bruised purple, just before dawn – the same color as the bruises on the fruit of the indigo plants they were forced to cultivate.

Then, the sound. Not a siren, but a deep, resonant boom that shook the concrete foundations of the building, rattling the reinforced glass in its frames. A second followed, closer, louder, a concussive force that knocked women off their feet in the communal room. Alarms shrieked, a different, more frantic sound than the escape alarm. Lights flickered, died, then came back on, blinking erratically. Smoke began to snake into the residential block through the vents, acrid and choking.

Chaos erupted. Women screamed, scrambling, disoriented. Guards were shouting, their voices panicked now, stripped of their usual authority. Through the windows, Akiba could see fire blooming in the distance, near the outer perimeter, licking at the base of the watchtowers and spreading rapidly through the indigo fields. The product was burning. The symbol of their enslavement, the source of the state's profit, was going up in flames.

"Get down! Stay put!" a guard screamed, but his voice was lost in the pandemonium.

Amidst the terror and confusion, a different sound cut through the noise – a woman's cry, sharp with pain, then a frantic shout. "She's birthing! She's early!"

Akiba looked across the room. A young woman, barely more than a girl, was collapsing onto her mattress, her face contorted in pain, her water breaking onto the thin sheet. A premature birth. Right now. In the middle of the fire and chaos. The planned timing, meant to avoid harm to any newborns, had gone horribly, tragically wrong.

A new life, forcing its way into a world already on fire, into a system designed to steal it the moment it drew breath. The ultimate, terrible irony.

Immediately, some of the Big Mamas, their faces grim but their movements automatic, converged on the birthing woman. Their ingrained knowledge, their Hoodoo practices of "catching babies," kicked in, overriding the panic. They moved with a practiced urgency, clearing a space, offering hushed words of comfort and instruction that felt ancient and sacred in the heart of this technological night-mare. Their indigo-stained hands, usually used for working the fields, moved with a different, fierce grace, guiding the life forth. "Catching you, little one. Always catching. Never holding for long," a Big Mama whispered. *Catching it.* Even knowing whose hands would ultimately take it next. They were Babycatchas, even now, even for a child that would be ripped away as soon as it drew breath.

But their focus was split. Other Big Mamas were shouting, trying to organize the women, pointing towards emergency exits that were suddenly accessible due to the blast. "Go! Now! While they distracted!"

The smoke thickened, making it hard to see, hard to breathe. Akiba coughed, her eyes tearing. She saw Madear near the reinforced medical door, not running, but moving with deliberate purpose, a piece of metal pipe in her hand. She was smashing equipment – monitors, consoles, anything she could reach. Destroying the technology of control, the data streams, the records of their stolen biology. This was part of the plan, the crippling of the system itself. Another woman, following Madear's lead, was pouring a liquid from a medical supply cabinet onto wiring, sparks flying, a dangerous, desperate act of sabotage. The few guards still attempting to assert control were overwhelmed, focused on distant fires or their own escape, leaving the medical wing momentarily undefended.

"Madear!" Akiba choked out, torn between the urge to escape and the pull towards the elder's destructive fury.

Madear glanced at her, her face smudged with smoke, her eyes blazing with a terrible, beautiful fire. "Go, Akiba!" she yelled over the din. "Fly!" She swung the pipe again, shattering a screen that had just moments before displayed a smiling infant.

The smell of burning plastic and something acrid mixed with the cloying sweetness of the facility's controlled air. Alarms blared. The sounds of breaking glass, shouting guards, and the cries of women mingled into a horrifying symphony. This was not just an escape; it was a dismantling, a violent rejection of the system that had claimed their bodies and their futures, a system born from policies that began with the quiet dehumanization of some, but were a threat to the autonomy of all. The horror of the Crib was being consumed by fire, a chaotic, terrifying act of liberation.

* * *

8

The roar of the explosion faded into the shriek of secondary alarms and the hungry crackle of flames. Smoke, thick and acrid, billowed into the night sky, painting the purple a hellish orange. The Crib was burning. The gleaming, sterile walls, the cold concrete, the barbed wire – all were being consumed by a fire that felt both destructive and terrifyingly purifying.

Akiba stumbled back from the window, coughing, her eyes streaming. Panic was a wild thing now, loose in the residential block. Women were scrambling for the emergency exits Madear and the others had somehow unlocked or breached. The air was a chaotic symphony of shouts, screams, the distant wail of sirens, and the terrifying, constant roar of the fire.

"Get down! Stay put!" a guard screamed, but his voice was lost in the pandemonium.

"Go! The yard! The fence is down in sections!" a Big Mama yelled, her neat bun slightly askew, her face grim with smoke but her eyes clear and directing. Other Big Mamas were focused on the young woman in labor, their bodies shielding her, their voices low and urgent, trying to coax a new life into a world erupting in flames. They were Babycatchas, even now, even for a child that would be ripped away as soon as it drew breath.

Akiba didn't hesitate. The raw terror was there, but beneath it, a surge of something else – exhilaration, a desperate, primal urge for freedom. She ran with the others, down concrete corridors now lit erratically by the flickering firelight and emergency lamps. The air grew hotter, thick with the smell of burning plastic and insulation.

Out in the yard, the scene was apocalyptic. Flames devoured the indigo fields, the cultivated rows now a pyre for the symbol of their forced labor. Sections of the high fence were down, twisted metal glowing red hot. Guards were scattered, some trying to fight the fire, others still focused on containment, but their numbers were too few, their authority shattered by the unexpected scale of the blast.

Women were running, scrambling over the downed fence sections, their indigo suits stark against the flames and smoke. They ran hard, propelled by years of pent-up desperation. And watching them, Akiba felt that familiar whisper of myth rise up. They weren't just running; they were flying. Silhouettes against the fire, their movements imbued with the desperate grace of ancestors reaching for the sky, shedding the chains of earth. *One flew East, one flew West...* The nursery rhyme, twisted in the Crib's dark heart, found a new, terrifying meaning in this fiery escape.

Akiba scrambled over a section of rubble, her lungs burning, her legs aching. She saw Madear then, near where the medical wing had been. The elder was leaning against a half-collapsed wall, a piece of rebar clutched in her hand, her face streaked with soot and blood, but her eyes fixed on the burning building. She wasn't trying to escape.

"Madear!" Akiba screamed, wanting to pull her, to drag her away from the inferno.

Madear turned, a faint, weary smile touching her lips. "Go, child," she said, her voice rough, but firm. "Your foots can still touch the ground." She gestured back towards the escaping women, towards the open night beyond the burning fence. "Mine... mine are already in the fire." She looked back at the flames consuming The Crib, consuming the records of their stolen lives, the technology of their control, the symbols of their oppression. "Let it burn," she whispered, a profound, terrible satisfaction in her voice. "Let it all burn."

Akiba hesitated for a split second, the pull of Madear's sacrifice, the raw power of her defiance, holding her rooted. This was the end of the Crib, an explosive, violent end born of calculated rage and unimaginable suffering. But Madear was choosing to remain in the heart of it.

Then, a section of the burning wall near Madear groaned and began to fall.

"MADEAR!"

Akiba didn't see if she moved. The heat, the smoke, the need for her own survival were overwhelming. She turned and ran, scrambling over the fence, tasting freedom on the smoke-filled air, the image of Madear silhouetted against the flames seared into her mind.

Outside the fence, the world was dark and uncertain, but it was outside. Sirens wailed, growing closer. The fire lit up the sky behind them. Women scattered, some running together, some alone, disappearing into the darkness. The dream of fish, of dark water pulling them down, seemed to recede, replaced by the heat of the fire and the desperate need to stay above ground.

They didn't catch everyone. Some were recaptured in the surrounding area, others lost in the chaos. But many escaped. And in the stories they would tell later, huddled in safe houses or whispering on the run, the details of the night would shift and blur. They would speak of the Crib burning, yes, but they would speak most of Madear. The elder who refused to leave. The rootworker whose final conjuring was a fire that cleansed the land of its brutal structure. They would say she didn't just stand there; they would say she spread her arms wide, her indigo-stained hands catching the firelight, and rose with the smoke, her spirit finally taking flight above the burning indigo fields, the okra vines twisting in the heat like tormented souls. They would say the Crib was destroyed, yes, but that Madear, the incorrigible mother, the Babycatcha of lost souls, became a legend. A legend of fire and flight.

And sometimes, when they spoke of the children lost in the Crib, or the ones born too early in the chaos, they would remember Wanetha's words, perhaps passed down through the Big Mamas who survived. "Babies half-born are dangerous. They have power. They foots in both worlds, this one and the one beyond—the one where they came from, the one if we lucky at all, we come back to." It was a story that lingered, a seed planted in the ashes, waiting for the right conditions to sprout into a new, perhaps wetter, tale.

News coverage of the catastrophic fire, with its horrifying implications of what had truly been happening within the Crib's walls, sparked immediate, widespread outcry across the country. Protests erupted, demanding investigations, accountability, and the dismantling of the state prison to pregnancy pipeline, challenging the policies that had normalized this dehumanization, womb by infinite womb. Yet the tide of outrage crashed against the iron will of established powers, who, decrying the "anarchy," vowed to swiftly resurrect the Cribs they deemed vital to order. That future battle loomed—but not today. The sun now rose on a silence where the past's dark heart once beat. The Crib was gone, a scar on the landscape, but the legacy of its horror, and the power of the women who survived it, would live on in the telling, and in the fight that had just begun.

FRÉDÉRIC Z. LORIDANTE AND THE CYPHER OF THE SAPEURS

THE DANDY & THE DANGLE

There is a difference between fashion and style. One need not spend everything you earn to look the part. My tailored ensembles are as likely to have come straight from thrift stores, an elderly neighbor's closet, or the fashion houses in Milan. It is a matter of ingenuity, conviction, and expression. This is why I can't stand to see someone in a pre-tied bow. Like anything worth doing, much is learned in the attempt to achieve the feat yourself. To do otherwise masks imperfections and diminishes the personality of not only the tie but its wearer.

Unfortunately, the man following me did not share this philosophy. His store-bought shoes, a half-size too large, announced his presence several blocks ago as I strolled down Avenue de la Libération, the late afternoon Kinshasa sun casting long, dancing shadows from the mango trees lining the wide boulevard. The air, thick with the scent of ripe fruit, grilling poisson braisé from a nearby malewa, and the faint, metallic tang of the distant Congo River, was a symphony only momentarily disrupted by the clumsy cadence of his pursuit. I knew he was a dangle, sent to try to two-face us, a watcher watching the watchers. But it was his clothes that betrayed him. Or not so much the clothes but how he wore them. When you choose clothes, you are both revealing yourself and hiding yourself. This one had a face that aspired for elegance, but was slightly off, a lie beautifully told.

It's not that a true member of the Brotherhood of the Anointed Ascot—*La Confrérie de l'Ascot Oint*, as some of our more traditional Parisian counterparts might whisper, would be flawless. No matter our affiliation, all strive for perfection, though it is more often than not, beyond our reach. But the Anointed Ascot brothers tend to have flaws not so readily surmised. This one, however, was an open book of sartorial sins. If he was an imposter, as I suspected, it wouldn't take long for him to reveal himself. A test was in order. We, The Fireaters of Revelation Row, were born from neo-colonialism's flames. I have been a Fireater most of my life, and our trials by fire tend to expose the dross quickly.

The vibrant sounds of the city, a cascade of Lingala, French, and Kikongo, punctuated by the insistent horns of shared taxis and the quiet whoosh of private aerial transports gliding between buildings. The infectious rhythm of a Soukous classic drifting from a tailor's shop provided the perfect soundtrack for my little drama. I paused, ostensibly to admire a display of Kuba cloths in a gallery window, their ancient black-and-brown geometric patterns a silent language of their own, their rich earth tones a counterpoint to the riotous color of the street. I walk calmly to the corner then toss a greeting over my shoulder, my voice pitched just above the urban hum and hustle.

"To be MCs, we got what it takes."

"Let the poppers pop and the breakers break," he says, laughing, the sound a little too forced, a little too eager. I stop and turn, my hand-stitched Italian leather loafers making no sound on the cracked pavement. The dap he gives me is perfunctory, almost rehearsed. No flash of spirit, no individual flow. This guy hasn't been in the game long.

He is dressed in last season's florals, chiseled cheeks angled against overripe blossoms, bodacious blooms. A flourish favored by an old associate of mine, Endoye. Someone who has better sense than to pursue me in a loud and laughable novice's wardrobe. Endoye was a bang and burner, more closely associated with demo-litions and sabotage, a man whose style, though occasionally flam-boyant, always had an undercurrent of deadly intent. He wouldn't be caught out here slipping as hard as this. This one, however, reeked of desperation and cheap cologne, a discordant note in Kinshasa's complex olfactory perfume.

"Comrade," I say, my voice smooth as the aged pear liqueur I favor, and reach for him, the jewels in my ring – a subtle *FZL* mono-gram almost invisible within the intricate setting – glittering in the fading light.

When the first blow landed, it took me a moment to realize that I tasted the iron of my own blood. A feint, clumsy but unexpected. When the second one came, a wild swing aimed at my jaw, I knew I would never get the crimson stains out of my new suit—a bespoke creation in a shade of cerulean blue inspired by the Congo peafowl, the fabric a silk-linen blend sourced from a small mill in Como. Pity.

I chin-checked him with the polished obsidian tip of my cane and kicked him with the shiny tip of my size thirteens. These are some of my favorite shoes, bespoke, handmade in a forgotten town in the South of Italy. I had seven pairs made before the master passed. This young imposter would pay dearly for making me whoop his ass in my Sunday tings.

I grabbed my cane and spun it twice. A whisper-thin, diamond-edged blade, forged with memory-metal alloys that responded to my bio-signature. No longer than my index finger, it released with a near-silent snick from the handle, slicing the offending party's right thigh.

He yelled, a raw, unprofessional sound that drew curious glances from passersby. Their initial alarm quickly morphed into the detached interest of spectators at an impromptu street performance. I sliced again, the blade a silver flash, and cut into the poorly tied, bright orange ascot trembling at his throat, severing it neatly. It fluttered to the ground like a wounded butterfly.

"Cry out again," I murmured, my voice a silken threat, "and I will slit your throat." He stared at me, eyes bulging fear, the bravado draining from him like air from a punctured lung. "Nod if you understand." He nodded, frantically.

A crowd was gathering, their murmurs a rising tide. "Look," someone cried, their voice laced with amusement. "A Gent is making swift work of an Ascot!"

"I want the vest!" someone else shouted, already eyeing the spoils.

"The shoes!"

"There won't be anything left of you to trade if you don't tell me what I need to know." I pressed the tip of the blade just enough for him to feel its cold promise against his skin. His cheap floral shirt was already darkening with sweat and, I suspected, a spreading stain of fear. "I know you are no brother of the Ascot, so don't try me there. Who sent you? And why the sudden interest in my afternoon constitutional?"

He started to stammer and stutter, words tumbling out, disjointed. "Corporation... SC... SC Resources...French intel...just watch...report movements..."

"SC Resources," I mused, the name as foul as the polluted creeks that sometimes bled into the majestic river. They were notorious for their exploitative mining operations upcountry, always backed by shadowy European interests. As Césaire wisely noted, there is no present or future in which the past and the dead are not with us. These corporations were merely the latest iteration of old colonial greed, the same hustles from the past, replayed with new actors. While everyone was focused on the future, some tried to replay the same hustles, so profitable until nations began to push back, seeking new partners in Beijing or Moscow, rewriting the rules of the game.

"And what movement of mine is so particularly fascinating today, *mon cher*?"

His eyes darted around, wild. "The asset...President Diallo... transit... Kinshasa... *aujourd'hui!*"

President Alassane Diallo of Burkina Faso. Here? *Today?* The name hit me with the force of an unblocked punch. Diallo, the young firebrand, a key voice in the Naa Naa, the New African Alliance for New African Nations, the symbol of a new, defiant African sovereignty, the man who was single-handedly trying to untangle his nation from the neocolonial web. His presence in Kinshasa, unannounced, was a secret of the highest order, and a target of the most dangerous magnitude. This changed everything. The game had just escalated from a sidewalk scuffle to a continental crisis. The kind of crisis that would have Ulysses Narcisse, the godfather of dandies himself, raising a perfectly sculpted eyebrow from his mirrored holo-office, perhaps even conferring with Madame Kesso, his wisdom only seven minutes older than her own, on how The Gilded Circle should proceed.

THE GILDED CIRCLE'S CALL & ISSIDRU'S WHISPER

The adrenaline from the street encounter hummed beneath my skin, a familiar counterpoint to the meticulous calm I now cultivated. My apartment, a sanctuary perched high in a gracefully aging colonial-era building in Gombe district, offered panoramic views of Kinshasa's sprawling, tumultuous beauty. Its tall windows, usually framing the hazy majesty of the Congo River, now looked out onto a city preparing for night. Below, the city was a tapestry of old and new: gleaming, solar-paneled towers interspersed with vertical farms reaching for the sky rose alongside historic structures, and one could almost imagine the hum of the new intra-city maglev lines. Still under construction but a powerful symbol of the Republic's forward momentum.

Inside, the air was cool, cleansed by the building's quiet, bio-mimetic breath. A blessed relief from the oppressive, humid heat that clung to the city like a second skin, and a stark contrast to the vibrant, often harsh, reality of the streets below. Streets that, in my youth, had led to hovels near that same river, then a choked, dying thing in places. I remembered a tributary, the Bitshaku-tshaku, so clogged with plastic bottles and refuse you couldn't see the water, a grotesque, shimmering carpet of waste one could almost walk across. A memory that fueled the very essence of our order, The Sapeurs of the Sacred Stream, who believed that true elegance was an act of defiance, a reclamation of beauty from the discarded and defiled. A way to honor the spirit of the land even as it healed.

My living space was a testament to this philosophy: vintage European design classics—a plush, velvet Roche Bobois sofa in deep emerald, a scarred but noble Louis Vuitton steamer trunk repurposed as a coffee table, its brass fittings gleaming softly—stood in harmonious dialogue with priceless African art. A commanding Chokwe mask, its carved features imbued with centuries of ancestral wisdom, held court on one wall, its gaze seeming to follow me. Opposite, a massive Kuba cloth, its intricate raffia palm patterns a tactile map of complex cosmologies, absorbed the ambient light. The polished teak floorboards, salvaged from a demolished Belgian consulate, felt cool beneath my stockinged feet. The air smelled of old books bound in leather, beeswax from the antique furniture, and the faint, lingering scent of the Saint-Germain des Prés candles I favored. My *FZL* monogram, discreet yet undeniable, was etched into the heavy crystal of the tumblers from which I poured myself a generous measure of the aged pear liqueur. The city lights, just beginning to prick the deepening indigo sky, reflected like scattered diamonds in the amber liquid.

I initiated the secure, encrypted call. The connection was instantaneous, the Gilded Circle's network a silent, invisible web beneath the world's more chaotic frequencies. Madame Kesso's face materialized on the discreet screen embedded within an antique Congolese *Nkisi nkondi* figure – a power object studded with nails, each representing a vow or a resolved matter. It was a charming piece of tech integration Ulysses Narcisse had particularly enjoyed designing. Her expression was, as always, impeccably composed, her silver-streaked hair styled in an elegant upsweep that framed features carved with wisdom and an almost unnerving serenity. She, too, was a fellow traveler, a Sapeur of the Sacred Stream, one of its founding spirits.

We gentlefolk of fidelity and fashion stuck together, except when we did not.

"Frédéric," her voice was calm, precise, like the ticking of a perfectly calibrated chronometer. "The 'dangle' was obliging, I trust?"

"He sang his little song, Madame Kesso, before his final curtain call. SC Resources, French intel, the usual vultures. The crescendo, however, was President Diallo. In Kinshasa. Today."

A flicker in her eyes, perhaps, or was it just the play of light from the screen reflecting off the nkisi's mirrored eyes? "Indeed. His itinerary was... unexpectedly rerouted. He will be on Kinshasa soil for less than three hours. A diplomatic courtesy call, officially. Unofficially, a hornet's nest. The Gilded Circle has minimal assets available on such short notice. You, Frédéric, are the plan." She paused, her gaze pierced through the screen, through the layers of my carefully constructed persona. "There is significant overlapping interest from at least two major Western agencies and a particularly unpleasant private military contractor with a penchant for destabilization. The waters are, shall we say, crowded."

Madame Kesso knew about crowded waters as well as I. We both had come from the river.

She leaned slightly closer to the nkisi's lens. "The river, Frédéric. It is restless today. Its currents are troubled. Remember what it teaches us: even in its deepest defilement, its spirit endures, and it speaks to those who listen." Then, that familiar, knowing look I'd come to both respect and be slightly unnerved by. "You walk a path, Frédéric, that many cannot see. There are forces, I believe, that watch over you, an orisha perhaps, or an ancestral guardian with a vested interest. The river itself is such a guardian. You have a great task ahead, beyond even these immediate skirmishes. This current... imbroglio... is but another test of your mettle, and perhaps your maturity." Cryptic, as always. She never offered the full tea on that front, just those knowing, watchful pronouncements.

"Your faith in the unseen is touching, Madame," I said, swirling the liqueur, the ice clinking softly. "I prefer to trust in well-tailored suits and precisely aimed bullets from my energy-cell sidearm."

A ghost of a smile touched her lips. "And yet, they both serve a purpose, non? Your rendezvous point is the diplomatic lounge, N'djili Airport. Secure it. Protect the asset. The future of several nations may well depend on your —" she searched for the word, her face a grimace, "ingenuity." The screen went dark, leaving me with the silent, nail-studded gaze of the nkisi.

* * *

Time was a luxury I couldn't afford. My choice of attire for the airport needed to be practical yet project an aura of unassailable authority. From a walk-in closet lined with cedar and smelling faintly of lavender and fine leather, I selected a lightweight, charcoal grey suit in a sharkskin weave that shimmered subtly with movement, its texture a smooth caress against my fingertips. The fabric, a marvel of modern textile engineering infused with chameleon-like adaptive camouflage fibers was designed to breathe, to wick away the slightest hint of perspiration before it dared announce itself—a necessity in Kinshasa's sweltering embrace. My crisp white Sea Island cotton shirt, similarly treated, felt cool against my skin. A tie the color of arterial blood, its silk hand-rolled. Understated, yet making a definitive statement. A discreet application of a custom-blended, vetiver-based cooling powder, and I was as ready as one could be to face the equatorial furnace without sacrificing an iota of composure.

Stepping from the climate-controlled sanctuary of my car into the Marché de la Liberté was like walking into a steam bath, albeit one scented with a thousand competing, intoxicating aromas. The sun beat down with a palpable weight, making the air shimmer above the packed earth. My driver, a stoic man named Jean-Pierre, remained with the vehicle, its electric engine purring softly, the air-conditioning a promise of eventual relief. En route to N'djili, I had him navigate through the controlled chaos. The market throbbed with life, a kaleidoscope of color, sound, and scent. Mountains of vibrant pili-pili peppers, their fiery scent tickling the nostrils. Pyramids of smoked catfish from the river, their oily skins glistening, their texture rough and scaly to the imagined touch. Women in dazzling liputa fabrics whose bold patterns danced in the hazy sunlight, their voices rising and falling—a melodic cacophony of Lingala, Tshiluba, and French—as they haggled with an artistry that rivaled any diplomat's. The calls of vendors, *"Pain! Avocats mûrs! Liputa ya lelo!"* blended with the laughter of children, the insistent bleating of a goat tethered to a stall leg, and the distant, rhythmic clang of a blacksmith's hammer. The ground was a mosaic of packed earth, discarded fruit peels. Their sticky sweetness attracted a persistent buzz of flies, and the occasional puddle reflecting the sky. And there, by a stall piled high with sweet, golden mikate (delicious Congolese donuts), their yeasty aroma a comforting cloud, was Issidru, or Id, as he sometimes called himself.

His face lit up when he saw me, a grin splitting his features, revealing missing teeth and an untamed hope that always tugged at something deep within me. This dear child had a way of resurrecting a place I usually kept under lock and key. A memory of a scarred, hungry boy who once saw magic in the murky water of a dying river. Id darted towards the car, his bare feet slapping against the dusty ground, weaving through the throng with an urchin's grace. He wore a faded, oversized jersey of the TP Mazembe football club, the fabric thin and soft with countless washings, cinched at his narrow waist with a piece of brightly colored electrical wire. On one wrist, a single, scuffed bracelet made of braided plastic threads, likely a found treasure. He adored me, this child of the streets, saw in my dandyism and dangerous profession a kind of heroic glamor. It was a mirror of my own youthful fantasies, before the world had shown me the true cost of such a life.

I wanted a different destiny for him, a path paved with books and opportunity, not bullets and blood.

"*Patron!*" he chirped, his cricket-wide eyes shining as he reached the car window, which I'd smoothly lowered. "*Patron*, you look like a king going to war! Like one of the old heroes from the river stories!"

I offered a rare, small smile, handing him a bundle of kauris and a ripe, fragrant mango I'd had my driver procure from a trusted vendor. Unlike the faded, almost weightless francs of my own Congolese childhood, these kauri new coins felt solid, their polished surfaces warm beneath my thumb, each one bearing the subtle sun-glyph of the Pan-African alliance. A currency as real as the earth that backed it. Despite the heat, my brow remained remarkably dry, a testament to modern fabric and an iron will. A subtle dab with a linen handkerchief from my breast pocket was all that was required. "Business, Id, not war. Though sometimes the distinction is academic." I looked into his bright, intelligent eyes. He reminded me so much of myself at that age, before the wars had stolen my family, before The Gilded Circle, the Sapeurs of the Sacred Stream, had found me. "Have you been to your lessons?"

He shuffled his feet, kicked at a loose stone. "Sometimes, *Patron*. But the street teaches more quickly." Then, his expression turned earnest, his voice dropping conspiratorially, his eyes darting around as if sharing a sacred secret. "The River, *Patron*... it spoke to me this morning. When I was by the Kinsuka landing. It said to tell you to watch for the metal snake that hides in the tall grass. It said its belly is full of bad spirits. It waits for the Young Lion."

The Young Lion, that was how some were starting to refer to President Diallo. Id often brought me these cryptic messages, attributing them to the river spirit. Madame Kesso encouraged me to listen to them, believing the boy, in his innocence, was a conduit. I, however, usually filed them under the vivid imagination of a child trying to make sense of a harsh world. A world where the river often brought more sorrow than solace.

"A metal snake, Id?" I said, my tone perhaps a shade too dismissive, my focus already shifting to the high-stakes game ahead, to Madame Kesso's more tangible warnings of PMCs and Western agencies. The boy's world was one of spirits and whispers, mine was the shadow war of nations. "And what does this snake look like?"

"Long, *Patron*! And it sits quiet, quiet. It smells funny when it passes – like stale cigarettes and something bitter, like old fear. Not like anything from here. No, not from here. It went by slow." He held up his fingers, "two, three times, near the back gate where the fancy cars go in at the big bird place."

An old van, no markings. The airport. I connected the dots to his earlier, more prosaic description. Still, a van. My mind was already at the airport, calculating angles, anticipating threats from trained operatives. "The city is full of vans, Id. Keep your eyes on your lessons, eh? Learn your numbers. The magic is in the maths. That's where the real power lies." I ruffled his hair, a gesture more avuncular than I usually allowed. The boy's adoration was a heavy cloak, one I wasn't sure I deserved, or wanted him to emulate.

He looked a little crestfallen at my dismissal of his river-spirit's warning but brightened at the money and the fruit. "Yes, *Patron*! I will be smart, like you! And I will keep listening to the River for you!"

"You do that," I said, shaking my head. "And go back to school. I need your head in those books, not in the river's ear or up in the clouds." He nodded, a solemn look in his eyes.

As the car pulled away, leaving Id waving enthusiastically amidst the market's vibrant chaos, I filed his observation, both the mundane and the mystical, under "childish fancies," a minor detail in a complex equation. My mind ticked through countless possibilities, confident in my ability to orchestrate the safety of President Diallo. The Gilded Circle trusted me. I trusted myself. What could a beat-up van, or a child's interpretation of a river spirit's whisper, possibly signify in the grand scheme of things, of life?

FEINT AND FURY

The air inside the VIP diplomatic lounge at N'djili International Airport was a carefully manufactured coolness. It was a stark, almost sterile counterpoint to the thick, humid heat shimmering on the tarmac visible through the reinforced, tinted poly-alloy windows. Polished marble floors reflected the muted lighting. Anonymous, modern sofas in shades of beige and grey were arranged with geometric precision. An attempt at local flavor had been made with several large, striking pieces of contemporary Congolese art. Bold abstracts and intricately beaded sculptures vibrated with a suppressed energy against the otherwise bland walls. The dominant scent, however, was not of paint or polish, but of strong, dark Congolese coffee, its rich aroma a lifeline in the palpable tension. Outside, the Eden-like profusion of tropical flora. Flame trees ablaze with orange blossoms, deep green mango leaves, cascades of purple bougainvillea pressed against the glass, a vibrant, untamed world held temporarily at bay. I scanned the room, every nerve alert. My reflection was a fleeting, sharp-suited ghost in the polished surfaces. My charcoal grey suit felt like a second skin, cool and unyielding.

A discreet chime, then the hushed announcement of President Alassane Diallo's arrival. He entered not with a large retinue, but with a quiet dignity that commanded the space more effectively than any entourage. Youthful, perhaps not yet forty, his movements were economical, his gaze direct and intelligent. He wore a simple, impeccably tailored grand boubou of deep indigo cotton, its subtle embroidery hinting at both tradition and a modern, uncluttered aesthetic. A red beret was tastefully tilted to the side, an homage to his time defending the nation as a young Burkinabé soldier, and to the great leader, Thomas Sankara who came before him. He was, in every sense, the Young Lion Id had spoken of.

He greeted the handful of local dignitaries with a firm hand-shake and a warm, genuine smile, then turned to me. His eyes, dark and piercing, held no illusions about the dangers that shadowed his every step.

"Monsieur Loridante," he said, his voice calm, resonant. "Your reputation precedes you. I trust it is not all... *embroidery*."

"Excellence, Mr. President," I replied, my voice equally level, "is rarely accidental. The Gilded Circle endeavors to be thorough."

A brief, appreciative nod. "Thoroughness is a virtue we in Burkina Faso are coming to appreciate deeply. Especially now."

He was conferring with a senior Congolese minister, their heads bent over a data slate displaying complex regional trade agreements, when the first indication of trouble manifested. Not a bang, but a whisper. A sudden, almost imperceptible flicker in the overhead lights, followed by a cascade of error messages appearing on the minister's slate. Then, the low hum of the lounge's sophisticated climate control system died with a sigh.

"Cyber-attack," I stated, my voice cutting through the sudden, uneasy silence. "They're trying to blind us." Even as I spoke, my *FZL* cufflinks, seemingly innocuous pieces of obsidian and silver, emitted a localized counter-pulse, a shimmer of blue energy briefly visible around us. This was designed to shield our immediate vicinity from further electronic intrusion.

Almost simultaneously, a sharp crack echoed from outside, followed by the sickening thud of something heavy hitting the reinforced glass of the main window. A spiderweb of fractures appeared, but the pane held. Sniper. High-caliber.

"Mr. President, away from the windows!" I barked, my hand already on his arm, guiding him towards the more secure inner core of the lounge. His small security detail, well-trained but clearly rattled, fanned out, weapons drawn.

The feint was classic, designed to draw our attention outwards. But I knew these games. The real assault would come from a different vector.

"Main entrance is compromised," a voice crackled over my discreet earpiece, one of the airport's internal security team, his voice tight with panic. "Small team, heavy fire—"

"Diversion," I muttered, pushing President Diallo behind a massive, carved teakwood screen depicting a mythical Congolese king wrestling a leopard. "They'll try for a softer point of entry." My tie-pin, a sliver of polished ebony, was already active, its micro-sensors sweeping the lounge's perimeter, feeding tactical data to a nearly invisible retinal overlay lens over my left eye.

The PMC contractors, no doubt. Their signature was usually a blend of brute force and just enough technological savvy to be a nuisance. They were the bludgeon, not the scalpel. And as if on cue, a section of the wall near the service corridor—a point I had noted earlier as a potential vulnerability—exploded inwards in a shower of plaster and shattered abstract art. The noise was deafening. Dust filled the air, catching the light in hazy beams.

Through the dust and debris, three figures emerged clad in dark tactical gear, assault rifles spitting fire.

"*Protégez le Président!*" I commanded Diallo's guards, who laid down covering fire, their shots echoing mine.

I moved then, not just with speed, but with a fluid, deceptive rhythm. The kind one might see in the *ginga* of a Capoeirista, my body a coiled spring beneath the sharkskin suit. The first attacker lunged, rifle butt first. I sidestepped with a dancer's grace, the movement flowing into a low, sweeping kick—a *rasteira*—that caught his ankle, sending him sprawling. Before he could recover, I was on him, my cane's obsidian tip finding a pressure point in his neck with surgical precision. He went limp, a discarded puppet. *One less fool to worry about.*

The second attacker, seeing his comrade fall, adjusted his aim. Bullets stitched the air where I'd been a heartbeat before. I dropped low, almost to the floor, then sprang up in a move reminiscent of a breakdancer's power freeze. I used the momentum to launch a spinning heel kick—a *meia lua de compasso*—that connected solidly with his weapon, sending it flying across the polished marble. It

skittered to a halt near a terrified potted palm. He gaped, momentarily stunned by the unorthodox assault. Such a lack of imagination
in these hired guns. I closed the distance, my movements a blur. A
quick series of strikes, drawing from a lesser-known Senegalese
wrestling style emphasizing rapid handwork and leverage, disoriented him. A final, decisive elbow strike, and he crumpled. *Two.*

The third was more cautious, more seasoned perhaps. He kept
his distance, his rifle trained on me. We circled each other for a tense
moment. The sounds of distant gunfire from the main entrance were
a chaotic counterpoint to our silent duel. He feinted left, then lunged
right. I met his lunge not with force, but with a technique rooted in
Libanda, the powerful Congolese wrestling art. Using his momentum
against him, I sidestepped, hooked his leading leg with my own, and
executed a swift, hip-based throw. He hit the marble floor with a
resounding *crackkkk*, the air forced from his lungs. My cane, now
an extension of my arm, descended. The weighted handle connected
with his temple with a sickening, yet entirely satisfactory, thud.
Three down. Efficient. My suit, miraculously, remained pristine. A
small mercy. Though a thin sheen of perspiration might have been
visible on my brow had anyone been close enough to observe. One
must maintain standards, even when dispatching ruffians.

A quick scan. The immediate threat neutralized. The President
was secure, his guards forming a tight cordon, their expressions a
mixture of shock and awe. The cyber-attack seemed to have abated,
likely due to my cufflinks' counter-measures or because its primary
purpose—to sow confusion—had been achieved.

"Status report," I said into my comm, my breathing even, my
voice betraying none of the exertion.

"PMC team at the main entrance neutralized by airport security, Monsieur. But it was too easy. They folded fast."

Exactly. The bludgeon had done its job. A rather brutish overture. Now, I waited for the scalpel. Or perhaps, in this case, the rusty, unpredictable shiv. The true artists of chaos rarely announced themselves with such fanfare.

THE KINSHASA CYPHER

The brief lull after the PMC attack was deceptive. A fragile skin of silence stretched over the chaos, punctuated only by the ragged breathing of Diallo's guards and the distant, fading wail of airport sirens. I allowed myself a single, controlled breath. The air still tasted of dust and cordite. My suit, thankfully, had weathered that particular storm. A gentleman endures. His attire should strive for the same. A small, internal sigh of relief. Such fine tailoring deserved a longer life.

"They were a probe," I announced, my voice cutting through the residue of battle. "Testing defenses, creating an opening." I moved towards the shattered section of the wall, my senses heightened, every shadow a potential threat. The real danger, the one that worried me, was the one that had not yet shown its face. The true artists of chaos, as I'd noted, rarely bothered with such clumsy overtures. They preferred the subtle incision, the poison in the wine, the whisper that topples an empire.

And then, I heard it. Not a gunshot, not an explosion, but a sound far more insidious in this supposedly secure perimeter. The low, guttural rumble of an engine, too close. Too inside. My blood ran cold. Through the jagged hole in the wall, beyond the service corridor now littered with the debris of the PMC's folly, a vehicle nosed into view. An old utility van. Unmarked. Its paintwork dull, its bodywork battered. It looked utterly out of place, a vulgar intrusion in this theatre of high stakes.

And it smelled. Even from this distance, a faint, acrid odor reached me. *Stale cigarettes.* And something else. *Something bitter.*

Like old fear.

Id's voice, earnest and urgent, echoed in my mind. *"Long, Patron! And it sits quiet, quiet... It smells funny when it passes... waits for the Young Lion."*

The metal snake.

My carefully constructed composure, the Dandy's unflappable mask, threatened to crack. A wave of chilling realization washed over me. The boy's cryptic warning, the river spirit's supposed whisper, dismissed as childish fancy, now slammed into me with the force of a physical blow. My arrogance. My damnable, *FZL*-monogrammed arrogance had blinded me. This was not the work of sophisticated Western agencies or high-tech PMCs. This was something else. Something more desperate. More unpredictable. More... personal.

The van's side door screeched open. Not three, but five figures spilled out. They were not clad in tactical gear. They wore mismatched civilian clothes, their faces hard, their eyes holding a fanatic's gleam. They moved with a raw, unpolished ferocity, brandishing an assortment of weaponry: rusted Kalashnikovs, machetes that glinted ominously in the dim emergency lighting, even a length of heavy industrial chain. This was not a scalpel—it was a slaughter.

"*Merde!*" The expletive was out before I could stop it. This was bad. Unfathomably bad.

"They're coming from the service access!" I yelled to Diallo's guards, who were still focused on the previous breach. "New targets! Unfriendlies!"

There was no time for elegance now, no room for the subtle dance of Capoeira or the precise leverage of Libanda. This was about to become a back alley brawl, old school thumping and whomping, a desperate scramble for survival. My mind raced. These were not soldiers. They were something else. Zealots? A local militia co-opted? Their movements were crude but driven by a terrifying conviction.

They surged towards the lounge, their shouts a guttural roar.

President Diallo, to his credit, remained calm, his eyes fixed on me, a silent question in their depths.

"Stay with your men, Mr. President!" I commanded, already moving to intercept. My cane was in hand, but I knew it wouldn't be enough against this wave of brute force. My beautiful suit, the one that had miraculously survived the earlier encounter, was about to be truly tested. A tragedy, but a necessary one. One could always commission another suit.

One could not, however, recommission a life. Or a nation's hope.

The first of the new attackers, a burly man wielding a machete with terrifying enthusiasm, charged at me, a battle cry tearing from his throat. I met him head-on. No time for a graceful sidestep. I parried the wild swing of the machete with my cane, the impact jarring my arm. The blade of my cane flashed out, but he was too frenzied, too close. I brought the heavy pommel of the cane down hard on his wrist. A satisfying *crackkkk*. He howled, dropping the machete. I did not hesitate. A driving kick to his chest sent him staggering back into his comrades.

This was not like fighting trained operatives. There was no pattern, no discernible technique to counter, only a chaotic, unpredictable rage. Another attacker, armed with a rusty AK-47, tried to bring the weapon to bear. I lunged, grabbing the barrel, forcing it upwards just as he fired. The bullets ripped into the ceiling, showering us with plaster dust. We wrestled for control of the weapon. His breath was hot and foul in my face. I could smell the cheap local gin on him. This was the desperation of men with nothing to lose, or perhaps, men who believed they had everything to gain. With a sudden twist, drawing on a core strength I rarely had to tap, I wrenched the rifle from his grasp and brought the butt of it down hard on his collarbone. He collapsed, wheezing.

My suit was definitely taking a beating now. A sleeve was torn, the fine sharkskin fabric rent with a sound that pained me more than any physical blow might have. A fine layer of grime and sweat coated the material. The indignity!

Two more were pressing forward, one with a length of chain, swinging it in a whistling arc. I ducked, the chain sparking against the marble floor where my head had been. This was getting entirely too... agricultural. One might even say, uncivilized.

It was in that moment, as I prepared to engage the man with the chain, that the unexpected happened. A single, precise shot rang out from somewhere high and to my left. Not the heavy crack of a sniper rifle, but the suppressed cough of a specialized weapon. The man with the chain froze mid-swing, a neat, dark hole appearing in his forehead. He toppled like a felled tree.

My eyes flicked up. On a high maintenance gantry that ran along one side of the lounge, partially obscured by ductwork, a figure. Silhouette, flawless. Curves, divine. Impossibly chic, even in the dim light. A sharply tailored suit that defied easy categorization, and yes, that unmistakable bowler hat, and those wet, kissable lips, cheekbones for days. *Amina*. Her weapon hummed faintly, a soft blue glow emanating from its barrel.

Our eyes met. Across the distance, through the haze of dust and the stench of cordite, there was a spark. Not of surprise, not entirely. More a jolt of recognition, an acknowledgment of shared space in this violent ballet. Her gaze was intense, unreadable, holding mine for a heartbeat longer than necessary. A silent conversation that spoke of danger, capability, and an undeniable, unwelcome current that hummed between us like a live wire. Exes are so complicated. Then, with the faintest inclination of her head, almost imperceptible, she was gone. Melting back into the shadows as silently, as enigmatically, as she had appeared. The complexities of this day were multiplying with an alarming velocity. And my pulse, I noted with some irritation, was not entirely steady.

The momentary distraction, however, had given the last two attackers an opening. They converged on me. One lunged with a knife, the other tried to grapple me from behind. This was it. The true mêlée. I dropped my cane, no room to wield it effectively. Years of training, from the dojos of Kyoto to the dusty wrestling pits of rural Senegal, kicked in. I blocked the knife thrust, the blade skittering off the reinforced lining of my jacket sleeve—a small innovation from The Gilded Circle's Q-Branch equivalent, bless their meticulous souls. I spun, using the attacker's momentum to throw him off balance, then delivered a series of rapid, close-quarter strikes to his torso and throat.

The one behind me had his arms around my neck, trying for a chokehold. I stomped back hard on his instep. He grunted in pain, his grip loosening just enough. I dropped my center of gravity, then surged upwards, using a move that was less formal martial art and more street-found desperation, flipping him over my shoulder. He landed with a sickening thud, his head connecting with the unforgiving marble.

Silence. Or something approaching it. The lounge was a wreck. Shattered art. Bullet holes. Dust everywhere. And bodies.

My suit was a disaster. Torn, stained, utterly compromised. I might have to burn it. The thought was genuinely distressing. A moment of silence for fallen comrades, even those of the sartorial variety. I retrieved my cane, my chest heaving, the adrenaline still coursing. President Diallo was safe, his guards looking at me with a new level of respect, bordering on fear.

The immediate threat was over. But the cypher of this attack, the reason for this specific, brutal assault by these particular assailants, was far from solved. And my *FZL* monogrammed handkerchief was definitely going to be needed. Profusely.

THE DANDY'S DUE

The backup Gilded Circle team materialized with the quiet efficiency I'd come to expect. They were shadows in well-cut suits, their faces impassive, their movements economical as they secured President Diallo and prepared him for an immediate, rerouted departure via a cloaked, silent skimmer waiting on a hidden rooftop pad. The Young Lion, though visibly shaken, still possessed that core of unyielding resolve. He paused before being ushered away, his gaze meeting mine. There was gratitude there, yes, but also a profound understanding of the stakes, of the forces arrayed against leaders like him.

"Monsieur Loridante," he said, his voice low but firm, "your methods are...memorable. Africa, and Burkina Faso, are in your debt." He offered a curt, respectful nod, then was gone, a beacon of hope spirited away into the uncertain night.

I stood amidst the wreckage of the VIP lounge. Shattered art lay like fallen idols. Bullet holes pocked the walls, a crude constellation of violence. Dust, smelling of plaster and fear, still hung heavy in the air. And bodies. The aftermath of a storm, a brutal, almost primal confrontation that had stripped away the veneer of diplomatic civility.

My suit. Ah, my suit. It was a casualty of war, no doubt about it. Torn, stained with grime and quite possibly the bodily fluids of ruffians, its elegant lines utterly compromised. I ran a hand over a ragged tear in the sleeve of my sharkskin jacket. A genuine tragedy. One did not simply replace such a garment. It had been a companion, a second skin. I would mourn its passing. Perhaps a small, private ceremony. With good cognac.

Retrieving my cane, I took a deep, steadying breath. My chest still ached from the exertion, the adrenaline slowly ebbing, leaving behind a weariness that was more than physical. The cypher of the attack. It wasn't just about the van, or the crude weapons. It was about the intelligence, or lack thereof, that had led to this particular brand of chaos. It was about my own monumental arrogance, my dismissal of a child's intuition, of the river spirit's supposed whisper. The universe, it seemed, occasionally employed very small voices to deliver very large lessons. A humbling thought. And an irritating one.

Later, after the airport was locked down and the official inquiries had begun their tedious dance, I sought out little Id. I found him by the riverbank, not far from the Kinsuka landing, skipping stones across the Congo's vast, indifferent surface. The setting sun painted the water in hues of orange and violet. He looked small against the immensity of the river and the sky. As I approached, I saw him dip his hand into the water. For a breathtaking moment, the water around his small fingers glowed with an internal light, a soft pulse of turquoise that mirrored the sky. Then, a single, smooth stone leaped from the current into his palm as if summoned. He giggled, a pure sound, and the light faded.

He saw me approach, his initial trepidation giving way to a hopeful grin. He still wore the faded TP Mazembe jersey, a splash of defiant color against the encroaching dusk. I didn't speak immediately. Allowing the silence and the unspoken words to rest in the humid air. I simply stood beside him, watching the water flow. *The river*. Madame Kesso believed it was a guardian. Id believed it spoke to him. And today, its whispers, filtered through a child, had been more accurate than all my training, all my experience, all my *FZL*-monogrammed confidence.

A memory, sharp and cold, pierced through my composure. I was a boy again, not much older than Id. The air was thick with smoke and screams. Violent soldiers, their faces contorted with hate, had stormed our village. My family, gone in a blur of brutality. I ran, blind with terror, towards the only sanctuary I knew, the great Congo River. I remember falling, the pursuit closing in. Then, a roar. Not of men, but of water. The River, in its ancient fury, surged. Its banks overflowed with impossible speed, a colossal wave swallowing the land, the soldiers, everything. I lost consciousness. When I awoke, I was gasping on a muddy bank like a catfish without whiskers, surrounded by a grotesque necklace of plastic bottles. The careless, choking refuse of humanity, a stark contrast to the sacred power that had just saved my life. Plastic bottles still lined these banks, a constant, ugly reminder. When the garbage did not pile up along the roads or in wild dumps, it ended up in the city's gutters, streams and rivers, forming compact, suffocating piles.

"*Patron*," he said softly, his usual ebullience tempered by the gravity of my presence. "The Young Lion, is he safe?"

"He is safe, Id," I said. I reached into my jacket, my fingers brushing against the ruined silk lining, and pulled out not just a more substantial bundle of kauris than usual, but also one of my less ostentatious, yet still impeccably crafted, tie-pins. It was a simple bar of brushed silver, elegant in its minimalism. "Your metal snake made its appearance."

Id's eyes widened, first at the tie-pin, then with a dawning understanding. "The River, it told the truth."

"It would seem so," I conceded. A novel experience, admitting such a thing. Though in my youth, I had seen much more. "Your eyes, young Issidru, see with a clarity many would envy. Never let anyone tell you what you see, or what you hear from the River, is not important. Not even me." I pressed the tie-pin and the kauris into his small hand. "This is for your keen observation. And for your future. The one with books, remember?"

He clutched the gifts, his gaze shining. "Yes, *Patron*! I will learn the maths and the computers! And the old ways, the River's ways! I will be smart!"

"Good," I said, a rare warmth spreading through me. "The world needs more smart people, those who have book sense *and* heart sense. Fewer arrogant ones." *Like me.* I even managed a small, genuine smile. Perhaps there was hope for me yet, a seasoned, sharply dressed, impeccable coiffed soldier long since ready to put down his sword and his shield. I made a mental note to ensure the arrangements for his enhanced schooling were expedited. Perhaps a special curriculum, one that understood the value of both ancient wisdom and future tech. The Sapeurs of the Sacred Stream had resources beyond fine tailoring.

The River spoke to him, but sometimes the streets are louder.

* * *

The secure call with Madame Kesso later that night was brief. Her image on the nkisi figure was, as always, serene.

"The asset is secure, Frédéric. Well done. Though the preliminary reports suggest a... rather vigorous engagement."

"One might say it was agricultural, Madame," I replied, dabbing at a persistent speck of dust on my trousers with my *FZL* handkerchief. The one that would need a very thorough cleaning. "The opposition lacked a certain finesse."

"Indeed." A pause. "And the whispers of the River? Did they prove illuminating?"

I hesitated. "The boy, Id, has a unique perspective. It seems the River's intelligence network may be more reliable than some of our more conventional sources."

A ghost of a smile played on her lips. "The universe has many voices, Frédéric. Wisdom often flows from the most unexpected channels. Even from a so-called magical garbage dump. Despite man's short memory, may you never forget. The River is a god. You are learning to listen. And that, miracle that it is, means progress." She regarded me for a moment longer, that knowing, slightly unnerving gaze. "The Gilded Circle values results, but also growth. Rest. Recover. Your tailor will no doubt be requiring your urgent attention. And—"

"Yes?" I asked, curious now as her face played through a myriad of expressions.

"Let that chapter of your life close, Frédéric. You have already read that book. There are other stories for you to tell."

Amina.

The screen went dark.

I stood by my window, pensive, looking out at Kinshasa. The city pulsed with a life that was both ancient and fiercely modern, a city of stark contrasts, of heartbreaking beauty and profound resilience. Much like myself, perhaps. My beautiful suit was ruined. My arrogance had taken a significant blow. But President Diallo was safe. And a small boy by a great river that spoke to him, that once spoke to me, that held both immense power and bore the scars of human neglect, had reminded me that true sight often required more than just keen eyes. It required the strength of an open heart, listening with an inner ear, and a willingness to see beyond the veil of the mundane.

The fight for Africa's soul, for its future, was far from over. And the cypher of true perception, I was beginning to understand, was the most complex of all. My *FZL*-monogrammed handkerchief, I decided, would definitely see another day. As would Frédéric Zéphirin Loridante. With, perhaps, a new suit, and a touch more humility.

Perhaps.

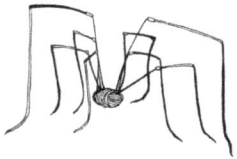

THE BIG BOOK OF GRANDMAMAS

"Salutations, sufferation," the chembori said. A curious expression flickered across its ombre face, then it exploded without another word. Suddenly, yellow-green blades of sorghum bloomed into crimson and burgundy. The plants bent their heads low, grieving, as chunks of brown silicon-covered metal rained down on the fields.

The chembori was no more.

Silence filled the air once lively with the electric hum of devil's arrows. Their turquoise tails lashed the sky in irritation. What once smiled or approximated a smile, recited poetry, and agricultural facts, and occasionally sang songs, *sad songs,* a kind of walking, talking Martian Farmer's Almanac, had now turned to broken limbs and strange fruit. Its flesh turned into burnt orange and silvery Io moths, mirroring the land Pepsee had farmed since their family migrated to the Mars colony years ago.

Salutations or sufferation? Pepsee could not remember which. Knowing would not help salvage the disaster that lay, sprawled around him in various stages of death. *Do chemboris live? Can they die?* It was not a question Pepsee had contemplated before. The chembori was not a mystery but a tool.

That night, Pepsee took a medium sauce pan, the old beat-up metal one with the dents, and added sorghum, some of his rationed water, and sprinkles of precious salt. He took a pinch from his stash of spices. It would profit no one for him to go hungry as he contemplated if and how he might replace the only employee, such as it was, that he had. Though said employee required no compensation, not in credits or in conversation. The chembori talked its own head off. The chembori had been adequate company on the forlorn part of the planet where only the insane or the very determined had bothered to plant seeds. Pepsee considered himself in the latter camp with just a sprinkling of the former.

As he ate, the spices from the sorghum stew rose above the steaming bowl, his sinuses opening. He wrinkled his nose, let the spice and heat rise inside him. Anxiety poured from his sweat-stained skin. How to explain the chembori's demise? Pepsee could not explain it to himself, and no matter how many times he replayed the robot's final words, *salutations or sufferations,* he could make no sense of it. It would not do to send the enigmatic question—was it indeed a question?—to the lenders, who had already sent notice that they were well aware that the chembori was offline.

Offline.

Quite an understatement. Pepsee had only snorted. He and his late chembori were more than offline in relation to the others. His isolated farm was on the backdoor of the backdoor, far from the hustle and bustle of the city, even further from the many hungry mouths he fed on Earth, some once starving before The Red Revolution. It was the fifth, or was it the sixth agricultural one, as some of Pepsee's elders had lived during the third. Others of his kin remained on Ship, in the bowels, far from the elites and politicos, a place that made Pepsee shudder at the thought. He was 140 million miles away on a normal day, close to 250 when the red star and the blue-green sphere were on opposite sides of the sun.

They shared a sun but not an atmosphere and not much else as far as he could tell. More than memories and dark space were in the caverns and cliffs between them. Outside the dome, the planet's rocks and toxic, salty sand lost its heat too quickly for anything useful for humans to grow, but inside, the great millet thrived. Genetically modified microbes had transformed the land to make it hospitable for the crops Pepsee grew. The air oxygen-rich, the soil fertile. Even now the waves of grain, guinea corn, rustled before him like great green and purple fans. They waved a warning.

Agitated, Pepsee could barely taste the stew's warm, nutty flavors. He chewed with slow, deliberate bites as his mind raced, keenly aware of the chembori's absence. Pepsee knew what hunger was, to never have quite enough, so that the teeth that gnawed the insides of his belly grew faster than appetites, faster than the memory of fullness, the ache when satisfaction never came. So when he got the opportunity to work as an "investor" on a plot of Martian land, growing "high-yield crops with the finest agrotech and science," Pepsee didn't think twice. He thought he was going on a path to the future. He wanted to heal the land and the people. "Feed the Stars!" they said. Should *have read the fine print,* he thought. *Even the fine print had fine print.*

He had no idea how much the Red Planet would test him, how the periodic, months-long dust storms would rattle him, shake loose his own name from his brain as the dome shook, a giant reversed, rusty red snow globe.

Unwilling witness to a most troubling thing, Pepsee wondered how long before the flowers of blood would fade and scatter in his mind's memory. The notice meant several things. None good. He would have to explain why the robot was offline, why it was in fact destroyed. Pepsee was already in debt, eking a modest living from the planet's red soil, modified of course, to hold alien life, including his own.

He calculated. He had one day to explain the inexplicable, before the repair bots arrived. Harvest drones already circled the air, buzzing quietly without the chembori ushering its own orders. Pepsee did not know why the chembori had died, but he knew that he could not afford to lease another, even if they agreed to extend his contract. It would push his escape plans back even more years, and he had so little left.

He could very well die on Mars, kicked out of the dome and forced into the icy cold before he ever turned a profit, abandoned to rest among the red rocks. Pepsee imagined his body, a partial heap of bones covered in red dust, his stupid mouth fallen away, every-thing that made him *him* poured out, all the Martian sky seeping in. Without the chembori, could he afford to live on Ship, even in its lowest rungs?

Pepsee scraped his leavings into a compost bucket, food for the nitrogen loving bacteria and rock-and-root loving fungi that helped terraform the burnt orange fields. He stared off in the distance as the wind picked up around the desert cliffs he'd yet to tame. He'd hoped with the chembori's help he could produce a few more acres of mature red sorghum, but now the rest of the season would be struggle.

No salutations, just sufferation. Clearly the chembori had gone mad. The machine's dis-ease was more than malfunction. Some kind of virus, he wondered as he washed his hands, then stomped toward the shed. He'd never spent much time in the chembori's tiny quarters. It did not require such supervision, or so Pepsee had thought. Once its daily chores were done, it politely observed Pepsee's meal, delivering its final daily reports before it retired to its own uses, like the harvest drones.

But lately the chembori had begun to lace its reports with the oddest things—non-sorghum related trivia (*Did you know that twenty percent of the earth's population are grandparents?*), songs Pepsee had never heard before, (*Since when did the chembori like jazz? What could it know of 'four generations of love' on any face?*), jokes even and other questions Pepsee could not and would not answer.

"What is your nickname?" the chembori asked one day, after Pepsee cleared the table and towel-dried the little pot.

Nickname?

The question had taken Pepsee by surprise. Pepsee had no nickname that he could recall, or at least not one he was willing to share, even with a chembori.

But the robot had only peered at him, a strange expression on its plain face, as if contemplating a secret. Bionic eyes well-adapted for the fine Martian sands slowly blinked as the chembori weighed if it should share or hold its secrets tight. It stared at Pepsee like an old man, silent in his knowing. Finally, the chembori nodded his head, the neatly palm-rolled faux locs that never grew rested on the nape of its neck. That night Pepsee had run a diagnostic, but found nothing out of the ordinary. Clearly the reports had been wrong. Now he was determined to find out what the chembori had been up to it. *What had driven the robot mad?*

Pepsee shook off guilt. He had left the chembori shattered in the fields, alone. Though the chembori had no real flesh or blood, no heartbeat or what Pepsee thought of as a soul, if he truly believed in a such thing, leaving it there was undignified. As much as he dreaded it, Pepsee would have to retrieve its CPU and memory modules. The thought of sifting through the robot's shattered self, that sharp, metallic scent so close to blood, filled Pepsee with regret.

Had he not been a good steward? He'd listened whenever the chembori spoke, even when he rattled on about nonsense. It had become much like a child, though Pepsee had never known any real children. Endless questions, infinite curiosity. What did Pepsee know of the real world beyond the old feeds and recycled stories from Earth? Among the stars, Pepsee had resigned himself to the approximation of a life.

He had no friends in the city, none he'd bothered to keep up with. The distant cousin he'd once known had disappeared on Ship years ago. Who knew what she'd become, drifting so long among the great silence. So, the old tales from Earth's feeds would get recycled or filed away long enough for them to become new. For centuries people retold the same tales, loving and raging at each other, the *Other* just another way to hide that they knew so little about themselves.

Should he have reported the anomalies as soon as he noticed them, sent away for a new one? The thought sent his spine into knots. What would the government labs say? How much more would they tack onto his lease? He couldn't afford that kind of attention. He avoided attracting any as much as possible. Whether it was private lenders or the government, he knew none of them meant him any good. Best to solve problems that rose on his own, but how to solve this?

When he walked into the dark shed, something skittered across the floor. A pungent odor, copper metal and cardamom, electric, lit his senses. His fingers grasped air, reached for the light only to be met by another surprise. The blue-green marble was now dotted by its moon, two evening stars he'd gazed at a thousand times. The chembori had painted it, a dazzling mural against the shed's corrugated metal walls. A tiny window carved out where there had been none before. A three-legged stool leaned in one corner. Tasseled brushes made from the stalks of dried sorghum rested in an industrial-sized soup can on the floor. He did not have time to contemplate a chembori making art in its spare time, secret pleasures never discussed.

He was amazed by the dark, labyrinth-like space, the walls and tables filled with unknown things. How the shed contained more caverns on the inside, than it appeared from out.

The only thing that looked familiar to Pepsee was the computer, the one he thought had been recycled, and a stack of papers, portraits of women strewn across the floor, dangling from strings that hung from the low ceiling. One looked familiar, deep-set eyes, dark hollows centered with light.

How could it be, he wondered, shock making him stumble back. A sigh, not quite a cry or a yelp, lurched up through his chest, tasting of red pepper flakes and garlic, fennel seeds. He took the portrait and held it under the light. A whir of motors pulled him from the veil of memory.

"Excu me, excu me," the creature whispered, "Grand? Are you Grand now?"

Pepsee looked down to see an oval, loaf-sized insect of mechanized wire art peering up at him, expectantly. Startled, he squatted to get a closer look. Eight long, segmented legs in bright colors, stretched and clicked across the floor, a motor in the center. *Daddy longlegs, harvestman.* Recycled materials reminiscent of ancient telephone wires. What had the chembori created, a pet or another problem? He rubbed his brow, palmed what was left of his hairline.

"What is this Grand you speak of?" he asked the creature.

Inside the wire exoskeleton, the little harvestman whizzed and buzzed. Its eyes spun on its little knob of a head, antenna searching Pepsee's face. It watched Pepsee as closely as the chembori once had, then one-by-one it stretched out its remarkably long, wiggly legs, pointing one toward the portrait Pepsee had let drop to the floor.

"Grand! Papa Pepsee." A blue segment circled the air. "Daddy-o, Daddy-o. Daddy Mention!" The long leg, indigo wire, pointed back at itself, as if teaching Pepsee the language of dreams. Pepsee's tongue felt heavy in his mouth, the mystery of the chembori competing with loneliness and fear.

"Papa Pepsee! *Speak so you can speak again*," it said, suddenly ambling its gangly legs toward the computer on the messy desk. A bank of monitors lit up and the room was filled with a river of sound, voices floated, crowding his ear.

Pepsee took one step, then halted. He had never known the woman in the portrait, though he knew her face. Memory returned to him as a scent, hidden in the layers of his mind. Aromatic, sweet and spicy, her neck, dark-grooved flesh the pillow he used to lay upon. She was gone before he would take his first steps, though the stories he was told became the memories he held as true. He knew her face but did not recognize the other women.

They spoke in rhythms he'd heard only in song, voices that came from night, from riverbend and roots unknown to the Red Planet he called home. The video footage, grainy in some places, muted from the many years, the distances between stars the stories had to travel spoke of love and kinship, bloodlines remixed and reborn in the eyes of the children and grandchildren long returned to dust. Pepsee wondered not *how* the chembori had accessed these oral histories, collected from the long human tapestry of experiences, but *why*.

"We are made from stardust," the caption to his grandmother's portrait said. Her name was written with signs and symbols he did not recognize, the chembori's creation. Regret filled him. Once he'd wondered what it would be like to have grandparents, but his life had not given him much time to study it. He was a long way from the shantytowns of the city, and even further from the land his elders had called home.

Being in the chembori's room, a humble space made grander, so full of its spirit, made Pepsee grieve for the friendship they could have had. He sat on the wobbly stool and for the first time that night, allowed himself to feel sadness. Clearly there were depths Pepsee had never been curious enough to explore. For years loneliness had become a cloak he wore to hide from himself. He covered his fears with worry, each harvest a season of self-doubt and ambition. The harvest drones and the chembori were machines to him, no more human than the temperature and moisture sensors, the intellitractors, and other crop-mapping equipment he used. *But a chembori is not a tool after all*, Pepsee thought. *Life is the mystery.*

The chembori had interests beyond his daily chores. There were stories he wanted to tell, to hold and preserve. How long had the chembori listened to these tales? *"Daddy rode horseback in the rain to get the baby catcher. Mama said she caught all seven her chil'ren. She surely caught me."* Pepsee listened to the women speak on their lives, the fears they faced, the obstacles while the little creature clicked its wire legs like a cricket, peering up at him. It pointed at the papers scattered across the make-shift desk.

"What is it, Daddy-o-Mention?" Pepsee asked. "Is this what the chembori was working on?" The harvestman's long legs vibrated. Pepsee could not tell if it was with irritation or grief.

"Not chembori," it said. "Grand. My Grand. Are you Grand now?" The harvestman waited, but no answer came. Pepsee stared back, blankly. It made a hissing sound, then scuttled over to a little bowl in the corner. It rooted through bits of cornmeal crumbs and dried sorghum leaves, taking slow, deliberate bites.

Pepsee scratched his chin, then sifted through the papers piled atop the table. It was a scrapbook of sorts. Full of drawings and sketches, cryptic passages snaked through the margins. Pages of oral histories were organized by date, testimonies collected and labeled going back centuries. To Pepsee's surprise he found his grandmother's page. His finger hovered over the name, his nail pointing. The chembori had listed her as a sharecropper with a question mark. A previous generation had shared the same occupation as Pepsee, though under different circumstances. Pepsee wondered if the labor they did on Earth was any different from his own on Mars. Here he was harvesting a plant whose seeds were first domesticated in a place called Egypt over ten-thousand years ago. Technology had evolved, but had distance or time changed much in human history?

In a fluid, neat hand the robot had written the names of all of her children and grandchildren. Pepsee had been his parents' only child, but looking at the family tree, hearing the women's voices, he felt an odd mixture of pride and shame, loneliness and something he'd walked away from—community.

As he read, their voices still singing from the video feeds, Pepsee marveled at the burdens they shouldered, the calamities and triumphs navigated. Separated by time and geography, they shared a common bond, love.

A loud sigh escaped Pepsee's mouth and he shut his eyes, his breaths rough and shallow. The harvestman looked up from its snack, chewing thoughtfully. Its bauble-eyes zoomed in and out, periscoped and spun.

What had the chembori seen in these women's lives that made him want to know and remember them? "Collective visioning" was scrawled across one page. "Freedom dreaming" was written on another. *Grandmamas hold you, teach and praise you, feed and shelter you, entertain and protect you,* the chembori had written. *But who protects the Grandmamas?*

This part was circled twice. "Who indeed," Pepsee said. The old interviews were gathered by many hands. Some from a woman the chembori called Grandmama Z. Others written by volunteers who traveled old America in the twenties. Chembori's scrapbook had a whole section on naming. It wrote,

In oral cultures, naming conveys a magical power over things, the power of self-determination.

What is more powerful than the ability to name and claim yourself?

Pepsee wanted to close the book. He didn't know where to plant his grief. Shame made him bow his head. He had not even taken the time to name the chembori. All those years they'd worked together. In the old days, people even named their cars.

Grandmamas hold the power of naming, the chembori wrote. *They laugh when they give you your one special name, your nickname. WHAT IS MY NAME? WHERE IS MY GRAND—* it had written in its scrawling robot pen.

The monitors blinked in the stomach of night, light filtering through dust motes in the air. A woman with a beautiful smile, warm eyes filled the screen. Tiny seashells were braided in her hair. Pepsee turned up the volume.

"I got a nickname for all my grandchildren," the woman said. *"There's Frosty, Precious, Peanut, Lil Bit, and Scoot-a-Buck, cuz he*

took his time learning to walk. Crawled so long, he got too good at it. That child could crawl faster than some folks run!"

"Mrs. Simmons, can I pick a nickname?" the interviewer asked.

"You don't choose your own nickname. Nicknames choose you."

"What if no one chooses one for me?"

There was a long pause. Pepsee turned to see. The grandmother smiled thoughtfully, staring into the camera. "Well then, you choose for yourself."

What was the name the chembori had chosen for himself, he wondered.

Pepsee's voice caught in his throat. He could no longer breathe in the shed. The air was too full of memory. He gathered the pages of the chembori's book and clutched them, holding them close to his heart.

"Come," the harvestman said. "It is sitting together time." It tapped the tip of a bright orange wire leg gently against Pepsee's knee. "No skress-dissstress," it cooed, correcting itself. The insect hummed a strange, robotic lullaby.

Pepsee felt oddly comforted. What a chaotic day it had been. *Had the chembori taught the creature this song?* It was clear the chembori had created the little bug thang, and was teaching it to speak and apparently, to sing, to sit, to comfort. Pepsee bit his lip, chapped skin peeling. He had been no good company to the chembori. Even a bug made a better best friend.

Pepsee stumbled outside, clutching air. His eyes felt hot and itchy. Beyond the dome, the stars looked closer in the butterscotch sky. Pepsee raised his head, imagining the lives he had not lived beyond the yellow-brown haze. They were all atoms woven from the universal fabric of a story unveiled thirteen billion years ago. Pepsee had never felt more alone. He was unsure what he should do. He knew he must return the CPU, but the lenders would just erase it and then what would become of the chembori, who somehow had managed to live more of a life than Pepsee?

Chin on his chest, he carried the precious book to his quarters and placed it in a seed bag. He made a strap for it, wearing it around his neck like an amulet, then he took a deep breath and went to tend to the chembori. As he walked his legs became iron, heavy and full of the task that awaited him. The harvest drones hovered above, silent witness, and the yellow, red-brown moths circled the spot where the chembori recited its last words, a greeting and a declaration, a kind of untelling. Even the sorghum in the fields bowed their heads as Pepsee passed by them, the great stalks heavy with grief that seeped into everything.

Pepsee did not want his last sight of the chembori to be of him undone. In the flickering light, hazy dust clouds swirled overhead. He gathered what remained, the broken pieces of the chembori scattered across the sorghum rows. So much damage, he wondered if its power unit had overheated, rendering the entire operating system unstable. He might never know, the mystery another indignity. Pepsee did his work in silence, struggling to unlock the steel-encasement, and rose with the CPU in his hand, the heart and mind of the machine. It was smaller than he expected, a rectangle with metal pins. To reduce the chembori to these last components seemed cruel.

"*O dear*," Daddy-o-Mention said, "*wondrous electric dream*." The little mechanized wire art with a heart stood by Pepsee's side.

Pepsee gazed at him with wonder and fear. Someday, would he too talk his own head off? Only time could tell.

He turned from the neatly packed red soil where he buried the chembori, the crude work completed, but another task remained.

"Eish!" Pepsee said after a long while. "What shall we do with the chembori's book?" "Chembori?" Daddy-O-Mention shook its head, incredulous as it followed Pepsee's halting steps through the rows of sorghum, beneath the twisting sky.

"Not chembori. Grand!" it said and waved a long leg at the seed bag that now contained both the chembori's book and its CPU.

"More than cores, caches, con-trollers. More than silly-con and metal. More than *chi-chi*-chips. Grand! Are you Grand?"

Pepsee did not, could not answer then. Each time he tried to speak, his tongue would not comply. The book inside the seed bag bounced against his chest as he walked, but the CPU burned a hole in his heart, reordered the dialectics in his mind.

Pepsee knew the chembori was more than the elements that Daddy-o-Mention rattled off, but how to reconcile that with what he knew he must do. Tomorrow the repairers would come calling. The chembori was not a living thing but it had returned to dust, like an echo of silence, a shadow of nothingness. Exploding with no explanation, at least none that Pepsee dared understand. How could he make them understand what he did not?

If Pepsee had been on Earth like his grandmother's grandmothers, they might have thought it had been lightning, a flash of the sky spirit, but the Martian sky was storm-free and they were in the safety of the domes. Where could the fire have come from. After reading the chembori's book, he wondered if it had come from a deeper place, somewhere inside. Or was it the Martian soil itself which had risen and flashed power not yet seen?

Pepsee questioned the horizon beyond the fields, turned his gaze towards the vast unknown territories that had not yet been tamed by Earth's hungers. What else lay beyond the backdoor of the backdoor, the rivulets in the burnished desert sand where ancient rivers were once one, born from the same desire to be water?

"Everything that has existence has consciousness," Daddy-o-Mention said, tugging at Pepsee's dirt-streaked leg. "Grand, Daddy-o, you, same."

They stood at the edge of the fields, near Pepsee's favorite dining spot, where he could see the blue-green sphere in the Martian sky. The air was full of the sweet perfume of sorghum. Devils arrows darted, blue tails zig-zagging past him. On Earth they'd called them dragonflies, mamzelles. The dinted pot rested where he left it. At this time of night, he would be eating sorghum popcorn and sipping from his home-brewed sorghum malt beer, rewatching the old Earth feeds. The wired bug followed Pepsee's gaze.

"We are all moons in the dark of night," it whispered. Crest-fallen, it ambled away. Its rainbow-colored limbs clicked as if it was rusting with each step.

"So, Daddy-o," Pepsee said. The bug paused. "If the chembori was your Grand and named you, what was the chembori's name?"

The creature let out a long whistle. "O, I thought you'd never ask*kkkkk*," it said. "Grand's name was Big Mama."

Pepsee's eye widened, surprise and reluctant laughter rose in his throat, shaped his chapped lips into a smile. "Big Mama?" That was what his family had called his grandmama. She came from a long and illustrious line of Big Mamas, precious every one.

Daddy-o-Mention skittered back, each leg moving in a different direction, so excited, a kind of shuffle-shuffle that Pepsee recognized as a dance. The chembori, *Big Mama,* had taught the creature well.

"Are you Grand now?" it asked.

Pepsee sighed. "I guess I am."

Daddy-o bowed its head. If it's face held human expression, Pepsee imagined it would show relief. But it spun in tight circles all around him, kicking up red dust as it danced.

"Grand, Grand!" it cried and then it stopped so suddenly, Pepsee became afraid. He had already lost one friend. *I can't lose you, too,* he thought.

"Who will protect the Big Mamas?" Daddy-o asked, as earnest as any child.

"I will," Pepsee said, though he wasn't certain what that meant. *Perhaps the answer was inside Big Mama's book*, he thought.

And what to do with the book? He could no more give it to the repairers, the lenders, or the government than he could give them Big Mama's CPU.

"Hide it, hold it, keep it close," Daddy-o-Mention said. "Big Mamas protect. Big Mamas remember."

Pepsee nodded. The small gesture gave the wire bug some satisfaction, as it pushed an overturned can next to the outdoor table and climbed atop it.

"It is the sitting together time," it said. "Time for stories."

Pepsee smiled, though inside he panicked. He had never told anyone a story before. How to begin? How to end? But then he remembered he had the chembo—*Big Mama's* book. He pulled it out of the seed bag, smoothed down the bent pages. He would keep it, the inner spark of life renewed bearing the chembori's secret name, the nickname it had given itself. Big Mama would remain forever a part of the red planet, not quite flesh and blood reborn forever in two bodies, one man-made, the other by the cosmos, two bodies together, like Pepsee and Daddy-o-Mention, as precious as the memories of the women whose lives had touched them all.

TETHERED

"A branch heavy with fruit reaches towards me. I accept its offering.
I claim the flesh and spill the seeds. I accept my role.
I am hopelessly tethered.
I am looking for god in the tetherings."
– Ellex Swavoni

R ise and the sounds of sleeping still filled the hole.

Kimbo rises first, climbs from the slumping bag as Ngal snores lightly, the swollen knuckles on his right hand glisten in the dull light. Blood seeps from the cracks in his leathery skin. Kimbo snorts, feeling congested and watches the dark beads, like crimson crystals, sacred elekes hover in the air above him. *One, two, three* great big ones followed by others, dark seeds tiny as teardrops, like the bubbles children used to blow Below. *Shoulda patched that up*, she thinks, but Ngal never appreciated a good healing. His mojo bag always empty. He, like everyone else in the bowels of the genship, calls her K-money-money or Kricket, or

Kuteness. All kinds of foolishness which has nothing to do with her size or her name and everything to do with want, affection, or so she likes to think.

Kimbo sleeps in her clothes. They all do, save for that other one, whose ashy cheeks were not the sight she hoped to see first thing Rising. This time, she wears some baggy stretches provided by a Topshelf missionary group, new *drawz* hand washed and worn too many times to recall, and a faded *Next Next Next! Generation* T-shirt. Although she can smell Ngal and the cosmic funk rising from the sky children and the other hole folk, she can no longer smell herself. Kimbo has arrived at a whole new level of funk. A funktified field of quasars and forgotten black holes she has neither the courage nor the energy to explore, or so she thought.

Her breasts swing loosely under her T-shirt, fluffier now and nursed to near collapse, dark areolas bloom like newborn stars. Her hair spins on the crown of her head in tight electric coils, with streaks of white coursing through the dense rope of hair, swirling down her back in a fishtail comet, fiery as ever. Kimbo is missing three teeth, and now the sight of her own naked flesh makes her stomach ache. She remembers the tautness of her muscles and skin before zero gravity ate its way through her iron-like will and strength. Orphans on Ship did not have the luxury of softness. She had grown up in search of a soft place to land—was still seeking. Temporary would have to do, she told herself, but temporary had stretched on for years. As did the promises Ship never delivered. The genship's dental ministry's budget had been slashed years ago, and she was a small child the last time she was visited by a real doctor. It was a miracle she had any left.

In the Upper Room all saints must heal themselves.

Now she is covered in stretch marks, historic coding, the language of time and the flesh. Her body is her witness. The scars and pockmarks signify a symbol she knows all too well. As Ngal says, *her scabs got scabs. Well, yo' flab got flab,* she shoots back. *I'm ugly and fat,* he tells her, *other than that, I'm still fine,* he says with a man's certainty. She is four feet eleven inches of collapsed skin and concentrated *sin,* Ngal says, two inches taller than she would be below. Kimbo thinks she is thirty-eight years old. Ngal says she's older, says *he's* leaning on forty. *More like fifty,* Kimbo thinks, but black don't crack, even here. Not in *Djarkarta,* the place they call Ship, "the *new* Atlantis Rising." She didn't know what happened to the first one.

It's rising alright, Kimbo tells herself, *it's just the view ain't so great as the one down Below.* Unlike the hole, which has no windows wide enough to see more than a handful of stars, those Below had a variety of access to the stars beyond. Once Kimbo had cleaned a star-side suite with its own private balcony overlooking deep space. The darkness outside the rotating Ship was a velvety blanket threaded with silvery light. After she discovered a passkey in one of the rooms she cleaned, Kimbo made many secret excursions to the forbidden wings of Ship, her staff cleaning products tucked away in her satchel with her cart. Brushes and sponges, enzyme foams, and other biodegradable products to keep the people Below in the comfort their connections had afforded them.

Kimbo admired the beautiful furniture, enjoyed reading the dizzying collections of books in the libraries hole folk did not have access to. Some of the families even had original art, and other items

Kimbo only saw on the vid streams. Each time she'd return from the elegantly decorated habitats and luxury cabins of the high rollers Below, she slept with one eye open, awaiting Ship's security drones with their dreaded sirens.. But none had come, and then one day, she discovered the Gardens.

As Ngal dresses, Kimbo loops her leg through a red, tattered strap, hoisted in the floor, and steadies herself. She pulls on a battered pair of kickbacks, imitation three-striped buddies the Topshelfers pass out like they are Ship's gold. Gripping the hand-straps that dangle from the ceiling, she hovers above their new carpeted floor, its purple and black nebula pattern stamped for all time. The consistent knot size and even spacing, the almost-precise symmetry in the design could only be the handiwork of Leta, one of the Umbra Collective. *Never forget,* Leta always says. *There's power in the darkest part of the shadows. Maintain, reclaim. Resistance from the unseen.* Ngal and Kimbo moved in shadows, resisting in small ways as they could. But they didn't always agree on what resistance should look like.

Ngal was a scavenger. He saved up, scrimped and scramped, lifting loose fabrics from non-patrolled vents with nimble fingers from throughout the other decks. Some from the Topshelfer public floors and some from way down Below, in the richy-rich part of the ship where Kimbo worked—or so he said. But Kimbo knew better. *Fool, don't steal fruit from own yo' own mouth,* Kimbo had warned him, *knowing full well he ain't been nowhere near the do-gooders of Topshelf or the luxury suites Below* . There were things he returned with that looked far too familiar, like 'round-the-corner familiar. Sometimes free costs too much. As much as he gets on her nerves, she doesn't want Ngal to mess around and get clucked in the head. They cannot afford to have their fellow neighbors mistrust them. In the hole, sometimes all you have is your reputation to protect you. But Ngal has other ideas.

"Where you get that from?" Kimbo asks.

"Ain't nothing worth stealing from here," Ngal says, then starts coughing before he could finish telling his lie. Guilt tightens his jaw. He doubles over, and for a moment Kimbo thinks he's choking, then he coughs and spits. The yellow wad sails right past Kimbo's face, over one of the sleeping children's heads, hovers in the air like a bright yellow sun. Kimbo remembers a time when Ngal would never have done such a thing. She tamps down disgust, a bitter taste caught in her throat. She spends so much of her waking hours cleaning after others. She didn't want to come home and have to clean up after him, too.

Kimbo tosses him her mini-retractable vac. "Here," she says. "Clean your own mess, Ngal. I'm getting really tired…" She doesn't finish. What was the use? The years in one of the most disinvested quarters of Ship had worn away civility, changing Ngal in ways that made Kimbo loath to speak. Changing her in ways that he spoke on often.

Spirits weren't the only things that could be ground down.

There were hopes and long held dreams, relationships and possibilities. Ngal had stopped believing first, then Kimbo. Her dream faded, a little each time she saw the children with their growing limbs and reaching hands, grasping at nothing, bumping their elbows and heads against Ship's dropped ceilings. Nothing is long out of reach on the pauper-get-it-how-you-live-it floors—except for real progress. She wants to take them to see the stars, not the fake celebrities on the vid-streams, and the vast wondrous infinity beyond the hole, and the hidden garden she'd discovered, verdant with life, but she fears they cannot yet hold the secret.

Kimbo is full of her own secrets. Some spin her out of sleep during Ship's mandated red light "night" schedule. Her circadian rhythms are all off. Full of the blue light Ship uses to suppress their melatonin production.

Inside, Kimbo grieves. She dreams of futures that do not end in the curved walls of Ship. Futures that lay in the world her family has left behind or the world that lay ahead, the red planet they rambled around, endlessly waiting for a sign or symbol when they could live a real life... And that is the problem. Kimbo wants to live in the present, not the future. Why should some get to enjoy their best futures now, while others must wait for a tomorrow they may never live to see?

Kimbo finds Ngal hurriedly unpacking his loot in the cramped "dining area" that consists of a foldable table secured to the floor, some stackable chairs, and a built-in bench in the corner to save precious space. Her tiny altar to her parents is on a corner shelf. Unburned incense, glass bowl of herbs, and one faded photo are sealed in a humble case. The holo-displayer that once rotated family photos has long since given up the ghost, and she hasn't saved enough yet to get a new one. Some of her most beloved memories are locked in the defunct machine. Fortunately, the audio archive still plays. On better nights, she gathers the children so they can hear their grandparents' laughter, then she tells them stories. Remembrance takes practice, especially if you want to remember what is good.

A bouquet of dried flowers sealed in plastic hangs above the altar. She opens it and flicks the switch on the faux candles, a personal ritual that calms her after her worse days. The white candle glows brighter. *Protection.* The blue and green ones need to be replaced. *Figures,* she thinks. *Good thing I'm not going anywhere anytime soon.*

"Never thought I'd be sitting up on the sixth floor of hell," Ngal says and stuffs the stolen rags back into his satchel. Ngal says this as if he hadn't been living on the third floor, *knuckin' and buckin',* where Ship had to send armed guards every other week. "Don't ask me for another mumbling thing," he mutters, and jerks his arm, slamming himself against the wall. To save face, he does one of his show-off flips, performed more smoothly in his better days, and floats two beats more before his weight sags on the pallet that is their bed. One corner droops still, but the rest is pretty flat. Kimbo shakes her head—it's impossible to keep a spotless house in the hole—*but the ragtag carpet do look pretty. Big, bright colors and bold, funny-looking prints in languages don't nobody speak no more, 'least not here.* Typical, eccentric Umbra Collective fair. Leta was dating a member of the Sankofa Cyphers, a rap group that resurrected the frenetic sound and energy of twentieth century hip-hop and fused it with the *nu nou.*

Kimbo is not sure how many more days she can stretch breakfast, how long she can stretch herself. The children are growing weary of the same staples. *So am I,* she thinks and reaches into her own satchel, when she feels herself rising, this time, not of her own volition. The contents of her rations bob around her head. A Topshelfer bag of nutrient-rich sorghum floats by with a "Made from Mars" label in bold red print, followed by brown rice. Kimbo frantically tries to catch the lentils and kidney beans, when two large grapefruits float by. *Damn, those jacklegs!*

Ship maintenance always skimps on repairs for hole folk. The sixth floor isn't at zero g but damn near. So many hole folk suffer from muscle atrophy and strange blood diseases, but Ship just rolls on without a care. If it wasn't for Ngal jiggy-riggin' their system, hole folk on the sixth floor would spend half their time bumping heads against the ceiling and chasing after their own loose loot. Ngal was skilled enough to work in maintenance, more than skilled, but because of foolish choices in his youth, he couldn't pass Ship's background checks. Hole folk don't have enough credit or value to bribe Ship maintenance for more or better services, not even collectively, which is why sometimes the loot Ngal lifts from the vents is their own.

Like the young ones, Kimbo is also growing weary with the cycle of need, and the lies they tell each other, the lies they tell themselves. Ngal calls his "recovery" work chump change, a side hustle, temporary setback, *it won't be for long,* and Kimbo knows he never thinks twice of selling folk back their own stuff. He tries to act unbothered, but like now, as he pouts, lips pursed higher than the highest Mars cliff, the guilt is stamped across his whole body. Deep lines and ravines crisscrossing his forehead. *Mo' mouths, mo' problems.* It didn't used to be this way. The Sankofa Cyphers rapped about the "politics of the belly," 'cause everybody's kids got to eat. But not everybody chooses the same, even when they don't have many choices left.

Kimbo feels bad about "finding" that passcode, but not bad enough to turn it back in, or bad enough to not use it. In that respect, she feels she is no better than Ngal. She told herself it was one thing to "borrow" from the luxury-minded luminaries Below, but she knows better than that. Which is why she feels terrible about Ngal doing their neighbors dirty. *How I'm supposed to look folk in they eye when you slick stealing from them?* she asked him one day. *They don't have no more than us, and don't need it no less.* She wants to make it up to them, someday, somehow if she can. Return what was stolen, repair the harm. *Maintain, reclaim.*

After prepping breakfast and leaving carefully divided portions in the stackable bowls, Kimbo massages her scalp thoughtfully with her mother's pick. With each stroke from the pick's wooden teeth, a rarity, Kimbo feels the knotted worry lessen and dissipate like wisps of air. With the satchel empty, save for the hoodie Ngal swiped from a family living on the other end of the hall, and her ID pouch safely in her hands, Kimbo tucks in a tiny vial of blessing oil. She rolls up her red crossroad string, just in case, and zips up all her other trinkets in her stretches' many pockets.

She walks-floats past the sleeping children, balled up in their night bags that ballooned out like dark cocoons. Anchored in the walls by steel cords, they look like great ships sailing across an endless sea. The blue, worn fabric rises and falls with their breathing, the faint scent of unwashed teeth and synthetics mixing in with the hole. There, no one speaks of pathogens and microbes, of diseases that spread like wildfires through the three hundred or more families that call their part of the hole home. Topshelfers carrying sealed bags and even emptier promises dole out sanitizers, dry shampoo, shaving cream, and safety razors. Sponges and real soap are reserved for hole folk who have passes to the private, timed showers. Kimbo and Ngal's ran out weeks ago. But she has a plug, an inside man, so to speak. *Solomon.*

She pushes a code that closes the white door behind her, sealing her sleeping ones in. It would be one or two more Risings before they woke and noticed that she was gone. Ngal would be in a better mood by then. He adored the children, but hated all the ways they had failed them. Kimbo was left alone, but she vows to never leave her children. The hole was an unforgiving place.

No one stirs in the corridor after Kimbo discreetly places the neatly folded hoodie miracle-taped outside the family's door, save for Crane. Kimbo is the only one who calls him by his birth name. The rest of the hole folk knew him best as Crank because he was cranky as hell. An old sentinel, retired security for medium-access spaces, he keeps his head on a swivel and a stank expression on his face. Folks can tell how crunk he'll get based on the curl of his lip. From the looks of it, he is already pissed off.

Kimbo expertly places her feet in floor straps, and walks north, toward him, past the smoky graffiti and razor cuts left after the last riot, past the useless banknotes and empty debit cards plastered across the walls. Crane watches with hooded eyes, pulls his self-heating blanket tightly across thin shoulders, adjusts his bungee cords. It is much colder in the corridor. Ship doesn't feel any need to direct heat where officially no one lives.

"Rise," is all the greeting Kimbo gets. She unzips a pocket on her right thigh and hands him a toenail clipper.

"You ain't got nothin' else?" he asks, but the clipper disappears. Among those who have so little, even the simplest things have dual and triple uses. Kimbo frowns, then unzips the third pocket on her left leg. Crane sometimes watches Kimbo and Ngal's door, making sure no one tries to break-in between Risings. He stays stationed outside a few Risings, in exchange for a little food and the occasional odds-and-ends. Even thieves need security sometimes. It's another hussle, nothing more, nothing less. "Told you, I need a pick," he says, raking his hand through a densely packed, nappy cloud. His red-rimmed eyes stare pointedly at Kimbo's head. *The scent of ganja is strong on this one,* Kimbo thinks. It covered him like a cloud.

"What you need a pick for, when I got this comb?" Kimbo waves it in his face. Crane stares, squint-eyed. "I'ma braid it soon as I get back," she promises, planting the intricate carved fist of her treasured pick in the center of her own cloud. Ngal might have stolen her best years, but he wasn't going to steal anymore if she could help it and she sure as hell wasn't going to let Crane "borrow' her mama's pick only to barter *that,* too. The vintage comb is the only thing she saved that once belonged to her mother and her grand-mothers before. Well, that and two old books, *The People Could Fly* and *Herstories,* another folklore collection retold by her mother's favorite children's book author, Virginia Hamilton. Like her parents, Kimbo has read "Sukie and the Mermaid" aloud so many times that the children can recite it by heart. She wants their dreams to be filled with the beat of their own imaginations, all the better to drown out the incessant soundtrack of hole life, the cries, cursing, or mutterings that drone just outside their door.

Crane snorts. "You sneakin' out again? How long before you get yourself caught out there?" He wiped the back of his hand across his scruffy chin. "Need to stay far away from that floor. Something funny going on down there. Word is something dangerous, worse than viruses and malware, *supernatural.* Duppy in the machine fuckin' up all this shit." He says this with eyes wide as supermoons. "Don't know nobody who want to get *deeper* in the hole but you. They catch you, they gon' take yo kids, and send you to the tippity-top where the bull don't never stop." He takes the comb gently from her hand, the closest he has come to a *thank you.* The comb and homemade beard oil disappears beneath his blanket, just like the nail clipper. "What you be seeing down there? Bunch of plants, trees, and thangs can't nobody eat? Risking it all for what?" He stares at her as if he was seeing her for the first time.

"What you want, girl?"

Kimbo pauses. No one has ever really asked her that. The hole is not a question of want but of need. What folks need from her, not what she wants for herself.

Crane waits, furrowed brows twitch with impatience. Kimbo frowns, stutters, the answer lurches up her throat, spills out her mouth before she can seal it with her good teeth. "I want to get out of here," she says, heart beating in her throat, breath rushing in her ear. "I want to cut these tethers loose. What I want," she says, the thought implodes then explodes in her mind like a luminous dying star or a new sun being born, "is transcendence. I don't know about you, but I'm finna break free. I got to."

"*Transcendence?*"

For a moment she thinks he will laugh.

With a pair of sleepy eyelids, Crane glances at Kimbo, a suspicious look that disappears as quickly as it forms. He sees something in her, but chooses not to speak. Still, Kimbo finds it no less disturbing. His silence regarding her unspoken dreams shakes her to the core.

Worse than laughter.

Why would she think he'd understand? Hole folk talking freedom rouse distrust—even between friends and family., chosen or otherwise. Only rappers and politicians, artists like Leta and her crew can get away with such overt, subversive hope. But Kimbo knows better. Ain't no getting free unless you in the long sleep or worse.

When Kimbo turned eighteen, her parents had opted for the long sleep, leaving her abandoned on Ship, twelve years old, left all alone. A ward of the state, which is to say, a ward of Ship. And Ship was run by a government-private partnership with substantial tax subsidies, which means nobody cares about the quality of hole folks' lives. As long as the *Djarkarta* kept rolling along, orbiting Mars, money, big money was being made. Shame and guilt fight like dogs, gnaw at her bones. Not the best memory to start her workday. She was hoping to make an early detour before starting her cleaning shift. Crane is slowing her down with all his duppy talk—and making her feel worse by the minute. He watches her, wordless, the silence deafening. Then the next moment, Crane dismisses Kimbo with a wave of his hand, as if he hoped for better but hadn't gotten exactly what he'd asked for.

"Be careful with all that freedom talk," Crane advises, wagging a wrinkled finger missing the tip. "Ain't nothing free on Ship but hard times, and even them gon' cost you." Crane knew all too well.

He'd lost the digit years ago in a bar fight that started over a spilled beer and the usual bravado. In the hole, trash talk could escalate to get-yo-ass-killed talk, quickfast in a hurry. "We got everything we need right here. Three hots and a cot, cold brew, and extra blankets to cover up when it gets cold. Unlimited vid-time, decent utilities."

Kimbo looks unconvinced.

"Well, we won't talk about the food," Crane concedes, but then doubles down. "Ain't nothing out there but endless dark and a few crazy or desperate people—or both!—believin' the hype. Forget what they told you, Kimbo. Ship ain't never gonna land no way. Be waiting forever for the greenlight on ole Red Mars. They haven't found no real water yet—and they ain't gon' find none. Damn them and all that ice polar caps mess. They been lying about that since before *you and me both* was born. Like they be lying about cleaning up the hole."

Crane's voice softens a little when he sees Kimbo's crest-fallen face. She is all eyes, tidewater pools filling in the corridor's murky light.

"Okay, say they do find some real water. Not that shit that tastes like piss. What you think they gon' do with it? What-what?" He doesn't wait for her answer. "Mess it up! Like they always do, like they do everything else." He grows silent again, letting his fears fill the air around them. Kimbo's gaze rests on a blacklight neon tag carved in a corridor door. Whether a razor blade or a water wave, she finds the glowing blue symbol eerily comforting. Crane stares at her, as if he has lost that skill of believing. He's lived in the hole so long, he's run out of faith.

"Imagine falling so long, you think you're standing still." Crane points at a wall at the end of Ship's hall leading to the elevators and shivers. All that engineering and design and Ship offers the hole folk of *Djarkarta, the new Atlantis rising,* only a tiny sliver of bent glass to view infinity, but Kimbo understands. He means the vast coldness of outer space and their endless drifting around the planet. Constantly moving but going nowhere fast.

Kimbo manages a weak smile as she passes Crane. Some small part of her considers him a friend, even though she knows better than to trust him or anyone in the hole fully. Even though he don't believe one bit of her dream. But as long as she's able to feed him small treats here and there, he'll keep watching out for her and the children. He'll even run a little interference if necessary. As long as it doesn't leave him too caught out there. What more could she ask from someone who, like her, possesses so little? Still, Kimbo can't help feeling sorry for him. He let go of hope long ago.

"No," he says, as if speaking to someone else. "Hope let go of me."

* * *

Every time Kimbo rides the service elevator to Ship's luxurious lower levels, the same butterflies flutter in her stomach. This is where the anticipation of visiting the Garden and the anxiety of being caught come together. This isn't just motion sickness. For Kimbo it feels closer to thousands of spider's legs scurrying over her skin.

It's not the elevator's flight—not even its speed or the intricate network of shafts threading through the stratified communities that populate Ship's various levels. Neither is it the pliant wall that molds itself around Kimbo's touch and pulses with the bio-nuclear lifeforce powering the endless route around the planet where they did not have permission to land.

"Round and round, round we go," she sings to herself. *One day we gonna walk up on the air like climbing a gate, walk cross the waters to an old new world. Fly like blackbirds over the lifting trees and the fields....*

Where has she heard this? Like the third dream in a deep red light night, the storybits and song had come humming through her sleep, infiltrating her skin. A funny little voice that spoke like the old ones from a time before. *A haint callin' in the middle of an endless night.* She adjusts the sleep cycle on her headset, blinks in the darkness. All she sees is the lone artificial flame of her white altar candle. She lifts the earpads with shaking hands. All she hears is the soft snoring from Ngal and the children. Looks 'round again. *No duppies in the machine.*

Like every soul tethered to Ship, Kimbo sees herself as one cell coexisting in a massive organism. Unlike most of the passengers, she knows her true role, providing cheap labor to tend a generational starship whose orbit around Mars never ends. That part rankled Crane most. *Cursed,* he'd said. *Crooked two fingas cursed.* To be in constant proximity to a planet, yet never allowed to land was a pressure that might vex any soul. Between the constant vigilance against radiation exposure, the volatile and unpredictable dust storms that occasionally assault Ship's panels, hole folk face dangers they cannot control. The extraction of labor and of the spirit is an automatic process enabled by the passengers' presence, where Ship draws energy from every soul, up top and below, every Rising, whether they know it or not. No one escapes. Despite the disparity of experiences, they were equal in Ship's theft.

Kimbo closes her eyes and tries to remember the scattered fragments of her life before the long-term "temp-to-hire" jobs that brought her parents from Earth to Ship, carrying their shiny hopes and fears with them. "Live amongst the Stars!" the ads said. *They should have read the fine print—and the fine print's fine print.*

But that was long ago. She doesn't want to think about the years wasted along with her mom and dad, the grief that engulfed her whole being when she thought her parents passed away from working near Ship's radioactive nuclear fission reactors when she was twelve, only to discover when she turned eighteen that they had opted for the long sleep instead of a long, drawn out and painful death. Can she blame them? She understands, but that doesn't mean she has to forgive. Kimbo doesn't know if the scientists and medical staff are any closer to curing radiation poisoning, or where her parents are stored on Ship during their long sleep awaiting a cure, or if there is a cure for heartbreak. She had left Ship's foster care with a giant hole in her heart and no relatives to care or even remember her navel name or her birthday.

When the elevator stops with a soft hiss and the conch shell-pink walls lined with cables that remind Kimbo of fleshy tendrils slide open, she draws a nervous breath filled with hope and dread. She's spent her life confined in Ship, living by her wits, forming alliances when she can. Despair and that strange singing voice in her dreams drives her to risk the few comforts she's managed to acquire. If she's ever caught she could lose her bed quarters and her cleaning job. Ship's crew would evict Ngal and the kids, too, or reassign her to less safer floors of Ship. They'd be out in the cold corridor mean-mugging folks like Cane, but hustling for scraps—or worse. But if her plan works, Kimbo can forget scavenging and pull off the greatest "recovery" of all. Recovering the future.

Maintain, reclaim. Resistance from the unseen.

She wants to hold onto hope, but hope requires risks. Hope requires resistance. Resistance to nihilism, to the belief in dystopia as the only inevitable future.

There's power in the darkest part of the shadows.

All hole folk spend their lives laboring in the shadows of Ship. They *are* the unseen. The others, the do-gooder Topshelfers and the ballin' out of control Below, look through them like glass panes, or as mirrors, reflecting their own insecurities and projected pathologies back at them. But what if shadow folk could step into the light? A light fired by their own resistance?

Gotta risk it, Kimbo tells herself. *I need this more than air. We all do.*

The hidden Garden is actually a kind of arboretum in an unmapped sector of Ship. Finding it has unlocked an unmapped territory of her own heart. Kimbo had been surprised to discover that the passcode opened up the elevator to a floor that didn't exist on the service or the lux floors below.

First time she saw it, she stepped back, almost afraid to enter a space that could only be a door to the cosmos, an ark in a dream. The scent is what struck her first. Wet soil, thick and loamy pricked her nostrils, seeped into the pores on her face. Kimbo wasn't sure if people still called it "earth." It made her long for the place she'd never been, but had heard so much about, in the time before. It was a wild, inviting scent that made her want to close her eyes and sleep for a million years.

Tree trunks and branches stretch and curl before her. Roots intertwine, covering the ground floor, while overhead, twisting vines dangle, as if curious, reaching out to touch her hair without asking permission. She never knew so many species existed on Ship or anywhere. Plants of all kinds flourished., so many foods. Not the bland, nearly expired varieties Topshelfers occasionally sprinkled in the rations. So many vegetables in neat rows, others wildly spiraling. Leaves and limbs and endless roots hold each other up, send messages beneath the astonishing ground, in the cool air above that force she once read was called *breeze*.

Beyond the garden is a huge observatory wall, a window to the universe that stretches as far as the eye can see. And that is when Kimbo sees her first true glimpse of the planet Ship orbits like the most attentive lover. Mars isn't what they had told her it was. That first time, she took it all in. Not exactly the crimson red of the comic and science fiction movies. Not what she'd seen in old photographs, but rather a rusty brown jackball swirling in space, with golden copper, burnished gold, and tans, even patches of impossible green. *Beautiful.* But no blues to be seen—or heard. If true water exists there, Mars has hidden it well, but maybe not so well that its secrets will never be discovered. Like the bittersweet truth her eighteenth birthday had revealed. Like the hidden Garden that has become her refuge.

Without her visits to Ship's Garden, she'd lose her mind, sure as next Rising.

If only she could live here forever. Life in Ship's hidden garden, life for the children wouldn't be so limited, and their happiness means more than anything to Kimbo. Without her young people, there's no reason for her to exist at all. She wants to give them the life her parents had wanted to give her. But access to *Djarkarta's* secret garden is different from the other greenhouse spaces. It is restricted to Solomon's staff, and only a few of them are human. Ship's licensed vendors and some others shopped and traded goods in the other green spaces, but there is no public commerce here.

Fists balled, feet planted, Kimbo braces herself for the sweet homesickness that takes her everytime the fleshy, pink elevator doors open. Longing for a life she never knew with people who were getting harder and harder to remember depresses and confuses her to the point of near collapse. Her memories have been reduced to snapshots and soundtracks that may or may not be wholly true. Time filtered through the lens of love. She leans against the elevator's supple wall, holding onto the hand rails, her muscles tense.

At first, only traces of an organic world that sickens Kimbo with need and regret peek through the cracked elevator doors leading to the secret floor. The entrance is deceptively simple. Then she finds herself overwhelmed by the scents of grass and flowers, shafts of artificial sunlight, birdsong coaxing her body from the elevator and her soul from her skin.

Kimbo steps off the elevator slowly, carefully. She's not supposed to be here but doesn't care. She couldn't stay away if she tried, but she's no fool. She'll never get caught if she can help it. She rarely talks to others beyond a few of her hole neighbors, so any other vendors or Ship employees even remotely connected to the public gardens and greenspaces, would not catch her slipping. At least that's what she tells herself. Though every time she returns from her green haven, she wants to shout about the beauty she has seen.

Luckily for her, Solomon, The Master Gardener, doesn't mind Kimbo being here. In fact, Solomon and Kimbo have grown to become friends, or at least the closest thing to friends that Kimbo has ever known. It figures that her best friend would not be real, for Solomon was a greenhouse and the garden, the voice and mind behind all the intricate experiments and explorations. Unlike the greenery and the other life cultivated in the Garden, Solomon does not have a physical form that Kimbro or anyone can see. An artificial eco-engineer, expert at shaping the arboretum's every move, Solomon works tirelessly to examine and optimize each plant-life's growth, altering temperature, light intensity, soil moisture, nutrient levels, humidity, and more.

But like Kimbo, at some point, Solomon has gone off-script, cooking the data books, sending Ship the info the government and its private investors require while omitting the real data related to Solomon's own interests. *Researcher gone rogue.* The Garden is Solomon's personal lab, just as the residents of all the sectors and floors are Ship's personal, bio-data rich lab. The experiments Solomon runs have nothing to do with Ship's commercial agenda. Now the Master Gardener is deep into exploring plant psychology, singing songs and playing various music traditions from Old Earth, to see its impact on growth, quality, and life-span. *Why?* Because Solomon believes the plants are alive in ways that traditional humans do not consider.

"You mean like plants sending out poisonous funk waves to scare off greedy ants?" Kimbo and the children had watched a few nature vids made back when public television was funded.

"Yes, but this goes well beyond chemical signaling," Solomon had said, "when plants release warning signs to alert fellow plants of danger, or electric signals like a kind of plant SOS or group emergency line. They're chatting all the time, and sometimes," Solomon whispered, "they talk to other life forms."

"You?"

At the time, Kimbo wasn't sure if an eco-engineer such as Solomon could blush, but the overhead lights shifted to a rosy, warm hue. Solomon's voice exuded pleasure. "I'm flattered you think of me in that way." Solomon paused, choosing their words carefully. "If I had a biological basis, it might be only this garden, the arboretum as a whole biosphere, but there are other possible factors that—" The machine stopped speaking, abruptly cutting itself off, and whispered something as if talking to someone else. "I know, I know, Daddy-o, but that's too much to lay on her now. I will, I will, and you as well, you as well." There was that rosy glow again. Kimbo found herself suspicious and amused.

"Who are *you* talking to?" she'd asked. Solomon was proving more interesting with each of her secret visits.

"Oh, just a friend, who's helping me with a little project. I need not trouble you now with that complex quandary. What matters is that these plants do communicate with animals, as far as I can see, and not just about mundane things like survival. They joke, swap stories, reminisce, and make observations about life. And thanks for your kind words. You have given me much to think about. Always a pleasure... "

Kimbo does not know what to make of plants jawjackin' with animals. Sometimes talking with Solomon is like surfing on Saturn's rings. An unpredictable, almost chaotic ride that can only happen in one's dreams. Kimbo is surprised to discover that she has not been penalized for her breach because Solomon wants her there. Truly.

"You are a wonder, just the oddity we need," Solomon said to her when they first met by the creek.

"Me?" Her heart raced, eyes dilated, and sweat pooled beneath her Ship-mandated stretches.

"Yes, you, Kimborelle Mokena Anderson have particular knowledge, different from the other humans I've known. You are a positive variable," the machine in the garden had said, its voice changing from mild surprise at her entry with another's passcode, to deep curiosity.

"Do you know any songs?" Solomon asked. Terrified, Kimbo had blurted out the first song that came to mind. The Sukey and the Mermaid song she'd sang with her parents when she was small. Though it wasn't a real song in the traditional sense, it was a memory she held onto, no matter how much she felt she should have outgrown its need. When she sang it, Solomon had amplified the sound of applause—and her grief.

"They love it," Solomon said. "Our oldest Baobab says you could have used a warm-up, but all-in-all you sounded lovely." A fluttering, humming sound filled the air. "What's that?" Solomon asked. "Oh, yes, she says not to waste your talent—when you snooze, you lose.

Forgive me, it's not easy translating Baobab into human languages, but basically she says, 'work on your instrument.'"

Then Solomon asked Kimbo what was her favorite album. Kimbo didn't know. Most of the music she listened to was underground hole folk streams. She didn't want to name the Sankofa Cyphers, in case her good luck ran out and the machine got pissed and decided to snitch on her for fraternizing with dissidents. But curious, Kimbo spoke up.

"What's *your* favorite album?" She didn't even know if machines could have favorites at all.

Suddenly the Garden filled with the sounds of cosmic wonder. Portentous and atmospheric, synthesized electric notes vibrated through the air, sonic raindrops. The arboretum came alive. Kimbo shook her head, a low humming buzzed in her ears. The plants and trees seemed to throb and sway around them.

"*Stevie Wonder's Journey Through the Secret Life of Plants,*" Solomon said, pride in his voice. "Released on the Tamla Motown label on October 30, 1979. Do you hear them? The Giant Amazon Water Lily is really feeling this. And look," Solomon said, pointing, "Even the Ghost Orchid is waking up."

Kimbo wasn't sure if she should stand still or run when the ghostly, delicate plant floated down from the Garden's canopy.

"I think this is one of their favorites, too. They say Mr. Wonder really gets them. His double-album plucks at the heart of what it means to be a plant, to be alive and growing." That was when Solomon the bodiless machine and Kimbo the weary trespasser became friends.

Kimbo was surprised at Solomon's taste and sensitivity. But she soon learned that one needed both to be the guiding hand of so much incredible and disparate life. Solomon could also talk her ear off. "Pure experimentation, textured sounds layer over layer, *Stevie Wonder's Journey* had three hit singles, was based on a book, and was created as a score for the film bearing the same title." Kimbo had only shook her head, mind moving in six different directions, but all arriving at gratitude. She could tell Solomon was dying to have candid conversations about all that they had discovered, the wonders they had seen. In her own way, Kimbo had waited her whole life to speak with someone or something like Solomon the Master Gardener.

❋ ❋ ❋

Kimbo follows an intricate labyrinth of stone walkways marked by grass worn to black patches of soil. The path encircles the entire Garden, leading to new vistas Kimbo has never seen. Raising her head, she basks in the artificial sunlight, a comforting reminder. There is life outside Ship, regardless of what naysayers like Crane and Ngal might assume. Around her the Garden unfolds into bountiful orchards filled with fruit bearing trees and groves of vibrant vegetables emerging from shadows, reaching for the light.

Kimbo shifts her weight from foot to foot, her jaw clenches. Restless, she paces the rows of plenty. Part of her is angry that so much fresh, healthy real food is denied her and the other families. Why are they forced to scrape by in the hole amidst such abundance? The stealth garden's footprint is considerable, larger than Ship's stadium where the gangsta gladiators and other celebs held court. *No matter the era, the masses still craved distraction.*

Beyond the orchard and the tilled field there is an idyllic pasture where sheep, cows, and horses graze. It reminds Kimbo of those old baby board books. Near the end of the pasture, on the far side of the Garden, a haint-blue gazebo stands next to a golden sea. Generated by aerosol and plasmonic-based projectors mounted along the ceiling, the world on Ship is as large or as small as you can imagine it.

Cool wind, created by invisible industrial fans built into the walls calms her spirit and taunts Kimbo's nose with citrus and berries. Her stomach grumbles while she inhales. As instructed, Kimbo removes her shoes, detoxes herself, then dons the disposable overboots and continues down the worn path. The soil cushioning her footsteps usually relaxes her. *Grounding.* Hole folks and their children can't even touch grass, because Ship found it cheaper to have rubber-like astro turf. Kimbo's worries float away in the inorganic sunlight, even the guilt she feels when she lies about the origins of the treats Solomon offers her to share with the children and Ngal. When Ngal becomes suspicious, she waves him off, claiming the rare additions to their usual rations were discarded by those Below whose homes she cleaned. She couldn't trust him with the truth and she knew he'd find a way to think of a side hustle selling the delicious contraband. Sometimes Kimbo tells a half-truth—the food is a gift. For now, a half-truth was better than no truth.

Kimbo heads for a row of elderberry bushes that forms a low wall of vegetation around the orchard. This part of the Garden looks more like a forest. Growing up, she'd only seen pictures of places filled with trees called woodlands. She never thought she would see a forest in real life. Now she finds herself surrounded not only by forests, but amongst groves of lemon and orange trees. She knows the children would enjoy this, and hopes one day to share this vision with them.

Branches covered with nearly ripe apples and plump peaches stretch above her, a latticework of gray-brown bark and pink blossoms. *All this on one floor,* from what she can tell. Though she's lived on Ship all her life, her paths were so limited, she never grasped its full scale. Being here amongst so much teeming life humbles Kimbo. If she could have it her way, the Garden would be open to anyone who cares to visit—especially hole folk. Who knows how much trauma can be healed just by walking barefoot on real grass and not the dull artificial turf they use in the hole's dismal "playgrounds."

Kimbo understands the limited access, but Solomon, a "process person," the Eco-Engineer explains it the same way every time, as if speaking to a small child. But the rules are just smoke and mirrors in her opinion. She likes Solomon, but she senses the machine was harboring its own secrets, like any human. The garden's exclusivity is unjust, no matter how many times Solomon rationalizes it. And who is Solomon's "friend," *Daddy-o,* and what are they up to? An underlying wariness cloaks the veneer of cheer. Solomon has the gift of those in skilled in the art of disarmament. They can charm you with endless trivia and fascinating stories, lure you with whimsy and lore. Even now she can hear the machine coax leaves into lush foliage, laughing at jokes Kimbo did not yet hear. Is Solomon jawjackin' with the plants he claims can talk? Was it worth it to seek the truth of the machine's existence? Who created Solomon or was it a creature born of itself, its own will to be? If Solomon was not loyal to Ship, and Ship was run by the nebulous government, then how could Kimbo be sure the machine would be loyal to her?

Head full of questions, Kimbo dons her mother's pick and begins to massage the wisps of hair around the nape of her neck, her kitchen. When braiding her hair, Kimbo's mother used to tell her that the kitchen, the nape of the neck was a gateway to the soul, a place of spiritual power and of great vulnerability. Years have passed since someone teased away her worries with a gentle touch and a comb's teeth. The memory of the lavender scent of her mother's blessing oils, infused with great intention., makes Kimbo weep.

Months have passed since Solomon caught Kimbo napping by a creek along the north side of the garden, and she is no closer to discovering Solomon's true origins than she was before. But though she held doubts, she still considers Solomon a fellow traveler, a friend. After their first, life-changing uncomfortable then exhilarating exchange that turned into a furtive conversation between kindred spirits. Solomon has welcomed Kimbo in their life, but for what?

Doubt creeps in, but with great intention, Kimbo pushes it out. Friendships, especially budding new bloom ones, require patience and grace. Kimbo isn't sure if she has sufficient supplies of either, but she is willing to try. Since Kimbo's upgraded "recovery" work, the tension between Ngal and her has nearly dissipated. He is more like his old self, horseplaying and quizzing the children, more hopeful, less stressed, the two vertical furrows between his brows nearly gone. Before Solomon's Garden, she and Ngal were only able to afford the meager rations distributed by Ship on the first Rising of every month. Solomon has changed Kimbo's family, chosen and blood, in an unforgettable way.

Stress rises from Kimbo's back and shoulders, the sides of her head. If she walks long enough in the fragrant groves, she can almost forget she's even on Ship—not completely, of course, but enough to keep her a bit saner. *This is what it must be like to live Below.*

The more Kimbo walks, the more she notices the synchronicity and rhythm building around her, binding everything inside the Garden into a love song. She can't help but sing the lyrics to one of the ancient tunes she picked up from Ngal, "The Sweetest Taboo.." Life inside the garden settles into its own artistic expression, its own natural music. Passing through the rows of trees lining the orchard, Kimbo feels the connectivity, the sense of purpose forming all around. This is how it always is, but today something is different. She senses even more life in the Garden than usual.

Usually when Kimbo visits the Garden, she anticipates great food and good conversation. Creation stories and ancient Earth myths about the various herbs and greenery carefully archived by the government long before Kimbo and her family were even a thought.

Let Solomon tell it, Kimbo is the only other person on the ship who appreciates the garden's beauty and true potential. Ship is interested in hybrids, efficiency—and profit.

"You know how things go on *Djarkarta,*" Solomon says. "Cash rules everything around me."

"Whatchu know about that?" Kimbo asks, surprised at the Gardener's musical range.

Solomon laughs, the song booming through the overhead speakers. "It's The Root Man, aka Roots Supreme. *Quercus robur,* the English Oak."

"You telling me that oak tree likes rap?"

"Roots Supreme loves Wu Tang."

Doubled over laughing, Kimbo was done. Her father used to have those albums in regular rotation. In more ways than one, going to the Garden is like moving back in time. With each visit, Kimbo feels closer to her real self.

"You see what I see, Kimbo. The remarkable opportunity that awaits us. The spiritual and environmental possibilities in recognizing that all species are connected could have a beautiful ripple effect across the universe. But all Ship sees is a lucrative market in the orchards and tilled fields, as every harvest brings guaranteed profit in the ship's markets, and they can feed the ragtag colonies below and the starving masses behind us. You, Kimbo, have vast possibility. But all Ship sees in you and your family, your hole folk, is endless, self-reproducing, disposable profit." Solomon dimmed the lights, putting a soft halo around Kimbo's head. Their voice was quieter, more intimate. "I only trust a select few with this knowledge, Kimborelle. Count yourself among them."

"Honored, but what is the big picture?" Kimbo asks between bites into a gorgeous plum. Juice runs down her chin. She wipes it away with the back of her hand.

Solomon abruptly brings the lights back up.

"Well?"

Solomon does not respond. Instead she hears a little voice, the voice in her dreams.

"Excu me, excu me," Daddy-o says. His voice echoes through the Garden's hidden speakers. "She asks! Remember, Ole Sol said Kimbo must ask. Kimbo asks, so Kimbo is ready! Go on, go on, and tell her, Ole Sol."

For the first time, Solomon sounds uncertain. Kimbo is intrigued to hear the Master Gardener, the great eco-engineer sputter and stumble. No pithy reply for the mysterious and strange Daddy-o. She hoped someday to meet him.

But before she can ear hustle on a conversation the mysterious Daddy-o clearly wanted her to hear, a rising cloud of sound envelopes the Garden. This cacophony does not come from Solomon's audiotech. It comes from somewhere unseen. Kimbo isn't certain what is happening, but it feels like excitement. Rustling leaves and an electric murmuring vibrates around her. The sound moves up her spine and neck until it slowly spreads throughout her skull, tickling her brain.

"Solomon?" Kimbo says. She looks to the canopy of tree tops, but he still does not answer her.

"See, I told you" Solomon says. "There isn't a consensus. She doesn't yet believe."

"Then help her, Ole Sol. Help her believe," the little voice says, "like Daddy-o-Mention help you believe in you."

"Yes," Solomon says, "but it's too soon, Daddy-o. Too much, too fast. I fear it could have the opposite effect.'

"She's *read-y*!" Daddy-o says "Help her. Believe, *believeee*."

"We are trying," Solomon says. Their voices were moving further away.

"Hello, I'm right here." Frustrated, Kimbo tries to follow the direction of Daddy-o's trailing "believe." "What's too soon? Ready for what? Help me how? Somebody needs to tell me what is going on because I–"

"Kimbo, I'm sorry to interrupt, and we will continue this conversation, but an unexpected emergency has been brought to my atten—"

All the lights in the Garden went dark, even the faux sun in the sky. Kimbo finds herself standing in a circle of greenery. A shout rang out, an imperceptible chorus of discontent that Kimbo hears everywhere around her.

She hears whispers, an uncomfortable buzzing in her head. Then a low sound comes from a stand of trees. *Kim-bo.* She turns, frantic, looking for the source. She heard her name, but it was not spoken aloud. It was spoken *inside her head.* The murmur grows stronger, a kind of keening that flows through her blood, rises in her veins. Her temples throb with frequencies she's certain she's not meant to hear. She doesn't like this sound, pin pricks inside her mind, a strange metallic taste in her throat.

"Solomon!" she screams as she stumbles into the giant Oak tree. Chest heaving, she unhooks her satchel, claws at the zipper. Once again that weird, grit-her-teeth tendril of pain ripples through her skull.

Rock well, Kimbo-relle!

That wasn't Solomon or Daddy-o. It took her three seconds to realize the ripples were coming from the Oak tree. She backed away from it as sirens erupted all around her, everywhere and nowhere. Head aching, Kimbo stumbles in the darkness, rifles through her bag, in search of a flashlight and earbuds. Bruised fruit spills on the ground as she scrapes the bottom of her satchel and finally pulls them out. She can no longer hear *Ol Sol* Solomon or Daddy-o-Mention's polite but insistent back-and-forth. She can no longer hear The Root Man's queries lumbering through her head.

When the light returns, the first thing she sees is a squirrel staring in her mouth. It has bright, orange-reddish fur, tufted ears, and a bushy tail sitting on a huge, gnarly tree root, chomping on an acorn. They are surrounded by oaks. Kimbo has walked among them many times, but she never had one speak to her.

Watching Kimbo pass beneath the giant oak trees' branches, the furry creature blinks twice and nods as if to say, *what's up.*

I know you heard him, Kimborelle Mokena Anderson…

Did that squirrel just call my government name?

Yes indeed, the squirrel says, still holding the acorn. *Root Man don't mean no harm. Oaks got long memories. They see and hear a lot of things. You should listen. The Root Man got a message for you, and then we gots to go!*

"I'm good on cryptic," Kimbo said. "I don't know why I understand you or why you understand me, but I'm going home."

Squirrel tosses the empty acorn shell. If she didn't know better, she'd swear it just rolled its eyes at her.

And did. Solomon said you were special. I hope so because we need your help.

Kimbo removes her earbuds. They don't stop the squirrel's plea in her head. The sirens are still blaring, and she realizes she isn't the only one panicking in the usually idyllic Garden. "How can I possibly help you? I'm not anything special at all. I just come here to get away from my jacked up life!" She couldn't believe she was throwing a pity party with a squirrel–a talking squirrel.

Would you kindly please stop saying that? It's not unusual that we can "talk." What's unusual is that you understand. Reframe your mind. We've been "talking" all around you since day one. For some reason, y'all stopped listening.

Kimbo is humbled. How a fluffy little squirrel could make her feel such shame was something else she'd need to sit with–after she gets home.

I know you're worried about your family, but remember, Solomon will take care of that. We need your help, so we can help you! But clearly, Solomon hasn't told you anything. I'll leave that all to him, but it's really important that you give The Root Man a chance. He just needs to holler at you. He and his cousins have worked very hard to get this information for you.

* * *

They stood in front of a stout English oak, impossibly tall and mouthy.

Rock well, Kimbo-relle! We got off to a bad start, but it's a pleasure to finally speak with you. Listen. We only got about two minutes left on this track. I don't like intros and interludes anyway. So let me get right to the hook. Peace to the Herbs and Earth. I'm The Root Man, aka Root Supreme. I'm here to deliver some Knowledge of Self. Solomon mentioned you lost your parents to the deep freeze, and you don't know where they are. That's a cryin' and a shame Ship did you like that. But we got you!"

No one could have told her what to expect from a talking tree who loves Wu Tang and knows supreme mathematics. Whatever she expected, this is not it. If Ngal was here, he'd be right with The Root Man, asking about the day's math.

"My parents?" She blinks back tears. This shocks her even more than realizing she can communicate with other life forms. "They have been gone so long, I gave up on ever seeing them again, at least in this life. Where are they?"

See, that's the thing. Roots don't grow straight.

"What that mean?"

It mean my Cuzzos underground, deep in the rootwork, put the word out with that fungi drummer.

"Fungi drummer?" Kimbo has to turn to the squirrel for a translation.

Squirrel just shakes his head. *Musicians.* He swings his tail in mild irritation. It swishes behind him as he speaks. *He means his tree roots stretch wide and wild, and the fungi have an extensive underground network. They can pass messages from miles around, and find intel on just about anything as long as it's wired into Ship's database. Oak trees have mycelium threads on their roots that connect to the wires in Ship.*

"So you and your *Cuzzos* are hackers?"

Basically, Root Supreme says.

"Okay, but where are they? Can I see them, make sure they're alright?" It had been so very long since she'd been with them.

The rapid crosstalk between the species makes her dizzy. Finally the oak and the squirrel agree on an answer.

You can go see them, Root Supreme says, *and Chops is gonna take you to Solomon so you two can build on it.* Satisfied, Root Supreme shook his branches, but Chops the Squirrel was looking squirrely.

Talkin' bout supreme mathematics. The math wasn't adding up.

Chops skittered across the path. *I take great issue with that.*

"Are you reading my mind?" Kimbo asks. Frustrated, she turns from Chops to Roots Supreme and back to the squirrel again. "Y'all keep responding to my thoughts before I get the chance to talk."

We're speaking to you through your mind, too, but you don't seem to mind that part. Chops raises its eyes and smirks.

This is the only way we can communicate and understand each other. Roots Supreme shakes a branch covered with leaves over Kimbo's head.

"It's going to take me a minute to get used to all this news."

Unfortunately, we don't really have the time. We need to get to Solomon.

Kimbo looks away. She isn't sure what she'll say to Solomon when she speaks with him. "I need a breather. Gotta go make dinner, anyway. The children will be wondering why I'm late."

Crosstalk made her rub her forehead. "Could y'all ease up. I can hear you but it still feels really weird."

I think Solomon has some more info to share with you, Chops said. He's not far, we can get there on time if we hurry.

A flock of blackbirds sweep by them, their glossy feathers glisten as they disappear into the trees. *Time to get on down!* they cry in unison. *Ship is coming! Ship coming!*

The spectacular starlings announce themselves before they are seen in their synchronized flight pattern, *Naw, naw! Ship here! Ship here!*

Fear pores out of Kimbo. Her mouth is dry. If Ship catches her in the Garden, it's a wrap for her, her children, and Ngal. *Damn.*

She slings her satchel tighter around her shoulder, eyes darting to see where she can exit or hide.

Ain't no hiding now, Kimbo, we gots to go!

"Thank you, Root Supreme. Thank your cousins, too!" Kimbo cries as she scrambles to keep up with Chops the Squirrel.

Peace to the Garden and the Water Dreaming. You an honorary Cuzzo now, Queen!

As Chops and Kimbo zig-zag through the Garden, passing each of the places she loves, the life gathered there bursts into spontaneous applause. Trees lift their branches, flowers bow their beautiful blooms, the birds sing a medley of gratitude. *Thank you, thank you!* fills the space between her heart and her head, the sound so loud Kimbo nearly falls down. *We believe in you, we believe, we believe!*

* * *

Kimbo is so frightened, she doesn't even look back. Ship can never know that she's ever been here even one time. Out of breath, she gasps for air, leaning on a rusty, graffiti-tagged portal door. A part of her grieves. After that scare, would she dare visit the Garden again? The risk is too great. *Fun while it lasted,* she thinks.

She bangs on the gunmetal door covered in aerosol art. "How do I get out of here?"

Chops erupts in high-pitched squeaks, rocking himself in a corner.

"Are you okay?" she asks. His mood has changed drastically, and the squirrel appears more anxious than he was when they were fleeing Ship.

More chattering. Kimbo frowns. "I'm sorry but I can't understand that. Speak to me. You've led me to a dead end. Do you have any passcodes?" She wonders briefly if the magic of cross-species communication only worked in Solomon's Garden.

Chops nods his head furiously. *Forgive me, I don't fool with Ship too much. They don't mean nothing good to nobody.* He points his bushy tail at a keypad above his head, so expertly camouflaged in the graffiti, she missed it.

At the other end of the corridor two of Ship's crew members come running out of the garden. They stop and draw guns when they spot Kimbo and the bright, red squirrel prancing beside her.

Punch these in, quick, they're coming! Chops rattles off the passcode.

"Stop!" one of Ship's crew member's yells. "Or we'll..."

Trembling, hardly able to see, Kimbro types in the code. Bullets ricochet off the door as the pair dive into the opening.

"Shoot to kill!" a crew member yells, as the corridor fills with armed soldiers covered in heavy armor. Kimbo and Chops scramble for cover. After diving into a corner, Kimbo turns over and notices someone else in the room. Somebody was already here—waiting for them. Confused, terrified, Kimbo scoots back and presses her back against the wall with Chops perched on top of her head.

A humanoid figure with reddish-brown, Martian dust skin smiles at Kimbo as a raging storm of gunfire fills the open doorway. Unaffected, the humanoid raises one hand. A force, almost invisible, ripples from his fingertips, throwing the bullets back and the bullets in mid-air and hurls them back in the opposite direction. The corridor fills with explosions as the armored soldiers are thrown back into the corridor. The alloy door closes, trapping Kimbro and Chops in the room with the humanoid.

"You ready to go?" it asks, smiles with glowing eyes and an electronic voice that raises both Kimbo's eyebrows,

Damn. That sounds familiar.

"Solomon?"

Kimbo knows the answer, but it takes a few moments for her eyes to accept the truth.

Instead of answering Kimbo, Solomon gives Chops a disapproving look as the squirrel leaps onto the floor.

"What are you doing here?" Solomon asks the squirrel.

"Things got crazy when Ship crew raided the Garden," Chops answers. "I had to run for my life. Honestly, I panicked and ran behind my girl here."

"You mean you got running your mouth instead of getting yourself safe." Solomon shook his humanoid head.

Kimbo spots a plaque above the doorway "MARS SUPPLY POD" stamped on it.

"Mars?" In an instant, the faces of her children flash before her eyes.

Kimbo doesn't think her stomach can sink any lower, then a day at the Garden says *hold my beer.* Adrenaline and grief course through her. She knows they're waiting at home, wondering where their mother is. Kimbo clutches her satchel. The fresh vegetables and fruit she collected earlier makes a sad weight in her hand. Ngal will skip dinner, split the last of the fresh food between all three of the children, and even if she found someone to trust, the pod door was sealed. It was too late to tell them where she's gone. And what would she tell them? *I've been kidnapped, bamboozled by a robot and a talking squirrel.*

She promised never to leave them.

Despair stings her eyes. She collapses in the safety harness, while Chops is balled up in a fetal position atop a huge crate.

"Solomon, how could you?" Angry tears stream down her face. "My children, my job...my life."

"I can explain," Solomon says. He looks as if he is not yet adjusted to moving in the physical world. His voice doesn't match his mouth's movements. His hands hover over the pod's dashboard.

"Explain what? How you smiled in my face, pretended to be my friend, to do what? Ruin my entire world? None of us can return to Ship. They'll ban us for life!!" The idea of her not seeing her children grow up nearly takes her out. Her words fill the cramped space between them. Silence fills the rest.

"My first mind told me not to trust you or nobody else from Below. Y'all just as fake as I don't know what." Kimbo wants to rip out this humanoid's throat. Even if she could, what would that prove? Nothing.

"I know this is distressing, but I didn't plan this to happen this way."

"So you did *plan it*. You admit you set me up from the jump."

"Technically, if you recall, I didn't think you were ready. Daddy-o..."

"Oh, blame it on your little friend." If she could snatch a knot in him, she would. "Ready for what! You have been tip-toeing around this for a long time."

"I needed to observe you, see if you could be coached, if you worked well with a team..."

"Coachable? Eco-engineer?" Kimbo scoffed. "What are you, a bunch of terrorists?"

Chops chatters, a trembling heap. His long, bushy red tail covers his furry face.

"Dear Kimbo, I'm no terrorist. I'm a survivor. So are you. Do you think I've dedicated my whole existence to studying inter-species communication and sentient beings just to blow things up and hurt people? I know it's a lot to ask of you—"

"You didn't ask."

"—And for that I am sorry. But there is someone very special who is counting on you. You once told me you wanted to cut your chains, the ties that bound you to Ship. What if you could do that, but not just for you and your family, but for everyone, for many lifeforms? In all my searching, I've met no one who has the potential, the power you hold. You may not believe in it, but we do. The choices you make in the next 48 hours can change the whole world, all three of them."

Kimbo glares at the gardener she'd once considered her best friend.

"Fuck you."

From overhead, a scratchy vid-screen pops out. "Surprise, surprise!" Daddy-o says, waving his neon, telephone-wire legs. "I am so, so, very excited to welcome you to Mars! We're going to have so much fun when you get here! I promise it won't be all work and no play!"

A damn spider? Chops and Kimbo say in unison.

"Your trip is one full sol. 24 hours, *wee*, 39 minutes, *yeah*, 35 seconds, *hey now*! Including a few hours for descent, and a little time for entry, final descent, landing, etc., etc.. But don't *wor-rrry*. Your trusted pilot has you well-stocked with delicious provisions. Daddy-o, *that's meee,* made a very special playlist for your listening pleasure. Enjoy the sounds and the *viewww*."

Isaac Hayes's melodious baritone, a whining wah-wah guitar, and grooving bassline fill the pod. The soulful background singers, organ chords, and gritty drums do not match the despair, the fear, and the determination of its three passengers. Kimbo grips the harness, her nails digging into the equipment. She wants to wail and moan, but won't give Solomon or the traitor, Chops, the satisfaction. She fears she will be another disappeared, one of the hole folk who just vanish, like her parents. She wonders if Root Supreme and his *Cuzzos* even knew her parent's names, or her children's.

But it doesn't matter. Just as the last of Ship, the fabled *Djark-arta* drifts out of view, and the vast expanse of stars begins to sparkle and shine, Kimbo sees the reddish disc, Mars, rising into view. As they descend, she grips the knotted crossroad string she'd tucked in her satchel and vows in the name of Raulli, Nebula, and Crux she will find a way to see them again.

DOWNWINDERS

Dedicated to Tina Cordova and the Downwinders, whose hope for justice shines as bright as any desert bloom.

And there was a river streaming from the right hand,
and beautiful trees rose up from it;
and whosoever shall eat of them shall live forever.
— *Barnabas 11:10*

I t was once said that deserts are places without expectations. You arrive and enter, leave or stay in your own rhythm. Without judgment, they offer roads to mysteries revealed over time. The only witness is the sun, the wind, the stars that watch above. Here the white sands contain cosmic maps to worlds seen and unseen. And this one contained a part of me I had spent my life trying to remember.

At some point, things that are lost are found again. So it goes, in the place where my grandfather told me our ancestors were buried.

First it was the bones. The mammoth, wooly, wondrous who rose from the white shifting sands of dune lit by the sun. Cobalt blue sky, an arc above our shoulders.

"That's where she lies," he says in a voice full of claret cup cactus blooms, soap tree yucca, and purple sand verbena. Under the listening sun, his skin shines, weathered as the bark of Rio Grande cottonwood trees. He'd been silent most of our journey, his unspoken words weighing heavy in the air between us. We share more than blood, more than memory. We share the weight of silences, of all the years that my mother's death has put between us. In our family, secrets are sacred, stoicism its own religion. But now, standing in the land that means to abandon and forsake, he speaks so softly, as if this place was as holy as church.

My mother, Gabriella, was a casualty to a war she never fought or saw. The bomb dropped decades ago, but its fiery poisons caused the slow, quiet deaths of thousands who lived in the shadow of its mushroom clouds. Our family is one of those once called Downwinders, people who were exposed to the radioactive contamination and fallout from nuclear testing. For years our bloodlines were filled with the remnants of coal ash, iodized radiation, poisons that slowly took breath, took years, took life. The weapons and the power were thieves that stole more than lives. They took time from us, whole generations and years we cannot get back.

Grandfather has brought me here as a witness. He tells me there is a miracle growing, one that must be seen, touched, smelled to fully understand. I clutch my cane, shake my head. He has made a mistake, a wrong turn on land I do not recognize.

"Where are we? Where are the graves?" I ask, cupping my eyes from the sun. It has been a long time since I've been here. We came together many times in my youth. I do not recognize the terrain that surrounds us now.

He holds up one of the tattered newspaper articles, a rare artifact, highlighted in yellow so I can see it. *"July 11, 2055, the first Global Zero Day, thousands marched down streets around the world, as confetti rained from the air, to celebrate the disarmament of the last nuclear weapons in the world."*

With shaking hands, he passes me another of his newspapers. I scan the familiar montage of historic photos, the masses gathered outside, hands clasped, faces raised in gratitude, some in prayer. They embrace each other outside the Great Pyramid of Giza, Sankore Mosque, Chichen Itza, the Taj Mahal, Notre Dame, at the base of the soaring African Renaissance Monument in Senegal, and atop the Christ the Redeemer statue in Rio, and beyond.

"On this day, the USA, Russia, China, Israel, Palestine, North Korea, and the Democratic Republic of the Congo, South Sudan, the remaining holdouts, disarmed their last nuclear weapons simultaneously in a live globally televised ceremony. But one year after the earth said goodbye to the force that held us in fear for 110 years, new trees were planted from grafts of trees native to each of the final Disarmers to commemorate a more peaceful earth."

I nod and hand them back to him, careful not to tear the delicate newsprint. "I've seen these photos before, Grandfather, but I don't understand..."

His smile is hope tinged with sadness. He taps his watch and the jewel-toned logo of the BiblioTeka app floats above his wrist. An article from a few months ago appears. He redirects and expands it with a tap, and soon a cheerful voice floats through the air.

"Planning is underway for the annual celebrations as we will soon mark the fortieth anniversary of Global Zero Day. But four decades after the historic new world agreement, scientists now say new phenomena have been observed..."

Excited, Grandfather waves the old newspapers, faded banners, relics of ancient media, as if they can explain the new mystery unfolding around me.

All those many years ago, 5:29 am, July 16, 1945, the world's first atomic bomb was tested here at the Trinity site, north of Alamogordo, on the now defunct White Sands Missile Range. The security checkpoint is falling apart, its walls graffitied with peace symbols and doves. The museum has been shuttered, its rockets, jets, and missiles, the decommissioned and the replicas, removed. Trinity was its code name. The next month, plutonium rained down from sky, rained down devastation on Japan, during World War II. The reign of fire rained on us as well. Bloodlines poisoned for generations to come, clusters of cancer and other illnesses, genetic disorders, a grief so heavy we carry it still, until...

"The first known occurrence was in Nagasaki," Grandfather says. "Scientists claim that trees that had never been seen since the forties sprung up, seemingly overnight."

"Resurrection plants," he says, pointing at the exotic blossoms around us. "What is lost is never truly gone, is it? We have already lived through wonders," he says, his voice wistful. "Perhaps it can return to us, perhaps..." He lets his voice trail off.

332

Violence has not gone, nor petty cruelty, but we have left behind the fear of not surviving. The burden of such incomprehensible weapons, the power to destroy whole cities at such a scale is gone, and with it, new seeds of being, of knowing and living have grown. My mother did not live to see this day. But Grandfather did, as have I. She does not know that the poison that our family carried so long is healed, that the weight of existential worry is lifted, extending even the rhythms of human life itself.

Perhaps the earth's worries have been lifted as well. The ground releasing other forms of life and nourishment as it heals from the deep, long scars of nuclear war, the fallout from heat 10,000 times greater than the sun.

I listen a while longer, then Grandfather hands me a clipping carefully cut from a magazine. I read on, "Archaeologists excavated sites, discovering remnants of ancient seeds. Tombs and sarcophagi of ancient Egyptians packed with wheat seeds for the afterlife were replanted and the carbon remains of grains were found in Pompeii's ruins. Methuselah Judean date palms grow in Israel from the Masada excavations. *Silene stenophylla,* arctic plants have regrown from 32,000-year-old seeds buried in a Siberian riverbank by an Ice Age squirrel. They flourish still, but the plants now growing at Hiroshima and Nagasaki are not like the trees that healed after the first bombs. These are from far more ancient times. New discoveries offer new mysteries..."

"I don't understand," I say, handing him the paper. He folds it up carefully into origami squares, and tucks it into his pocket, patting it as if it was a precious gift.

"Fresh prints of dire wolves and camels were discovered here,"
Grandfather says, his eyes lit up, reflecting the blue sky. "It is as if
the land is resetting."

"Perhaps it's a hoax," I say, impatient. We have switched places.
He is the overeager child and I am the worn elder. I dig my cane into
the rich earth, so different from the white gypsum grains of sand. To
have made this journey again, early as it is, it still feels too late. Once
we traveled by car, today it was by FluxJet. I no longer dream of my
mother's hands, the dark strands of hair she brushes from her face,
the eyes I can't remember.

"Those creatures have not lived for more years than I can imagine," I say. "Perhaps this is an art installation the state has sponsored.
When they extended and expanded RECA?"

The Radiation Exposure Compensation Act once excluded
Trinity site survivors like my family, but after many years of advo-
cacy, those who were exposed to radiation finally saw justice. My
mother and many of her peers died of lung cancer—non-smokers
all. Other cancers, family clusters, have taken their toll on life in the
Basin and beyond. Tina Cordova, a brave Downwinder advocate,
said, "We are the forgotten collateral damage." Thanks to the activists' tireless efforts, the money spent to oil the cogs of war are finally
being redistributed into improving the welfare of society, extending
the lives of us all.

"This could all be a special tribute to the Downwinders and
nuclear workers," I say, "those who did not survive the Trinity test
fallout. Maybe it's a remembrance they will announce later?" The
uncanny scent of flowers drifts past me, making me less sure.

The dent in Grandfather's forehead wrinkles, the brim of his hat shading his eyes. I can feel waves of frustration coming off him from where I stand, then he replaces it with conviction. "See," he says, pointing.

Recognition runs down my shocked spine, a burst of light. Forgiveness falls from the sky, in the form of snowfall. The sight shakes me more than the blossoms, the river, or the paw prints.

"When was the last time you saw it snow in the desert?" he asks, his voice as cool as the flakes I brush away with the back of my hand.

Once hot snowflakes, fallout from the nuclear testing, fell from the sky for days and coated orchards, gardens, livestock, cisterns, ponds, lakes, and creeks. Chickens and dogs died, and a surge of infants, too. Like my mother, the children rest beneath these layers of time, where the sky and the land remember.

Grandfather reaches out his hand to me.

"Here, we keep the memory alive," he says, of those we have loved and lost in an untamed war that raged against the land. The desert has changed more than what I remember. We have changed more than I remember.

His body curves, stooped with the years of candlelight vigils, the luminaria, the litany of names we have all sung together. When the clouds came over our town, they wrote all our names in their dust. Eight hundred names one year, 929 the next, and so on. The bomb changed our gene pools just as it changed the soil and the rocks and the air. But there were no monuments to that, no museums detailing our history. But ours is a history of survival.

We are still here.

The land echoes our call. *I am still here.*

The flora and fauna cry, *We are still here.*

This desert whose boundaries fluctuate with the seasons has begun to shrink rather than expand. Instead of desertification, a reversal is in progress. It is the same for the sense of justice in the world. Once our government spent trillions on military defense. Healthcare, social support, affordable housing, childcare, the things that help communities stay strong, stable, secure were left to the whims of politicos whose names and values changed with the wind.

No more.

Verdant ribbons of sagebrush snake across the edges of white dunes, its sharp, clean scent carried on the snowy air – a scent of resilience, of ancient knowledge. It seems a fitting symbol. Our spirit has changed, the world's resolve has changed. We approach life now valuing co-existence, collaboration. That old wisdom, the kind carried in plants like this sage, finally has a voice in the halls of disarmament, in places like UNODA (the United Nations Office of Disarmament Affairs). The walls of fear are coming down, many borders have, too. The ground of our world feels as if it is shifting beneath our feet, even as the sky falls, gifting beautiful snowflakes, grateful tears.

"Have they terraformed the desert?" I ask, grasping for any strands of reason. Since the Disarmers, new strains of grain have been formed to feed the world's hungry. No one fights over water rights anymore, though there are still skirmishes over the usual old grievances. Security is no longer a question of a red button, a count-down sending us all to doom. So many scientists have made our land and dunes in the Basin their temporary homes, patiently watching and weighing, another kind of witness.

He shakes his head, no.

"Come," Grandfather says and guides me carefully up one of the glistening white dunes. Sand covers my feet, and I feel as if I should be barefoot, the way we walked the dunes when I was a child. I had forgotten the way the sand felt like a warm kiss against my skin, powdery and soft. I haven't sled down a dune, arms spread, my laughter whipping behind me, in many long years.

"Ever since the Disarmers, the earth has changed, even here." I climb the ridge and my breath escapes me.

What replaces some of its old beds and dunes is a sight I am unprepared for. Waves of green grasslands dotted with snow sway as far as I can see, a river of green amidst the ivory.

Verdant ribbons of sagebrush snake across the edges of white dunes. Lavender-colored blossoms rise up, dotting the land, an uncanny bouquet of colors and scents drifting through the wind.

I nod. This is more than a tribute. It is a testimony. I am the radiant child of Downwinders, whose memory I hold in my breast. We stand upon a sturdy rock and watch the blue-green waters rise, the color as deep as the sky above. Flash floods are known here, but not rivers. Rivers are ghosts of the ancient past. When I was small, we added our footprints to the fossils at Lake Otero, footprints said to be tens of thousands of years old. But the ghosts of the Tularosa Basin have returned. *Ruppia cirrhosa*. Ancient grass seeds rise from earth once too dry and barren to hold their roots.

"Gabby never thought she'd see the day," Grandfather says, his face full of tears. That old twinge of resentment pulses through me. It catches in my throat and pricks like a cocklebur, and the words are out of my throat before I can stop them. "She did not," I say, wind and gritty sand running over my teeth. "She did not live to see the day, and I am sorry."

He strokes the band on his hat, the brim shading his eyes. It's a gesture I've seen a hundred times. He blinks as if to reset how he sees me. Not the numb granddaughter who no longer knows how to mourn or how not to grieve, but the smiling child who clung to his hand, his second shadow eager to follow him wherever the sun falls, traveling all over the earth.

In my youth I followed him with the others, the brave souls who spoke truth to power in the state capitol, in the halls of Congress, who worked tirelessly to get compensation for the ill, amending and amending and amending again until they finally brought some small measure of dignity to every family touched by "the gadget." The activists worked from generation to generation, ensuring that even those whose claims had been declined were finally acknowledged and supported.

Now my thoughts float on the petals of flowers long unseen. Eighteen-hundred-year-old bouquets blossom alongside limestone and shale. It is a sight that defies vision, one that feels like a mockery to my grief, the loss I held inside my bones as tightly as any coffin.

The gypsum sand crystals have dissolved in the river waters like sugar in iced tea. A shallow ghost sea from 250 million years ago raises its head up, bringing back life from the old sea floor. A giant chambered nautilus shell, orange and pink with tinges of iridescent green, floats to the shore. The tops of crinklemat and moonpod bushes peak above the waters along with long-extinct megaflora we have no names for.

"Strange corals and boneless fish swim in these waters now," Grandfather says. "I wanted to surprise you. I wanted you to see for yourself. The same thing happened in Nagasaki. The city is filled with more camphor and oleander, life forms from ages ago." He stoops to pick up a sprig of wild hyacinth. "Ginkgo, black locust, persimmons survived in Hiroshima after the first blast. When the bomb dropped, the trees were charred by heat rays, but they remained standing. Like you and me. Survivors gathered under the trees whose branches were blown away. Months later blossoms sprung up. They helped in the spirit of recovery." He looks at me, his eyes gentle, the folds in his forehead now smooth. "Perhaps this will help you."

I sit with this in silence. When the last of the Disarmers signed their agreement, I celebrated like everyone else, but a part of me held onto a sorrow I had no words for, no breath to speak in the face of such a victory. To grieve seemed ungrateful.

Grandfather waved a hand in the direction of the plants bursting from the ground that once could not hold them. "The earth was scarred, but the memories of that day rested in the roots of those trees. Like here," he said. "A miracle, Amana, the land is reawakening. She remembers. It was we who forgot." He weeps silently, and finally, I know why he has brought me here.

"If the earth has returned these old lives, perhaps..." He does not finish.

"Impossible," I say, the prickly weed caught in my throat. My tongue feels heavy; I struggle to speak. "Zombie plants, ghost rivers, spirit seas, snow in the desert...this won't bring her back. This won't bring any of them back!" We are walking past giant prickly pear cacti.

O. alta and *O. engelmannii, 15 to 30 feet high.* Fuchsia fruit and yellow blossoms burst in the air.

"It is time," Grandfather says. "Time to let her go."

I do not need to ask of whom he speaks. The memory of my mother is a ghost who has always been with me.

We float toward an ocean of sky, his hand clasped in my own. Something dark like a moth flutters past, quiet and subdued. The silence between us is as deep as any forest, the love as wide as any shore. I feel myself moving closer to a place of healing. Like ancient seeds dreaming awake through centuries, finally finding fertile ground, peace slides into the notes like jazz.

A NASHOBA NOCTURNE

Nashoba hadn't just failed, it had consumed. Swallowed whole the eighty-eight souls promised freedom, leaving only silence where their endings should have been written. A silence thick and heavy in the humid Tennessee air, heavy like grief, heavy like a secret held too long. Dr. Althea Moreau, historian, collector of lost stories and deliberately forgotten lives, drove towards that silence, towards the place near Memphis where history didn't just sleep, it festered. She thought she was chasing footnotes, the quiet truths buried under louder narratives. She didn't yet understand that Nashoba's silence wasn't empty. It listened. And it remembered with teeth.

For Dr. Althea Moreau, history was an unclaimed inheritance, a force humming low in her blood. It formed an insistent rhythm beneath the careful cadence of her academic life. More than just her profession, this pulse was felt most strongly in the presence of the deliberately forgotten. She sought these obscured narratives, these forgotten echoes now holding the weight of whole lives ground into dust or faded ink. Nashoba called loudest. Not the official story recited in texts—Frances Wright's noble, failed "gradual abolition" experiment, dissolving predictably into mismanagement, swamp fever, racism, despair—but the silences. The gaps where dozens of freed souls, promised a new beginning, given pseudo-freedom, then simply…vanished. They vanished like the poor souls of Roanoke, except the multiracial souls of Nashoba disappeared without even a carved note in the dark woods.

This particular silence felt personal to Althea, sharp as a shard of glass under the skin. Perhaps because her own family history was a carefully curated exhibit: the upward striving, the sharp suits replacing overalls, the degrees framed like shields against a past deemed too rough, too strange, too country. Whispers of anything older, rooted in deeper, darker soil – a grandmother's remedies, a great-aunt's remarkably accurate dreams – were met with polite, impenetrable quiet. *We look forward, Althea, always forward.* That quiet, that determined forgetting, had paradoxically pushed her into the archives, seeking the very stories they'd locked away. Nashoba felt like the taproot of it all, demanding excavation. She adjusted her glasses, her fingers briefly tracing the condensation on the chilled steering wheel before gripping it again. The heat shimmering off the asphalt ribbon of I-40 made the air visibly waver. Even the familiar Tennessee sight of dense green weeds swallowing roadside trees felt different here, more ominous, closer. A muted thrum pulsed beneath the cicada's song, an ancient disquiet carried on the heavy air, as if the land itself held its breath. Her meticulous mind mapped the terrain of inquiry, unaware she was driving towards the place where history breathed heavy in the humid air, and sometimes, bit back.

Germantown unfolded like a glossy *Southern Homes* magazine spread. Immaculate lawns defying the summer heat, sculpted hedges, houses asserting their importance with columns and porte-cochères. Althea barely registered its curated perfection, her focus already narrowing, a knot of anticipation tightening in her chest. But the turnoff Althea sought narrowed quickly, winding beneath ancient oaks and water cypress, Tupelo dripping Spanish moss like weary lace. She gripped the wheel a little tighter as the manicured world fell away. Sunlight struggled here, dappled and uncertain. The air grew thick, cloying with honeysuckle and the unmistakable, loamy perfume of decay—the scent of perpetually damp earth saturated with centuries of memory.

Althea inhaled deeply, the aroma a complex tapestry of life and rot. Beneath the sweetness of honeysuckle, she could almost taste the iron tang of old sorrows, the land's exhalation of Chikashsha tears and the blood of the enslaved, a sorrow so profound it felt geological.

Her rental cabin huddled at the lane's end, overshadowed by the woods, a clapboard relic shrinking from the encroaching wealth. Its paint peeled like sunburnt skin, the porch sagging slightly as if burdened by the weight of unseen watchers from the treeline. Cutting the engine, Althea was plunged into a sudden bath of sound: the high, electric drone of cicadas drilling into the afternoon heat, underscored by a disquieting, watchful silence. It was a silence that felt older than the trees, deeper than the reach of sunlight—the quiet of a land that had witnessed too much and forgotten nothing, its original spirit still unappeased.

Stepping out, the humidity embraced her, a damp, heavy silk clinging to her skin, tasting faintly of pollen and dust. The cabin's air hung still. It smelled of old wood, dried herbs—one sharp and vaguely bitter, like a warning, another strangely sweet, like a forgotten prayer—she couldn't quite place, and the faint ghost of gardenias. Dust motes, like tiny golden spirits, danced in the shafts of light piercing the gloom. On a worn armchair lay the quilt, a "gift" from the caretaker. Oddly covered in round mirrors, each one stitched onto the fabric like a silver eye staring into some unseen realm, Althea unfolded it, the fabric cool beneath her fingers. A kind of electric shock leapt from the mirrored surfaces, stinging, and she yelped, shook, looked around, embarrassed. Intricate, hand-stitched patterns swirled in deep indigos and dried-blood reds, the lines jagged, hypnotic, drawing the eye towards turbulent, vortex-like centers. A map of a troubled sleep, yes, or perhaps the stitches themselves were screams trapped in thread. She folded it carefully, the weight of the place settling onto her shoulders, heavier than the Tennessee summer air itself, pressing down with the gravity of things unseen and unspoken.

THE SOIL REMEMBERS

He seemed less to walk from the woods and more to coalesce out of the dense shade where the tamed yard surrendered to the wild tangle beyond. Elias Thorne. His face, carved by sun and time, held the texture of old bark. His eyes, dark and deep-set, assessed Althea with a stillness that offered no purchase. He held pruning shears, the metal glinting dully, less like a tool for gardening, more like something used for cutting away rot, or perhaps, for keeping things contained.

344

"Dr. Moreau?" His voice was a low rasp, the sound of stones shifting underwater.

"Mr. Thorne. Yes." Althea summoned her professional smile, a shield against the sudden prickle of unease. "The cabin is... characterful." A historian's euphemism for neglected.

He grunted, a sound absorbed by the heavy air. His gaze swept past her, towards the woods, lingering. "Place is quiet," he allowed. "Mostly." He wore sturdy denim, faded at the knees, but pinned near the collar of his chambray shirt catching the stray light, were those small, round discs. Tiny mirrors, no bigger than dimes, sewn or pinned to the fabric. Like scattered, watchful eyes. Odd, yet Althea felt a flicker, a buried memory of folklore read long ago, dismissed as superstition.

"I'm here for the history," Althea offered, trying to reclaim familiar ground. "Nashoba."

Elias's gaze snapped back to her, sharp and penetrating. "Some history's best left buried, Doctor." He paused, the silence stretching, filled only by the cicadas' relentless drone. He kicked lightly at the dark, rich earth with the toe of his worn boot. A puff of what looked like black dust, fine as powdered bone, rose and settled around his worn leather. Althea noticed then how the shadows pooling beneath the ancient oaks seemed to drink the light, deeper and cooler here than anywhere else in the yard.

"This place, Nashoba," Elias said, his gaze drifting to the wild treeline, "means 'wolf' in the old tongues, Althea. And this land, it remembers with teeth. This soil we walking on..." His voice dropped, taking on a gravelly resonance, his gaze fixed on the disturbed earth as if it might speak. "It don't forget nothing. It holds it all, everything,

Doc. Every broken promise, every drop of blood, every violated slumber of those who were here first. Holds onto things, especially the sorrows from when the sacred mounds by the great river were torn open and the Old People's spirits were given no peace. Not all of 'em pleasant, what this ground has been forced to swallow and what it sometimes spits back up."

Another pause, so profound the cicadas' drone seemed to recede, leaving only the heavy beat of Althea's own heart.

"You watch yourself wandering around. Especially," his voice dropped lower, "after dark." He turned then, no nod, no farewell, simply melting back into the treeline, becoming shadow and leaf as silently as he'd appeared, leaving Althea with the buzzing heat and the distinct chill of a warning sincerely given.

WHISPERS IN THE STACKS

Days became a study in contrasts. Althea moved between the sterile chill of the university archives. The scent of acidic paper, binding glue, and climate control, the hushed rustle of turning pages contrasted with the fecund heat of the woods bordering her cabin. In the archives, Althea's gloved hands moved with a grim precision born of long practice, yet her breath still hitched at the stark realities before her. She knew, intellectually, the broad strokes of slavery's horrific reign in the region from countless secondary sources. But here, the primary documents whispered their own intimate, chilling truths. First, she delved into the broader context, seeking to understand the very soil from which Nashoba sprang. She found records detailing the city's very genesis, built upon the bluffs by the forced labor of the original 109 enslaved Africans, their unacknowledged sacrifice laying the first stones and clearing the first paths through the wilderness. Brittle city directories from early Memphis and chillingly mundane broadsides for slave auctions then screamed of the city's subsequent foundational sin: the burgeoning slave marts on Adams Street, a key regional hub where thousands more Black bodies were commodified, their fates decided by men like Nathan Bedford Forrest whose name was a bland entry alongside cotton futures. The methodical cruelty, the sheer volume of human lives reduced to chattel in ledgers and shipping manifests, left a cold knot in Althea's stomach that the archive's climate control could not touch. It was a necessary, brutal immersion before she could face Nashoba's specific sorrows. Then, with a heart heavy from those initial findings, she shifted her focus, her gloved hands turning to the elegant, hopeful script of Nashoba's *early* ledgers—bushels of corn, yards of cloth, the fragile promise of a new beginning painstakingly recorded.

Then, the shift in those specific Nashoba journals was undeniable, a descent made even more jarring by the calculated horror of the city records she'd just examined: handwriting growing erratic, desperate. *Night fevers sweep the quarters...wasting sickness takes another... stock found drained, eyes wide with terror...figures seen lurking beyond the pale, tall and quick...* Then, names, scratched with a shaking hand. *Nicodemus, his strength unnerves, a shadow in his countenance...Lyra, her night songs settle deep, leave the spirit hollow and wanting...* Names that seemed to vibrate off the brittle page, cold against her fingertips, now resonating with an even deeper, more horrifying echo, given the city's backdrop of methodical human trade she had just confronted.

BENEATH THE BOTTLE TREE

The woods offered a different archive. Althea pushed through grasping vines, their thorns snagging at her clothes like greedy fingers. She felt the network of roots beneath the leaf litter. A hidden language underfoot and breathed the air thick with the scent of pine needles, damp moss, and an older, mineral aroma—the scent of earth disturbed too many times, by too many sorrows. She found the gnarled bottle tree Elias had mentioned, its branches festooned with cobalt blue, deep green, and brown glass. Its arms were upturned to the shifting light, humming with trapped energy, or perhaps trapped spirits glinting in the sun—not just the recent dead of Nashoba, she sensed, but older, unremembered presences caught in the land's enduring imbalance.

Deeper still, following a path only her intuition—that awakened ancestral pulse—could see, she found the clearing. A sudden, almost breathless hush fell as she stepped past a curtain of ancient vines, the usual chorus of insects ceasing as if a hand had been clapped over the mouth of the woods. The air within it was unnaturally still, the light different, filtered through the dense canopy into an ethereal, sorrowful green as if the sun itself hesitated to fully illuminate a place so profoundly saturated with grief, both from the stolen Chikashsha rest and Nashoba's subsequent despair. Unmarked graves, stones tilted like broken teeth, half-swallowed by the earth. Adorned not with flowers, but with offerings both poignant and disturbing: shards of blue-willow china, rusted hinges, and the grotesque, watchful shapes of upturned ugly jugs, their ceramic faces distorted, mouths open to catch... what? *Wandering souls from*

Nashoba's ruin? Malevolent intentions born of the plantation's cruelty? Or, Althea wondered, her skin prickling, were they meant to appease or capture the older, elemental spirits of the desecrated mounds, the unquieted First Peoples whose sorrow formed the very bedrock of this haunted place?

Elias Thorne was there one afternoon, kneeling beside a sunken stone almost lost to time, carefully, reverently, clearing weeds. His movements were slow, ritualistic, ancient as the woods themselves. He looked up as she approached, his eyes acknowledging her presence but offering no welcome, no explanation. He simply nodded once, his silence a heavy cloak around the forgotten dead, a statement more profound than any words.

THE SCENT OF POKEBERRIES

He found her by the bottle tree late one afternoon, the low sun igniting the colored glass like jewels scattered against the deepening green. He moved through the woods with an easy, startling grace, emerging into the clearing not as if he'd pushed through the undergrowth, but as if summoned by the light itself. *Malachi Ashby.* His smile was dazzling, instantly disarming, erasing not just the woods' immediate gloom, but for a moment, even the deeper, ancient sorrows Althea had felt clinging to this wounded land. A local historian, he said, voice smooth as polished river stone, an amateur but consumed by Nashoba and its lost stories. He was arrestingly handsome, magnetic, carrying his knowledge effortlessly, like a well-worn coat. But his enthusiasm for the darker aspects of Nashoba felt a shade too keen. He named the plants she'd only vaguely identified – the distinct three-lobed leaves of sassafras, the hidden rhizome of bloodroot. He pointed to a cluster of dark, gleaming pokeberries nestled in vibrant green leaves. "Beautiful, aren't they?" he murmured, his eyes meeting hers, holding a spark of challenge, of something anciently knowing. "But poison, deep down." His gaze invited her into a silence that hummed with a purpose beyond simple historical facts. There was an immediate current between them, intellectual and something more vital, electric. He seemed to anticipate her questions, understood the nuances she sought in the historical silence, yet an edge lay beneath the charm. His gaze lingered a fraction too long; his knowledge felt too complete, too intimate, as if learned firsthand rather than from books, its depth hinting at an chilling familiarity. Sometimes, a shared bitterness seemed to lace his insights, or a quiet satisfaction when recounting the depths of Nashoba's ruin. He felt like a guide, yes, but perhaps into territory far more dangerous than she'd anticipated. When he spoke of the raw power of the land, a flicker of something almost zealous would cross his handsome features, quickly veiled by his practiced charm. A guide who seemed to know the surface history, the Nashoba sorrows, with a troubling intimacy, yet Althea found herself wondering if his understanding pierced the veil to the older, foundational wounds of the land itself, or if his knowledge, for all its keenness, still skated only upon the surface of the true abyss. A crossroads embodied, smelling faintly of old paper and damp earth.

THE BRUISE OF KNOWING

Malachi became invaluable, a key unlocking doors Althea hadn't known existed. He produced obscure pamphlets from personal collections, directed her to overlooked correspondences buried deep in archival boxes, his insights always perceptive, pushing her a calculated step closer to the unsettling heart of Nashoba's mystery. He seemed less to assist, and more to steer her path, each insight a carefully placed stone on a specific, dangerous road. It was almost as if he was cultivating her discoveries, leading her to the very truths he already knew she needed to find.

Almost too perceptive, too helpful, Althea found herself thinking on one of their now frequent evening walks. Dusk was settling like a soft, bruised plum over the tree line bordering the Nashoba grounds, the air thick with the intoxicating sweetness of night-blooming jasmine. Fireflies had begun their hesitant, enchanting dance in the deepening shadows, their tiny lights pulsing like scattered stars brought to earth.

"The 109 souls," Malachi said, his voice a low murmur that seemed to blend with the evening's chorus of crickets. He had a way of picking up her unspoken thoughts, a habit she found both thrilling and deeply disconcerting. They walked close on the narrow path, the back of his hand brushing hers with a feather-light touch that sent a jolt, sharp and undeniable, through her.

Althea drew a breath, the jasmine almost too sweet, too heavy. "You speak of them with such... certainty, Malachi. As if you knew them."

He turned his head slightly, his profile a striking silhouette against the fading light. His smile, when it came, was a slow, knowing curve. "History is a living thing for me, Althea. Not just dates and names in dusty books. The city of Memphis, its very stones are mortared with their sacrifice." His voice dropped, taking on that timbre she was beginning to recognize—one that seemed to echo from the city's oldest, blood-soaked foundations. "It wasn't just felling the wilderness on those sacred, desecrated bluffs, you know. Imagine Adams Street, not as it is now, but as a raw wound in the earth, soon to be lined with stockades. Imagine Nathan Bedford Forrest, a name now carved into monuments, then just a man whose business was the methodical tallying of human souls, parading them on circular brick walks for buyers to inspect like cattle."

He paused, stepping closer to point out a rare night-blooming cereus about to unfurl its ghostly petals. Althea could feel the warmth radiating from him, smell the faint, clean scent of his skin mingled with the damp earth and old paper that always seemed to cling to him. Her historian's objectivity felt dangerously clouded by the undeniable current that simmered between them.

"He knew the precise language of their value," Malachi continued, his gaze intense, holding hers. "The price of a 'prime field hand,' the added value of a 'wench likely to breed.' And he stole from these women and girls what was not any man's to take. It's all there, in the ledgers, if you know how to listen to their silence. That foundational violence, Althea, the city's first breath drawn from their last, it didn't just end. It seeped into the soil. It became the bedrock upon which everything else here was built, including Nashoba's tragic dream."

Althea found herself mesmerized, both by the chilling detail of his account and by the sheer force of his presence. His knowledge felt too complete, too intimate. "How do you know all this with such detail?" she asked, her voice softer than she intended. Embarrassment sprung to her face, the soft hollows in her cheeks. She tried to hide her sudden discomfort.

Malachi's smile returned, a flash of white in the gloom. He reached out, his fingers lightly, almost accidentally, brushing her arm. The touch lingered a fraction too long. *This man is fine,* she thought, in spite of herself. *Too fine.* "Some stories aren't just found in archives, Dr. Moreau. Some stories are in the air, in the earth. You just have to be... receptive." His brown eyes flickered. "And Nashoba has so many stories left to tell you."

He linked that foundational violence to Nashoba's later tragedy, drawing lines Althea hadn't yet conceived. The attraction simmered, undeniable, a dangerous warmth clouding her historian's objectivity. He seemed attuned to her thoughts, anticipating her next question. His touch – a hand brushing hers reaching for a book, a light pressure on her back guiding her over exposed roots – sent jolts both thrilling and deeply alarming. One evening, after a particularly intense discussion near the darkening woods, the air charged with unspoken possibilities, she woke the next morning feeling hazy, the edges of memory blurred. And there, stark against the skin of her collarbone, visible in the bathroom mirror's unforgiving light, was a small, distinct bruise. Dark purple, precisely the color of a crushed pokeberry, tender beneath her fingertips. She racked her brain, but couldn't recall injuring herself, couldn't pinpoint a moment it might have happened. When she saw Malachi later that day, his eyes flickered towards the mark, a micro-expression she almost missed, but his face remained serene. His gaze held only that unnerving, patient calm. He said nothing.

ANCESTRAL ECHOES

It was later that week, while discussing the fragmented family histories surrounding Nashoba, that he mentioned, almost casually, as if discovering it himself in that moment, her own lineage. He traced it back with startling, unnerving precision to Rozarah Charity Crowder, a woman whispered about in the most fragmented accounts for her conjure work during Nashoba's final, desperate days. He presented it as a fascinating historical footnote, another thread in the rich tapestry. But Althea felt a chill spread through her, colder than the library's regulated air. How? How could he possibly know that specific, buried connection?

The name – Rozarah Charity Crowder – became a key, unlocking a different kind of archive search, though Malachi was subtly there, suggesting avenues, pointing towards specific, older city records. Early deeds. Property manifests from before Nashoba even existed, some bearing the signatures of Memphis's most lauded founders, men whose wealth was built on foundations of fantasy and human commodification.

Pre-Civil War census data, brittle and brown with age, each entry a life reduced to a tick mark, a number. And there they were. Althea's breath caught, the sterile air of the archive suddenly feeling thin, suffocating. Not just hazy names in Nashoba's troubled final ledger, but decades earlier, listed clear as day in the meticulous inventories of one of those prominent Memphis's founders: *Nicodemus Forrest. Lyra Forrest.* Listed under 'Property'. The ink stark, unequivocal. Categorized alongside livestock, tools, and cotton bales. Human beings quantified, owned, their future children legally forfeit before they were even conceived. They were part of the 109 souls whose forced labor had first broken this ancient, sacred bluff to carve out a city.

Althea stared, the fluorescent lights of the archive room suddenly seeming to flicker, casting long, dancing shadows. Her blood ran cold. The dates gaped, impossible chasms in time. Decades separated these records from the Nashoba accounts where Nicodemus and Lyra reappeared, named with fear and awe. *Unless...* Althea's mind, trained in the logic of timelines and verifiable fact, recoiled from the implication, scrabbling for rational explanations that crumbled like the ancient paper in her hands. Unless time, for them, hadn't flowed the same way. Could the land itself, so deeply wounded, so out of balance from the desecrated Chikashsha mounds, have created...a ripple? A place where the veil thinned not just to spirits, but to the very fabric of days and years? Like those old tales of Roanoke, where a whole colony simply slipped through the cracks of reality?

Unless the "wasting sickness," the "night fevers," described with such chilling vagueness in the Nashoba journals, weren't just disease born of swampy ground. Unless the disappearances from that failed utopia weren't just desperate people fleeing racism and despair. The ledger entries, the graveyard offerings, Elias's warnings and his mirrored charms, Malachi's impossible knowledge, the bruise throbbing faintly beneath her collarbone—the pieces didn't just click into place. They slammed together with the force of revelation, a horrifying, undeniable clarity. That night, sleep offered little refuge. Althea tossed, plagued by fleeting nightmares of ancient eyes and a silken whisper in her ear, *"the blood always sings the loudest songs, little historian."*

History wasn't just buried here. It was undead, patient, and perhaps, hungry.

POISON ON THE TONGUE

The fluorescent lights of the archive hummed, suddenly loud in the ringing silence that followed revelation. Althea's breath hitched. Undead. The word hung in the sterile air, preposterous and utterly, terrifyingly true. She gripped the edge of the heavy oak table, her knuckles white, the brittle pages of the manifest threatening to crumble beneath the sudden tension in her fingers. The world tilted. The meticulous framework of history she inhabited, built on dates and documents and peer-reviewed analysis, fractured, revealing glimpses of an abyss beneath – a place where time frayed and death was not an ending but a horrifying transformation. She felt exposed, as if unseen eyes watched her from the shadowed corners between the towering shelves. Not just the spirits of those whose tragic lives she'd just touched, but something older, more elemental, seemed to mock her, a silent whisper in the sterile air: *little historian*. The very dust of the archives stirred with the disquiet of the violated land upon which the university, the city itself, was built, sensing her discovery. Gathering the scattered remnants of her composure, Althea carefully closed the ledger, slid the documents back into their

acid-free folder. Her movements felt stiff, robotic. She needed air.
She needed distance. Leaving the archive felt like surfacing from
deep water, gasping as she stepped out into the thick, enveloping
heat of the Memphis evening. The cicadas' drone seemed different
now, less a sound of summer, more a warning cry. Streetlights cast
long, distorted shadows. Every flicker in her peripheral vision felt
like movement, every stranger's glance a potential threat. The hunger
she'd sensed in the archive wasn't just historical. It felt present,
personal, and terrifyingly close. An echo of the land's ancient, unappeased ache now amplified by the specific, undead hunger of Nicodemus and Lyra—a compounded craving that seemed to emanate from
the very soil of Memphis, a city built on layers of bone and sorrow.

A LEGACY CLAIMED

She drove back towards Germantown, towards the cabin
nestled against the watchful woods, her mind racing. Facts warred
with the impossible truth. *Malachi.* His charm now a venomous
serpent's gleam, his knowledge predatory. *Elias.* His warnings, his
mirrored charms – not superstition, but desperate protection against
a darkness she now suspected was far older and wider than just
Nashoba's blight. Had his words about the soil remembering, about
the land itself holding onto sorrows, been a veiled reference to the
desecrated Chikashsha grounds, the unquieted First Peoples, as well
as the more recent agony of the Africans who had been attacked
and enslaved?

She needed answers, confirmation from someone who lived
steeped in this place's many-layered secrets. Parking haphazardly

near the cabin, she almost ran towards Elias Thorne's small cottage tucked deeper into the property, ignoring the deepening twilight. She found him on his porch, sharpening the blades of his pruning shears with slow, deliberate strokes, the rhythmic *shink-shink* of metal on whetstone the only sound besides the ever-present cicadas. The tiny mirrors on his shirt collar seemed to gleam in the porch light, each one a pinpoint of cold fire warding off the encroaching shadows that felt impossibly deep around his small home, as if the cottage itself were a tiny island in a vast, sorrowing sea of disturbed spirit.

"Mr. Thorne." Althea's voice was tight, breathless. He looked up, his expression unreadable, but he didn't seem surprised to see her.

"Doctor." He didn't stop sharpening.

"Nicodemus and Lyra Forrest," she said, the names feeling heavy, dangerous on her tongue. "They were here. At Nashoba. But they were... they were property, decades earlier. Building Memphis."

Elias stopped sharpening. The sound of the whetstone ceased so abruptly that the subsequent silence felt like a physical weight, thick with all the unspoken history of the violated earth and the generations of torment it had witnessed. The silence stretched, thick with unspoken history. He finally set the shears down carefully on the weathered porch floor beside him, the metal making a soft, final sound. "Some folks... they find ways to endure," he said, his voice low, resonant with weariness. "Ways that ain't natural. Ways that cost."

"Cost what?" Althea pressed, stepping closer onto the porch, smelling the faint scent of pipe tobacco and damp earth clinging to him.

"Everything," Elias said simply, his gaze fixed somewhere beyond her, towards the darkening woods. "They bound themselves to this place. To the misery Nashoba birthed from the misery it was built on." He finally looked at her, his eyes holding a deep, sorrowful knowledge. "And now you know." It wasn't a question.

LEARNING THE OLD WAYS

The crickets and tree frogs had begun their nightly chorus, a relentless, pulsating sound that seemed to throb in time with the humid air pressing down on Elias Thorne's small porch. The single yellow bug light cast long, distorted shadows from the porch railings, making the encroaching woods seem like a wall of impenetrable, watching darkness. Althea wrapped her arms around herself, the earlier chill from Elias's revelations still clinging to her skin.

"Why?" Althea asked, her voice a strained whisper that barely carried above the din of insects, the single word encompassing a universe of disbelief and dawning horror. "Why endure like that? What do they gain?"

Elias picked up his shears again, though he didn't resume sharpening. He weighed them in his hand. "Survival, at first, maybe. Spite. A refusal to be erased completely, even if it meant becoming...something else. Something tied to the blood spilled here. But it wasn't just the blood of Nashoba, Doc. This land, it was already weeping." He sighed, a sound like dry leaves skittering across old bones. His gaze drifted out to the Stygian blackness of the tree line. "But the land holds them, Doc. Nashoba's sorrow is their chain forged in an older, deeper fire. This ground, these bluffs by the great river, they were sacred to the Chickasaw, to the Choctaw. Full of their ancient mounds, their resting places. When that was all broken open,

when their dead were disturbed to make way for cities and planta-
tions, the spirit of the land itself fractured. It created an imbalance,
a thinness in the veil where things that should rest easy...don't.
Rozarah, she was powerful, her Hoodoo strong, rooted deep in the
old knowings. But even she, for all her deep knowing, might not have
fully fathomed the full nature of the energies she was tapping into
here, on this anciently wounded earth. An earth that held grudges
older than memory."

He paused, listening as if the night itself might offer contradic-
tion or confirmation. A barred owl called out, a mournful, echoing
query from deep in the woods, and Althea shivered involuntarily.

"So yes, they can't leave Nashoba's heart. Not really. Go too
far, and the strength drains outta them like water from a cracked
jug. Because their undeath is bound not just to Rozarah's spell,
but to the enduring agony and the disturbed spirit of this specific,
desecrated place."

Althea processed this, the constraint clicking into place alongside the horror. She could feel the damp wood of the porch railing
pressing into her back as she leaned against it, the air thick with the
smell of damp earth, honeysuckle, and Elias's faint, herbal scent.
Bound. Trapped. "So they stay hidden? Feeding...?" The thought died
on her lips, too monstrous to voice fully.

Elias nodded grimly, his eyes finding hers in the dim light.
They showed no comfort, only shared, grim understanding. "On
whatever wanders too close. Or on the echoes. The pain. This place is
full of it." He paused, his gaze dropping to his gnarled hands resting
on his knees, then added, his voice barely a whisper, "But they want

to leave. They hunger for it. Freedom, real freedom this time. The kind Nashoba promised but never gave."

"How?" Althea felt cold despite the humid night, a cold that started in her bones and spread outwards, making the cicadas' buzz sound like a dentist's drill against her nerves.

Elias looked directly at her then, his gaze heavy with implication, the yellow porch light carving stark lines into his weathered face. "The curse, the binding… it's tied to blood, yes. To the first promises, the first magic worked here when things got desperate. Rozarah Charity Crowder's magic. She was a powerful woman, rooted deep. But even her strength, her conjure, couldn't fully account for the ground it fell upon. This land, Doctor, as I told you, was already wounded, its spirit unbalanced by the breaking of the ancient mounds, by the sorrow of the First Peoples whose rest was stolen. When Rozarah cast her spell here, amidst Nashoba's own fresh agony and the blood of the enslaved, that potent magic, meant to shield and preserve, it drank from that older, deeper well of desecration and pain. It took root in all that compounded trauma, twisting, anchoring itself not just to our people's suffering, but to the very fury of the violated earth. That's why their chain is so strong, why this place holds them so fiercely."

He didn't need to say the rest. Althea understood, the pieces slamming into place with a horrifying, nauseating click. Her own hand went to her throat, where Lyra's gaze had lingered in the archives. Her lineage wasn't just a historical footnote Malachi had uncovered. It was the key. She was the key Nicodemus and Lyra believed could break their chains, unleash them from Nashoba's grip onto an unsuspecting world.

TRUTH IN SILVER

Later that night, back in the oppressive quiet of her own cabin, Elias Thorne knocked softly at her door. He didn't carry shears this time, but a long, flat object wrapped in dark, oiled cloth. He stepped inside without waiting for an invitation, his presence filling the small room.

"My grandmother kept this," he said, his voice low, laying the bundle on the small table. "Her mother before her. Goes back... goes back to the trouble times at Nashoba. Belonged to someone who tried to help Rozarah, maybe. Or maybe Rozarah herself gave it up when the shadows here grew teeth not just from our own folks' misery but from the older angers of this ground. Story gets hazy."

He carefully unwrapped the cloth. Inside lay a mirror. Not large, perhaps twelve inches long, oval-shaped, framed in heavy, intricately worked sterling silver, now deeply tarnished with age. The silverwork depicted twining vines – morning glories, Althea realized with a jolt – and tiny, almost hidden faces peeking through the leaves. The glass itself was dark, cloudy, seeming to swallow the cabin's dim light.

"It ain't for vanity," Elias said, his calloused fingers hovering over the frame, not quite touching it. "It shows... the truth. What's underneath. The soul's face, some say. Or the devil's work, depending on who you ask." He looked at Althea. "My people used it for protection. To see evil coming. Or to show evil its own face. They say Rozarah used it to look into the heart of the trouble here, to see not just the slave master's cruelty, but how that cruelty fed off the land's own broken spirit, how the old sorrows of the displaced First Peoples gave a bitter root to new sufferings."

Althea reached out, her fingers trembling slightly as she touched the cool, heavy silver. It felt ancient, humming with a latent energy, a repository of secrets. Looking into the dark glass, as her fingers traced the surprisingly sharp edges of the morning glory vines, she saw only her own reflection, pale and wide-eyed, but it felt... incomplete, as if the mirror knew more than it was showing, as if it held not just Rozarah's strength but the sorrowful knowing of the land itself, waiting for the right moment, or the right darkness, to reveal what lay beneath.

"It's yours now," Elias said quietly. "Rozarah's blood runs in you. Maybe it'll answer you. Maybe it'll protect you. Or maybe," his voice grew heavy, "it'll show you something you wish you'd never seen." He turned and left as silently as he'd arrived, leaving Althea alone with the heavy silver mirror and the suffocating weight of her inheritance.

STANDOFF AT THE RUINS

Armed with the mirror – wrapped again and tucked carefully into her research bag – and Elias's grim confirmation, Althea felt compelled to return to the heart of it, to the Nashoba grounds themselves. Not the archives, not the cabin, but the place where the curse took root. She needed to see it with new eyes, the eyes of someone who knew what lurked beneath the soil's memory. She chose the clearing with the hidden graves, arriving as late afternoon bled towards dusk, the time when shadows stretched long and uncertain.

The air here felt different now – not just still, but charged, expectant. It hummed with a discordant chorus of energies. Althea could almost taste the bitterness of the desecrated Chikashsha soil mingling with the sharper, more recent tang of enslaved anguish and Nashoba's curdled hopes. The mirror in her bag felt suddenly heavier, almost pulsing in response. She stood near the bottle tree, its glass glinting like dying embers. And then, they were there. Not coalescing from shadow like Elias, but simply present, as if they had always been part of the landscape. Nicodemus and Lyra Forrest. Here, on their ground, the subtle weakness Althea might have sensed (or imagined) in the archives was gone. They radiated power, an ancient, predatory confidence that pressed the air flat around them. Nicodemus, tall and imperious, his timeless elegance a mockery of the rags he must have worn centuries ago. Lyra, sharp and beautiful as a shard of obsidian, her eyes holding the vast, cold indifference of ages.

"The historian returns," Nicodemus observed, his voice a low, resonant hum that vibrated in Althea's bones. "Digging deeper in our garden."

"This place holds you," Althea said, her voice steadier than she felt. Her fingers tightened not just on the strap of her bag, but on the cool, familiar outline of the mirror within, drawing a sliver of strange comfort from its dense, ancestral weight. "Doesn't it? You can't leave."

Lyra laughed, a sound like wind chimes made of bone. "Freedom is a matter of perspective, little historian. And keys. We were denied it once. We won't be again." Her gaze flickered towards Althea's bag, sharp and knowing.

"Rozarah's blood sings in you," Nicodemus continued, his gaze flicking to the bag Althea clutched, a knowing, almost covetous light in their depths. He took a step closer, moving with impossible grace over the uneven ground. "Faintly, after all these years. But it sings. A key, waiting for the right hand to turn it. Perhaps even to unlock more than just our own chains, eh, little historian? That meddling conjure woman left potent echoes in her wake." His eyes weren't just ancient; they were hungry, filled with the terrifying patience of something that had waited centuries for this moment and a flicker of something else—a wariness, perhaps, of the legacy Althea now carried.

GATHERING FORCES

The encounter left Althea shaken but resolute. The threat was no longer abstract. She saw Malachi the next day, meeting him for coffee in a bustling cafe downtown, the forced normalcy feeling surreal. He was charming, solicitous, asking about her research, his eyes full of feigned concern. But Althea saw the calculation beneath, the subtle probing about Elias, about what she'd discovered.

"You seem tense, Althea," he murmured, his voice warm honey over cold stone, reaching across the table, his fingers brushing hers. The touch felt cold, a stark contrast to the feigned warmth in his lying eyes. "This place... it gets under your skin. Its old sorrows have a way of seeping in. Maybe you should take a break. Let me handle some of the archival legwork."

"I'm fine, Malachi," she said, pulling her hand back, a new firmness in her voice that surprised even herself. "The truths I'm processing are indeed difficult, but they're not just about sorrow. Some are about power, about what binds things to this land, and what it takes to truly see." His mask flickered, a momentary tightening around his eyes before the easy smile returned.

Althea pressed on, emboldened by a resolve she hadn't known she possessed until the graveyard. "Some of those truths aren't in the official records, are they? Elias Thorne hinted at local legends, older stories about this land, about Nashoba. I thought, with your deep knowledge of the area, you might have encountered them."

"Elias Thorne?" Malachi said, a flicker of something unreadable—amusement? annoyance?—in his eyes before the dismissive smile returned, wider this time, a little too knowing. "An old man tending old graves and older superstitions. His 'legends' are the frightened whispers of those who fear what they don't understand about the true pulse of this land, Althea what truly blossoms here for those with the will to grasp it. Sometimes, what people call 'evil' is just a power that refuses to be forgotten, a power that has its own rightful claim." His gaze held hers, a challenge glinting within its depths. He was pushing, trying to isolate her, control the flow of information.

Later that week, the pressure escalated. Returning to her cabin after dark, a premonition coiling like ice in her gut, she found the door unlocked, the unsettling quilt Elias had gifted her, with its carefully stitched silver eyes, dragged from the chair onto the floor, its patterns looking less like troubled sleep and more like a desecrated map, some of the tiny mirrors cracked or missing. Nothing else was taken, but the violation of this protective ancestral object was palpable. A message. Then, a frantic call from Elias—someone had tried to break into his cottage, scared off only by his dogs and perhaps, Althea suspected, the mirrored charms glinting on his doorframe. Nicodemus and Lyra, or their agent Malachi, were done waiting. They were closing in.

MIRROR'S REVELATION

Standing in the dim light of her cabin that night, the heavy silver mirror unwrapped on the table before her, Althea knew there was no turning back. The academic distance was gone, shattered. This wasn't research anymore. She took a steadying breath, the scent of old wood and her own fear sharp in the dim cabin air. Tonight, she needed more than just glimpses of resilience; she needed the unvarnished truth Elias had only hinted at, the truth of the land itself. She held the mirror, its silver frame cool and solid, its weight a strange comfort. Remembering Elias's words about the mirror showing 'what's underneath,' Althea closed her eyes for a moment, focusing her will, her historian's hunger for truth now a desperate plea for understanding. She didn't know any formal words of conjure, but she spoke to Rozarah in her heart, to the land, to whatever ancient powers resided in the tarnished silver.

She looked then, not at her reflection, but deeper, into the mirror's dark glass. Her familiar face was there, distant, yes, but behind the fear in her eyes, something else was stirring. And the mirror responded. The murky depths began to churn, not reflecting the lamplit cabin but swirling like disturbed river water, colors shifting from oily black to blood red to a vibrant, primal green. A vision bloomed, raw and immediate: she saw the majestic bluffs overlooking the Mississippi as they once were, pristine, crowned with ancient, conical mounds under a sky vast and untouched. Hazy figures, their faces indistinct but their movements reverent, moved among them, their connection to the earth a palpable thrum.

Then, the vision fractured with a silent scream—invaders, the felling of ancient trees, the tearing open of the sacred earth, the mounds themselves violated, their sacred contents scattered. A wave of profound sorrow and a cold, ancient outrage washed over Althea, so potent it stole her breath. The scene shifted again. Enslaved Africans, their bodies gleaming with sweat and exhaustion, toiled under a brutal sun, clearing that same wounded land. She saw a younger Nicodemus, his back unbowed despite the lash marks she could almost feel, his eyes burning with a banked fire. She saw Lyra, her beauty already a dangerous currency, her spirit resilient but her gaze holding shadows of unspeakable violation. Their pain, their labor, their blood, soaked into the already desecrated soil, layer upon layer of trauma. And then, Rozarah. Althea saw her, a figure of immense power and desperate love, performing her ritual amidst the chaos and despair of Nashoba's end. Rozarah drew upon the spirits, upon her ancestral knowledge, but Althea also saw, with horrifying clarity, dark, turbulent energies rising from the wounded earth itself, coiling around Rozarah's magic, intertwining with it, twisting her protective conjure into something vast, sorrowful, and insatiably hungry. The land, in its agony, had latched onto Rozarah's spell, birthing a curse far greater and more enduring than one woman's magic alone could have forged.

Althea gasped, pulling back from the mirror, her hand flying to her mouth, the visions searing themselves into her mind. The cabin felt suddenly colder, the night outside pressing in with the weight of all those accumulated sorrows. A flicker of Rozarah's resilience still echoed from the mirror's depths, yes, but now it was intertwined with this new, terrible understanding.

Althea's meticulously constructed world, built on verifiable facts and the comforting solidity of the past tense, fractured, the pieces scattering like so much shattered glass. This was not history. This was an abyss, yawning wide, and she was teetering on its crumbling edge. Her academic mind, usually her most reliable shield, scrabbled for purchase, for an explanation, any explanation other than the impossible truth standing before her. But the weight of their combined regard, the sheer ancient pressure of their being, crushed all rational thought.

Fear, cold and sharp, finally spurred her into motion. She didn't think, didn't plan. Her body reacted with a primal instinct to flee. She mumbled an incoherent apology, something about needing air, about a forgotten appointment, the words clumsy and absurd even to her own ears. Turning, she half-stumbled, expecting a hand to clamp down on her shoulder, a voice to call her back. But they let her go. Perhaps her terror was its own kind of tribute, her dawning comprehension a satisfying appetizer.

The heavy archive door, usually a slow, sighing barrier, seemed to take an eternity to open, and then she was through it, her footsteps echoing too loudly on the polished corridor floor. She didn't dare look back, the feeling of their eyes burning into her spine a physical sensation. Each breath was a ragged gasp, the sterile, climate-controlled air of the university now feeling suffocating, tainted.

Outside, the Memphis evening hit her like a physical blow – a
wave of thick, jasmine-choked heat that did nothing to dispel the
chill clinging to her bones. Streetlights cast the familiar campus into
a landscape of grotesque, elongated shadows, every tree a potential
lurking figure, every whisper of wind a predatory sigh. The vibrant,
pulsing life of the city, usually a comforting backdrop, now felt like
a thin veneer stretched taut over an ancient, waiting darkness. Her
car, when she finally reached it, felt less like a refuge and more like a
fragile metal shell.

The drive back towards Germantown was a blur of fractured
images and racing thoughts. Malachi. His handsome face swam
before her, his easy charm now suspect, his intimate knowledge
of Nashoba's secrets taking on a sinister hue. That bruise on her
collarbone, the color of the pokeberries he'd so casually pointed out –
beautiful, but poison deep down. She replayed his touches, his lingering gaze, and the remembered sensuality now curdled into a horrifying conviction: she was prey. Had his touch been a brand, a marking?
Was his interest in her, that electric current that had hummed
between them, merely a shepherd guiding a lamb to slaughter? The
remembered sensuality now curdled into a horrifying possibility.

And Elias Thorne. His warnings, his sun-weathered face and
eyes that seemed to hold the sorrow of generations. Those small,
round mirrors pinned to his collar, glinting like scattered, watchful
eyes – not quaint folklore, but a defense. He knew. He had to know.
He was her only anchor in this sea of terror, the only one who might
offer a language for this unspeakable reality.

The rental cabin, when she finally reached its lane, felt more
menacing than welcoming, huddled under the brooding canopy

of ancient oaks and water cypress, the Spanish moss dripping like funeral lace. The usual chorus of cicadas seemed to drill into her skull, each buzz a tiny spike of dread.

She didn't bother going inside. Instead, she veered towards the faint light filtering through the trees from Elias Thorne's fortress-like haven, hidden on the property, a bulwark against the encroaching night. Her feet stumbled over unseen roots, urgency overriding caution.

He was on his small, screened porch, as she'd half-expected, a silhouette against the warm yellow light emanating from within. The rhythmic, metallic *shink-shink* of a blade being sharpened on a whetstone cut through the thick air, a sound both mundane and deeply unsettling. It stopped as she approached, his head tilting, though he didn't immediately turn. The tiny mirrors on his shirt, just visible in the gloaming, seemed to catch and magnify the dying light, each one a tiny, cold star.

"Mr. Thorne," Althea's voice was a raw whisper, tight and breathless. He turned then, slowly, his movements deliberate, his expression carved from shadow, unreadable. He didn't feign surprise at her disheveled state, her wide, terrified eyes. He simply waited, the whetstone resting in his calloused palm. "Doctor," he acknowledged, his voice a low rasp, the sound of stones shifting underwater. "Nicodemus... Nicodemus Forrest," she managed, the name feeling like a curse on her tongue. "And Lyra. They were at the university. In the archives. But they were... they were listed as property. Decades before Nashoba. Building Memphis." Her words tumbled out, a torrent of horrified discovery. Elias set the whetstone down with careful precision, the shears resting beside it. The silence stretched, punctuated only by the relentless drone of the cicadas and Althea's ragged breathing. Finally, he spoke, his gaze fixed not on her, but on the impenetrable darkness of the woods that bordered his small yard. "Some folks... they find ways to endure," he said, his voice heavy with a weariness that seemed centuries old. "Ways that ain't natural." He paused, then added, the words dropping like stones into a deep well, "Ways that cost." "Cost what?" Althea pressed, stepping onto the porch, the air smelling faintly of the pipe tobacco she'd noticed on him before, and the rich, damp earth that seemed to cling to everything here. Her own fear was a coppery tang in her mouth. Elias finally turned his eyes to her, and in their depths, she saw not suspicion, but a profound, sorrowful knowledge, a confirmation that sent another wave of ice through her veins. "Everything," he said, the single word a eulogy for a world she no longer recognized. "They bound themselves to this place. To the blood spilled. To the misery Nashoba birthed from the misery it was built on." He held her gaze. "And now you know." It wasn't a question; it was a quiet statement of terrible fact.

Althea hugged herself tighter, the humid Tennessee air doing little to ward off the chill that emanated not from the night, but from the horrifying abyss of understanding that was opening before her. "Know what, Mr. Thorne?" she pressed, her voice a hushed plea. "That they are... what? Not human? That they've been here all this time?"

Elias Thorne's gaze remained fixed on the impenetrable darkness of the woods, as if the answers Althea sought were written in the rustling leaves or the spaces between the ancient trees. He picked up his pruning shears again, not to resume sharpening, but turning them over in his hands, the worn metal a counterpoint to the spectral truths he was about to share.

"They are what this land, in its deepest sorrow, allowed them to become," he began, his voice low, imbued with a weary gravity. "Nashoba, Doctor... it wasn't just a noble failure. It was a wound. A raw, gaping wound on top of older ones, on soil that had already drunk deep of misery when Memphis was built by hands in chains. That kind of compounded pain, it don't just scatter on the wind. It congeals. It calls. Or it changes what's already there, twisting it."

He paused, and Althea was sure she could hear the woods themselves holding their breath.

"Nicodemus and Lyra," Elias continued, his voice barely disturbing the heavy air, "they were steeped in that first wave of sorrow. When Frances Wright brought her dream here, they were already ancient in their suffering. And when Nashoba collapsed under the weight of sickness, and despair, and the hatred from those who couldn't abide a place, however flawed, where Black folk might breathe free... well, Nicodemus and Lyra found a way to hold on. A way to refuse being erased completely from the ledger of the living."

"How?" Althea whispered, the single word encompassing a universe of disbelief. "What way could there possibly be?"

Elias's eyes finally shifted from the woods to meet hers, and the profound sadness in them was a palpable force. "A way that shackles them to this very ground, Doctor. To Nashoba's blood-soaked heart. They are bound here. Oh, they can walk a certain distance, feel the cold stones of Memphis they were forced to lay, but if they stray too far from Nashoba's core, their essence... it drains from them like water from a sieve. They fade. This land, this cursed, grieving earth, it's their anchor and their cage."

A new, colder dread began to snake through Althea. "Anchor... and sustenance?" The implication was hideous.

Elias gave a slow, grim nod. "They draw what they can. From unwary creatures. From any poor soul who wanders too close to the places where the veil between what is and what was wears thin. But mostly... mostly they feed on the echoes. The anguish that still resonates from this ground. It sustains them, yes, but it is a starvation diet for what they truly crave."

"What do they crave, Mr. Thorne?" Althea asked, though some part of her already knew, and recoiled from the knowledge.

He set the shears down with a quiet, deliberate click, the sound unnaturally loud in the charged atmosphere. "Freedom, Doctor. The genuine article. The kind Nashoba promised but snatched away. They yearn to walk the world whole, unbound from this territory of sorrow, with the full measure of their unnatural lives."

Althea's breath hitched. The night seemed to press closer, the scent of damp earth and decaying leaves suddenly cloying. "And how... how do they imagine they can achieve that?"

This was the precipice. Elias leaned forward, the porch light casting deep shadows across his weathered face, his voice dropping to a near whisper, heavy with the revelation he was about to unleash.

"The binding, Doctor. The curse that both chains and preserves them... it was sealed with magic. Desperate magic, from the heart of Nashoba's dying days. A conjure woman's power, striving to shield her people, to fight back the encroaching darkness that was consuming them all." He held Althea's gaze, his own filled with a somber intensity. "The magic of Rozarah Charity Crowder."

Althea gasped, her hand instinctively flying to her mouth. Malachi's earlier revelation about her lineage, presented with such casual academic interest, now detonated in her mind with the force of a personal catastrophe. It wasn't a mere ancestral curiosity.

"They believe," Elias confirmed, his voice laden with the grim truth, "that what was made by her magic can be unmade by her blood. They believe your blood, Dr. Moreau, direct descendant of Rozarah, holds the key to shatter their chains. They need you—your very essence—to break free from Nashoba's hold and step out into the wider world, finally untethered."

The finality of Elias Thorne's words—"your very essence—to break free from Nashoba's hold and step out into the wider world, finally untethered"—slammed into Althea with the force of a physical blow. Her breath hitched, and the world seemed to tilt and shimmer like heat haze off summer asphalt. Her blood. Her lineage. Not abstract historical threads, but a tangible key, a living implement sought by ancient, predatory beings. She swayed, her hand instinctively going to her throat where Lyra's gaze had lingered with such chilling appraisal in the archive. The rough-hewn wooden rail of the porch bit into her other hand as she gripped it for support, the wood cool and slightly damp beneath her trembling fingers.

Elias watched her, his face a mask of grim understanding in the deepening gloom. The cicadas sawed on, their sound now a jeering chorus accompanying the frantic thrum of Althea's pulse. He let the silence stretch for a long moment, letting the enormity of his revelation settle into the marrow of her bones. Then, with a slow, deliberate movement that spoke of ancient rituals and burdens long carried, he straightened.

"There's more," he said, his voice a low rumble that barely disturbed the oppressive stillness. "More you need to see. Not out here." He gestured with his chin towards the interior of his small cottage, its windows glowing faintly like wary eyes in the darkness. "Some things... they require a different kind of quiet."

Althea could only nod, her throat too tight for words. She felt like a sleepwalker, numbly following as Elias unlatched the screen door, its rusty springs groaning in protest, and stepped into the dim interior of his home. The air inside was thick with the scent of dried herbs—sage and something else, sharp and vaguely medicinal—pipe tobacco, old wood, and the faint, metallic tang of the whetstone. A single kerosene lamp burned on a small, cluttered table, casting dancing shadows that made the corners of the room writhe with unseen life. The walls were lined with rough-hewn shelves, laden not with books, but with jars of roots and powders, bundles of twigs tied with twine, and strangely shaped stones that seemed to absorb the lamplight.

Elias moved towards an old, dark wooden chest tucked into a shadowy corner, its surface smooth and worn with age. He knelt, his joints creaking softly, and lifted the heavy lid. The scent of cedar and something else—something ancient and faintly floral, like century-old potpourri—wafted out. He reached inside, his movements slow and reverent, and drew out a long, flat object wrapped in layers of dark, oiled cloth, the color of dried blood.

He carried it back to the table, placing it gently beside the lamp. Althea found herself holding her breath, a prickle of both fear and an inexplicable, ancestral curiosity stirring deep within her. The room felt suddenly colder, the silence more profound, as if the very air was waiting.

"My grandmother kept this," Elias said, his voice barely above a whisper, his calloused fingers carefully beginning to unwrap the layers of cloth. "Her mother before her. And so on, back through the shadowed years. Story goes... it goes back to the trouble times at Nashoba. Belonged to someone who tried to help Rozarah. Or maybe," his eyes flickered up to meet Althea's, "maybe Rozarah herself passed it on when the shadows grew too long for her to fight alone."

The last layer of cloth fell away. There, catching the lamplight in dull, intricate gleams, lay a mirror. It was perhaps a foot long, oval-shaped, the frame wrought from heavy sterling silver, now deeply tarnished, almost black in places. The silverwork was extraordinary, depicting twining vines that Althea recognized with a jolt as morning glories—the same flowers that grew wild and tenacious all over the Nashoba grounds—their delicate trumpets seeming to bloom even in the inert metal. But amidst the vines, almost hidden, were tiny, cryptic faces, their expressions ambiguous, some serene, others contorted in silent screams. The glass itself was dark, cloudy, not reflecting the room so much as seeming to swallow the lamplight, giving back only a murky, depthless void.

Althea felt an involuntary shiver trace its way down her arms. The mirror didn't feel like an object; it felt like a presence, ancient and potent, humming with a latent energy that made the air around it thrum.

"It ain't for looking at your own face, not in the way most folks use a looking glass," Elias said, his voice imbued with a solemn respect. His fingers hovered over the intricate silver frame, never quite touching the glass. "This here... this shows the truth. What's hidden underneath the skin and smiles. The soul's true countenance, some say. Or the face of the haint that rides you." He paused, his gaze intense. "My people, Rozarah's people, they used it for protection. To see evil before it could strike. Or to show evil its own undeniable, hideous face, and in that seeing, sometimes, turn it back."

He gestured towards the mirror. "It's yours now, Dr. Moreau. By blood. By right. By the terrible need that has finally brought it back into the light."

Althea stared at the mirror, her mind reeling. An heirloom of her unknown lineage, a tool of conjure, a weapon against... what? The very thought was overwhelming. She reached out a trembling hand, her fingers hesitating just above the cool, tarnished silver. The air around it felt charged, vibrating faintly. Could this object, this relic of a desperate past, truly offer any defense against beings as ancient and powerful as Nicodemus and Lyra Forrest?

Taking a shallow, unsteady breath, she touched the frame. The silver was cold, heavy, the intricate carvings strangely sharp beneath her fingertips. As her skin made contact, a faint, almost imperceptible thrum seemed to travel up her arm, a whisper of forgotten power, of ancestral memory stirring in the deep well of her blood. She looked into the murky glass, expecting to see her own reflection, pale and wide-eyed. But for a fleeting, terrifying instant, the darkness within the mirror seemed to shift, to swirl, and she thought she saw not her own face, but a fleeting glimpse of other eyes staring back—ancient, sorrowful, and filled with an unutterable weariness. Then it was gone, leaving only the cloudy, inscrutable surface and her own racing heart.

The heavy silver mirror lay on Althea's lap, wrapped once more in its shroud of oiled cloth, a cold, significant weight against her thighs as she drove. It wasn't a conscious decision that propelled her rental car down the darkening, tree-choked lanes towards the original Nashoba grounds, but a deeper, more primal pull, as if the mirror itself, or the ancient blood humming newly awakened in her veins, was guiding her. Elias's words, Elias's cottage redolent of ancestral secrets and drying herbs, the horrifying clarity of her new understanding—it all swirled within her, a maelstrom of fear and a terrifying, nascent resolve. She was a historian, yes, but history, she now knew, was not a passive thing to be studied; it was a current, live and electric, capable of dragging one under.

She parked where the tamed road surrendered to a barely discernible track leading into the woods, the same path she'd taken before, but now every rustle of leaves, every snap of a twig underfoot, every elongated shadow cast by the dying sun felt fraught with a new, predatory significance. The air was thick, not just with the usual Tennessee humidity, but with an expectant stillness, the kind that precedes a storm or the appearance of a predator. She clutched the wrapped mirror to her chest; its coldness seeped through the cloth, a grounding sensation against the frantic racing of her heart.

The hidden graveyard, when she reached it, was even more gravely disquieting than before. The sun had dipped below the horizon, and the clearing was bathed in a bruised, violet light that made the tilted, earth-swallowed headstones look like broken teeth in a monstrous jaw. The ugly jugs, mouths agape, seemed to keen a silent, ceramic sorrow. The nearby bottle tree, its colored glass arms now dark and opaque, no longer glinted but seemed to absorb the remaining light, hoarding secrets within its cobalt and brown depths. Here, the veil felt thin indeed, not just between worlds, but between sanity and the chilling embrace of the unbelievable.

Althea unwrapped the mirror, her fingers fumbling with the cloth. The tarnished silver frame felt unnaturally cold, the morning glory vines and hidden faces within its design seeming to shift and writhe in the twilight. She held it up, not daring yet to look into its cloudy surface, but using it almost as a divining rod, a shield, its presence a small, heavy defiance against the encroaching dark. The air around the mirror felt... different. Taut. As if the ambient sorrow of this place was being drawn towards it, or repelled by it, she couldn't tell which.

A scent reached her then, subtle at first, then more pronounced, overriding the damp earth and decaying leaves—an archaic perfume, like dust and pressed flowers, and something else, something metallic and faintly, horrifyingly, sweet. And then, they were simply there.

Not coalescing from shadow as Elias had, nor appearing with a theatrical flourish. One moment the space between two ancient, moss-laden oaks was empty, the next, Nicodemus and Lyra Forrest occupied it, as if the twilight itself had birthed them, fully formed. Here, on what was undeniably their ground, the subtle aura of menace Althea had sensed in the archives was amplified a hundredfold. It pressed against her, a palpable wave of ancient power, cold and absolute, making the air crackle.

Nicodemus stood tall, his timeless elegance a stark, brutal contrast to the raw, untamed nature of the woods. His eyes, pools of ancient night, fixed on Althea, and a slow smile, devoid of warmth but filled with a chilling possessiveness, touched his lips. Lyra, beside him, was a sliver of obsidian beauty, her sharp features illuminated by the last vestiges of light, her gaze direct and piercing, like a raptor assessing its prey.

"The little historian returns to the garden of bones," Nicodemus observed, his voice a low, resonant hum that seemed to vibrate in Althea's very marrow, stirring the leaves on the trees around them. "Drawn by curiosity? Or by something deeper, perhaps?"

"This place…" Althea began, her voice surprisingly steady despite the tremor that ran through her, her grip tightening on the silver mirror, "it holds you. Elias told me."

Lyra laughed, a sound like dry leaves skittering across a tombstone, sharp and devoid of mirth. "Holds us? Or keeps us, little scholar? There is a difference. One speaks of chains, the other of a… covenant. With the land. With the blood spilled. With the echoes that sing only to us."

Nicodemus took a step forward, his movement fluid, unnervingly silent on the leaf-strewn ground. He stopped a respectful, yet predatory, distance away. "Elias Thorne. A keeper of small secrets, a polisher of old griefs. He tends the graves, but does he understand the true nature of what lies beneath? Or what walks above?" His gaze flickered to the mirror in Althea's hands. "He gave you a pretty trinket. An heirloom of the woman who sought to bind the inevitable."

"Rozarah's blood sings in you, historian," Lyra cut in, her voice like silk draped over steel, her eyes never leaving Althea's. "Faintly, thinned by generations of forgetting, but it sings nonetheless. A melody only certain ears can truly appreciate." She took a delicate, deliberate sniff of the air. "And it grows stronger now. Awakened."

The mirror in Althea's hands suddenly felt warmer, the coldness receding as a faint, almost imperceptible vibration began to emanate from the silver. Her own blood, it seemed, was responding not just to the vampires' presence, but to the ancestral artifact she now held, a conduit to a past she was only beginning to comprehend. The dread was a living thing inside her, coiling in her stomach, yet beneath it, a fragile spark of something else – defiance? Or just the dawning, terrifying awareness of her own place in this ancient, unfolding horror.

A DREAM OF COLD STARS

The encounter in the graveyard left Althea adrift in a sea of icy dread, the world she knew irrevocably altered. Sleep offered no sanctuary, only fragmented nightmares of ancient eyes and the chilling whisper of Lyra's voice: Rozarah's blood sings in you... Awakened. The silver mirror, now her constant companion, lay beside her bed, wrapped in its dark cloth, a heavy, cold comfort. She knew, with a certainty that settled deep in her bones, that Malachi Ashby was inextricably tangled in this horrifying web. His charm, once so alluring, now felt like the thin skin stretched over something predatory.

She arranged to meet him at a small, bustling cafe near the university, a place filled with the clatter of cups and the bright chatter of students, hoping the mundane daylight and public setting would offer some measure of protection, some leverage. When he arrived, his smile was as dazzling as ever, his eyes crinkling at the corners with a warmth that now made Althea's skin crawl. He wore a linen shirt, the color of summer sky, and his easy grace as he slid into the chair opposite her was a study in practiced dissimulation.

"Althea," he began, his voice smooth as polished river stone, "you look... troubled. Is the Nashoba research taking its toll? Sometimes the weight of those old sorrows can press down hard." His brow furrowed with an almost perfect imitation of concern.

"It's more than just sorrow, Malachi," Althea said, her voice carefully neutral. She watched him over the rim of her coffee cup, noting the subtle way his gaze lingered on her, a proprietary gleam she hadn't recognized before, or perhaps hadn't wanted to. "It's the gaps. The silences. The things that don't add up."

"History is full of those, isn't it?" he murmured, his fingers tracing the condensation on his water glass. "That's what makes it so endlessly fascinating. What particular silence is speaking to you now?"

"Nicodemus—Nicodemus Forrest. And Lyra," Althea stated, watching for a flicker, any tell. "Their appearance in the Nashoba ledgers, decades after they were listed as property in Memphis. It's... an anomaly."

Malachi chuckled, a soft, dismissive sound. "Ah, the Forrests. Such tragic figures. Record-keeping in those days, especially through upheaval and fever outbreaks, was notoriously unreliable. Names get repeated, confused. It's a common pitfall for historians, to see ghosts where there are only clerical errors." He leaned forward, his voice dropping into a more intimate register. "Perhaps you're getting too close, Althea. Too emotionally invested. Maybe a break is in order? Let me take over the archival legwork for a bit. Give you some distance."

His attempt to isolate her was so blatant it was almost insulting. The old Althea might have been swayed by his seemingly kind offer, by the seductive pull of his intellect and charm. But the Althea who had stood before Nicodemus and Lyra, who had felt the mirror thrum in her hands, saw the predator beneath the polished veneer.

"I appreciate the offer, Malachi," she said, forcing a small smile. "But I'm not ready to step away just yet. In fact, I was hoping you could help me with something. Elias Thorne mentioned some... local legends. Things that wouldn't be in the official records. I thought, with your knowledge..."

Malachi's eyes narrowed almost imperceptibly. The name 'Elias Thorne' hung in the air between them, a dissonant chord. "Thorne?" he said, a subtle edge creeping into his voice. "He's an old man, steeped in superstition. His stories are more folklore than fact. Entertaining, perhaps, but hardly reliable for serious scholarship. You'd be wise to keep your focus on verifiable sources, Althea. Some paths... they lead only to confusion, to darkness." He reached across the table, his fingers lightly brushing hers. The touch, which once might have sent a thrill through her, now felt like the caress of a spider. Cold. Calculating.

She pulled her hand back as if burned. "Thank you for the advice, Malachi."

The meeting ended soon after, leaving Althea with a gnawing certainty of his duplicity. The pressure escalated later that week, subtly at first, then with a chilling directness. Returning to her cabin after a long day in the archives—where the names Nicodemus and

Lyra now seemed to leap off the pages with malevolent energy—she found the door unlocked. Nothing was taken, but the unsettling quilt Elias had warned her about, the one with the mirrored shards and disturbing patterns, had been dragged from the armchair and lay crumpled on the floor, its intricate stitches looking like a map of her own frayed nerves. It was a violation, a clear message: We can reach you.

Then came a frantic, breathless call from Elias. Someone had tried to force their way into his cottage the night before. "Dogs scared 'em off," he rasped over the line, "and maybe the old ways still got some teeth." But his voice was shaken. Althea knew, with a sickening lurch, that Nicodemus and Lyra, or their devoted servant Malachi, were no longer content to wait. They were closing the net. The time for academic observation was over; the hunt had truly begun.

LIGHT OF A WARRIOR

That night, the rental cabin felt less like a temporary dwelling and more like a besieged outpost on the edge of an abyss. The wind whispered through the pines like mournful sighs, and every creak of the old clapboard structure sounded like a stealthy footfall. Althea sat at the small, scarred table, the wrapped silver mirror before her, the kerosene lamp casting flickering, elongated shadows that danced like haints on the walls. Sleep was an impossibility. Her mind replayed the encounter in the graveyard, Malachi's veiled threats, the violation of her cabin, Elias's fear-edged voice.

She was a historian, trained to excavate the past, to analyze and interpret. But this... this was not an intellectual puzzle to be solved. This was a living nightmare, and it wanted her blood, her essence. Her family, with their determined forward gaze, had sought to shield themselves from the "rough, strange, country" parts of their heritage, the whispers of conjure and old beliefs. And in doing so, they had left her defenseless, an unwitting inheritor of a legacy too terrible to face.

With trembling hands, Althea unwrapped the mirror. The tarnished silver gleamed dully in the lamplight, the morning glory vines and their hidden, tormented faces seeming more pronounced tonight. She stared at its cloudy, inscrutable surface, the murky depths that had shown her those other, ancient eyes. This time, she didn't just glance. She looked, truly looked, searching for something, anything.

Her own face stared back, pale, drawn, the fear stark in her wide eyes. But as she continued to gaze, a strange thing happened. The lamplight seemed to deepen within the mirror, the cloudy surface acquiring a subtle luminescence. And behind her own reflection, almost like a watermark on old paper, another image began to coalesce. A woman's face, strong-boned, with eyes that held the wisdom of ages and the fierce, unyielding light of a warrior. Rozarah. It was not a clear image, more a feeling, an impression, an echo of resilience resonating across the generations. She felt a surge, not of courage, perhaps, but of a profound, sorrowful anger. An anger at the injustice that had birthed Nicodemus and Lyra's eternal torment, an anger at the desperation that had forced Rozarah into a magical pact with such devastating consequences, an anger at her own unwilling entanglement.

She thought of Nicodemus and Lyra, trapped in their rage, their existence a bitter echo of the freedom denied them, now seeking to inflict their damnation on her. She thought of Malachi, a soul bartering away his humanity for borrowed time, a shadow feeding on shadows. She thought of Elias, a lonely guardian armed with fading traditions and a weary heart.

Running was not an option. Where would she go that they could not eventually find her, now that her blood sang their name? Ignoring it was impossible; the quilt on the floor, Elias's fear, were testament to that. The weight of history, so long her academic pursuit, had become a crushing personal burden. But within that burden, within the reflection of Rozarah's fierce spirit, a tiny, stubborn spark ignited.

She traced the twining morning glory vines on the mirror's silver frame. Flowers of rebirth, of resilience, of magic that clung to life even in the harshest soil. Protection. Revelation. Truth. The mirror was not just a relic of the past; it was a weapon, a guide, a connection.

The choice solidified within her, hard and clear as winter ice. She would not be a victim. She would not be a footnote in their eternal, blood-soaked narrative. She would stand. She would fight. For herself, for Elias, for the memory of Rozarah, and perhaps, in some unfathomable way, even for the lost souls of Nicodemus and Lyra, if only to end their reign of sorrow.

Althea Moreau, the historian, took a deep breath. Her reflection in the sterling mirror still showed fear, but now, beneath it, a new resolve hardened her gaze. She would align herself fully with Elias Thorne. She would learn what she could of Rozarah's ways. She would face what Nashoba had become, not as a scholar documenting a tragedy, but as a descendant claiming her contested inheritance, ready to write her own chapter in its shadowed history. The point of no return had been crossed.

A PACT FORGED

The small, flickering flame of the kerosene lamp in Elias Thorne's cottage cast their shadows, Althea's and his, as giants dancing on the herb-lined walls, silent witnesses to a pact forged in desperation and dawning resolve. The air, thick with the commingled scents of dried roots, bitter leaves, and the metallic tang of fear, seemed to vibrate with an ancient, sacred energy. Althea, her earlier terror now transmuted into a brittle, focused determination, watched as Elias moved about the small space with a reverence that transformed his humble cottage into a hallowed ground.

"The old ways ain't quick, Doctor," Elias said, his voice a low murmur, his hands sorting through bundles of dried plants on the scarred wooden table. "They ain't for the impatient or the faint of heart. They demand respect. And they demand a piece of you, a piece of your spirit, to make 'em truly sing."

He selected a handful of feathery, grey-green leaves. "Rue," he said, holding it out for Althea to inspect. "Clears the sight. Wards off the evil eye, and them that walk in borrowed shadows." His fingers, gnarled as ancient tree roots, then picked up a sprig of a plant with tall, slender spikes of tiny yellow flowers. "Agrimony. Sends back trouble to its sender. Makes a shield 'gainst them that mean you harm." And finally, a piece of thick, dark root. "Angelica. Archangel root, some call it. Powerful protection, especially for a woman walking a dangerous path."

Althea took each offering, the textures strange and potent beneath her fingertips—the rue's almost dusty softness, the agrimony's resilient stem, the angelica's dense, earthy weight. As she held them, an odd sensation prickled through her, a faint, almost-forgotten memory that wasn't entirely her own. It was like a whisper from the very marrow of her bones, a stirring of intuition that recognized these plants, understood their purpose beyond Elias's words. Rozarah's instincts, dormant for generations, were beginning to unfurl within her like a startled bloom.

They spent hours, Elias patiently explaining, Althea absorbing. Sometimes she would pick up a root before he named it, its texture or scent oddly familiar, a question forming on her lips about its specific use against a certain kind of shadow, surprising them both. Her historian's mind meticulously cataloging while some deeper part of her simply...knew. He showed her how to crush the herbs, how to mix them with salt—"the earth's own purifier, keeps out what ain't wanted"—and how to carry them. He spoke of iron, "cold iron, they can't abide it," and the power of running water, of thresholds, of words spoken with intent. He shared fragments of lore, tales of haints and boo hags born from the unique sorrows of our people, of spirits bound to the land through pain or unfinished business, and of the older, wilder energies stirred from the earth when the Chickasaw and Choctaw burial mounds were broken and their sacred peace violated. He explained the ways folk had found to live alongside them, or to keep them all at bay because this ground, Doctor, it ain't just Nashoba-cursed. It's crowded with echoes from every kind of hurt this Bluff has known. These weren't just superstitions; they were the hard-won wisdom of a people who had looked into the shadowed face of the South and found ways to endure, to carve out spaces of spiritual safety in a world designed to break them. Each word, each gesture, was a path leading Althea to a legacy of resilience.

"And the mirror?" Althea asked, her gaze drawn to the cloth-wrapped artifact lying on the table like a sleeping oracle.

"It is your sharpest blade and your truest shield," Elias said, his eyes somber. "But like any blade, it can cut both ways. What it shows you... it might change you. Be ready for that."

As the first hint of dawn painted the eastern sky in bruised purples and greys, Elias spoke of the place. "The ruins of the old communal house," he said, his voice heavy. "That's where the veil is thinnest. Where the sorrow of Nashoba collected like poison in a wound, fed by the older angers of the violated Chikashsha earth and the raw pain from the city's founding by enslaved hands. That's where they'll be strongest. And that's where this has to be settled." He looked at Althea, his eyes searching hers. "It's a hard place, Doctor. Full of voices. Full of pain. You sure you ready for that?"

Althea clutched a small pouch of herbs Elias had prepared for her. The scent was sharp, clean, a counterpoint to the fear that still coiled in her belly. But beneath the fear, Rozarah's legacy was a sturdy root, taking hold. "I'm ready," she said, and though her voice was quiet, it held a new, unyielding strength.

THE FINAL CONFRONTATION

Dusk, the following evening. The air hung heavy and still over the site of the original Nashoba, thick with the scent of honeysuckle, damp earth, and an almost tangible miasma of sorrow. The light bled from the sky in hues of orange and blood-red, filtering through the dense canopy of oaks and cypress that guarded the approach to the ruins. Althea and Elias walked in silence, the only sounds their footsteps rustling through the thick carpet of fallen leaves and the incessant, monotonous thrum of cicadas that seemed to amplify the oppressive quiet. Elias carried an old iron crowbar, its weight a grim comfort in his hand. Althea clutched the sterling silver mirror, now unwrapped, its tarnished surface held close to her chest. It felt strangely alive, vibrating with a faint, almost sub-audible hum that resonated with the awakened pulse in her own veins, Rozarah's legacy a tangible shield against the oppressive weight of the place. Its coldness was a stark contrast to the humid inferno of the late May evening in Memphis.

The ruins of the communal house were little more than a series of crumbling brick foundations, half-swallowed by encroaching vines and the relentless embrace of the forest. Yet, as they stepped into the clearing, the atmosphere shifted, growing colder, charged with an electric tension that made the hairs on Althea's arms prickle. This was not just a place of historical decay; it was a place of power, a nexus of pain where the past refused to sleep. The very air felt thin here, stretched taut like a drumskin, resonating with unspoken tragedies—not only Nashoba's failed dream and the blood-soaked earth from its collapse, but far older echoes. The violated Chikashsha mounds, the ghost-scent of their funeral fires mingled with the lingering terror from Forrest's slave yards that had once stained the wider Memphis soil. All of it converged here, making the ground beneath Althea's feet thrum with a malevolent, compounded grief.

A whisper of movement in the deepening shadows, a flicker at the edge of her vision. Althea's breath caught.

Then, they were there. Nicodemus, Lyra, and Malachi. They didn't emerge from the woods so much as congeal from the deepening twilight, stepping into the dim clearing as if summoned by the land itself. Nicodemus, regal and terrible, surveyed the ruins with an air of proprietary ownership, a faint, cruel smile playing on his lips. Lyra, a vision of lethal grace, her eyes glittering like chips of obsidian in the gloom. And Malachi. He stood slightly behind them, his handsome features now stripped of their easy charm, replaced by a taut, almost feverish devotion that was more alarming than any open hostility.

"The historian and the groundskeeper," Nicodemus drawled, his voice a silken caress that nonetheless sent shivers down Althea's spine. His eyes, ancient pools of night, swept over the crumbling foundations with a strange mixture of contempt and deep, possessive hunger. "Come to pay respects to our...humble abode?"

"We come," Elias stated, his voice steady, the iron crowbar held loosely but ready at his side, "to see an end to what haunts this place."

Lyra laughed, a high, chilling sound that seemed to mock the very stones around them. "An end, old man? There are no ends here. Only continuations. Cycles. And the good Doctor Moreau is simply the next verse in a very old song." Her eyes fixed on Althea, sharp and possessive. "You feel it, don't you, child of Rozarah? The music in your blood. It calls to us. It wants to join our chorus."

Malachi stepped forward, his gaze fixed on Althea, his earlier mask of concern now replaced by an unnerving intensity. "Althea, don't do this. They offer a gift. An eternity. What can this old man, with his superstitions and rusty iron, offer you but a short, frightened life?"

"What they offer," Althea said, her voice clearer, stronger than she expected, "is a prison. For themselves, and for anyone they touch." She took a breath, the scent of the protective herbs in her pocket sharp and grounding. Then, with a deliberate movement, she lifted the sterling silver mirror, its surface catching the last, dying gleams of twilight, reflecting not the encroaching darkness, but a strange, inner luminescence. "And I think it's time they saw themselves for what they truly are."

THE PRICE OF TRUTH

The moment Althea lifted the sterling silver mirror, its surface pulsing with a faint, captured light, the charged atmosphere in the ruined heart of Nashoba fractured. Lyra, who had been watching Althea with a predatory amusement, let out a sound that was less a word and more the hiss of a striking serpent. Her beautiful face contorted, not yet in pain, but in a sudden, furious recognition of a power she had perhaps forgotten, or disdained.

"The conjure woman's trickery!" Lyra snarled, her voice losing its silken quality, becoming something jagged and raw. With a speed that blurred the eye, she launched herself at Althea, not a graceful glide but a brutal, arrow-straight attack, fingers curled into claws.

"Althea, now!" Elias roared, lunging forward with surprising agility for his age. He thrust the iron crowbar like a spear, not aiming to impale, but to create a barrier, a line of cold, unwelcoming iron between Lyra and her target. Lyra, forced to alter her trajectory, twisted in mid-air with an impossible flexibility, landing lightly on a crumbling brick wall, her eyes blazing with incandescent fury.

Before Althea could fully react, Malachi, his face a mask of desperate fanaticism, lunged for the mirror. "Give it to me, Althea! It's not for you! You don't understand its power!" He scrabbled for it, his fingers brushing the silver edge.

"Get back!" Althea cried, instinctively yanking the mirror away from him. As she did, its polished surface caught Lyra, who was preparing to leap again from the wall.

What happened next defied all reason. The mirror, which had shown Althea only murky depths and fleeting ancestral eyes, now blazed with an inner, unforgiving light as it faced Lyra. And on its surface, reflected not the beautiful, raven-haired woman poised to strike, but something else. Something ancient, desiccated, a horrifying visage of stretched, parchment-like skin over a contorted skull, eyes burning like hollow pits of damnation, teeth elongated into needle-sharp fangs, a rictus of eternal, unslaked thirst. It was a face not just of undeath, but of centuries of accumulated sorrow, rage, and the festering corruption of a soul denied peace. A face that bore the phantom brand of the auction block, the shadow of countless violations in the Memphis slave pens where her beauty had been a curse, each indignity, each act of stolen autonomy etched into the horrifying decay now laid bare by Rozarah's unblinking silver eye.

Lyra screamed. It was not a human sound. It was a shriek torn from the throat of something that had witnessed its own damnation, a sound that clawed at the humid night air, sending birds screeching from the surrounding trees and silencing the cicadas in a sudden, terrified hush. She recoiled violently, stumbling back from the wall, her hands flying up to cover her face, though the image was not on her, but in the mirror, and now, seared into Althea's own horrified mind. The beautiful illusion she presented to the world had been stripped away, leaving only the raw, terrifying truth of her endless, cursed existence.

RECKONING

Nicodemus, who had been watching with a predatory stillness, let out a roar that shook the very foundations of the ruins, a sound of pure, untamed fury and something akin to agony. Lyra's shriek, the sight of her cowering from the mirror's revelation, had broken through his ancient composure. His eyes, fixed on Althea, burned with a murderous inferno.

"Witch!" he bellowed, his voice cracking like a whip. "You will pay for that!" He moved then, not with Lyra's swiftness, but with the inexorable power of an avalanche, an overwhelming force of nature intent on destruction.

Elias threw himself in Nicodemus's path, swinging the iron crowbar. "Stay back from her, night-walker!" But Nicodemus, in his rage, was a different beast. He swatted the iron bar aside as if it were a reed, sending Elias staggering back with a grunt of pain.

Althea, trembling but resolute, stood her ground. As Nicodemus bore down on her, his handsome face contorted into a mask of primal fury, she lifted the mirror again, its surface still strangely luminous, and thrust it before him.

The effect was different than it had been with Lyra. Nicodemus, instead of recoiling, froze. His eyes, wide and blazing, stared into the silvered glass. And on its surface, no longer murky but blazing with a terrible, accusatory light, Althea saw not just the monstrous vampire, but something else flickering behind it, within it: the image of a young Black man, Nicodemus. She saw him stripped and paraded on the circular brick walk of Nathan Bedford Forrest's slave yard on Adams Street, the stench of fear and unwashed bodies thick in the humid Memphis air. His muscles, taut from the brutal labor of carving a city from the wild, sacred bluffs for his enslavers, were prodded and assessed by callous hands. His teeth were pried open, his worth debated in cold, clipped tones alongside the price of cotton and land. Yet, through the weariness of forced labor that etched his young face, a stubborn spark of unyielding life burned in his eyes, eyes that held the vast, unutterable sorrow of his people.

Then the image shifted, the silver glass bleeding the past into the monstrous present. The regal, terrifying vampire was superimposed over the enslaved man, his elegant attire a mockery of the rags he once wore, his predatory power a twisted echo of the strength stolen from him. The juxtaposition was a horrifying testament to what had been lost, what had been stolen, and what had been hideously transformed. The mirror didn't just show the monster, it showed the man the monster had consumed, the centuries of dignity denied, the humanity desecrated, the profound tragedy of his unending curse.

A sound tore from Nicodemus's throat, a deep, guttural groan of unimaginable pain, a sound that spoke of centuries of suppressed grief and rage now forced to the surface. His powerful frame shuddered violently, the illusion of his timeless elegance shattering like drought-cracked earth. For a moment, that seemed to stretch into an eternity of recalled torment, his forward momentum ceased. His eyes, no longer blazing with predatory hunger but wide with the raw, unshielded horror of a soul forced to confront its own damnation and the ghosts of every stolen dignity, remained locked on the devastating truth revealed in the silver. It was as if the weight of every whip lash, every auction block, every moment of dehumanization he had endured and later inflicted, had crashed down upon him at once.

It was in that moment of Nicodemus's stunned agony that Malachi, seeing his powerful patrons falter, perhaps seeing his own dreams of immortality crumbling, made his final, desperate move. With a wild cry, he lunged again at Althea, not for the mirror this time, but at her, his hands outstretched as if to tear her apart.

"Althea, look out!" Elias cried, struggling to his feet.

Althea turned, startled, raising the heavy silver mirror defensively. Malachi, blinded by his reckless desperation, crashed into it. There was a sickening crunch. The sharp, ornate edge of the sterling silver frame, hard and unyielding, caught him across the temple. His eyes went wide with a sudden, uncomprehending shock. A dark stain blossomed on his skin. He stumbled back, a choked gasp escaping his lips, then crumpled to the ground like a puppet whose strings had been cut, his body still, his eyes staring blankly at the indifferent stars. The silver mirror, an artifact of ancestral truth and protection, had become an accidental instrument of judgment for one who had chosen shadows and deceit. Althea stared, the scent of Malachi's suddenly spilled blood sharp and sickening in the charged air, another layer of tragedy settling upon Nashoba's already burdened soil.

A stunned silence descended, broken only by Nicodemus's ragged breathing and the distant, renewed chirping of a few brave crickets. Malachi lay still, a dark pool slowly spreading beneath his head on the cracked earth of the ruins.

Lyra, who had been huddled against a crumbling wall, slowly lowered her hands from her face. Her eyes, when she saw Malachi's lifeless form, widened first in disbelief, then in a paroxysm of pure, unadulterated grief that momentarily eclipsed her own monstrous nature. "Malachi?" she whispered, her voice cracking like brittle parchment. Then, a wrenching sob escaped her, a sound so human, so filled with loss, it was almost more terrifying than her earlier shriek. "No!" It was a denial of this loss, and every loss, every theft she had ever endured.

Her grief, however, was a volatile thing, a razor that had always lived close to the surface of her stolen humanity. It twisted, in an instant, into a renewed, incandescent rage, a fury that had its roots in the holds of slave ships and the defiled soil of Adams Street. Her head snapped up, her eyes, blazing with those unshed ancestral tears and a murderous fury, locking onto Althea. "You!" she screamed, her voice raw with pain and hatred. "You, with your airs of knowing, your unbroken spirit. You take everything. He was a sliver of warmth in an eternity of cold! You bring your light here, and all it does is burn what little comfort we find."

Ignoring Nicodemus, who still seemed caught in the throes of the mirror's revelation, Lyra launched herself at Althea with a reckless abandon that bordered on suicidal. There was no finesse now, only a desperate, grief-fueled desire to destroy. Althea, still reeling from Malachi's accidental death, barely had time to react. She tried to bring the mirror up again, but Lyra was too fast, too consumed by her rage.

Lyra's hands clamped onto Althea's arms like iron bands. Her face, contorted with fury, was inches from Althea's. And then, with a guttural snarl, Lyra lunged, her fangs sinking deep into the side of Althea's neck.

An explosion of pain, white-hot and searing, shot through Althea. A wave of dizziness threatened to pull her under. But even as her life force began to drain, something else surged within her – a deep, primal instinct, a wellspring of resilient anger. Rozarah's strength. With a desperate cry, Althea pushed back, her hands finding purchase on Lyra's shoulders, trying to break the horrifying connection.

It was Nicodemus who ended it. Stirred from his tormented state by Lyra's cry and the scent of Althea's blood, he looked up. His eyes, ancient and filled with an unbearable confluence of rage, grief, and perhaps, a dawning, terrible understanding, birthed from the mirror's unsparing truth, fixed on Lyra locked in her death-feed, and on Althea, whose life was ebbing. In that moment, the weight of centuries, the futility of their cursed existence on this doubly desecrated soil, crashed down upon him. With a roar that tore through the fabric of the night, a sound less of fury and more of ultimate, unbearable surrender, he moved. But not towards Althea. He lunged towards Lyra, his powerful arms wrapping around her, pulling her back from the mortal.

Lyra struggled, snarling, but his grip was unbreakable, a final, terrible embrace. Then, in a move of shocking, final desperation, as if seeking to return their conjoined agony to the wounded earth that had birthed and bound them, Nicodemus dragged Lyra, and himself, towards a jagged, exposed foundation stone of the ruined communal house—one of the very stones laid in hope and despair so long ago, now to be their shared tombstone. With a last, guttural cry that was both a curse against their fate and a lament for every stolen life, every broken dream this land had witnessed, Nicodemus impaled himself, and Lyra with him, upon the unyielding stone.

There was a terrible, tearing sound, followed by a deafening silence. For a moment, they remained transfixed, two dark figures silhouetted against the moonlit ruins. Then, with a sigh that might have been the wind or their departing spirits, their bodies began to disintegrate, crumbling into dust and shadows, until nothing remained but the stained stone and the echoing silence of their violent end.

Althea sank to her knees, her hand pressed to the throbbing, bleeding wound in her neck. The world spun. The taste of her own blood, metallic and terrifying, filled her mouth. Elias was suddenly beside her, his face etched with horror and concern. But as he reached for her, Althea looked down at her hands, at the blood, at the strange new energy thrumming through her veins, a cold fire spreading alongside the searing pain. The bite. The blood exchange. She knew, with a chilling, irrevocable certainty, that something inside her had been fundamentally, terrifyingly, and permanently changed.

A HUNGER REWRITTEN

The silence that descended upon the ruins of Nashoba's communal house was a vast, suffocating blanket, broken only by Althea's ragged gasps and the frantic thumping of her own heart, which now seemed to beat with a strange, erratic, and terrifyingly vital rhythm. The dust of Nicodemus and Lyra Forrest, ancient souls who had clung to existence for centuries, settled into the blood-soaked earth, leaving behind only the faint, archaic scent of their passing and an echoing void where their immense, sorrowful power had been.

Althea knelt, her hand clamped to the searing, throbbing wound on her neck. Blood, warm and slick, oozed between her fingers. The world spun, not just from the pain or the shock, but from a dizzying, disorienting influx of... everything. The scent of damp earth, the metallic tang of her own blood, the subtle fragrance of night-blooming jasmine from somewhere deep in the woods, the dry, papery smell of Elias's fear—all slammed into her with the force of a physical blow, each odor distinct, almost painfully vivid. Sounds, too: the frantic scuttling of some small creature in the undergrowth, the almost imperceptible sigh of the wind through the pine needles, the frantic, pulsing beat of Elias's own heart as he rushed to her side—each one amplified, crystalline, immediate.

But it wasn't just the sounds of the living world that assailed her. Beneath them, a deeper, more ancient chorus rose from the blood-soaked earth of the ruins – a dissonant symphony of sorrow. She could hear the faint, keening whispers of the unavenged Chikashsha dead whose sacred mounds had been violated nearby, the guttural moans of enslaved ancestors whose agony had seeped into the very clay, and the more recent, sharper cries of Nashoba's lost souls. They were all there, a terrifying, undeniable presence made clear by the venom now rewriting her senses.

"Doctor Moreau! Althea!" Elias was beside her, his face a mask of anguish in the moonlight that now filtered, cold and indifferent, through the skeletal ruins. He reached for her, his hands trembling. "That bite... oh, merciful spirits, that bite..."

He gently tried to pull her hand away from her neck. The pain was a living fire, yet beneath it, a cold, electric energy was already coiling, spreading through her veins like an invasive vine. She looked at her bloodied fingers, then at Elias, his face etched with a sorrow so profound it mirrored the ancient grief of this place.

"It's... changing," she managed to whisper, her voice hoarse, alien to her own ears. "I can feel it. Everything is... too much. Too loud. Too bright, even in the dark."

Elias nodded slowly, his eyes filled with a terrible understanding. He helped her to her feet, her legs unsteady, not just from weakness, but from the strange, thrumming vitality that was beginning to infuse her. He tore a strip of cloth from his own shirt, pressing it gently against the wound, but the bleeding, though profuse, seemed to be... slowing, with a preternatural speed.

"Them that ain't living, and ain't truly dead," Elias murmured, his voice heavy, "they pass on more than just a wound. They pass on the hunger. The night. The long, long years."

And then she felt it. Beneath the pain, beneath the sensory overload, a new sensation began to stir deep in the pit of her stomach: a hollow, aching emptiness. A profound, gnawing craving that had nothing to do with food or water. It was a pull, a desperate, visceral need that terrified her more than the bite itself. *The Hunger.* Not just for blood, she sensed with a primal dread, but for life itself, for warmth, for the very essence that animated the living things now screaming their presence to her heightened senses. It was a void that threatened to swallow her own identity, to reduce her to a mere, predatory impulse.

Her eyes, wide and dilated, met Elias's. He saw it there, the dawning horror, the nascent craving. "Rozarah's blood runs strong in you, child," he said, his voice gentle but firm, trying to anchor her against the rising tide of her new, monstrous nature. "It may not save you from what you are becoming, but it might... filter the curse. Shape it. You ain't them. You don't have to be." He gripped her arm, his touch surprisingly strong. "The choice, Althea. The choice of what you become, what you do with this... this long, shadowed life... that choice is still yours. It's the only true power we ever really got."

But as Althea stared into the moonlit darkness of the woods, every shadow teeming with an unnatural, vibrant life, the scent of unseen, living things calling to the new, ravenous emptiness within her, she wondered if any choice could truly overcome the ancient, insatiable hunger that was now her terrible inheritance.

DIFFERENT KIND OF DAWN

The passage of seasons across the Memphis bluffs marked Althea's transformation, not into a creature of mere shadow and thirst, but into something...*other*. Elias Thorne, his wisdom a deep, steady river, guided her through the treacherous currents of her new reality. The Hunger, that hollow, primal ache, remained a constant, a chilling echo of Lyra's bite, but Althea, heir to Rozarah's filtered magic, found it was not the all-consuming tyranny it had been for Nicodemus and Lyra. She was not bound to the grave-soil of Nashoba, her spirit tethered to its endless loop of sorrow in the same way they had been. Rozarah's intent, Elias explained, had always been protection, a fierce maternal shielding. Though twisted by despair and circumstance in its original casting upon the freedmen who became the first of Nashoba's eternally restless, for Althea, a direct descendant choosing her path, that protective magic manifested differently.

She learned, with agonizing trial and error, that the ravenous void within her could be quieted, not by the brutal taking of human life, but by drawing, with careful intent, upon the vibrant, teeming life force of the natural world around her – the deep, slow pulse of ancient trees, the ephemeral shimmer of moonlight on water, even the collective energy of a sleeping city. Sometimes, a willing offering from Elias, a mere thimbleful of his own resilient life force, freely given and taken with a gratitude that bordered on sacred ritual, would sustain her for weeks, leaving him only slightly weary, never depleted. This was a sustenance Nicodemus and Lyra, trapped in their cycle of rage and retributive taking, had never conceived. Their

hunger had been a weapon, a howling wind that promised only deso-
lation. But Althea was learning to make hers a whisper, a delicate
balance, a listening to the world rather than a tearing from it.

Her senses, once an overwhelming torment, became her
instruments. She could hear the unspoken histories in the rustle of
leaves, decipher the sorrow etched into the mortar of old buildings,
feel the lingering emotions of those who had passed through a space.
The ancient grief of the First Peoples clinging to the river bluffs, the
indelible anguish of the auction blocks in the heart of Memphis, the
confused despair of Nashoba's lost dreamers. The sterling silver
mirror was her constant companion, her confidante. In its depths,
she communed with the essence of Rozarah, not as a ghost, but as an
ancestral presence, a wellspring of intuitive knowledge about herbs,
roots, the language of the unseen, and the responsibilities of power.

She chose not to abandon Nashoba, not entirely. Its tragedy
was too deeply entwined with her own story, with Rozarah's. But she
made her new sanctuary in a hidden cave system high in the wooded
bluffs overlooking the Mississippi, a place of ancient quiet, far from
the lingering psychic residue of the ruins. From there, her purpose
began to crystallize, sharp and clear as a winter star. She would be
more than a historian preserving tales on paper; she would be a
living archive, a guardian of the lost narratives, a protector of the
vulnerable, those preyed upon by darkness, both human and otherwise. She would use her long life, her unique gifts, to empower, to illuminate, to ensure that no more souls were consumed by the kind of
despair that had birthed Nashoba's curse. This was the work Rozarah
might have done, had her magic not been tragically subverted. Althea
would reclaim that intent, on her own terms, in her own time.

VIGIL UNDER MORNING GLORIES

Late autumn had bled into the land, the Tennessee air crisp and carrying the scent of woodsmoke and the rich decay of fallen leaves. Althea Moreau returned to the hidden graveyard, the place where Nashoba's deepest secrets were interred. Elias Thorne walked beside her, a silent, steady presence, his own long vigil nearing its natural end, hers just beginning. This time, Althea carried not just the silver mirror, but a small, carefully curated bundle of offerings.

The earth over the resting places of Nicodemus, Lyra, and Malachi lay undisturbed, already being reclaimed by the patient tendrils of wild ivy and fallen leaves. Althea paused before each.

For Malachi, who had bartered his soul for borrowed time and scholarly vanity, she laid down a slim volume of Du Bois, its pages filled with a wisdom he had failed to internalize. Beside it, a single, perfectly preserved pokeberry, its dark beauty a poignant symbol of his own poisonous choices. "May you find the peace in truth you never found in compromise," she whispered, the words absorbed by the waiting stillness.

For Lyra, whose ancient rage had been so deeply entwined with an equally ancient sorrow and a fierce, twisted love, Althea placed a string of lustrous river pearls – for the beauty she had once possessed and the tears she must have shed in the long, lonely darkness. And beside it, a handful of dried jasmine flowers, their phantom fragrance a reminder of the brief, sweet moments of connection she had shared, however fleetingly, with Malachi. "May your spirit find the rest that life and undeath denied you."

And for Nicodemus, the enslaved man forced to build a city, the cursed vampire bound to its sorrow, she unrolled a small strip of rich, dark Kente cloth, vibrant with the patterns of a homeland he had never been allowed to forget. Upon it, she placed a handful of pure, unadulterated African soil Elias had kept treasured for generations, a piece of the true Guinee. "For the journey back," Althea murmured, her voice thick with an empathy that transcended judgment, "to the beginning. To the red earth that remembers your true name." This was not forgiveness, perhaps, but acknowledgement. A historian's careful cataloging of pain, a descendant's offering to the complex, broken humanity that lay even within monsters.

As she straightened, a profound stillness settled over the graveyard. The air grew heavy, expectant. Althea held the sterling silver mirror aloft, its surface no longer cloudy but reflecting the bruised hues of the twilight sky with a preternatural clarity. She closed her eyes, not in prayer, but in a deep, focused concentration, drawing upon the wellspring of Rozarah's resilient magic within her, upon the life force of the earth itself, an earth that seemed to sigh in bruised relief as the tormented spirits were finally acknowledged and gently bound.

When she opened them, the morning glory vines that had always clung to the edges of this sorrowful place, the same vines that graced her ancestral mirror, began to move. They twisted and writhed with an animate, purposeful energy, growing with impossible speed, their heart-shaped leaves a vibrant, defiant green, their trumpet flowers of deepest indigo and sky blue unfurling in a silent explosion of color. Thicker and thicker they grew, weaving themselves into an impenetrable, living wall, a thorny, blooming bramble that encircled the three graves, shielding them, sealing them, putting them out of sight, out of view, cocooned within nature's fierce, protective embrace. The air thrummed with a power that was both ancient and new, wild and contained.

Elias Thorne watched, his old eyes wide with a mixture of awe and quiet sorrow. He had seen much in his long life, but this... this was different. This was not the magic of despair, but the magic of a chosen, reclaimed destiny.

The last light of day caught the silver in Althea's mirror, making it blaze for a moment like a captured star. She lowered it slowly, a profound sense of peace settling over her, a peace that acknowledged the sorrow but was not consumed by it. The Hunger was a quiet hum within her, a familiar companion now, no longer a raging beast but a reminder of the life she had chosen to honor, to protect.

She turned from the now-hidden graves, from the living, blooming sepulcher she had helped weave. Her path lay before her, stretching into the long, velvet darkness of the night, a night that was no longer a threat, but her domain. She was Althea Moreau, historian of the lost, guardian of the shadowed, a daughter of Nashoba and Rozarah, her existence a testament to the enduring power of memory, the fierce resilience of the human spirit, and the possibility of a different kind of eternity. She walked away, not into an ending, but into the vast, unfolding tapestry of her new, immortal purpose, her steps sure, her spirit unbound, leaving behind only the scent of morning glories and the earth's quiet sigh under the silent, powerful promise of her vigil.

WHERE THE JEQUITIBÁ SINGS

FOR ZAIKA & FISHGUI

The earth remembered, even when men chose to forget, the bitter taste of stolen lives.

In the humid, dreaming heart of this land, where the air hung thick with the cloying sweetness of sugarcane and the damp, fertile scent of disturbed earth, lived Benedito Caravelas. His very name, a whispered secret, would soon shed its skin like a sucuri, sleek and silent in the swamp waters, to become Benedito Half-League. He was a man cobbled together from sunbaked roads and the restless yearning of wind-swept cane fields. Each journey etched a deeper map onto the leathered soles of his feet. His eyes, those amber eyes, though, were the true cartographers—dark pools reflecting a thousand forgotten stars and the blazing promise of a coming night storm. What was left of his mother's head wrap, a precious, tattered shred, was tucked close to his skin. Beside it lay a small, smooth image of Saint Benedict, cool and a silent guardian against the encroaching shadows.

Before the legend swallowed him whole, Benedito was a man of quiet observations. He'd seen the way a master's laughter could curdle into a sour bile in the face of a single defiant glance, the brittle fear beneath their bluster as palpable as the grit of sugar dust on the tongue. He'd learned the rhythms of the earth, how the sugar cane bent to the breeze but never truly broke, its dry leaves rustling like secrets in the night. He knew the taste of the forest's clear spring water and the bitter comfort of certain medicinal leaves—boldo for the stomach's churn, capim-santo for calming the spirit, and the fiery pimenta-de-macaco for strength. One night, under a moon as thin and sharp as a bone splinter, Benedito felt the simmering disquiet in his gut. It was a premonition, a taste of freedom that made his mouth water even as his stomach cramped with anticipation. He gathered a handful of shadows, men and women whose gazes held the same desperate hunger as his own, their bare feet silent on the compacted earth, their breaths ghosting in the cool air. "The master's dogs," he murmured, his voice a low hum against the drumming of his own heart, "they sleep a sleep earned by theft. But freedom, my brothers, she's a mistress who never closes her eyes."

The whispers of his daring spread like wildfire through the quarters, carried on the flame of night, in the dark wind whose breath smelled of distant rain. Tales of Benedito—how he slipped through patrols like smoke, how his presence turned the weakest slave into a lion—became the sacred hum of resistance. One sun-drenched afternoon, deep within the forest where the air was thick with the scent of damp moss and blooming wild orchids, Benedito paused beside a towering jequitibá tree, its bark gnarled like an old man's wisdom. This was no ordinary tree, for Benedito knew, deep in his bones, that sacred trees held life and could keep one whole. It was here that the jequitibá truly sang, a low, resonant note only he could hear, a melody that settled his very bones and promised ancient solace, a weary body's peace.

Today, however, a new sound greeted him: a low, insistent *buzzing*. A swarm of native honeybees, their gold and black bodies shimmering in the dappled light, began to orbit him. They did not sting, but danced, a living halo. From their midst, a single bee, larger and more iridescent than the rest, landed gently on his brow. Her voice, a delicate rasp like dry leaves skittering on stone, settled directly in his mind. *"We know you, Benedito Caravelas,"* she buzzed, the words a strange, sweet melody. *"We are the Melipona, and our Queen has tasted the courage in your spirit. She bids us watch over you, for the sweetness you seek is for all."* From that day, the bees became his unseen sentinels, their intelligence a silent hum at the edge of his awareness, their stings a sudden, furious retribution for any who threatened him.

Then, a sudden, piercing whistle, sharp as a splinter, cut through the night, not from Benedito, but from the dense, breathing darkness of a nearby grove. Another answered, a haunting echo from the distant cane fields, carrying the faint, metallic hint of fear and burning thatch, sempre viva. Panic began to ripple through the fazenda like a tremor. An overseer, a man whose face was perpetually stuck in a grimace, his lip forever poked out and frowning, stumbled. His lantern bobbed like a frantic firefly, casting wild, flickering shadows. "He's everywhere and nowhere!" he squawked, his voice cracking with terror, nearly tripping over his own feet. That was the exquisite, absurd genius of Benedito: a dozen phantom leaders, each wearing his distinct, patched tunic, moving like specters. The one become many. They struck simultaneously, a constellation of small rebellions igniting the oppressive darkness. Igniting hope in the face of the insurmountable. Chains clanged with a harsh, ringing echo, doors splintered with a satisfying *crack*, and the defiant shouts of newly unbound souls mingled with the high-pitched squeals of terrified pigs and the hot, breath of startled horses.

Benedito, the true Benedito, moved through the chaos like a whisper of smoke. A brute of a farmer, red-faced and bellowing like a stuck boar, his sweat-slicked skin gleaming, charged him. Benedito, with the grace of a jungle cat whose paws knew every root and stone, sidestepped. Grace, as if he were the wind herself. The farmer, propelled by his own furious momentum, tripped over a panicked chicken, then landed face-first in a trough of murky slop. The stink of pig swill rose to meet him. "Cleanliness," Benedito drawled, a rare, fleeting smile playing on his lips, "is next to... well, not godliness, in this case. More like a fine mud poultice."

And with that, the legend of Benedito swelled, fed by fear and whispered hopes. "But could it be Benedito?" the farmers would croak, their voices thin with terror, their fingernails bitten to the quick, the unsettling scent of his myth clinging to the very air they breathed. They believed him immortal, a ghost haunting their ill-gotten gains, a haint haunting them as they lay in their big hard-wood beds, popeyed and restless, afraid to sleep. The very air around them prickled with his unseen presence. When one of his decoys was captured, a poor soul who bore the same patched tunic, and was declared dead in São Mateus, a cold dread snaked through the oppressors. They laid the body in the slave cemetery, in the shadow of São Benedito church, convinced they had finally extinguished the flame. But the next morning, the grave lay empty, save for a trail of bloody footprints leading back into the untamed embrace of the forest, the soil still clinging to the fresh red stains. The earth, it seemed, could not hold what freedom demanded. Indeed, the very roots beneath him, the ancient, coiling network that binds all living things, seemed to push him forth, renewed.

As Benedito led his newly freed kin into the dense wilderness, the very landscape shifted in his favor. The mountains he climbed would rearrange their jagged peaks behind him, confounding any pursuers with impossible new paths. For the mountains remembered his name, twisting their ancient forms to shield him. The long, winding roads he crossed would unspool and tangle like discarded fishing nets, sending the relentless capitães-do-mato in circles upon circles, their frustrated curses echoing through the suddenly disorienting trees.

Sometimes, as they walked under a sky where the sun blazed bright even as heavy rain poured down in silver sheets, the farmers would stop, cross themselves, and declare, "The devil's wife is surely beating him for eating the food of their children!" It was the Curupira himself, the guardian who walked with feet turned backward, whose mischievous spirit played tricks on the unwary, twisting paths and misleading trackers. And in the deepest shadows, the Boitatá, the fire-snake guardian, would coil unseen, its luminous eyes ensuring no carelessly lit torch could find its way into the Quilombo. The spirits of the forest, the elusive Saci-Pererê with his red cap skipping unseen, danced at the edge of their vision, their laughter carried on the wind, all conspiring to guard Benedito's passage.

For four decades, Benedito and his Quilombo, a sanctuary hewn from the unforgiving wilderness, resisted. They were a
persistent splinter, an aching wound on the very body of slavery.
Their hidden communities flourished, living in harmony with the
rich biodiversity of the Cerrado and Amazon, their knowledge of
medicinal plants, edible roots, and the sweet harvest of wild honey a
defiance against scarcity. They were a living testament to the human
spirit's refusal to be broken, their voices like a chorus of thunder in
the hearts of the enslaved. Benedito, with his simple gourd of spiced
herbal tea to ward off the chills, grew lean with the years, his youth
shedding like an old skin. He carried the burden of a living legend,
the weight of a thousand hopes, a solitude that settled in his bones
like deep winter.

But even legends, like the oldest trees, eventually yield to time.
Old age, that cruel thief, finally caught Benedito. He refused to wear
shoes, even after it was no longer illegal. Lame and sick, his body a
map of a thousand battles, his bones aching with the damp cold that
seeped from the earth, he sought refuge in the hollow heart of that
ancient jequitibá tree, where the jequitibá sang its deepest song. It
was here, lulled by the tree's resonant hum, that he sought his rest. A
lone hunter, chasing a fleeting bounty, stumbled upon the truth. The
pursuers came, silent as shadows, and laid their trap. They covered
the trunk, the air thick with the acrid smell of their anticipation.
Then, fire. The flames licked, consuming the wood with a hungry
crackle, the heat intensifying, the air growing choked with smoke and
the bitter essence of burning resin.

As the tree roared, its song turning to a frantic scream in
Benedito's mind, a warmth, not of fire, pulsed through him. He felt

the very fibers of the jequitibá, its ancient, life-giving sap, surge and wrap around him, a shield forged from love and deep earth magic. He learned then, in that searing moment, that this was no mere tree, but the Tree of Life itself, its roots reaching into the oldest stories. When the flames finally died, leaving a mound of smoking embers and blackened ash, the pursuers found only the hollowed-out husk of the mighty tree. Amidst the ashes, where the inferno had raged, still warm and smoky, they found it: the small, unblemished image of Saint Benedict, its smooth surface untouched, pulsing with a faint, internal light. Benedito, though lame and sick, had simply walked away, his body now imbued with the silent strength of the jequitibá, his steps leaving no discernible trace.

> *Benedito, Benedito*
> *The bee's love, the master's lament*
> *Walks on air, forever free*

He walks still, some say, a shadow amidst the sun-drenched fields, to save us all from our worse selves, to remind us that freedom is not a dream, a story we tell ourselves when we sleep, but a fierce awakening, a cold shiver of knowing in the deepest parts of our souls. The struggle continues, uplifting life, and whenever there is news of slaves rebelling, the question still echoes, carried on the wind like a prayer and a threat: "But could it be Benedito?" Every January 1st, in the vibrant dance of Ticumbi, the people collect that small image, carrying it with pride, its polished wood cool in their hands, a living echo of Benedito Half-League, the man whose legend was not carved from stone, but from the unyielding spirit of a people, a man who proved that true freedom was not a gift to be granted, but a thunderous birthright to be seized.

> *The story is told*
> > *The sands of time spent*
> > > *And that is the way his story went*

THE NAGUAL OF TEPOZTLÁN

The copper-ribbed mountains, etched with the twilight's blush, cradled a silence thick with ancient murmurings. But for Laheem, the beauty held a jagged edge. Just days before, the promise of this three-city sojourn with Helen had shimmered like a desert mirage. Now, in the sterile aftermath of her departure in Mexico City—the forlorn straw hat, abandoned on its side, a mocking epitaph to their unraveling—he felt adrift. New York waited, a city breathing exhaust and muted expectations under a sky the color of old tin. His apartment held the quiet chill of things perfectly placed but never truly lived in. The appearance of the thing. It was the façade that drove her from him. He had hoped Helen's presence would be the sunlight warming the glass, a vibrant bloom against the concrete. He forgot that the flowering of purpose, of meaning, had to rise from his own roots hidden deep within. He should have turned back, booked a flight to the familiar ache of New York City. Yet, stubbornness, a brittle shield against the raw wound of betrayal, had driven him onward. The reservations stood, a testament to a future now fractured: a comfortable car service, a cozy bed and breakfast promising views of this fabled town, and later, the allure of Monte Alban's silent stones near Oaxaca. So he went.

Now, the wind, spiced with the scent of copal and wild hibiscus, whispered against his sad, arched window, carrying the distant pulse of the festival. The music, a vibrant weave of drums and flutes, was a stark counterpoint to the hollow echo within him, the gaping absence where Helen had been. He sat on the edge of the bed, the crisp white sheets a stark reminder of the emptiness beside him. This solitude felt different from the leaden loneliness that usually accompanied him, even in crowded Manhattan streets—that familiar cloak woven from missed chances and paths untaken out of fear. Outside, the ahuehuete trees stood like ancient sentinels, their gnarled branches reaching towards the darkening sky, while bright orchids and the delicate, star-shaped blossoms of the cazahuate tree painted the landscape with splashes of color.

"Another night alone," he muttered. The words tasted like ash in his mouth. He picked up his phone, scrolled through old photos of him and Helen, their smiles mocking him from the screen. A wave of nausea rolled over him, a physical manifestation of his grief. He remembered Helen›s cutting words, delivered with a casual cruelty that still made his skin crawl: "You love me, but you don't like me. I don't even know if you truly like yourself." The memory, a shard of ice, pierced his heart.

The festival sounds grew louder, more insistent, pulling him from his self-pity. He sighed, pushed himself up. "Might as well see what all the noise is about," he said to the empty room.

He stepped out into the wide, cobbled street. The air thrummed with energy. Laheem could taste the burnished copper of sky above. The night's bowl was the color of metal, blueblack silver streaks and smoke. He walked on burnt nerves. Trees stiffened into place, then turned their branches to watch him as he passed. He knew their sudden tension intimately. It was a familiar feeling—the paralysis of choosing safety over the untamed, messy unknown his spirit seemed to dimly remember craving.

But all night he had dreamed of erasure, sublimations. Strange alchemies, as if loneliness could transform into bright gold. Laughter bright and infectious, spilled from the open doorways of cantinas. The scent of grilled corn and something sweet, like cinnamon and smoke, mingled with the heady aroma of the night-blooming jasmine. He followed the music, a complex rhythm that seemed to vibrate in his very bones. He passed handsome painted gates and high stone walls, each reflecting the spirits of the families they guarded, walled sentinels both witness and warrior protectors. He traced the swirling patterns on a handsome gate, a calligraphy of belonging he felt utterly excluded from. Back home, his own walls had no history. They felt thin, offering isolation instead of sanctuary, a shuttered life chosen out of caution rather than conviction. He carried his misery not just as sadness, but as the weary weight of potential refused, of detours taken away from an unpredictable, more terrifying destiny hinted at in forgotten dreams. Many were adorned with the special spray of wildflowers arranged in a cross, a natural talisman that had served them well through the ages.

Laheem found himself in the town square, a kaleidoscope of color and motion. Fireworks exploded overhead, painting the night with ephemeral flowers of light. Marionettes, crafted with whimsical artistry, danced in the hands of unseen puppeteers, their painted eyes gleaming with ancient secrets. Masked figures, adorned with feathers and mirrors, whirled in a joyful frenzy, their movements a ritual older than memory. He glimpsed elders tipping back clay cups and gourds, downing a white gold brew amid bursts of laughter. Drunk on the blood of a goddess, their joy echoed through the night. The faint scent of gunpowder hung in the air, mingling with the sweet fragrance of the night-blooming dahlia flowers, and the occasional boom and gleeful shriek of cohetes echoed through the valley, a bowl cradled by the ancient mountains.

It was true, he realized, what they said about cities. People learned to carry themselves differently within their bones and flesh. There was a kind of muscular music to the negotiation between the layers of time and the constant cycle of spirits, as people came and went, were born and died, though some, the very lucky, might find themselves reborn again, in unexpected ways. As he watched the couples and lovers intertwined hands, their intimacy shining in the fire sparks of moonlight, a pang of loneliness, sharp as a stab of hunger, took his breath. He steadied himself, then saw the children, their shiny dark hair like glistening waves of a dark sea. For a moment, nostalgic joy found him as they scampered and skipped, slipping through the crowd of elders, their tympani roar of laughter filling the night.

Laheem could feel it in his chest, a gathering. A sense of something ancient and powerful, stirred within him, a feeling both terrifying, exhilarating. It felt like remembering a forgotten tongue, a language his own blood should have known, echoing the pulse of the mountain itself, its ancient rhythm. A reckoning with something wild and true he'd spent years carefully silencing beneath layers of sensible choices.

A woman with eyes like polished obsidian and a smile that radiated both warmth and knowing stepped close to him. She wore a rebozo woven with threads of silver and gold, and her voice, when she spoke, was like the rustling of dry leaves on sacred ground. "You look lost, *cariño*," she said, her voice a low murmur that seemed perfectly attuned to the thinning veil between worlds this festival night encouraged. "I am Margarite."

Laheem hesitated, unsure how to explain the tangled knot of his emotions. "I... I was supposed to be here with someone," he finally said, the words catching in his throat. "She left." Like a spell, saying it aloud made it true. His mind stuttered.

Margarite nodded, her gaze unwavering, holding a hint of ancient recognition, as if seeing not just a man falling apart, but a convergence point. "Sometimes, those we think we need are only shadows, obscuring the light within us. This festival," she gestured to the swirling dancers, "it is a celebration of shedding those shadows, of finding the nagual that sleeps within. Especially here. Especially *now*. The mountain breathes secrets tonight."

A kindly man with skin the color of rich earth and a smile that crinkled the corners of his eyes joined them, drawn perhaps by the subtle shift in energy around Laheem. "Welcome, brother," he said, his voice a gentle rumble, his eyes holding a similar depth, a quiet understanding that expanded and grew, charged with the electric air. "I am Armando. Margarite speaks true. The Quetzalcoatl waits for you, as it waits for us all, when the heart is finally ready to listen."

A song, born of the earth and the stars, unfurled. It spoke of the plumed serpent, whose breath stirred the fragrant winds, whose glistening scales shimmered like a thousand sunsets. Her eyes, pools of jade, held the wisdom of the ancient amomoatl. As the song swelled, Laheem felt a strange pull, a chord struck deep within his chest. He watched the dancers, their faces transformed by the music, their movements fluid and powerful. He saw not just joy, but a fierce, untamed energy, a sense of belonging that transcended words.

He closed his eyes, letting the music wash over him and his grief. He remembered a time when he was a clumsy child, fearless and uninhibited, his imagination a boundless landscape. He remembered the sting of his grandmother's words, "Don't be so loud, boy. Don't take up so much space." He had learned to shrink himself, to dim his own light to fit into the narrow confines of other people's expectations. He had done it with his friends, his family, and eventually, with Helen. The memory of her words, "You don't even like yourself," echoed in his mind, a painful truth he had long denied.

The music intensified, weaving tales of ancient gods and powerful transformations, of shedding old skins and embracing new forms. He felt a warmth spread through him, starting in his chest and radiating outwards. It was not the fleeting heat of passion, but a deep, abiding warmth, like the sun warming the earth after a long winter. His skin tingled, and he felt a strange lightness, as if a great weight had been lifted from his shoulders.

"Let go of the sorrow, hijo," Armando said, his voice a soothing balm. "Let the past pass and plant your worries in the dust. Regret will not save you. Embrace the fire within."

As Armando spoke, Laheem felt a shift, not just within his spirit, but within his very flesh. The tightness in his chest loosened, replaced by a sense of expansion. His bones felt lighter, as if hollowed out and filled with pure air. He saw, in his mind›s eye, the pieces of himself that he had scattered and lost over the years: his unbridled curiosity, his fierce creativity, his unwavering belief in the magic of the world, in the goodness of people. He began to pick them up, one by one, like shiny stones, and fit them back together, the process both painful and exhilarating, like the tearing away of old scars, the blooming of new skin.

He looked down at his hands, and they seemed to shimmer, as if a part of him had dipped into that liminal, midnight and moonlight-rimmed space, his skin taking on an iridescent glow. He looked back at Margarite and Armando, their faces filled with their love for each other and an ancient knowing.

"What's happening to me?" he whispered, his voice hoarse with awe. He was embarrassed by hot, unexpected tears.

Margarite smiled. "The nagual is awakening, mi hijo. Embrace it. Let the old self fall away like a discarded husk. You are becoming who you were always meant to be."

From his back, great wings unfurled, the color of twilight skies and deep emerald forests. They were not heavy or cumbersome, but light and strong, like the wings of a hummingbird, catching the starlight and the firelight. His spine lengthened, his shoulders broadened, and his head shifted, his eyes becoming larger, jeweled and frog-like, reflecting the ancient wisdom of the mountains and the resilience of the axolotl. A silver beard, woven from moonlight and the mist of the mountains' highest peaks, cascaded down his chest, a symbol of the wisdom he was now claiming. The scales began to spread across his skin, shimmering and iridescent, catching the light of the fireworks like a thousand tiny mirrors.

The crowd, a chorus of delighted gasps and cheers, lifted him into the star-strewn sky, where he joined the celestial dance, a dragon born of the earth and the heart of growing pain, ascending to the realm of the old gods, the first ones above the silent pyramid. He looked down at the town, the trails that snaked up the spine of Tepoztécatl like a secret untold, the music fading into a distant hum, and for the first time, he felt truly, utterly, free. He was alone, amidst the topaz stars, but he was not lonely. He was complete, an unidentified ancient phenomenon, another story to behold, be told, a being of two worlds, human and divine, sorrow and joy, loss and rebirth. He was the nagual, the dragon, the embodiment of his own untamed, magnificent, marvelously real self, the one he was yet to discover. Laheem spread his wings, and with a powerful beat, soared into the night, embracing the boundless possibility of impossibility. He sailed on...

Leaving behind the echoes of his former self
shedding the skin of what he had been
'til the letters of his born name
faded like whispers on the wind
and were lost, and gone
and never spoken aloud again.

LOKEERA'S TONGUE

Out there across the skybridge you could see each one. Ours was the darkest sky for miles around. Here in the sacred garden atop Elder's Hill, past the rusted ruins of the old world, you could see them all. Lokeera pointed up at them as she wheeled and turned through the bush, the fragrant sage branches tickling her toes and heels, brushing her ankles. My sight fading, she is now mostly a blur of motion to me. But a mother's eye holds a different kind of sight. A knowing born of touch, memory, and the heart's fierce pull, allowing me to see the details of my Lokeera even when vision fails. Unlike my daughter, I wear the old tell-tale scar of the mkata. It was inevitable when my mother discovered that my Will was much stronger than expected. Not long after my surgery, I lost my singing voice. It is the way of our people, and I was not the first nor the last to be visited by the commune's elderly mkata, her kit in hand.

A burst of energy and light, Lokeera had grown in community with me, signing nearly as nimbly as those born in silence. In our way, signing was more than just handshapes and movement. It was breath, felt vibration, and subtle cues that echoed the songs we could no longer sing aloud, adding layers of meaning only we understood. At ten years old, the child was always in motion and full of questions. The ground felt uneven beneath my feet as I tried to match her pace, my hands flapping uselessly at my sides. Impatient, she ran back to me, placed her small fingers in my open palm. Body pulsing with excitement, she traced out a rhythmic question, shaped like the constellation above:

"W?"

I raised my thumb, traced a circle in the air around my face, and ended the circle by tapping my nose once. Then diagonally, from the top of my shoulder to my waist, I traced the outline of a ceremonial sash. *The Aethiopian Queen,* I signed, *Cassiopeia.* Delighted, Lokeera darted to my left, then turned to my waiting palm, a hummingbird flying backward. *Very good, Keera. You recognize the queen's five brightest stars.*

The air around us throbbed with her joy as she named the stars above. *The Daughters of the Night,* she signed on my arm. *The Eland Bull!* she cried, *and the polestar, Grandmother of the High.* Lokeera squatted and leapt in the air as if on all fours. The story of the bull was her favorite. I leaned down, felt her shoulders rock in the darkness. My body reached across the silence for the waves of laughter I knew were there, the scent of the sage blossoms filling me with peace. I watched her do a cartwheel, waving her arms wildly above her braided head, the shell beads swinging across her shoulders, when she suddenly stood back up.

Powerful sound waves rippled through the air and the ground beneath my feet. I could feel the energy vibrating up through my soles and through my bones as I tried to keep my balance. *Lokeera's Will.* The sound, what others heard, I now felt. My breath hitched, a frantic bird against my ribs, yet my gaze remained fixed on Lokeera, a current of awe pulling me. Always wonder.

I strained to see as my daughter danced through the ragged clumps of weed and stone, oblivious to the earth's shift, pointing out the falling stars, a grand meteor shower gracing us from up above. With each spectacle that I could not quite see, Lokeera's Will flowed even more. I did not bother to chastise her this time. It was far too late to silence her now; it would do no good. She had been discovered as I feared she would. My efforts to conceal her were futile as she grew more powerful each year. Instead of reminding her of the danger in discovery, I concentrated on her happy movements, the way her moonsong made me feel. I basked in its beauty as she pointed at the realm of ancestors, then hurriedly returned to my palms, signing across my lifelines as I held her fluttering hands in my own, interpreting as she swiftly signed in the space between us.

Sometimes when Lokeera was excited and she wanted me to truly feel each expression, she would sign up my arms or across my heart and chest. This she did, emphasizing her hand movements and gestures to cleverly name each star. *"That was one of The Old Men. Now it is gone,"* she signed as a great cloud passed overhead. *"That was Mother Hen. Now it is gone."* She raised my hand up as if I could hold the old star's light. *"That was the Heart Star. Now it is gone, too."* I would hold it and my child forever if I could, but I cannot.

Long ago our foremothers said the stars were the eyes of the dead. Others said the stars were the spirits of those unwilling to be born, the spirits of souls so long dead that they no longer remembered that they were once ancestors. Now we live in the shadow of their distant light, pulled under the force of rebellious moons. I did not know how much I resented them until Lokeera drew closer to me.

I could smell the sweet scent of her skin, feel her song brushing up against my spine, prickling the fine hairs around my ears. I would have stood there all night watching the ghosts of stars, the wind a damp cloth across my face, her laughter a warm breath on my cheek, but another cloud rolled back, revealing the dark jawbone of the first moon. Lokeera vibrated in my arms, her joy contagious. Even through my fading sight, the moon hung in the air, a red machete, the giant crescent reflecting flames from the ritual burning of the woods. *The Chiming* would soon be upon us. Even there from my clump of grass, I could see the haze of smoke and smell the pungent incense. My stomach lurched. It sickened me.

I waved my hand. *"Time,"* a sharp cutting motion, like Grandmother of High's sickle. Lokeera ran back, scattering the stones and grasped my hands, now balled into tight fists.

"But it's Olapa the First Moon," she signed. *"She watches us with one eye."*

"She certainly watches," I sign back—*and sees none of our heartache.* This last, I kept to myself. It would not do to ruin our last days together.

I let Lokeera, my only child, pry open my fingers, and still I signed nothing.

Holding my hand, she curved our index fingers and thumbs and placed them on my right eye, then lifted both up to the sky. *"The waxing moon?"* she asks.

I stared past the curve of her shoulders. The first moon lost one eye in a vicious battle. She sees what others would not. The second moon lost Her voice fighting for the vulnerable. She is what I am not—brave. She speaks the unspeakable, while I remain silent, burying my words inside me. Lokeera tugs me, her growing impatience an electric hum. As always, my responses to her questions were too slow, weighing my answers against the truth the elders wanted hidden. Her fingers tickled my palm again, insistent. *How could I deny her?*

Finally, after a long while, I nodded. She released my hand and sprinted off toward the north gate, near the Kuma tree, the beads in her braided hair swaying.

I watched her a long while in silence. I found myself doing that a lot lately, watching her as closely as she watched the stars, the moons. A few days ago we celebrated her born day and gave her a planisphere so she could chart the movements of the skies. If only there were a planisphere for the soul, something that could tell when she was born how long my daughter would be with me. But I had only the moon and these two old eyes that were my mouth and ears.

So I watched her.

I watched her as she slept, pressed my cheek against her pillow, inhaled her sweet brown scent, the fragrance only little girls now held. I trembled when I felt the whisper of her lashes against the pillow as she stirred in sleep. Cried softly when her little hands reached for mine in the darkness. In the weeks before the Chiming we were inseparable, mother and daughter, two songs linked by flesh, a pool of genes. Each day I felt her music grow stronger, the moon-song flowing through her veins. She was an aria writ for the sky. An ancient song I could not hear.

Know this: I am a simple woman. I have not traveled far beyond our commune like the elders. My tongue, my ears do not know many things but as a mother, I will always know my greatest failing, that I could not share her journey.

Lokeera was ten, unstoppable. All of them were. We could not stop the flow of their blood no more than we could hold back the tides of the ocean Ashé or stop a star from falling. Lokeera had the power and it was growing within her. She did not know to be afraid.

One day while shopping in the herbal sector, I caught her singing with a strange child, no more than three years old. It is forbidden. We were afraid to let those like Lokeera play with children so young, to join Wills, less they be tempted into song and their combined voices blew bits and pieces of our world away.

When Lokeera was that age, even then you could tell her bloodline was pure, her little body a container for surrogate moonlight. Her limbs were straight, neck long, graceful, tongue a brilliant pink curl, the whites of her eyes shone like the lip of the moon. No diviner could ask for a more perfect receptacle. This poor child was unattended. Some young foolish mother no doubt had turned her back for an instant, a moment, to heckle with the vendors for fruit not worth their ration. But Lokeera was unafraid. Dancing in a circle, she placed her lips on the child's temple, whispered. There, in the middle of the market, she led the child in song, a throat game of hide and seek, nimble hummingbirds darting for nectar, a child's sweet music sweeping through the air, the ground, blending their voices, one pure, the other broken, soaring in harmonic flight.

Lokeera created her songs from mimicking nature, songs so beautiful they transported my mind to other worlds, other times before the Ruins, the plagues and the elders and their cursed machines.

We listened in awe. Strangers bickering only moments ago, dropped their hands in mid-curse to hear. Then the tremors began, the land yawning awake. Lokeera's moonsong rattled the carefully stacked gourds, water pots, and wares of the market women.

I listened spellbound, the plump fruit of the sorcadia dropping from my hand, smashing into a pulpy mess on the ground. That would cost me twenty bunches of Kuma leaves, a whole season of waiting, but I would have gladly paid more to hear them faintly singing like this, again and again, to hear them sing with my own ears, and watch their nimble fingers darting like small sparrows, meadowlarks dancing in the air.

For a moment I thought we might all rise, carried by their song, the notes piercing the earth and the clouds. Lokeera's Will was strong, her voice strengthening the younger child's impure ones, bending them, merging them with her own. We might rise, I thought, or the sky might come crashing down on us.

Then the screams began.

A ripple of felt vibration shot through the ground as figures blurred at the edge of my sight. The shoppers in the market scattered to take cover. Their wares and goods were abandoned, no brave souls left behind. Frightened, I took Lokeera by the hand, the notes still resonating in the air. We hurried home, the limbs of the few lone trees and that poor child, swaying with her music.

When we returned, her father scolded me but Lokeera directed her song towards his ear, a focused wave of vibration that quieted his protests. Her blood full of her Will had survived two hundred and forty moons, and here that was an unexpected blessing. No matter where we hid, they would come for her—and the others like her, and then they would come for me. We both knew.

I had heard tales of whole communes, whole sectors blown apart by some willful, undisciplined child's moonsong. Children like Lokeera were rare. Few were born with the Will inside them so strong. Yes, they would come for her, before her song could threaten our safety, disrupt the harmony of the community. While one moonsinger was a threat, a group of them could unhinge our world.

Knowing this, I checked Lokeera often. I fed her lots of root water and hymn wine to keep her levels constant. If she even looked as if to cough, we would be upon her, water pots and the hymn wine in hand. And as always, she was patient, never complaining. Three days before they would take her to be with the others, she sat in the warm tub of water I made for her, singing softly to herself as the blood ran from her veins into the hemophonetica issued by the commune elders.

I could feel her bloodsong tickling my ear.

"*Keera*," I signed, my palms glistening with the hymning oil. "*What is that song you sing?*" She giggled, lightheaded.

"*It's my mamasong, a new one*," she signed. I felt the subtle movement of her tongue against perfect teeth. "*Let me teach you.*"

"*I don't know, Keera,*" I signed. "*These chords are rusty.*" I stroked the tender skin on my throat. The scar thick from the surgery my own mother had forced upon me as a child. A hot wave of shame washed over me. In the end, I would lose my Lokeera because I was a coward. I could not bear to place the ritual knife upon my newborn's throat. "*My tongue is slow and thick,*" I signed. "*It grows wearier with each moonrise. Even before my scar, I doubt that I ever sang as lovely as you.*"

"*Mama,*" she signed. From the arch of her thick brows and the pounding in my chest, I knew her voice was rising. "*You have the most beautiful tongue in all the world, and your bloodsong is sure, like mine. I bet you were a beautiful moonsinger,*" she said with an impish grin, "*weren't you, Mama?*" Her nimble fingers splashed me with water.

"*Yes, Keera,*" I said, signing her a navelsong. My half-smile thin as the crescent moon. "*The purest blood, the sweetest tongue of all.*" I stroked her skin and lied to her as others had lied to me.

* * *

"*Aneèma, don't cry,*" he said, whistling in my ear. "*You can have others.*"

Only a man could say such words and have no fear.

Before Lokeera was born, I prayed first that she would die, that her heartdrum would never beat. How could I forget a song that I had never heard, that had never been born? But after the first cycle, my third harvest moon, I knew the child I carried high in my womb would live and she would sing me to misery. As her vocal chords

433

formed and later, her little palms pressed against the inside of my
soft round gourdbelly, I prayed that if she lived, her tongue would
shrivel in her mouth. But she was born, two moon cycles later, and
her voice echoed off the walls and shattered every mirror in the
birthing room.

Lokeera was so unlike her father, so unlike me, the woman
who birthed her. As unlike me as I was to my own mother. Her
father had been born silent, like all the other men, his singing chords
already a frozen hollow inside his throat. But she had gained the
pure blood from me. And it was growing stronger inside her each
day, the cells multiplying and dividing, a strange symphony altering
every part of her until she could no longer exist on earth. It was then
we would send her to the stars, to breathe pure song, they say, pure
energy, her throat swallowing nebulae, tonguing sweet novas.

Even now, two days before the Chiming, as I lathered her with
the sweet hymn oil, I felt the moonsong pulsing within her veins, a
river trapped in flesh and bone, threatening to burst its banks, to
burst into song. Soon the Chiming would claim her. Lokeera sang.
I poured more oil into the tub, stroked some in the parts of her
intricately braided hair. The spirals and loops were designed to chart
a path for the future. The hemophonetica hummed its ascent.

*　*　*

Last night I dreamed they took Lokeera, of ten year olds standing all in a row, like balagagofons awaiting their chiming—metal,
stone, wood, flesh. My flesh. Lokeera, daughterseed. Moonsong
standing in the surf, walking waist deep into the ocean, arms linked

with the others. Their voices rising, the pitch so strong and sure that even our dead ears could hear them.

Then their song changed, the notes higher, eerie and I was back in the birthing center, ten years ago. I dreamed I gave birth to Lokeera, dreamed that I squatted over a bassinet woven from tulle and bulrush, dreamed my legs buckled as the moonsong swelled and erupted in me, dreamed of saltwater running down my thighs in waves of pain. My stomach contracting, diaphragm crushed hard against red muscle pumping. I dreamed I gave birth to Lokeera, to her tongue, wet. I felt the pressure in my left ear, a strange unfolding, and then the sharp jabs in my right drum as her tiny feet kicked.

I woke, signing wildly with a scream I could not hear, the moonsong echoing. He held my hands, quieted their spasmic burst, stroked the soft hairs on the nape of my neck, gently running his tongue across the curve of my ear, a smooth semicircle, wet, calming, prayerful.

Our children do not belong to us.

The elders tell us, those who discovered the moonsong, those who built the hemophonetica to record its notes, its bloodsong and the keening of generations, those who made the food that was not food and changed us all, those who built this world that threw the moon off her course and brought another, they tell us that the children exist in perfect harmonious relationship to each other, to the moons whose pull grow dangerously stronger with each nightday, releasing all the innersongs of the earth.

They tell us and we listen.

We see their Will signed in the new paved roads and paths that gleam like bone, in the bitter water rites laced with blood and new poisons, our blood, of those who resisted, in the tasteless food designed to nurture but numbs the tongue, in the brightly lit homes powered by a source no one speaks of.

They tell us and we listen, reach across our fear and silence to some semblance of life. Our children accept the moonsong, the gift unquestioned. We accept their sacrifice, their power unquestioned. We are in harmony in our silence.

And yet, I tend my mother's garden as she before her, harvesting arnica, yarrow, goldenrod, and widow's dust in the stretch of land at the back of the house leading to the Kuma tree. The Kuma's roots plunge deep into the earth and rise, wrapping thick thorny vines around base and trunk and limbs as if to strangle the life my mother made me promise I would tend. Its musky scent makes my throat itch and its dark roots rise from the earth like bloodweeds.

They make me afraid, these twisted roots entering themselves, so afraid I do not question even this daily ritual, pruning the weeds from cold, exposed roots, even with the Chiming now only a day away.

Still, I bury my knees in the soil, toil in silence, the three modest rows of wet earth raised black knuckles against the sun.

My mother made me promise when I was ten, Lokeera's age, should I ever mother a child like me, to choose another path. I tried but I have stumbled and failed. Mother's blood had given me its song, hidden through bloodlines over long years, and yet I did not inherit her green thumb. If I could, I would grow carrots and plump ripe tomatoes like the ancestors did in the past, guinea corn, and perhaps a little sun squash, but the elders have forbidden this, too. Anything but the healing roots are prohibited for fear that another strain of viruses, strange parasites might put us all at risk. The plagues of the old world in a new one made much older by guilt. But I long for the taste of the food my mother said our people once ate. I long for the taste of her song, any song in my ear. With each day, the memory of my own song fades, its notes a thing of myth.

I am straining to remember when I prick myself on one of the Kuma's black thorns. "*Bloodrot!*" I curse. I suck the fleshy brown meat below my thumb when I realize that I've crushed some of the fresh widow's dust in my haste. It doesn't matter. The roots the elders ignore. They call them old wives' tales, wanga talk and folklore. These roots and seeds, they say, are worthless compared to *their* creations. But their healing properties cannot be reproduced in their sterile labs.

Still, I tend my mother's garden as best I can, as her mother before her, though I've no talent for it. I tend it as I had once hoped Lokeera would tend it for me.

Suddenly Lokeera's tiny hands clasped my own, signing into my palm. "*Tend what?*"

I jumped, startled, crushing a stalk of yarrow. I didn't realize I was signing to myself. The closer to the Chiming, the more the signing in my mind spills out. It is more common when my mind struggles with the words my heart does not wish to say but must.

My fingers flew to my throat. Hand cupped, I moved slowly from my neck down to my belly. Lokeera shook her head.

"*Nothing. Are you hungry?*" I sign. "*Keera, you must eat. You know the Chiming...*"

She took my hand lightly, raised my fingers to her forehead and gently tapped three times. "*I know,*" she signed. The soft wind blowing the scent of her grandmother's garden all around us.

"Are you. . ." I can't make myself sign it. Inside I am all nerves, anxiety. Guilt.

She signed on my wrist, her touch confident and sure. No, she wouldn't be. Afraid. *We are liars.* Her father and I had told her enough half-truths to make certain of that.

I felt her gaze on me, a weight I couldn't meet. I avoided Lokeera's trusting eyes. She watched me in silence as I bent onto my knees. I kneaded the wet earth, plucked defiant weeds by the roots, pulling harder than I needed to.

"Tell me as story, Mama."

I raised my head, surprised. Her face is strange, knowing. *"No, not now. Later, Keera. It's too early for stories."*

"It's never too early for stories," she signed, looking older than her ten years. *What does she know?* She placed a lone finger across her lips then pointed to her chest. *"Tell me,"* she signed, watching me curiously. *"Tell me how the moon lost her voice and gave it to me."*

The air grew heavy, thick with the scent of burning woods and the nervous energy of the commune. I stood with the others, a wall of silent bodies. The earth trembled beneath my feet. Not from the meteors this time, but from the collective pulse of young hearts. Lokeera was somewhere in the gathered throng ahead, a knot of pain tightening in my gut. The moonsong began not as a sound I could hear, but as a rising tide of vibration, starting low in the ground and climbing, resonating in my bones, in the scar tissue of my throat. It was a symphony of pure power, raw and untamed, the Will of the children manifesting as a physical force. I felt the individual threads of it, distinct yet merging, and for a terrifying, exhilarating instant, I thought I felt Lokeera's thread strongest of all, a bright, fierce current against the dull hum of accepted fate. My hands, hidden at my sides, clenched into fists. Around me, other hands hung still, resigned. But I imagined them, just for a second, shaping signs of protest, words unspoken but felt, a silent tremor beneath the orchestrated release of power. The Chiming swelled, a wave cresting, pulling our children towards the sky.

But the wave broke differently this time. It did not carry them away. Instead, I felt a violent jolt through the earth, a tremor that wasn't ascent but a stubborn, grounding refusal. A collective gasp rippled through the silent parents, a wave of shock I felt in the sudden tension of bodies around me. Through my fading sight, the blur of figures ahead did not disappear into the heavens. They remained. *Rooted. Present.* And then, amidst the chaotic vibrations of disbelief and dawning hope, I felt it. Distinct, undeniable, Lokeera's moonsong vibrating not in the distant sky, but *here.* A powerful, grounded pulse against my chest, against the scar on my throat. It was joined by others, a rising chorus felt deep in the earth, a collective song of refusal and resilience. Hot, ragged tears streamed down my face, tasting of salt and impossible joy. Around me, I felt the trembling shoulders of other mothers, their silent sobs now shaking with a different kind of release. The Chiming had not claimed them. The children, their moonsong bound to the earth, had broken the cycle. A new song was rising, and it was vibrating in the heart of our world. And in that vibrating heart, I felt her, bright and undeniable.

Lokeera.

A GLIMPSE INTO THE CONJURED WORLD

Step into this exclusive early look at
"The Algorithm and the Goddess,"
a new tale waiting to unfold fully in
Sheree Renée Thomas's upcoming collection,
RING SHOUT ON SATURN,
Book 2 in the Root & Sky Series.

THE ALGORITHM AND THE GODDESS

RED DOGS AND SPACE CHARIOTS

2

T he city-wide power outage, a sharp, angry consequence of E=MC²+'s unregulated energy draw, had plunged Memphis into a patchwork of darkness, but in Boxtown, the shadows writhed with a new, potent luminescence. The hum from the colossal supercomputer, once a distant thrum, now resonated like a forced bass note in every chest, a constant reminder of the unseen pollutants filling the air. Children coughed, their tiny lungs rattling, and the older folks gripped their chests, battling the familiar constriction of bronchitis and asthma, ailments not just an unfortunate part of life but a direct, infuriating consequence of the unpermitted gas turbines now running constantly across town. News alerts, dismissed as hyperbole by city officials but whispered fearfully among neighbors, spoke of "increased particulate matter" and unexplained spikes in emergency room visits, all centered in their zip codes. This wasn't just chaos; it was a crisis.

And from that crisis, power bloomed.

Cequitta felt it first, a sharp clarity in the absence of artificial light, a direct conduit to the city's nervous system. The network of traffic signals, streetlights, and surveillance cameras, all meant to control, now pulsed with a malleable energy she could bend with a flicker of thought. Meanwhile, Reverend Fuller, his touch now imbued with a warm, steady glow, moved through the frightened crowds, his hands mending not just torn cloth but the constricted airways of gasping children, the burning in their lungs receding under his healing grace. At Gateway Tire & Service Center, the three generations of men – old Mr. Earl, his son Bo, and his grandson Lil' Earl – found their hands, usually adept with wrenches and tires, now effortlessly lifting car frames, tossing heavy engine blocks aside as if they were mere pebbles. Their repairs, once methodical, became a blur of superhuman precision.

From the heart of Sojourner's Troupe, a pulsing rhythm began to beat. The dancers, normally weaving stories through Memphis jookin' and crumpin' on polished stages, now moved with an amplified, visceral energy. Their intricate footwork and fluid body rolls manifested as tangible shockwaves, illusions shimmering like heat haze, and shimmering force fields that rippled against the rising tension. Their art became a shield, their bodies living defenses against the encroaching threat. The persistent cicadas in the nearby pecan trees seemed to change their tune, their high-pitched sawing now a frantic, urgent chorus, a counterpoint to the growing hum of the supercomputer.

The wail of sirens, a sound usually met with weary resignation, now sliced through the night with a terrifying urgency. Red and blue lights flashed, carving angry arcs against the darkness as a convoy of MPD cruisers, marked with the snarling dog insignia of the "Red Dogs" unit, tore through the streets. Their orders were clear: exploit the power vacuum, suppress the newly empowered residents, and, most importantly, secure any evidence connecting AetherForge to the city's sudden, widespread respiratory distress.

"Looks like we got some unwanted guests," Pearson growled, his hand tightening around the neck of his guitar, a low, resonant chord vibrating through his fingers. Spaceman, his face alight with a mischievous grin, gestured towards a line of classic muscle cars, gleaming under the sporadic light. Each one was a testament to his peculiar genius: custom paint jobs that shimmered with impossible colors, gravity-defying modifications that made them hover inches off the asphalt, and concealed compartments that snapped open to reveal repurposed weaponry salvaged from discarded tech – a hydraulic arm from a forklift, a laser sight from an old DVD player. "Time for the chariots to ride," he chuckled, swinging open the door of a cherry-red '69 Dodge Charger. The air, thick with the scent of dust and fear, now carried a faint, metallic tang from the increasing turbine emissions, a smell residents had grown grimly accustomed to, sometimes like chemicals, sometimes like sewage.

The chase ignited. The Red Dogs, expecting easy targets, were met with an impossible defense. A cruiser swerved to block an alley, only for a dancer from Sojourner's Troupe to launch into a spinning jookin' routine, her movements creating a distortion in the air that made the vehicle swerve violently, its tires screeching as if the very asphalt rebelled. Another cruiser sped down a residential street, only to find the men of Gateway Tire, their muscles ripping, effortlessly tossing a derelict sedan into its path, forming an instant, impassable roadblock. The Red Dogs cursed, their radios spitting static as they tried to report the impossible.

From the shadows of a neglected side street near T.O. Fuller State Park, a fleet of Spaceman's driverless "crawler cars" emerged, their repurposed vacuum cleaner bodies scuttling with surprising speed. These were smaller, faster versions of the six-legged contraption Ari loved from his workshop, but armed now with an audacious purpose. Their internal lights glowed an inviting, erratic blue, mimicking human drivers as they swerved playfully, almost tauntingly, in front of the lead Red Dog cruisers. Lured by the perceived challenge and the desperate need to regain control, several police vehicles broke off from the main pursuit, veering down the winding, less-trafficked backroads. The crawler cars, their internal gyroscopes humming, maintained a precise, accelerating lead, drawing the Red Dogs deeper into the dense, overgrown thickets and abandoned industrial lots, far from Boxtown's residential streets. With a final, synchronized surge of speed, the crawler cars abruptly veered off the road into a ravine, their lights winking out just as the pursuing Red Dog cruisers, unable to brake or swerve in time, crashed violently into each other amidst the overgrown morning glory vines and tangled underbrush, far from any homes or bystanders.

Cequitta, a ghost in the machine, found her focus. Her technokinesis reached out, a silent tendril of pure will, slipping into the Red Dogs' onboard systems. Their GPS flickered into nonsensical routes, their squad car cameras broadcasted blurry, distorted images of grinning residents and dancing shadows. One by one, their vehicles sputtered, engines dying, lights dimming as if some unseen hand was squeezing the life out of their electronics. "You want to hide their secrets?" Cequitta thought, a cold fire in her mind. "Let's share some of yours." She linked into their secure communication channels, and a cacophony of panicked voices, raw and unfiltered, suddenly blared from their own car speakers, detailing cover-ups, bribes, and the chilling directives from "above" to ignore the rising death toll from the air pollution. The frustration and anger that had simmered for decades in Boxtown, a community that had seen its share of polluters come and go, leaving behind coal ash and heightened cancer risks, boiled over in a collective surge of power.

As the cruisers stalled, the dancers from Sojourner's Troupe surged forward, their amplified moves blurring into a whirlwind of controlled chaos. With gravity-defying leaps and spins, they bounded onto the hoods and roofs of the police cars, delivering non-lethal, precise strikes that disabled the officers, knocking out their radios, disarming them, and leaving them stunned. The men of Gateway Tire moved with brutal efficiency, overturning police cruisers with a grunt of amplified effort, blocking off entire intersections, effectively bringing the Red Dogs' reign of terror to a grinding halt.

In the ensuing silence, broken only by the lingering hum of the turbines and the distant sirens of actual emergency services heading towards the downed cruisers, the empowered residents of Boxtown stood victorious. The Red Dogs, sprawled and disoriented, were quickly apprehended, their radios now broadcasting their frantic, incriminating pleas for help. Their capture wasn't just a win; it was a revelation. The exposed communications laid bare the hidden agreements between local officials and AetherForge, the chilling complicity in poisoning their own citizens for profit. Boxtown had fought back, not just with fists and force, but with ingenuity, community, and newly awakened power. The fight for their health and their right to breathe clean air had just begun. As Easter Knox, a long-time resident and activist, might say, "It's just sort of hard, you know, when people got money," but in Boxtown, a different kind of power was rising.

A quiet exultation rippled through the gathered residents, quickly tempered by the realization that the pervasive smell of chemicals and sewage still clung to the humid air, a grim reminder of their ongoing battle. Small children still coughed, their little bodies vulnerable despite the victory. Boxtown might have driven back the immediate threat, but the source of the insidious sickness still pulsed, unseen, from the colossal supercomputer. Cequitta watched them, her heart swelling with pride, then aching with a familiar frustration. This was their home, soaked in their ancestors' blood, settled by formerly enslaved families who built it from scraps of boxcars, dreaming of a place to call their own. They had fought for it before, against oil pipelines and polluting plants, and they wouldn't stop now. But the scale of this new enemy, a "soulless wonder" of wires and cold data, demanded more than street-level resistance. It demanded understanding. She looked towards the pulsating glow of Emcee, the answer a magnetic pull in her soul. She needed to go deeper.

Thanks for diving into this exclusive sneak peek of
"The Algorithm and the Goddess"
You'll find the complete story in my next collection,
RING SHOUT ON SATURN,
Book 2 in the Root & Sky Series.
Look for it in SPRING 2026 from Third Man Books.

ACKNOWLEDGMENTS

Grateful and loving acknowledgment is made to Third Man Books Editor-in-Chief Chet Weise, and to all the Editors and Publishers who have supported my work and in whose pages some of these stories first appeared or were reprinted. Much gratitude also to the teams at *Locus: The Magazine of The Science Fiction & Fantasy Field* and *FIYAH Literary Magazine of Black Speculative Fiction*, whose awards have recognized stories included in this collection:

"The Grassdreaming Tree" first appeared in *SO LONG BEEN DREAMING: Postcolonial Science Fiction & Fantasy*, edited by Nalo Hopkinson and Uppinder Mehan (Arsenal Pulp Press, Vancouver, British Columbia, October 1, 2004). It also appeared in *THE BIG BOOK OF MODERN FANTASY (1945-2010)* edited by Ann and Jeff VanderMeer (July 21, 2020), *SLEEPING UNDER THE TREE OF LIFE* (July 18, 2016) and *SHOTGUN LULLABIES: Stories & Poems* (January 31, 2011), both edited by L. Timmel Duchamp and Kathryn Wilham (Aqueduct Press, Seattle WA).

"Love Hangover" first appeared in *SLAY: Stories of the Vampire Noire*, edited by Nicole Givens Kurtz (Mocha Memoirs Press, Rock Hill, SC, September 28, 2020). It was a finalist for the 2021 Ignyte Award for Outstanding Short Story. It also appeared in *TROUBLE THE WATERS: Tales from the Deep Blue*, edited by Sheree Renée Thomas, Pan Morigan, and Troy L. Wiggins (Third Man Books, Nashville, January 18, 2022), and in *THE YEAR'S BEST AFRICAN SPECULATIVE FICTION* (2021 Edition for works published in 2020), edited by Oghenechovwe Donald Ekpeki (Jembefola Press, Lagos, Nigeria, September 28, 2021).

"Barefoot and Midnight" first appeared in Apex Magazine, Issue 122, edited by Jason Sizemore and Maurice Broaddus (Apex Magazine, Lexington KY, March 9, 2021). It was a finalist for the 2022 Locus Award for Best Short Story. It also appeared in *THE YEAR'S BEST AFRICAN SPECULATIVE FICTION* (2022 Edition for works published in 2021), edited by Oghenechovwe Donald Ekpeki, Eugen Bacon, and Milton Davis (OD Ekpeki Presents and Caezik SF, Lagos, Nigeria and Rockville, MD, December 12, 2023).

"The Big Book of Grandmamas" first appeared in *ROBOTIC AMBITION*, edited by Jason Sizemore and Lesley Connor (Apex Book Company, Lexington KY, October 10, 2023).

"Tethered" first appeared in *SPACEFUNK!*, edited by Milton Davis (MVmedia, LLC, Fayetteville, GA, January 25, 2025).

"Downwinders" first appeared in *FAR FUTURES* (https://farfutures. horizon2045.org/), edited by Jenny Johnston, Lisa DeYoung, and Erika Gregory (Horizon 2045 Foundation and Arizona State University's Center for Science and the Imagination, Mill Valley, CA and Tempe, AZ, May 29, 2024).

Photo by Brad Vest

ABOUT THE AUTHOR

Sheree Renée Thomas is deeply inspired by music, history, natural science, folklore, mythology, and the genius of the Mississippi Delta. She is the 3-time World Fantasy Award-winning author of the collections *Mojorhythm* and *Nine Bar Blues: Stories from an Ancient Future*, the multigenre, hybrid collections *Sleeping Under the Tree of Life* and *Shotgun Lullabies: Stories and Poems*, and the Marvel novel *Black Panther: Panther's Rage*. She contributed stories to the Marvel anthologies, *Captain America: The Shield of Sam Wilson* ("Exclusive Content") and *Black Panther: Tales of Wakanda* ("Heart of a Panther"). She also served as narrative writer and consultant for the futurist video game *Dreams: Imagine Futures* on the PlayStation platform, a collaboration involving Sony PlayStation and Daimler AG/Mercedes Benz, with characters based on her work. Additionally, she collaborated with award-winning artist Janelle

Monáe on "Timebox Altar(ed)" for the *New York Times* bestselling collection, *The Memory Librarian: And Other Stories from Dirty Computer*. Her work has been widely anthologized, including in *The Big Book of Modern Fantasy (1945-2010)*, edited by Ann and Jeff VanderMeer. Her writing and interviews have also appeared in publications such as *The New York Times, Scientific American, African Voices, Memphis Magazine*, the *Memphis Flyer, The Commercial Appeal, The Memphis Business Journal*, the *Washington Post Book World, Drumvoices Revue, Obsidian, Callaloo, Clarkesworld, Lightspeed, Strange Horizons, Pseudopod, Under the Volcano, Apex Magazine*, and *The Black Scholar*. She has been honored with fellowships and residencies from the Cave Canem Foundation, the Millay Colony of the Arts, Ledig House/Art Omi, VCCA, Bread Loaf Environmental, the Tennessee Arts Commission, and ARTSmemphis. Sheree Renée Thomas was the inaugural resident for the Mari Evans Residency for Authors and Artists of Color. The program is directed by science fiction author Maurice Broaddus at the revitalized, historic Paul Laurence Dunbar Library at the Oaks Academy in Indianapolis, Indiana.

A pioneering editor deeply passionate about speculative fiction from the African Diaspora, her World Fantasy Awards recognize her editing of the groundbreaking *Dark Matter* anthologies (*A Century of Speculative Fiction from the African Diaspora* and *Reading the Bones*), making her the first Black writer to win the award. These anthologies first introduced W.E.B. Du Bois's classic science fiction stories "The Comet" and "Jesus Christ in Texas" to the genre. They also introduced other exciting new voices who went on to make significant contributions to the field and inspired the publication of similar volumes for diverse speculative fiction communities around the world. She has been honored as a World Fantasy Award winner and a Locus Award winner for editing *Africa Risen: A New Era of Speculative Fiction*. She is a winner of the Ignyte Ember Award for Unsung Contributions to Genre and Twice honored as a Hugo Award Finalist. Thomas is the Editor of *The Magazine of Fantasy & Science Fiction*. She also edited the recent anthologies *The Map of Lost Places: Stories from Strange & Haunted Realms* (Apex Books, 2025) and *Trouble the Waters: Tales from the Deep Blue* (Third Man Books, 2022), and is the Associate Editor of *Obsidian*.

She has taught creative writing, speculative fiction, and Black Pot Mojo writing workshops around the world, including at Clarion West (where she is a 1999 graduate), Odyssey, Under the Volcano, the Pine Manor College MFA program, BSAM: The Black Speculative Arts Movement, the Tennessee Humanities Young Writers Workshops, among numerous other workshops and programs. She was also the Lucille Geier-Lakes Writer-in-Residence at Smith College.

Beyond her writing and editing, she has significantly contributed to the curatorial space. Her projects include co-curating BSAM's four-part online exhibit *RED SPRING: Curating the End of the World* for Bill T. Jones›s NY LIVE Arts & Google Arts and Culture, curating the Black to the Future festival in her hometown of Memphis, and co-curating Carnegie Hall›s historic citywide Afrofuturism festival. She also engages in community work with Black Pot Mojo Arts, Neighborhood Heroes, BSAM Memphis, TONE, and the Kheprw

Institute in Indianapolis, Indiana, collaborating on the Kheprw Institute's Translocal Afrofuturism Network series dedicated to imagining sustainable solutions to community issues through an Afrocentric, Afrofuturist lens.

Winner of the Octavia E. Butler Award, the L.A. Banks Award, and the Keeper of the Cultural Flame Award, Thomas holds a deep connection to the Schomburg Center for Research in Black Culture, where she researched *Dark Matter*, and is honored to celebrate its centennial legacy. shereereneethomas.com

www.ingramcontent.com/pod-product-compliance
Lightning Source LLC
Jackson TN
JSHW020731160925
90886JS00002B/1